TOYWORLD

HOME OF THE CHRISTMAS THIEF

TONY BERTAUSKI

Copyright © 2022 by Tony Bertauski

All rights reserved.

No part of this book may be reproduced in any form or by any electronic or mechanical means, including information storage and retrieval systems, without written permission from the author, except for the use of brief quotations in a book review.

1

I'm not the hero in this story. Far from it.

To tell this story properly, we need to start at the beginning. It was a night like any other. I had folded the covers back and smoothed the wrinkles. I drank the remains of chamomile tea, still warm, with a lemon wedge resting on the bottom of the mug. In my silk pajamas, cool and smooth, I slid into bed. I lay in the dark, listening to the downstairs grandfather clock count the seconds.

The house was empty. As usual.

An annoying red glow filled my window from across the street, strings of lights on my neighbor's gutters. I stared at a small water stain on the ceiling that I had yet to repair, and counted all my life's failures. It wasn't something I enjoyed doing. Just something I'd always done. Part of the ritual.

Then I took three deep breaths, exhaling slowly with each one, and closed my eyes. The breathing technique was something my father taught me as a child. It was habit. Comfortable. I made the mistake, once, of telling him of a dream I had. *Dreams are wasted thoughts,* he said with a voice as hard as an icy driveway. *Foolish entertainment.*

He believed in two things: hard work and harder work. The only thing that was real was what could be seen and touched. Dreams were stupid. It wasn't like I could stop dreaming, nor did I want to. There was no television in the house, and computer time was strictly monitored. Dreams were my only escape as a child. I recorded them in a notebook and hid it between my mattress and box spring. I would get so nervous he'd find it that occasionally I would burn it. A few weeks later, I would start a new one.

This night, where the story begins, I had a dream like no other. I traveled to somewhere beyond the galaxy. I floated without a spaceship, breathing as if air existed in the vacuum of space. Coasting weightless and effortless, past planets and moons, stars and black holes. I saw things I never imagined. It was the loveliest of dreams.

I didn't remember waking up, but I'd opened my eyes to stare at the water stain on the ceiling. Only it wasn't there. The grandfather clock wasn't ticking. I wasn't in my bed.

I was slumped on a shelf, frozen in postdormital sleep paralysis, locked in my body, staring helplessly across a room. How I got there was a mystery. This didn't feel like a dream. What else could it be? I was a grown man, a rational man. This was a dream; it could be nothing else.

A small Christmas tree was in the corner, casting a red glow across the room. I was thinking of my neighbor's repugnant lights. The light, however, caught pairs of eyes in dim corners. There were dozens of them. I'd had this dream before, being stalked by predators. Never like this, though. I'd read a fair share of dream books and knew they represented my fears. As always, I couldn't outrun them. Powerless, I endured their judgment. They weren't blinking. Neither was I.

I wanted to escape, to run away. *Wake up!* I thought. Sometimes that worked.

A terrifying jolt racked my entire being. I tumbled forward like a puppet. I heard the wind, then the hollow clatter of plastic sticks on laminate flooring. It sounded like pieces of an unassembled model dumped out of a box. I still remembered that sound like it was yesterday. Horrifying.

I was bones. Red, red bones.

Fibulas and tibias, phalanges and ribs. Crimson and polished and expertly crafted. No wires or twine, no glue or ties. I sat up with a clatter. One of my arms fell from my shoulder. Pulled from the socket, it looked like a chew toy the dog had forgotten. There was no time to panic. The predators were circling.

Keys jingled on a key ring. Long tubes of light flickered on the ceiling. Giants entered the room. *Ah, of course. They've come to grind my bones.*

They wore puffy coats and stocking caps. Boots crusted with snow. A man and a woman and a child in between. I gave them quite a fright, scrambling into the corner like a feral cat. The man spilled coffee. Imagine seeing a trembling pile of bones. I expected them to swat me with a broom.

The father, I correctly assumed, turned to the mother and said with all the nonchalance of calling attendance in homeroom, "I thought they were blank."

The mother looked more confused than terrified. She went to the shelves, which, by the way, weren't filled with predators, and picked up a stuffed dog with floppy ears, squeezed the nose on a giant orange cat. "This never happened before," she said, looking at me. "Christmas is ten days away."

Never happened before? I couldn't parse the meaning. Like this had never happened before, or this had never happened *ten days before Christmas?*

The girl walked around a workbench covered in bags of white stuffing, sewing needles and thread. A backpack strapped to her shoulders. She was ten years old or twelve. I'm not good with kids.

Madeline Bells.

That was her name. I didn't know how I knew it. The name just popped into my head. She picked up my lost arm like it was a stick. I squeezed into the corner, my joints protesting. Right about then I was thinking this dream was different. Like no other dream I'd ever had. I was about to pop another limb off my body when the mother said to the girl, "Easy, hon. He's frightened."

This was weird. Even for a dream. They squatted in front of me like I was a puppy who had just piddled on the floor.

"Hello, Viktor," the mother said. "We just want to help."

I was jammed into a corner with nowhere to go and wondering who Viktor was. Then I noticed a tag on my arm. The one Madeline was holding.

Viktor the Red.

Viktor was my family name of sorts, from the old country. I would wake up soon and write all of this down, tease out the symbolism. The predators were my father; I was bones that lacked self-worth or identity or fill in the blank. It would all make sense, it always did. When I woke up.

The mother popped my arm back into the socket. Her touch was warm and gentle. Madeline looked at her mother and said, "Can I keep him?"

I never forgot that, for as long as I lived. It was the way she said it. It filled me with a warmth I'd never felt. It was so kind. I began to melt.

I woke in my bed. In my home, in my silk pajamas. My pillow damp with sweat. I leaped out of the covers and touched my chest and stomach, ran my hands down to my toes. I went to the bathroom and looked in the mirror. There I was, in my forty years of flesh. Wrinkles had never made me so happy.

I showered in cold water till my teeth chattered, then sat in the kitchen with a cup of tea till it was time for work. I was different that day. Madeline's words were butterflies. *Can I keep him?*

I once read the barrier between reality and dreaming was gossamer thin, and the two were irrevocably inseparable. One side tugs on the other. I couldn't explain why the dream felt so real. I only knew one thing.

I wanted to go back.

2

His name was Hiro. A bit on the nose for a story, right? Why not call him Prince or Excalibur? It's quite simple: that was his name. He wasn't named after a grandfather or famous uncle or anything like that. They liked the sound of it. It's on his birth certificate, look it up. It's all very legal.

Our Hiro, as some of us called him, was eight years old when it began. He had no idea who he was or what was about to happen. No one did. This is all a fairy tale, you might think. And you can believe that if you want. It won't make it any less true than believing the world is flat.

His adoring parents were watching their son carefully peel tape from a Christmas present when this story began. His stack of gifts was almost as high as he was, sitting on the floor. Being an only child had its perks. This year was the year for a chemistry set, designer pants and name brand shirts, and a monogrammed parka for camping, if he ever went camping. There was also a telescope with a digital display, a block and hammer cityscape for budding engineers, a marble chess set with hand-carved pieces, an advanced magic module to expand last year's set, and, perhaps his favorite, hardcover books signed by his favorite authors.

This was the most favorite time of year in the Tanaka household.

"Do you like it?" his mother said.

Hiro unfolded a monogrammed apron. He liked chopping vegetables, stirring soup and watching bread rise. He liked making cookies best of all, licking batter from the spoon. But the apron wasn't for cooking. There were sketchbooks wrapped inside it and a set of graphite pencils, colored markers, paintbrushes and watercolors.

He would be embarrassed if friends saw the apron with his name stitched on it. Ah, but that was the one and only benefit of being a loner. No one to make fun of you, no one to prank you or always coming over to visit or talking to you. Hiro rarely spoke, even when a teacher called on him. He always looked at his Devin Claire shoes and muttered just above a whisper.

Imagination can be your very best friend, his grandfather used to say. He was a loner, too.

"Look at this." His mother pulled out three journals. "One for you, one for me and one for your father."

She passed them out, each of them splashed with glitter, the words written calligraphy style and surrounded by finely detailed mazes. *Dream Journal,* it read. His mother didn't click a button for Christmas. She made it. *That's the true spirit,* she would say.

"Now we can write them down," she said.

This was perhaps Hiro's favorite gift that Christmas (which, by the way, would turn out to be the last Christmas). It was such a simple gift. At breakfast, they always told each other their dreams from the night before. His father would go first, then his mother. He enjoyed hearing their dreams as much as he did telling his own. *Dreams are gateways,* his mother would say.

She had no idea how right she was.

Does it make you sad, a boy telling his dreams to his parents this way? Shouldn't he be spending the night with friends, playing video games, talking about girls or boys or whatnot? Don't be. Our Hiro was very happy.

"Coffee," his father announced. He shoved off the couch, tousling Hiro's hair.

Hiro dug a pencil out of the apron, turning it in the sharpener, watching the wood curl in scalloped leaves. When his father returned, they took turns reciting their dreams from the night before. His father didn't write his dream down. Hiro wasn't sad he didn't use the dream journal his mother had spent so much time on, since his father had had a very long dream about an elevator falling twenty stories. It was a bad dream, but his mother insisted there was no such thing as bad dreams. Only challenging ones. All dreams had something to say.

Hiro wrote his dream as he told his parents. It was about Santa Claus and his reindeer. He heard the bells and the hooves on the roof, the sleigh scuffing the shingles. His mother asked questions, to help him remember, her lips thinning in a broad smile. Hiro still believed in Santa. That would end soon enough. And not for reasons you might be thinking.

They played chess that afternoon. His father beat him three games, but the last one was close. Hiro helped his mother make cookies, then read his books in front of the fireplace. The whole scene was ripped from a Christmas calendar, it was all so very perfect.

And when *it* happened—the very reason for this story—no one felt a thing.

They didn't hear a sound or feel a tremor, didn't see a flash of light or smell a change in the air. It was much too subtle to know that everything, in that very moment, changed around the world.

Hiro went to his room that night, his belly full of melted marshmallows and lemon drops. The Christmas lights drooped from the eave outside his window, casting a white glow across his pillows. He stopped in the doorway, his hand reaching for the light switch. A purple monkey waited for him on the edge of his bed.

Yes, a purple monkey. You think you've heard this story before? Not even close.

Hiro didn't move for a full minute. You wouldn't think a stuffed animal would be surprising. Hiro had never owned a stuffed animal. He had toys from when he was very little, but never a doll or a teddy bear. A troll doll, once, with green hair that stood like flames. But that was it. Never a stuffed animal big enough to hug.

Hiro wrapped the long, skinny arms around his neck, the fur tickling his cheek. He fell asleep with a smile. In the morning, for some reason, he forgot to ask his parents who had put the monkey in his room. That wasn't like him to forget. His manners were impeccable. He was on Santa's gold star list.

But Hiro wasn't the only one who forgot that Christmas.

3

Long, crooked fingers scratched the bedroom window, an ancient creature that woke during winter storms. It wanted inside to hide under the bed, to crouch in the closet. Hiro no longer believed in those things. He was older now. Occasionally, though, he checked under his bed. Childhood beliefs never go away. Not entirely.

He opened his eyes, stared at the eggshell ceiling, listened to the *scritch, scritch, scritch* on the frosted pane. It was still dark. The outline of a tree branch, dusted with snow, swayed outside.

Thoughts of bedtime monsters dissolved like a snowball against a brick wall. He did not like feeling frightened of his own mind, the way his thoughts seemed to live in his head. He wasn't a child anymore. At the same time, he loved the way imagination created worlds to explore. Sometimes, though, it seemed imagination was beyond his control. That was exciting. At the same time, it made him nervous.

Tucked beneath thick blankets, a dream lurked just beyond reach. He relished these moments, waking before the alarm yanked him into a hard and cold world. Last night's dream wasn't frightening or whimsical. He didn't go to school in his underwear or forget to study for an exam. It was a big dream. A black and empty dream.

His grandfather would say memory was like a misty day. Names and places, thoughts he would have just moments before, would disappear in the fog. He knew they were out there, just beyond his reach. But some days were clear skies, and memories were as easy as picking apples. Hiro's dream wasn't lost in a mist. It was just so far away. Like reaching across an infinite galaxy.

The alarm blared from his dresser. He threw the blankets off, plunging into the cold air. He dressed quickly in beige pants, a white shirt and a black sweater with the school insignia, then made his bed and fluffed his pillow. The smell of coffee greeted him downstairs. He stopped next to the front door, stood in front of a mirror to straighten his collar. His hair was black and shiny, falling over his forehead, just above his eyes. A timid shadow darkened his upper lip. He leaned closer, combing the trace of whiskers with his finger. A lone hair had sprung from his chin like a weed. It took three attempts to pluck it.

The streetlight shined through the bay window, filling the front room, pale and yellow. The furniture had been rearranged, the couch shoved aside and the chair against the wall, leaving the corner of the room empty. His parents did that every year, the first week of December, pushing stuff around, then sitting down to read their phones or watch a program. In January, it went back the way it was before. One year, his father put a coat rack in the corner. They hung their coats on it, put their shoes beneath it. Now it was like they were expecting the delivery of a large appliance that never came.

"Good morning," Hiro said.

"Morning to you." His father was at the kitchen table, wearing a white shirt and skinny black tie, a tight knot cinched against his throat. He worked from home now, remotely, but still dressed up. He sipped coffee as black as his tie.

His mother offered a blanched smile, her complexion pale in the harsh kitchen light. She'd stopped wearing lipstick shortly after the art program was dropped from the school curriculum and cut her hair, a severe crop just below her ears. She'd been reassigned to teach technical writing. Her attire was as colorless as her lips. A silver beaded necklace was across a white blouse beneath a gray jacket.

Breakfast and a glass of water waited on the table.

Hiro wondered what his father had done differently this morning. The eggs looked like a wet sponge. He poked at the yellow mound, strings of cheese stretching across the plate. He rearranged the eggs in the center.

"Did you dream last night?" Hiro said.

His father chuckled, distracted by something on his phone. His mother smiled thinly, chewing with lips curved slightly downward. Hiro pulled a chunk of egg from the blob, twanged the cheese string with his fork.

"Don't play with it, Hiro," she said.

"I had this dream. It was different. Have you dreamed like that before? Like you, I don't know, went somewhere?"

"Can't say I have," his father said.

"It was like... *space*. Lots of it. Like a galaxy." He poked the eggs. "There was a planet."

"Did you finish your science proposal?" his mother said.

His father pointed. A more relevant question for breakfast conversation. Because dreams were just leftover thoughts, a symptom of a chaotic mind struggling to make sense of the world. Hiro couldn't remember who said that.

He told his mother he'd finished it. He wasn't exactly lying. *Is anything ever really finished?* She used to say that in art class. When there was an art class. He rearranged the eggs like satellites orbiting a space station, the stringy cheese tethering them together.

"I'm leaving in ten minutes. I can't take you home after school. I have a conference." His mother rinsed her plate.

"I wonder where the journals are," Hiro said.

"They're in your room," his father said.

Hiro wasn't talking about schoolwork. He searched the cabinets above the stove, then the pantry while explaining the journals they once had, where they wrote their dreams down at breakfast instead of scrolling through newsfeeds. It seemed like forever since he'd seen them. His mother had made them a long time ago. He couldn't remember why.

"They're not in the pantry, Hiro."

"I'm looking for salt."

"Why?"

Hiro didn't want to say the eggs were bland. They were bland. He didn't ask his father if he'd done something different with breakfast. It tasted like soppy cardboard. Hiro found old packets of salt and pepper from a restaurant. His mother returned with a square briefcase, watching him dust his eggs. His parents glanced at each other.

"It's supposed to rain this afternoon," his mother said. "Can you pick him up?"

"I've got a meeting at two," his father said.

"He can wait for you. I'd rather he not catch a cold." She brushed lint from her jacket. "I'm leaving, Hiro."

He took another bite, then washed the rest down the sink, wiping his mouth and checking his sweater for food that might have spilled. He stopped in the front room. The yard was washed in a gloomy soup, the sun struggling to find its way through the aluminum sky. Mother's car breathed ashy clouds from the tailpipe, staining the modest snowbank along the driveway. His mother honked.

"She might leave without you." His father sipped his coffee.

Hiro looked at the empty corner. "Why do we move the furniture every year?"

He shrugged. "That time of year."

That was all he said. It was something they did because they always did it. And forgot why they did it in the first place.

Jacob Herrington's shirt hung out from the bottom of his sweater. The desk etched an arc on the waxed tiles when he turned it, making a terrible sound. Jacob scrolled through his photos. James Popper nodded at him and said, "Do it, do it."

Jacob thumbed his phone. They looked across the classroom. A few seconds later, Missy Cabernet saw what Jacob had posted on the Social. They were laughing. She wasn't.

Hiro felt trapped in his desk, the way it wrapped around him, the way the molded plastic didn't quite fit his bottom. He tried not to fidget. The hardware creaked. Jacob and James looked at him. Hiro stared at the blue lines on his notebook. If he didn't look up, he would become part of the desk. Just another object in the room. Nothing worth noticing.

The door swung open. Silence seeped in like fog, leaving only the hard clap of Mr. Corker's shoes: a punishing sound that haunted the hallways. It could be heard around corners and across the gym, sending shivers down freshman spines. *Heel-toe, heel-toe.*

He stopped at the podium, sharpshooter eyes snapping on each student. They locked on Jacob. Corker turned his head, looking down the row. Flicked his fingers. Jacob turned his chair to fall in line with the rest of the chairs, as straight as Corker's spine. Five rows of chairs in perfect order.

Corker went to the closet and brought out a box. Setting it on the desk, he called for a volunteer. Gabriel Mankowicz—third seat, second row—wasted no time. Corker pulled out folded papers, maps and drawings, notes and calculations he did in his spare time, and stacked them on the desk. He threw his black tie over his shoulder and climbed onto his desk with legs as long as fishing poles. The shoes were black mirrors. Shoes he buffed in the teacher's lounge, so perfect a student could see their distorted reflection in the toe. He unfurled skinny fingers like a spider, and Gabriel reached into the box to hand him what was inside. He hung three planetary models from the ceiling.

"Thank you, Ms. Mankowicz."

Gabriel returned to the second seat in the third row. Corker reached into his pocket, blew his nose into a white handkerchief like someone playing an instrument poorly. Then promptly folded the contents into a neat square and returned it to his back pocket. Aimee Steiner looked away.

"Proposals are due." He touched the screen on the wall. A list appeared. Two names were in large, red font. "Mr. Jenkins and Mr. Tippitt are remiss."

He nodded. Two boys slid out of their seats to stand at attention. Corker's reprimand began, reminding all of them of their responsibility. Or as he called it, their *pupil duty*. Hiro kept his eyes forward. He stared at the mobiles hanging from the ceiling, the planets gently swaying on thin lines, each making a slow and wobbly course around their prospective stars.

"Sit," Corker said. He paced back to the podium, hands locked behind his back, stamping the floor. *Heel-toe*. "Proposal feedback will be posted tonight. You will respond in agreement or support your disagreement by tomorrow. Your report will be due upon our return from winter break. Ten pages with proper footnotes and a minimum of five legitimate references." He held up his hand. *Five*. "Social boards are not legitimate. It must be peer-reviewed publications of preapproval."

He paced with locked arms, reviewing examples of acceptable topics that had been submitted, primarily interstellar discoveries from the last one hundred years. Anything on a planet, other than the one where they currently existed, or moon or asteroid, comet, black hole or other galactic thing they'd covered in class was acceptable.

Penelope Partridge raised her hand. "Can the report not follow the proposal?"

He paused. "Elaborate, Ms. Partridge."

"I mean, if we decide to write about something other than our proposal?"

"Precisely!" He stabbed a skinny finger at the ceiling tiles. His favorite expression looked like popping a child's balloon. "This is the scientific method. Science is based on learning from mistakes. Mistakes are part of the process." A smile creased his face like a knife through a block of cheese. "Diverge from your proposal but do so with great care."

He marched stiff legged. His voice rose and fell on the sharp edge of consonants, enunciating words with a watchmaker's precision, reviewing various proposals, their weaknesses and strengths: discoveries on other planets and moons, current interstellar travel and, for the ambitious, the warping of time and space. A palpable haze of boredom hung over their heads, eyes glazed with milky condensation.

Hiro was thinking about breakfast.

An epiphany began taking shape. Shapes and colors projected in his imagination. Hiro pretended to be taking notes but didn't write a single word. A circle filled the page with hatched lines to capture tones and shapes. It felt like a planet, but not a planet that resembled one from Corker's mobile. Squiggly lines emanated from its atmosphere, jutting out into space. Color pencils ached to capture the vivid blends he was seeing.

Once upon a time, this classroom had been where his mother taught art. Hiro had helped her hang decorations after school when he was younger. He remembered long strands of artificial greenery and shiny orbs. A small tree in the corner and a vague memory of happiness.

Hiro sketched the outlines of land masses. There was distant laughter, a sound outlawed from Corker's class, but Hiro was too immersed. He had to grab the details while they hovered in his imagination, before they disappeared into the fog. The squiggly lines should be glowing. Yes! That was what he'd dreamed. Glowing, squiggly lines. If he had a yellow pencil, he could outline them. Instead, he applied a soft layer of shade.

He didn't hear the clapping of hard soles. Only saw the polished shoes, in perfect alignment, next to his desk, triggering an adrenaline flood in Hiro's chest. He slammed the book closed.

Corker's fingers unfurled like a clammy creature. Hiro had no choice. Corker studied the drawing, lips pursed like a lemon squeezed under his tongue. The longer he looked, the sourer it became. He squinted at Hiro and grunted. Perplexed was not one of Corker's personality traits. But, for a moment, he was exactly that. He took long, deliberate steps. The shiny shoes sounded like axes on a marble slab.

"Come."

Hiro was a petrified version of himself, an immovable carving that resembled a sixteen-year-old boy fused to a plastic seat. Cold vapor filled his legs; his cheeks could cook an egg. The students were looking at him. Some smiling. This was the only time everyone paid attention: a championship bout between a heavy favorite and a hopeless underdog. *Ding, ding.*

Corker taped the drawing on the wall. Hiro gripped the desk like he'd been pushed from a plane. Corker nodded ever so slightly. Then let the silence bake Hiro like a Thanksgiving turkey. Sweat tracked his spine. The silence was a microwave beam. Hiro let go before he was fully cooked.

He shoved his hands in his pockets. His legs were cold steel. He bit his lip to keep it from quivering. It wasn't just the march up to the front that disemboweled him or the twenty-five pairs of eyes that brought earth-shattering panic. *Mother will hear about this.*

Corker offered the podium like an honor. And then, to make matters worse, he abandoned him up front, walking stiffly down the aisle and folding his lanky body into Hiro's empty desk.

There were snickers and whispers that, ordinarily, Corker would snuff out with a cold eye. But he let them go. Sweat popped up on Hiro's upper lip. He tasted something metallic on his lower lip. Corker nodded, and Hiro knew what that meant. It had happened before when Jenny Skarsgard was caught on her phone. Corker hadn't sat in the audience when she marched up front. Hiro looked at the faux wood grain of the podium.

"Um." Hiro reflexively swallowed a rock in his throat. "This is—"

"Hands from pockets, Mr. Tanaka," Corker said. "Address the class."

Hiro swallowed again, but the rock wouldn't go down. He quickly grabbed the podium to keep his hands from flying off. Their eyes, all their eyes, were mini microwaves. He could smell his hair burning. Perry Parsons had his phone where Corker wouldn't see it. Hiro closed his eyes briefly. If Corker made him let go of the podium, he would crumble like a wooden puppet.

"Um, this is... I was—" He started to point at the drawing and quickly latched back onto the podium. His mouth filled with cotton. "I was working out my proposal."

"Proposal?" Corker said.

"I wasn't sure, you know, what to write yet. I started drawing."

Corker nodded with dead eyes. Hiro stammered. He wasn't sure if words came out.

Paul Baker raised his hand. "What is it?"

"The drawing?" Hiro said.

"Yeah. The drawing."

"Planet."

"Which one?"

Hiro shook his head. He didn't know.

Margaret Bleeker said, "What are the lines coming off it?"

Hiro didn't know what those were, either. He couldn't admit it was a dream. Not in front of the class. Corker raised his hand like one of the students. He didn't lower it until Hiro nodded.

"Where are the words?"

"Words?"

"Yes, words. It is a written assignment, five pages, and sourced. *Woooords*." The class chuckled, and Corker let them. "Where are the words?"

"It's just, I was... ideas... and..."

"The lines are wormholes," Hazel Melblank said. "*Worlds Apart*. It was a movie where space is an illusion and—"

"There are no such things as wormholes." Corker turned a darker shade. The first sign he was human with a heart that pumped blood instead of antifreeze. He turned his icy lasers back to Hiro. "Why did you draw it?"

"Because I wasn't sure—"

"That's not what I'm asking. Why did you draw *that*?" He jabbed a finger at the wall behind Hiro.

"I-I-I don't know."

"You don't know?"

Hiro shook his head. Admitting it was a dream could make this last even longer.

"So you made it up?" Corker's eyes narrowed into deadly slits.

Hiro nodded. Corker rapped his fingernails on the desk like chisels. His lie detector was spinning. Hiro wasn't budging.

"*Worlds Apart*," Hazel said. "He probably saw it and—"

"Enough."

Corker vacated the desk and stepped aside. They watched Hiro return to his former bubble of anonymity, sitting in the perfectly straight row of perfectly matched uniforms. Hiro concentrated on not collapsing, grateful he hadn't fainted. Or worse.

"This is not a movie or a comic book," Corker said. "In this class, we work with facts. Things we know. A little thing we call proof. The purpose of this assignment is reality, not fantasy. It is not what you *wish* for, it is not about what you *believe*. No flying saucers or little stuffed animals running the world. No wormholes." He looked at Hazel. "Do not trust your senses. Trust only facts. This is science."

Hazel raised her hand, and Hiro wished she hadn't. "If we can't trust our senses, then how can we read facts? We need our eyes to see, which is one of our senses, and—"

Hiro could feel the heat shift to her side of the room. "Enough entertainment for the day, Ms. Melblank. Let's continue our class in reality. Because this reality is all there is. Mr. Tanaka, you will meet me after school to discuss reality a bit further."

Corker stripped the drawing off the board, wadded it into a tight ball and tossed it.

"That is where that belongs." He pointed at the trash can. "Precisely!"

Hiro put his pen down, held an apple by the stem. It rotated one way and then the other. He should be working on his outline, using words for his report instead of drawing, but couldn't stop thinking of round things hovering in space.

He closed his eyes. The conversations at other tables, the occasional glances in his direction, went away. The dream was still in the fog. The colorful planet surrounded by a radiant atmosphere. Glowing lines like ethereal vines twisting in solar winds, reaching into the galaxy. It was so real.

A chair scraped the floor. Hazel dropped her sharp elbows on the table. She leaned in, her eyes big and round, an amused smile half twisted into her cheek.

"You going to eat that?" she said. "Kidding. No one eats them." She took the apple from him, cupped it like a snowball. One of the points of her collar was tucked inside her sweater. The other one curled up. She whispered, "You're a terrible teacher. No offense. I mean, you had the floor. You could've said anything. But you sort of didn't."

Hiro stared at his notes.

"He's a turd, Hiro. Yeah," she said, "a turd. The kind that attracts flies." *Is there another kind?* "He's supersmart, like genius smart, and should be building rockets or something instead of designing sadistic teenage mind games. Maybe his mother didn't tuck him in at night or his father made him eat beets or someone didn't love him back. Although I can't see Corker loving anything. Either way, who pays the price? We do. We pay."

Hiro covered his writing with both hands, for some reason. He was uncomfortable with the way she looked at him, like she could see his thoughts and anxiety. His eyes were glassy portals that revealed the quivery dance his brain did whenever someone looked at him this long. And his notes would somehow betray him even more, like clues to his not-so-secret fears.

She leaned back, still watching. He hoped she'd get bored if he didn't look up; she'd go back to regular life and leave him alone. His stomach was pulling alarms in his head. He closed his notebook and started packing.

"Where is this?"

She unfolded a wad of paper and smoothed it on the table. The wrinkles made the squiggly lines crooked and wayward. The planet he drew was smudged.

"Did you really make this up?" she said. "Or were you trying to draw something else?"

He pulled the drawing closer. It was better than he remembered. If he closed his eyes, it would look just like his dream. All it needed was color.

"I dreamed it."

The words came out like snowflakes on a whisper, drifting in the cafeteria noise. She caught them with wrinkles between her eyes.

"I don't remember the last time I dreamed. Except..." She looked up, like her thoughts were floating near the ceiling. "Do daydreams count?"

She recounted, unabashedly, how she'd daydreamed about wearing shorts to school, like, really short ones. And didn't shave her legs.

"So are they?" She dropped her finger on the squiggly lines. "Wormholes? Like I said, remember? *Worlds Apart,* shortcuts through space. You never saw that movie?"

He shook his head. He didn't know what the lines were. Although they felt like tunnels, which, if they were in outer space, would make them wormholes.

"You should include that in your paper," she said. "The drawing. Staple it to the back."

His spine shivered. He could feel his legs solidify. Just the thought of Corker seeing his drawing on the table raised a fleet of perspiration. He even had the thought of putting it back in the trash in case Corker went looking for it. Hiro already had one detention to stay after school. When his mother found out, there would be more.

"Corker and his facts," she said. "What kind of facts did we have before microscopes? Germs were invisible fairies until the microscope was invented. And there was the one guy, the famous one, I don't remember his name, I should, but he said the sun doesn't orbit around our planet when everyone else said it did. And what did that get him? They threw him in jail or something. I guarantee you Corker would've marched to his house with pitchforks and torches because facts, Hiro. Facts!" She chopped the air. "Nothing exists without facts!"

People were looking at them. He covered the drawing.

"Look, what I'm saying is we don't know everything. Am I right? Like how'd we get here? Why are we here? What's the point? Corker can't answer that. No one can."

She stabbed the drawing with her finger.

"You put that with your report, make it part of some historical research. You know, like write about what astronomical science was like before the telescope when people thought gods made it rain when they threw someone in a volcano. What's the worst that can happen? He'll give you a bad grade because you had a dream?"

"My mother."

He bit his lip hard enough to taste it. His thoughts dripped from his brain and escaped out of his mouth. He had to get away before he confessed to something he didn't do. He gathered his notebook, put his pen in his pocket.

"Your mom, right," Hazel said. "Didn't she teach art? She can handle it, Hiro. I'll bet she'll be proud if you use the drawing."

He shook his head rabidly. She didn't know his mother. She was different now. The chair nearly tipped over when he stood. He didn't need it slamming on the floor like a gavel to get everyone's attention.

"I'll text you." She held up her phone. "Or I can email you, class chat, whatever. I'm not charging you; this advice is free. But if you want to help me with *my* report, we'll call it even. Help me help you help me."

Hiro dropped his pen. His hands were shaking.

"Or not," she said.

He took a deep breath, moving slowly, deliberately. No sudden movements, nothing to see here. Just two people talking. Or one person talking. But it was nothing, just a boy and girl and an apple. He started to walk off, then remembered the drawing. She snapped a picture of it.

"You on Social?" she said, taking three more pictures before he got it. "Stay off for a while. Perry Pinhead posted your guest lecture."

The sweat down his back turned into morning frost. Perry had had his phone out when Hiro was at the podium. Hiro wasn't on Social. And he'd never have known it was posted if she hadn't told him.

"You can still be a teacher." She took a bite of the apple, then spit in her hand. Wiped her tongue and made a face, then said, "Just saying, everyone doesn't start strong."

4

Corker wasn't in his classroom.

Maybe he forgot Hiro was coming. He doubted Corker had ever forgotten anything. Hiro was early; he wanted to get this over with. He'd never had detention before, didn't know what would happen. Maybe Corker would have him scrub the floors or straighten desks with a ruler. There was a hope, a tiny hope, that if he did everything just right, his mother wouldn't hear about it.

When this was his mother's classroom, there had been lamps in the corners and candles on the teacher's desk. Music played from a small speaker. The desks were never in the same place; sometimes they were arranged in a circle or facing different directions. Sometimes students sat cross-legged on a rug.

Now it smelled like a hospital.

Hiro sat in his assigned seat. His legs shook, so he walked up and down the aisle. Corker's desk was orderly. No candle wax drippings, no coffee cup filled with candy. There was a calendar with a stack of envelopes, names without addresses. December 25 was circled on the calendar. Maybe he was going on a trip for winter break. It was hard to imagine Corker on a ski slope or lounging on a beach.

The planetary mobiles hung from the ceiling, slowly turning in the draft from the ventilation ducts. The box was on the floor. Hiro went to the podium. He didn't shake or bite his lip. It was easy standing up there without all the eyes on him. Hazel was right. He should have done something besides grip the podium like a toy soldier.

"That's right," he whispered, "I dreamed of a planet. It isn't against the law. Just because no one else does or, or, or if they do, can't remember them. I did nothing wrong."

He looked at the empty seats, imagining his classmates no longer snickering. Their expressions slowly changing. They were nodding along. Perry was still secretly filming him. They all had their phones out now, not even trying to hide it.

"I'll bet you dream, too," he whispered, pointing. "Wishing for something different. Thinking something is missing. Dreaming the world could be different. I'm not different than you. We're the same."

Someone would say, *I had a dream, too!* And then someone else would say it and someone else. Mitzy Bennigan would be the first one to stand on her desk, because that was something she would do. Corker would tell them to be quiet because he wanted to hear what else Hiro had to say.

"*That* came from my imagination." Hiro pointed at the empty wall where Corker had taped his drawing. "I don't know where it came from. It spoke to me. It can speak to you. All you have to do is listen."

They would start clapping now. Corker would stand up with the others, walloping those big spidery hands together and then climbing onto the desk, his head brushing the ceiling.

Hiro went to the wall and pretended to take the drawing off. The cheers would be so loud the principal would come down. And once he saw the drawing, he'd burst into tears. Hiro's mother would rush into the room and hug him. They would be posting about him on the Social, where his inspiration would spread around the world.

"This is my dream."

Hiro thrust his empty hand above his head. Metal objects crashed on the table. Wires circled around his arm. He'd knocked one of the mobiles off the hook Corker had set into the ceiling tile.

Without hesitation, he climbed onto the table. The wires were tangled but hadn't kinked. The hook had fallen off the ceiling. He had to search for it, straighten out the planets and climb back onto the desk. He wasn't sure where Corker had exactly put it. The wires rang in his shaky hands. There was no way to know, so he just hung it above the podium. He moved it two times, stepping back, examining it, trying to remember where it had been exactly.

There were footprints all over the table.

He looked around, found a towel in the cardboard box where Corker had stored the mobiles. It sat on top of a stack of notebooks. Big sheets of folded paper were wedged between them. Hiro saw bright colored lines, and despite the paralyzing anxiety, his curiosity made him look.

He unfolded a large map on the table. There were dozens of them in the box, drawings of interstellar constellations crisscrossed with red lines and blue lines, orange and green and yellow. A thick purple line had clusters of Corker's indecipherable writing; words underlined with exclamation points. Calculations with symbols and numbers, things circled. Nothing he could understand.

It felt familiar.

Maybe it was because it had to do with space, and that was all Hiro could think about: space. The notebooks had dates and times, long rambling entries without paragraphs or punctuation and barely a word he could read, a scribbling mess of lines from someone whose mind worked too fast for his hand to keep up.

Click-clack.

The heel-toe warning was coming down the hall. Hiro rushed everything back into the box, started for his seat, then ran back to wipe his footprints off the desk. The footsteps grew closer. There wasn't time to get back to his seat. He stood against the whiteboard as the door began to open. He tossed the towel into the box.

Corker stopped. His nostrils flared. Eyes shifting around the room, landing on the mobile above the podium still swaying. He blinked heavily.

"Sit."

Hiro went to his assigned seat far away from the front of the classroom. Corker looked inside the cardboard box. Hiro held onto his desk to keep from running away. Corker put the box in the closet, then went to his desk, sat down and began writing. This went on for several minutes. The dry scritching of a pointed pencil, the stabbing punctuation and abrupt folding of paper. He tucked the letter in an envelope, licked the flap and added it to the pile.

Maybe this was detention, listening to a teacher handwrite letters. Corker put the pencil down, tidied the desktop and stood up. Hiro stiffened as he walked down the aisle. He took the desk in front of Hiro, turned it around and folded his lanky body into it. With his back straight, he stared with dead eyes.

Corker was more gray than pink. His cheeks drawn, cheekbones protruding. He barely looked real, like a hollow version of a bitter physics teacher in a wax museum. A ghost who didn't want to be there any more than the students it haunted. His lips slowly parted.

"Did you take the drawing from the trash?"

"My what?" Hiro smacked his dry lips. They stuck together. Corker blinked with impatience. "Oh. No. No, I didn't take it from the trash."

Corker waited with heavy eyelids. His fingers unfolded, hand extended. Palm expectant. Hiro swallowed. There was no point in drawing this out. He dug his drawing out of his backpack.

"I didn't take it."

"Then why do you have it?"

"I found it in the cafeteria."

"How did it get there?"

Hiro sat still. He didn't shrug or lie. Nor did he say anything that would get Hazel in trouble.

Corker smoothed the drawing on his desk. He appeared to study it, nodding and grunting to himself. Following lines with a fingernail in need of trimming. He pondered it like a detailed map.

"You dreamed this?"

A cold rush of blood froze the hair on his head. He knew. He knew Hiro had dreamed it.

"How many times?"

"How many?"

"Yes. How many times did you dream this?" He held the drawing up.

"Just last night."

"Why?"

"Why?"

"Why did you dream *this*?"

That didn't make any sense. Why does anyone dream? "I, uh, I don't know."

Corker grunted, not satisfied. It was better not to lie, not even a little. Corker had lie detectors as good as Hiro's mother.

"Nothing more you'd like to share?" He drummed the fingernails like daggers. "About the dream?"

"No, sir."

"Anything else besides this?" He shook the drawing.

"No. No, I just remember that, that's all. I swear."

This was weird. Nothing about not paying attention in class or lying about taking it. Corker seemed distracted, but, thankfully, there was nothing more. If Hiro had dreamed something awful and embarrassing, he would have to say it to be spared the X-ray vision that was peeling through his thoughts like a card catalog. Corker narrowed his eyes, grunted.

"You are best served to stay in this world, Mr. Tanaka. Not fantasy land."

He methodically folded the drawing twice, running his finger down the crease, and handed it to Hiro. He crawled out of the desk, turned it around and put it in line with the others. Hiro watched him pace up front to resume letter writing.

"You may leave," Corker said without looking up.

Hiro wasn't sure if he'd heard that correctly, so he didn't move. It wasn't until Corker waved his hand that he grabbed his backpack. He ached to get away from the antiseptic smell and the sound of the pencil. He stopped with his hand on the doorknob. He couldn't explain what happened next. From somewhere unknown, a thought slipped over his tongue before he could stop it.

"I'm changing my proposal."

Corker stopped what he was doing. "Pardon?"

"I want to do a historical review of discoveries. Like what we believed was true before microscopes. I mean, we didn't know single-celled organisms existed. People thought spirits were causing disease. And telescopes, too. Before that, the sun orbited around the planet, and anyone who said different got punished. I think, you know, it would be interesting to look at how facts evolve with technology. Maybe this is a dream." The drawing quivered in his hand. "But what if it's more than that?"

Corker put his pencil down. The temperature dropped a few degrees. Hiro wanted to say more, like shouldn't the scientific method be curious? Maybe Hazel was right and these were wormholes that were somehow communicating through dreams like radio waves. If all we had was our senses to observe reality, why did we ignore dreams? Because this dream felt as real as the paper in his hand.

"Dreams, Mr. Tanaka, are thoughts. And thoughts are nothing more than thoughts." He half-heartedly pointed at the ceiling. "Precisely that."

He pushed away from his desk. His heavy, calculated footsteps pounded Hiro's chest like a hammer. Corker's hand wrapped around the doorknob. He looked down on Hiro like a superhero tired of saving the world, desperate to escape.

"This is science, not fiction writing. Keep your feet on the ground till after winter break. Whoever is teaching this class when you get back may feel differently than I do."

"You're not coming back?"

He pulled the door open and gestured. Hiro stepped into the hall. The heel-toe footsteps faded behind him.

5

Fifty-one days without dreaming.

I knew the exact number because I started a journal. I read a book about lucid dreaming, and that was what it said to do. I had dreams during that time, but they were petty: going to work in my underwear, house flooding. Those kinds of dreams. Still, I kept a notebook on the nightstand and wrote them down as soon as I woke.

I'd lost hope. *It was just a dream,* I told myself. *A vivid, lucid dream. It wasn't real. I wasn't a toy.*

On the fifty-second night, I smelled popcorn. I hate popcorn. Gets stuck in my teeth, always messy. *Why would I make popcorn?* I thought. I started to panic, thinking I'd left the stove on. I was going to get out of bed, check the kitchen.

A furry orange cat startled me. He was the size of a middle school child, slouched in the corner with round eyes. I was on a dresser. A purple monkey on one side, a floppy-eared dog on the other. Both wide-eyed and slumped over, staring at posters of puppet bands. A mobile of a solar system hung from the ceiling. There were planets and moons I'd never seen, like something a third grader would make.

There she was, Madeline Bells, lying on her bed, tapping on a laptop. Humming to a song in her earphones, watching a video. Face lit with electric light. Her hair was longer than the last time I'd seen her, when she picked my arm off the floor, crouching down while I cowered in the corner.

The air was crisp, but not cold. Like inhaling effervescent evergreen. It was so different than the air at home. It was vibrant, scintillating. Alive. I wanted to cry. *Am I breathing?*

I was wrapped in a flannel blanket. I squirmed until it fell from my collarbones. Two arms. I had two arms. And the tag, the Viktor the Red tag, was gone. Madeline looked up. I held still like the toys next to me. It was instinctual, automatic. Like I'd done something wrong. She pulled the earphones out. We stared at each other, and then slowly she slid off the bed and crept out of her room.

Music bled from the covers. Not a song I knew.

She returned with her mother, carefully stepping into the doorway, peeking inside. I could feel their apprehension. Their emotions were palpable, like I was running my fingers over tissue paper, feeling grains of sand beneath. Like the air between us was gritty.

Her mom whispered. Madeline approached with a hopeful smile.

"I wrapped you up so you wouldn't get cold." She looked at her mom, back to me. "Can I pick you up?"

I didn't say yes or no, but I didn't fight it when she reached for me like I was a feral cat. Her hands were warm. The warmth seeped through me like bathwater and all the goodness of innocence. That weepy feeling filled me again.

"I'm so glad you're back." She hugged me like a puppy.

"Gentle," the mom said.

It didn't hurt. She could squeeze as hard as she wanted.

"Can you hear me?" she said. I was too emotional to nod. "Can you talk? No? It's okay." She turned to the mom. "Where's Dad?"

"In his office. Why don't you show him around, and I'll get him."

Madeline gave me the grand tour of the house. I wrapped my boney arms around her neck, and she giggled, pointing out the kitchen, her parents' bedroom, and the bathroom. Her dad's office was in the back of the house. A fireplace was blazing in the living room. Fuzzy, red stockings hung from the mantel. Three of them. A Christmas tree in the corner, presents stacked beneath it. A half-finished puzzle was on a coffee table, a book on a beige sofa.

"It's the strangest thing," the mom muttered. "I can't explain it. He's back."

"How long has it been?" the dad said.

"Almost a year."

A year? I thought. I would solve that conundrum later.

The parents watched Madeline explain the puzzle to me. They did one every Christmas. It was a tradition. The dad had streaks of gray in a tightly clipped beard. He wore a black tie and white shirt. Creases in his slacks. He stared with intense fascination. It was a weird mix of surprise and curiosity. There was a living toy in their house. That didn't seem to be the root of his surprise, like of course the toy was living. It was something else.

"This is my dad, Philip."

The dad reached out his hand. I just looked at it, then realized what he was doing. I wrapped boney fingers around two of his fingers. Warm, like Madeline.

"Pleased to meet you, Viktor," he said.

"And you've met my mom, Polly. She made you. You're not a box job. You're original."

That sounded special.

"Is he talking?" the dad said.

"Let's not push it," the mom said. "He needs to acclimate."

"Maybe we should go into town."

"Not yet. I want to keep an eye on him today, not overwhelm him. Hon, keep holding him; I want to scan his charm."

The mom left the room. The dad looked me over, complimented my bone structure, how sturdy I was. The mom returned with something like a cell phone. This was what babies must feel like, all the fuss and smiles. The dad stepped back, made way for the mom and her cell phone.

"Okay. Um, this won't hurt, Viktor. I'm just going to wave this in front of you."

I squeezed Madeline's neck. When someone with a foreign object says this isn't going to hurt, it's going to hurt. The mom heard my bones shaking and stepped back. She pulled a silver marble from her pocket. It was an oversized ball bearing.

"See that?" Madeline said. "You have one just like it." She touched my head. "Usually, it's in the chest, but since you're all bones, Mom put it up there. Can we show him?"

"I don't think that's a good idea."

"Isn't that what you do to help with stabilization?" the dad said. "Once he sees the core, he'll know who he is. Right?"

The mom was thinking, and I was getting more nervous. She started nodding because, evidently, toys had come to life, and she'd done this before. I felt Madeline's hand cradle the back of my head. Once again, the warmth filled me with pleasurable wonder. She shushed and rocked me. A smile grew inside me. Her fingers were at the base of my skull.

There was a click.

I couldn't move. I'd lost all feeling in my bones, but I could see what was happening, hear what they were saying. Madeline held a silver marble like the one her mom had pulled from her pocket.

"This is you," she whispered.

This dream was impeccably detailed. I wasn't the toy. I was a marble inside the toy. The red skeleton was a vehicle. A body. That was how this worked. I had no idea how it could possibly work, but there was some logic to it. Like a brain inside a body.

"I think he's got it," the mom said. "You can put it back."

There was another click as the marble slid back into my skull. A little trapdoor closed. I was back in her arms. I made the mistake of touching my forehead, heard the hard plastic of my fingers touch my skull. It wasn't till my finger slipped inside an empty eye socket that I sort of lost my cool—scrambling on Madeline's shoulder to run away from the queer sensation.

"It's all right, it's all right." Madeline held me tight. That helped. Immensely.

The mom waited till I was no longer shaking to hold up the cell phone instrument. She told me, again, it wasn't going to hurt. I clung to Madeline. I would have closed my eyes if I had eyes.

She waved it over my head, then studied the reading. "Good. He's stable. Let's watch him for a bit. Want to put him down?"

Madeline lowered me to the floor. I hadn't thought about standing on my own. It was a bit like walking on stilts. I was a child all over again, waving my arms, dragging boney feet over the hardwood floor, knocking puzzle pieces off the table. It was like ice skating for the first time.

"Wow," the dad said. "He's not good at walking."

"Yes," the mom said. "I built him as a blank prototype, not expecting him to wake up. It's like some consciousness crossover occurred."

"From another toy?"

"What else could it be?"

The dad scratched his beard. "It's just, he acts like a newborn."

"I'll check around to see if a nearby toy went blank. Maybe there was some synchronous thought transmission that cross-connected with another charm. It's happened before, one toy moves into another if the frequencies suddenly match."

"The odds on that are—"

"A billion to one. Yes. What else could it be?"

"What about, I don't know, *somebody* switched into the wrong toy?"

I felt the chill between them. I didn't know what that meant, exactly, or why I felt it. I'd followed what they were saying up to that point. If my consciousness was inside that marble—they called it a charm, I guess—then perhaps it could sync up with another marble, like a wireless toy leaping from one toy to another. But when the dad said *somebody*, that meant something else. Something chilling.

Somebody switched into the wrong toy.

"No. That's not possible. There's not a switch bank near my shop," the mom said. "Even if there were, a person couldn't accidentally occupy a random toy."

"I know," the dad said. "Still."

The mom shook her head. "I'll check around, see if any activity matches up. What time did he wake?"

They noted the time I woke up on the dresser. And the date and time they found me in the toy shop, which, apparently, had been a year ago. It hadn't been a year when I last dreamed of this place. They were clearly confused. Not as much as I was, and not as much as they should be.

That night I was put on the dresser with the purple monkey and floppy-eared dog. I didn't sleep. Just sat there, listening to Madeline sleep. In the morning, I was still there, wrapped in the flannel blanket.

❊

They wore puffy coats and stocking caps. I had a green cloak the mom had fashioned from a blanket. It had a hood and tied around my neck, dragged behind me like a cape. Madeline didn't want me getting cold. I looked like a fairy tale.

The outside of the house was simple. Thick shutters, brick chimney, a cracked sidewalk. A car puffed smoke in the driveway, not a model I'd ever seen before. It was boxy, very wide. Madeline explained what snow was. It went up to my pelvis when I stepped in it. It wasn't cold. Slightly chilly, maybe. It felt like sponge cake.

Madeline and I got in the back seat. We drove past small houses decorated with ornaments and lights. Neighbors waved as we passed them. In the distance, the hills rose around this valley village that was quiet and friendly. It was all quite normal. Until we got downtown.

That was where the toys were.

There were teddy bears and skinny dolls, furry animals and action figures. Walking and talking, sitting inside cafés, dancing across the road. A panda bear dressed as Santa, ringing a bell in front of an empty bucket. Farther down, a fabric doll was facedown on a storm sewer. People walked past them without acknowledgment, as if they were pigeons in search of crumbs.

Toys are people.

This explained everything. It wasn't impossible, the more I thought about it. Technology could program a metal ball with artificial intelligence and insert it into a body. How the neural connections were made to control it, I had no idea. The proof was walking down the sidewalk. Although *I* wasn't artificial intelligence. If I were, would I know it?

This is a dream, I reminded myself. *An incredibly long, detailed dream.* I decided, for once in my life, I would stop trying to solve the equation and just go for the ride.

"That's where you woke up," Madeline said.

A small shop was tucked between a shoe store and an electronics repair shop. Words were painted on the window. *Toy Stitchery.*

I recalled, as the store receded through the back window, jolting awake on the shelf, losing my arm. It seemed like so long ago. So frightening. And now, it almost seemed normal to see toy elephants staring at pastries through a shop window and holding trunks.

According to Madeline, toy stitching ran in the family. The skill passed down from generation to generation. It went all the way back to the Great Toy Migration. I wanted to know more about that, but, seeing as I didn't know how to talk, I had no way to ask.

"I'm going to build my own shop in the city," she said. "Maybe you can be my assistant."

Well, here I was, not more than a day old in this dream and I already had a job.

Toys of different stripes and colors were queued up along an old brick building. I couldn't tell what they were waiting for, but they were dirty and wet. Matted fur and marred plastic. A yellow toy truck was missing a wheel. The car stopped in front of us. Someone threw a pink piggy out the window. It tumbled like a pillow, four short legs pointing at the blue sky, at the end of the line.

"Pull over," the mom said. She was out of the car before the dad had come to a complete stop. "Hey, no! You don't toss her like that."

The car drove off. The mom went a few more steps, still shouting at the driver. She came back to the car. "I need to see why the shelter isn't open. Can you go down to the experience café, engage Viktor's senses? I don't want him seeing this. I'll meet you down there."

The mom picked the pink piggy up, brushed her off and helped her get in line. She spoke to the toys on her way past them, unlocking the front door to let them in. Madeline wasn't looking. Her nose crinkled, dark eyebrows pinched. I thought she was avoiding me. I tapped her arm.

"It happens every Christmas." She put her arms around me. "It won't happen to you."

For the next two days, we sat around the fireplace and told stories, went to town to see the mom's workshop, built a snowman in the front yard, visited experience cafés, where I learned the full array of toy senses. We were working on the puzzle when the house started beeping. The room was suddenly cold. An alarm clock was making noise.

Then I was staring at a water stain on the ceiling.

6

A plywood boardwalk was beneath naked bulbs swaying on black cords, sharp shadows dancing on boxes of the old and forgotten: a baby crib, a hermetically sealed wedding dress, a plastic dog carrier. Hiro's father, bundled in a winter coat, breath steaming in the white light, walked between the rafters. Hiro hated the cold. His skin always tired beneath layers of sweaters.

"It's down there." His father pointed. "I think."

They walked to the end of the plank. He pulled the string on the last bulb. It swung over his stocking cap like a great idea. Hiro shivered, hugging himself, as his father pulled out boxes and glanced inside. Coffee mugs and glassware, wooden spoons and moldy towels.

"I've been looking for this." His father held up a meditation bench. Looked around. "We're getting warmer. I can feel it." *No, we're not,* Hiro thought.

They found a bronze sculpture of a stout little figure. That was from when Mother used to sculpt. When she used to make stuff. Her studio, in the back of the house, had smelled earthy. She would stay back there all day, coming out with more clay on her hands than there was dirt in the backyard. She would be glowing. Now that room was an office.

"Help me with this," his father said.

Hiro helped slide a long box onto the plank. He rubbed a layer of dust off the label. "Why do we have an artificial tree?"

"Why do we have these?" He opened a box of smooth black rocks with a pouch of white feathers. "Your grandparents were always bringing stuff back from their travels. We just put them up here."

They dug deeper, carefully stepping on the joists to keep from going through the ceiling. There was a cylinder of ornate canes, a pottery wheel, and a unicycle missing a pedal.

"Here we go." His father held a box in the light. There were brushes and pallet knives and rags stiff with paint. He handed it to Hiro, who set it on the boardwalk. "Why do you all of a sudden want art supplies?"

He shrugged. "Something to do."

"It wouldn't have anything to do with Mr. Corker's class, would it?" He paused with a grim smile.

Hiro thought he'd gotten away with that. Missteps were usually dealt with at dinner or, at the very latest, breakfast. It had been two days since detention. His mother hadn't said a word to Hiro. But, apparently, had said plenty to his father.

"Your mother said he's a good teacher, Hiro."

Hiro grunted, then covered his mouth.

"All right, a challenging teacher. A bit unusual, maybe. But there's a lot you can learn from him."

"He made me get up in front of class."

He turned with a jar of marbles. "Are you injured?"

"What?"

"Did you bruise a kidney?"

"He embarrassed me in front of everybody."

His father handed him the jar and pulled off his mittens, breathing into his fists. He nodded, thinking. The temperature was dropping by the second. Hiro wanted to cup his hands around the light bulb for warmth.

"There was this Buddhist temple. All the students there were very diligent about their studies. Among them was a foul old man. He cursed if someone bumped into him. Spat on the sidewalk during walking meditation. Then one day, to the relief of everyone, he decided he'd had enough and left the temple.

"The students were all excited. They approached the teacher and said now that the old man was gone, they could get serious about their meditations. The teacher asked if they really wanted to practice. They all agreed. Of course they did. That was why they were there. So the teacher left the temple. He returned two days later with the old man."

Hiro waited for the end of the story. "That's it?" he finally said.

"The best teachers push buttons, Hiro. They graciously reveal your shortcomings that you cannot see. They are neither naughty nor nice. They do what's required of life."

Hiro nodded. Even though it didn't make sense. "Someone put the whole thing on Social. They recorded me."

"So? You went in front of class, and you did it. You faced it and owned it. That, my son, is courage."

"I didn't have a choice."

"Sure you did."

Is he joking? It was hard to tell with the shadows across his face. *Choice?* This would be a very different conversation if Hiro had refused to do what Corker told him to do.

"Remember this?" His father reached into the clutter. Boxes tumbled over. Red paint flaked from the rails. Lacquer peeled from the boards. He handed it to Hiro. The sled dropped on the boardwalk with a bang.

He remembered this when he was little. There was this long slope in the park. In winter, everyone would bring disks and toboggans and sleds. Hiro's parents and grandparents would stand at the top with the other parents. Hiro remembered the park was decorated with lights and shiny round things in the trees.

There was this one time a kid asked if Hiro wanted to wax the rails, make it go faster. Hiro wasn't ready for just how fast it would go.

The wind whistled in his ears. He tried to steer away from the hump the big kids would hit. He was launched into the air. The landing knocked the wind out of him, and he tumbled all the way to the bottom. The big kids were down there, laughing. Someone called him a banger.

Hiro pulled the sled back up the hill. His ribs ached. He couldn't catch his breath. When he reached the top, his parents said that was probably enough for one day.

"And what did you do?" his father said.

"I went again."

"Why?"

Hiro insisted it was because he knew if he didn't, he'd be too afraid to ever go again. He avoided the hump the second time, went all the way to the bottom and climbed back to the top. Then they went home.

"Do you know what everyone has in common with heroes?" His father leaned the sled against a rafter, put his hands on Hiro's shoulders. "They're scared, too."

"Tomo!" Mother called from downstairs.

"That's my cue," he said, rubbing his arms. "Turn off the lights when you come down."

His footsteps echoed down the boardwalk. Hiro watched him climb quickly out of sight. He considered following him downstairs, where it was warm, but after that talk about heroes, he felt like he should keep looking. Not like there were dragons in the attic.

He carefully climbed through the rafters, ducking to avoid the pitched roof where nails were sticking through. They'd found the brushes. The rest of the supplies were somewhere. He pulled open flaps and dug through boxes of books, found a stash of old music on silver discs and a CD player. He'd never heard of any of the artists. The cover art was things like snow and strings of lights, warm fires and evergreen trees.

He lugged a box to the boardwalk to take downstairs and went back for more. He decided to keep going till he reached the corner. One of the plastic bins had spilled a stack of books. He put them back in the bin. The pages sparkled in the white light. The glitter had worn off the covers. His mother's handwriting had faded.

The dream journals.

The pages crackled when he opened them. Hiro's journal was half full of words and pictures, the pages dogeared and torn, sketches in the margins where he'd try to show his parents what a dream looked like during breakfast. But there in the middle, where the writing had stopped, the dreams were shorter. The drawings scarce. He couldn't remember when he quit writing them down. Or why.

His mother's journal was mostly poems written in flowing handwriting; so stylish it was as enticing to look at as it was to read. Her lyrics were like candy. They grew shorter and trite. Ending with one final thought, a single line without punctuation. *And to all a good night.*

To Hiro's surprise, his father had recorded a dream. It was only one. As dreams go, it was strange in the familiar way dreams distort reality into something believable until waking. A dream of waking on a wintery morning, his head filled with sugar plums and candy canes, running downstairs in bare feet to open presents.

It sounded nice.

Boxes tipped over, and a bigger mess lay before him. He was getting careless and would freeze before he finished. He didn't want to be a hero. But when something scampered beneath the clutter, he jumped back, nearly stepping through the ceiling, and stood on the boardwalk, bumping his head on the light bulb. The light swayed into the corner. Perhaps he hadn't caused the avalanche after all. It was a rodent. Or something bigger. Like the things that lived under his bed when the lights went out.

He reached for the drawstring on the light, prepared to run all the way to the ladder. An object rolled out of a box and bounced off the insulation, dribbling onto the boardwalk. Hiro picked it up. It was round and smooth and shiny with a hook made from a paperclip. A picture was pasted to the side. *Hiro's First... something.*

The last word was missing. *My first what?*

He looked as far back into the shadows as he could see, then grabbed a golf club from a moldy bag. Squeezing the rubber grip, he advanced like a swordsman, jabbing and poking. As the minutes went by, nothing scampered, nothing moved. It was his imagination that made this mess, a mess he would clean up after he warmed up in front of the fire. The last box he poked spilled colorful tubes crimped at the bottoms. Markers and pencils followed. The art supplies were buried under a tangle of lights and silver bells. He scooped them into the box and turned to leave.

The hair stood up on the back of his neck.

It was that feeling of someone breathing behind him. Of something beneath the bed. His knuckles ached around the golf club. He backed out, careful of where he stepped, when he saw something staring at him. The light caught two unblinking eyes. Hiro held still. He nudged a paper bag aside and peeked around the rafters.

It was furry.

❄

THE SILVER DISC whirred in the player. The label, written in black marker, spun past a transparent window. It was his mother's handwriting. The player was too old for wireless earbuds. Hiro plugged headphones, the kind with spongy foam over the speakers, into the jack.

He propped pillows against the headboard. It was old-people music. You couldn't dance to it, wouldn't blare it from a car. There was no bass to boom. There were strings and bells. He wouldn't describe it as good. But it made him feel good.

He finished his sketch. Now he added color. The details were sharp. He'd dreamed the dream for the second time, the exact same dream, which was weird. It was like seeing a world through the most powerful telescope. The deep blue oceans and craggy chunks of land. He used a white pencil to color the polar caps and a cerulean blue marker to capture the atmosphere.

The squiggly lines were harder to reproduce. Their colors, in the dream, were always shifting from sienna to burnt orange to scarlet, forest green to navy blue to bright pink. He tried combining the colors, but they ended up murky. The planet looked the same in both dreams, but something was different about the second one.

Someone grabbed his foot.

Hiro leaped from the bed, and he wasn't sure, but he might have screamed. He definitely threw the CD player against the wall. The headphones ripped from his ears. Pencils and markers scattered on the floor. He stood beside his bed, covering himself, even though he was wearing three sweatshirts and two pairs of sweatpants.

"Your dad let me up," Hazel said. "He was calling you. You didn't answer."

Hiro retrieved the player. The lid was cracked. He threw it on the bed and wound the headphone wires. His heart was spinning faster than the disc. For a second, when he felt her grab his foot, he thought something had come down from the attic.

"He's nice, your dad. We talked for, like, ten minutes." She lifted a cup, holding a saucer below it. "He made tea."

She took a sip, then tossed her bookbag on the bed. Pencils and markers bounced on the sketchbook.

"Nice. You're going to use this for the report? I knew you would." She compared the colored drawing to the sketch he'd done in class, squinting back and forth.

"What are you doing here?" he said.

She frowned. "You're not as nice as your dad."

"I just mean... why are you in my house... my room?"

"So you can help with my report. Your dad was impressed. You know, teenagers on winter break doing homework, that sort of thing. I think that's why he made tea. These are different." She held up the drawings. "You're missing lines in this one."

That was it. There were fewer squiggly lines in the second dream. It was hard to remember the first dream. Maybe he had it wrong.

"I dreamed it again. Last night."

"Same dream?"

He nodded. He couldn't explain it, but it wasn't so much seeing the colors he remembered but how they felt. The squiggly lines *felt* sienna, burnt orange and scarlet. *Are there really fewer lines?*

"You're good," she said. "I wish I could draw like that."

She unpacked a laptop from her backpack. The monitor lit up. She sat on the corner of the bed, humming as she doodled the touchpad.

"Do you really need help?" he said.

"Yessss," she said. "But that's not why I'm here."

The rings on her fingers danced against each other as she tapped the keyboard. By the looks of it, she'd painted her fingernails cherry red a month ago and chewed at them ever since. He stepped around the bed. She slid the laptop toward him.

It was the Social with photos and comments and emojis: little hearts and angry faces, thumbs up and thumbs down. A video was streaming, the heading below it in all caps: TEACHER OF THE YEAR.

Hiro felt like he'd eaten a bad mushroom. His stomach recoiled. The image of Corker's classroom reached out from the screen and buried a fist in his gut. It wasn't Corker behind the podium, but a chalky student, eyes wide in terror. He wanted to slam it shut.

"They're on your side," she said. "Mostly. The video went viral. There's, like, I don't know"—she peeked at the screen—"over a thousand comments calling out bullies for putting this up. It's totally backfiring on them. I don't know why they haven't taken it down, but good."

"Why are you showing me this?" he stammered. "I-I-I never would've known."

"Because of this." She scrolled through the comments.

Hiro couldn't take his eyes off the disaster: his trembling lip caught between his teeth, sweat glistening on the bridge of his nose. And the whole world saw it.

"Here, look. Read that. Just read it." When he didn't read it, she turned the laptop back around. *"Who is this? Please tell me who you are. I dreamed that picture!* You hear that? She dreamed that sketch you did. You're not on Social, no one has your number or email. She knows nothing about you, and she said she dreamed what you drew. I thought you'd want to know. I mean, what are the odds?"

"She's just, she's playing along."

"Maybe." Hazel shrugged. "I messaged her. She sent her email. So, you know, that's it. You want it?"

"Want what?"

"Her email. Maybe there's, like, a viral dream going around, and you two are connected. Maybe it's, like, your future wife. Wouldn't that be a story? Tell your grandkids you met through this video. Sort of sweet."

He shook his head. He didn't want the email. He just wanted that video to go away. There were two weeks before they went back to school. How long did a viral video last? He knew nothing about these things.

"Look, sorry. I didn't mean to upset you. I just thought if she was for real, you should know. Maybe I shouldn't have showed you. I shouldn't have. But then you wouldn't have believed me. Anyways, I'll let you get back to whatever you're doing. Can I?" She aimed her phone at the new drawing and snapped a pic. "You want the rest of this?"

She offered the tea. When he didn't answer, she put it on the dresser.

"Oh, hey. Where'd you get this?" She grabbed the purple monkey by the gangly arms, pressed the Velcro hands together and looped them around her neck. The monkey hung against her like a baby in need of a serious bath.

"Found him in the attic." He didn't add how much it scared him. The way the purple monkey had been sitting there like a puppy.

"She smells old."

"She?"

"Yeah, she." She made a face. *Duh.* "She likes you more than me."

"She does?"

"Maybe." She took another sip of tea. "I can make up stuff, too."

She plopped the dusty monkey back on the dresser and packed

her laptop, humming again as she strapped the backpack over her shoulders.

"Anyways, bye," she said.

"Wait." Hiro went to his desk, shuffled through notebooks, found a stack of folders with bent corners. She was tickling the monkey's stomach when he handed them to her. "These are just, like, old notes and references. I'm not writing on the topic anymore, so you can use them, you know, if you want."

"Sure?"

He nodded vigorously.

"All right then. I didn't lie to your dad, then." She pulled fingerless gloves over her hands, the chipped fingernails poking through stubby holes she had cut with scissors. "It's nice to hear you say more than three words."

"Yeah, well. Okay."

"That's it?" She tilted her head, waiting. "Shouldn't you say something like…"

"Oh. Um, thanks, Hazel."

"Haze. My mom calls me *Hazel*."

She threw up two fingers, shouted, "Toots!" and headed for the stairs. Hiro stood in the doorway, heard his father ask if she was leaving already. They talked for a couple of minutes. He'd been working from home too long. When the front door closed, Hiro went back to his room. He didn't know why he'd thanked her. Then saw a scrap of paper on the bed.

It was an email.

7

The wire mesh was drawn aside; the heat from the fire blasted out like a furnace. Hiro stabbed the logs with a black poker, stirring the embers. Sometimes he'd sit in front of the fireplace until he tasted perspiration on his lip.

He stared at the mantel. Framed photos of family vacations, his grandparents, the time he played soccer in third grade (*why is that still up there?*). There were candles, too, and a painted gourd and one of those ugly mugs his mother used to sculpt. Nothing had changed. But it felt like something was missing.

"Your turn," his father said. "Hiro?"

"Sorry."

Hiro rolled dice across the board, then moved his piece, collected a power card. His mother organized her decks with one hand, eating popcorn with the other. Hiro had lost track of how many magic points he needed to advance his pod. His father had assembled a brigade of trolls outside his territory.

"Pass," Hiro said.

His father frowned. It wasn't like Hiro to pass, but he cared little about winning tonight. His mind was crowded. He found himself at a party of strange thoughts, all of them new and uninvited. There wasn't space to strategize. His father rattled the dice, tossed them on the board.

"Did you know a girl came to visit Hiro today?" he said.

"A girl?" his mother said.

"A very nice girl." He tapped his piece on the corner of the board. "We talked for several minutes. She was charming. She liked my tea."

"She liked your tea? That is charming."

Hiro shuffled his defense deck, pretended to focus. His mother held the bowl of popcorn out. Hiro shook his head.

"Who was it?" she said.

"Nobody."

"Nobody?" she said. "Does Nobody have a last name?"

"Haze," his father said.

"Haze," Mother repeated.

"You know her?"

"Hmm-mm."

Hiro's father ignored her, smiled at Hiro. "You should invite her over," he said. "There's room on the board for another player."

"She doesn't know how to play." Hiro had no idea if that was true.

It was his mother's turn. She played a strong-3 card and stacked a carriage of gnomes in the battery. Hiro took his time, played a series of giant cards and squeezed a gate across the moat. The fire crackled, and his mother dug through the popcorn in silence. His father jotted down some notes before throwing the dice.

"She's helping Hiro with his research project," he said. "She must be smart."

"Helping him? That's interesting."

Hiro scuttled away from the fire. He was suddenly hot. His stomach was twisted and empty. Ants marched up and down his skin.

"Everything all right?" his father said.

"I'm fine. Whose turn is it?"

There was nothing he could say that wouldn't make this worse. The truth would be worse than a lie. Besides, he couldn't make sense of the truth enough to tell them. The dream, the email. All of it.

His father said, "Is it the viral video?"

"No."

He'd told his mother about the video, how Corker had made him get up in front of the class, how one of the students had recorded it and posted it. Hiro looked at his socks, could feel his parents looking at him while his father gave her details of the video that only a person who had watched it would know. So now his father was on the Social. Hiro couldn't get any smaller. He didn't say anything about the comments. *Please tell me who you are. I dreamed that picture!*

There was a long pause. Then his mother took her turn and went to the kitchen. Hiro rushed through his turn. The game wasn't going to end soon enough. His father rattled the dice, dropped them on the board.

"You know, there was this girl in college—"

"I don't like her," Hiro said.

"Well, I liked this girl at college." He glanced at the kitchen, then scooted to the edge of the couch. "She was tall with long black hair that shined like a majestic bird."

"A bird?"

"Yeah, a bird. She had a magnetic smile, these big brown eyes like, like chocolate." He always struggled for analogies. "Anyway, she was very popular. She was president of a sorority, organized student activities, went to parties. Always impeccably dressed in the latest fashion."

"And you married her. I get it."

He slapped Hiro's knee. "I went weeks without saying a word to her. I was trapped in the lab or my apartment, wearing the same clothes for days at a time. There wasn't time to brush my teeth—don't tell your mother. I only thought about school and barely looked up when I walked across campus. This girl was in my English lit class, sat in the front row. I would stare at her hair, the way it flowed over her shoulders."

"Her bird hair."

"I'd wait for her to turn her head to catch a glimpse of her face. I'd get lost in daydreams. When class was over, I'd stay at my desk, pretend to write notes until she left."

"You sound a little stalkerish."

"I couldn't move when I was around her. She was this planet, and I was in her orbit. I wanted to be an asteroid soaring through the universe, but when I saw her, I just went round and round her. Like my body would fill with sand and my legs froze. I don't think I could swallow."

He shuffled his cards.

"I was coming out of a café with coffee. It was starting to drizzle, and I was waiting for a ride when she came walking down the sidewalk. She was on her phone, a sparkly scarf around her neck, her hair pulled back from her face. I was back in orbit. The coffee was shaking in my hand. She was going to see me staring, but I couldn't look away. She stopped next to me, answered a text. Her smile wrapped around me."

"I don't need to hear—"

"I opened the car door and then stopped. She was still there. And then I did it. I put the coffee on top of the car and turned around. I stuck out my hand." He held out his hand. "Hello. I'm Tomo, I said. At first, she didn't know I was talking to her. She looked up from her phone and smiled. She shook my hand. It felt like ice cream melted inside me. We're in lit class together, I said. She had no idea who I was or how much I'd studied the back of her head, but she smelled so nice. Fireworks were going off.

"It's nice to meet you, she said. I shook her hand way too long, and she was giggling, and I think I was laughing. My hand was sweaty when I let go. All I could do was nod. Then I waved, and she waved back."

He squinted across the room, seeing it happen.

"I started to duck into the car. I remembered my coffee and grabbed the door. The roof was slick, and the cup slid. Just as I was coming out of the car, it fell. The lid popped off, and all that coffee went over my head and inside my collar. It soaked my shirt, burned my back. I think she said something, but I was just... I was mortified. And you know what I did?"

"You asked her to marry you."

"I got in the car and went to class. I was completely embarrassed. The tight chest, the rotten stomach, the heat in my cheeks. I noticed the thoughts I was having and just let the sensations be there."

Another meditation lesson. Hiro had heard more than he could count. They were usually obvious, like the old man in the temple. He hadn't seen this one coming.

"I took the risk. And the next time I did it, it was easier. Still hard." He raised a finger. "The next time, I introduced myself to this lovely woman at a study group. A beautiful woman who loves to eat popcorn when she plays board games."

"I don't like Haze."

He shrugged. "You know what your grandfather always says. Jump—"

"Jump in the pool," Hiro said. "I know. I'm not asking her out."

❄

"Where'd you find these?"

His mother returned to the game with the dream journals. Hiro told her they had been in the attic when he was looking for art supplies. She played a few cards, then opened one of the faded books, sliding her fingers over the yellowed pages. She couldn't remember making them.

Hiro's father made a card play, then opened one of the journals. Hiro's newest sketches were dated over the last couple of days.

"What's this?" he said.

It was the dream he'd told them about at breakfast, he explained. He'd had the same one almost every night, floating in space, looking down on a strange planet with squiggly lines. He didn't bother telling them there were fewer squiggly lines each time he had the dream. It would be hard to describe why that felt important.

"Do you ever think we don't see something when it's in front of us?" Hiro said.

"Like what?" his father said.

"You know the science project? Mr. Corker only wants us to use facts. But facts change. Like before microscopes were invented, no one knew about microorganisms. But they were still there. There could be planets out there, things we don't know about. Maybe someone or something is trying to tell us about them through dreams."

"Sounds like someone doesn't want to do a science project," his father muttered.

"What if I wrote a report about single-celled organisms causing disease instead of evil spirits?"

"You'd fail," his father said.

"But I wouldn't be wrong."

"He won't accept drawings of imaginary planets, Hiro," his mother said sharply. "Work with what we know.

"And don't get an F." His father put the dice in front of him.

How could someone be punished for the truth? They were right, though, if he was honest. He could make up anything and say it hadn't been discovered. He pushed a dragon scout through the primordial tunnel to open a hole in the wall of ogres and grabbed a gold card from his father's stack.

"So don't take risks, that's what you're saying," Hiro said.

"Hiro," his mother said sternly.

"Something on your mind, Hiro?" his father asked.

He shook his head. Heroes were courageous. They took risks to discover the unknown. But his parents wanted him to follow the rules. Hiro wondered how many risks his father had taken since spilling coffee on his head. Did he still jump in the pool? Or did he wait to get pushed?

"Take calculated risks." His father dropped a magician's net on the board that snared Hiro's dragon scout and claimed half of Hiro's gold. "There are consequences."

8

Hiro inhaled through his nostrils. Each breath was slow and fluid while he focused on an imaginary point in his mind. His heart rate settled. The meditation bench from the attic was solid. He rarely meditated on his own. It was only when his parents made him do it during Sunday morning ceremony.

Now seemed like a good time.

When he was done, he paced around his bed to the other side and back, slowing down just enough to read the email on his laptop before making another lap. His heart was racing again. Finally, after ten laps, he stopped in front of the mirror. The purple monkey, propped against an alarm clock, watched him fuss with his collar.

He'd already changed sweaters twice. The shirt beneath it once. No matter what he did with his hair, it always fell back into place. His hair was reliably straight, even when he got out of bed. He rubbed his finger over his teeth, tested his breath.

"Hi. Hi there. Howdy." He cleared his throat and loosened his collar. "What am I doing? Or, nothing. Just, you know."

Meditation didn't help. He went back to pacing. If he walked fast enough, he could outpace the claustrophobic feelings. But anxiety trailed like a tether of tin cans. He kept moving, glancing at the email, went back to the mirror. He turned the monkey toward the window, then turned him back around. He needed to practice in front of someone. Even a stuffed monkey.

He cleared his throat, pulled back his shoulders, and smiled. He looked like an advertisement for life insurance. "Hello. It's nice to—"

His phone buzzed. Hiro stepped back like it was the rodent from the attic (which he still hadn't told his parents about). A number popped up. *Oh, God. She's calling me.* It was a local area code, so it couldn't be her. He touched the screen.

"Hello?" he said.

"Hey." It took a moment to recognize her voice. Haze said, "I was going to text, but didn't. You still drawing?"

"How did you get my—"

"Your dad gave it to me." Hiro thought for a second, recalled their cell numbers taped to the refrigerator. "I was going to come over," she said, "but I didn't want your parents getting the wrong idea. And your mom's a little intense. So, hey, here I am. I was just—"

"What do you want?" he said.

There was a long pause. "You need to work on manners."

"Sorry." Tension had slung the words out of him. There were more that wanted out, and he couldn't stop them. "She wants to video chat."

"Who?"

"The girl. The, uh..." He studied his laptop. "Pride204. You know, from the video. The email?"

"Awww, you emailed her. I'm proud of you, stepping up like that. That's why I called, mostly. Also, to tell you they took the post down. Your video is viral no more. There were, like, a thousand comments, and they were all sticking up for you, talking about how brave you were to get up like that."

Brave? He didn't *want* to get up in front of the class. Certainly didn't want the world to see it.

"Anyways, when you calling her?" she said.

"I'm not." He looked in the mirror, phone pressed against his ear. "What would I say?"

"Most people start with hello."

"That's not what I mean."

"Talk about the drawing, Hiro. It's not a date."

Words didn't come easy for him. When he looked at someone, a snowstorm blew into his brain. The words were in there; he just couldn't see them. Then he ended up staring at the other person, and that never went well.

"What if I freeze?" he said.

"That's what you're scared of? You don't have a terminal disease, Hiro. You live in a house with heat and food and a mom and a dad. You'll survive. You've already been embarrassed in front of the class. You went up there, everyone was looking at you, and you were just staring back at us, biting your lip and hanging onto the podium like it teetered over a volcano. And then someone put it on the Social and—"

"You're not helping." He returned to pacing.

"Do you know how to ride a bike?"

"No," he lied.

"You don't know how to ride a bike?"

"Yes, I know how to ride a bike."

"You didn't do it the first time, did you? Same thing. Just click her number, stand back and say, 'Hi, my name is Hiro.' Here, practice. Do it now."

"It's easy for you. Everyone likes you."

Genuine laughter erupted. She snorted and sighed. "That's why I'm calling you on a Friday night, because everyone likes me. Please. What people think of me is none of my business. You're scared, Hiro. You can feel scared and call her at the same time."

"You sound like my mother."

"Aww. Take that back."

She sounded like she meant it. Haze only knew his mother when she was in teacher mode. Although teacher mode had become her default mode.

"Why are you doing this?" he said.

"Doing what?"

"Calling me. Helping."

"I don't know." He imagined she was chewing her nails. "You and her dreamed the same thing. It's weird, but it's also, I don't know, important. Or maybe I just wish I dreamed, too."

"I wished you dreamed this, too." Then she would be making the call. It would be easy for her, and she would love it. *Why me?*

"I'm not calling her, Hiro. Push the button. Oh, and one more thing. I need more notes for the report. And maybe you can write a paragraph for me, you know, just to get it started. Help me get in the flow. You don't have to write much, like half a page or a page or two, you know, if you find yourself in the flow and—"

"You're using me, Haze."

"Aww. That's sweet. Tell me how the call goes."

❄

The laptop was on the bed, the desk chair facing it. Hiro adjusted the screen so the camera would capture the bookshelf behind him. He moved a family photo so it would be over his right shoulder, then adjusted the books so the most important ones were in frame. They were smart books, ones he'd never read. He considered lighting a candle.

He'd selected a maroon sweater that fit nicely. Made his shoulders look sharp. He experimented with different postures: slouching forward looked too casual; legs crossed was too proper. He tried the chair backwards and rested his chin on the back.

He opened the bedroom door. The television could be heard from downstairs. His father would be on his laptop, and his mother would be curled beneath a comforter. Hiro moved his dresser to block the door. He didn't have a lock.

After a few trips around the bed, he plopped down. Waiting was making it worse. Wading into a cold pool was a bad way to get in. *Just jump.* He tapped the keyboard and closed his eyes, stopped himself from slamming the laptop shut, forced himself to sit there and open his eyes. The call was spinning. She wasn't going to pick up. *At least I tried.*

A face appeared.

Her complexion was dark, lips full. Her eyes brown and wide, staring back from another dimension. Hiro started to bite his lip.

"Hi," he said. "My name is—"

The screen was a blur. He saw palm trees and a deck, then a door. A stove briefly flashed by. "Where are you going, young lady?" someone said, their voice fading. Hiro watched stairs with beige carpeting swing past. Heard a door slam. The ruffle of blankets. Then he was looking at a ceiling fan slowly turn. There was the sound of shuffling papers; the phone tipped to reveal a messy desk.

A painting filled his screen. Her fingers clutched the page, switching it to a drawing, then a sketch, then another drawing. There were five or six of them.

"How many times have you dreamed this?" She shook the paper. Flakes of paint fell off. "Wait, don't tell me. Write down your answer. We need to be objective. Do it, write it down."

Hiro turned to his desk, then hid an index card on his lap. She counted down to zero, and they both showed their answer to the camera. They both had dreamed it five times.

"I'm on the phone!" She left the screen and turned on music. She returned, her face filling the entire screen. She whispered, "It's not a dream. I mean, it is, but it's more than that. It's a place. It's a place, Hiro. She told me about a book. Look."

She left again. Things tumbled out of sight. A purple cover was suddenly on his computer. *Lucid Dreaming.*

"I found it at the library. It's old, really old. But it explains what's happening. Dreams aren't just dreams, they're windows. Not windows. *Doorways.* Most nights we're just looking through them, seeing what's over there. But you can crawl through a window if you open it. I thought the dream was noise until I saw your drawing. Your drawing! She told me you'd been going there, too. That's when I knew, I just knew she was right."

Haze told her? "What's that music?" Hiro said.

Everything was spinning so fast, he barely heard the song in the background until the bells began to chime. And then he recognized the tune. The words. It was what he'd heard on the CD. The music he'd found in the attic.

"Christmas music." She smiled. "You forgot about it. We all did. That's why we're dreaming the dream." She shook her drawing. "This is what took Christmas away. I started searching the library. There's this corner with really old books, where I found this one. It had fallen behind some other books. It's about Santa Claus and reindeer and snowmen…"

She continued naming names and things he'd never heard of but seemed distantly familiar. Like a memory from a time in the cradle, ushered from the fog by the timeless music. Was he really remembering it, or just thinking he did?

"Do your parents move furniture around this time of year?" she asked.

Hiro fidgeted. He began to shake.

"My parents chop down a tree and leave it in the backyard, like they don't know what to do with it. She told me they—"

"Who told you?" Hiro said.

"Someone who—never mind. You'll think I'm crazy."

That was exactly what he would have thought. If she didn't have those drawings. Didn't say that about the tree. *We have a tree in our attic.*

"We need to stick to facts," she said. "Fact, we're having the same dream. Fact, we live in different parts of the world. Fact, our drawings look the same, almost exactly. And this one, the last one… let me see the last one you did."

He showed it.

"See! Look, there are fewer portals."

She traced the squiggly lines.

"It's how we get there," she whispered. "And they're disappearing. If we don't get there soon, they'll be gone. She said he's cutting them off, one by one. And when the last one is gone, we'll never see Christmas again."

"Christmas?" He shook his head. *Why would that be important?* "Who's telling you all this?"

"Chase!" someone shouted.

She looked away. "I'm coming!"

"Mom said we're going!" someone replied.

"I said I'm coming!" She carried her phone to the corner of the room. "Don't ask your parents about Christmas. It'll upset them. Like something they want to remember but can't. Just, for now, don't say anything. And meet me there tonight."

"Where?" What was he going to do, board a plane?

She thumped the purple book. "Wake up inside the dream. It's all here. When you go to bed tonight, keep looking at your hands. I don't know why it works, but that's what they say. Look at your hands and ask yourself if you're dreaming. When you have a tiny doubt that you're not awake, then you're in the dream." She got up and peeked out the bedroom door. "I'll meet you there."

"Wait!" Hiro said. "How do I... are you serious?"

This wasn't what he expected. He didn't have time to be nervous. *Stick to the facts. And the facts are there.*

"Hello?" he said. "What do you mean by—"

She fumbled the phone. It bounced on the floor. He was looking at her dresser. The drawer was half open. He waited for her to pick it up, he had so many questions, and then he saw something that made all the doubt go away. All those facts were trumped by what was sitting on top of *her* dresser. The long arms with purple fur.

A monkey looking at him.

9

Most nights I made the journey.

Sometimes Madeline was sleeping, curled up with the purple monkey (I wasn't the cuddly type. Couldn't argue that). Other times no one was home. This morning, I smelled bacon and went to the kitchen.

"Good morning," Madeline said.

Madeline was always excited to see me. Like I'd sailed overseas and was home on leave. Truth was even stranger. I had done the math. Time went faster here. On an average night of sleep, I would be here for two and a half days, a one-to-seven ratio. One day at home was seven days here. I hadn't figured out where *here* was.

I climbed onto an empty chair and bumped knuckles with the dad. I'd never been cool. Not even a little. They were eating breakfast. Just a normal day with a normal family. With a red skeleton.

"I wonder if Viktor dreams," Madeline said to the mom. "Do you dream, Viktor?"

I shook my head. I didn't like to think about that. The more time I spent here, the more it made me dizzy. *Am I a man dreaming about being a toy, or the other way around?*

The mom put a bowl on my placemat. It looked like porridge. I smelled it first, let the aroma of cinnamon and sugar fill my senses, then stirred it with my finger. If I had eyes, they would have rolled back into my skull. Flavors surged through my bones. The satisfaction utterly complete. Food wasn't nourishing, not that I was aware of. The experience, though, was blissful. The sweeter, the better. I once dipped my feet in a bowl of peppermint corn syrup and wept in ecstasy.

"Off you go," the dad said. "See you after school."

Madeline packed her bookbag and went to school. The mom kissed the dad, and off to her workshop she went. The dad finished breakfast, and off to his office he went. I stirred the cinnamon porridge for thirty minutes.

The thing you don't understand about being a toy is that nothing else matters but the present moment. When I was here, I was completely content. Even cleaning the kitchen was fabulous. I never grew bored. Think of the greatest thing you've ever done in your life, the sweetest moment you've ever experienced—your first kiss, the perfect job, winning the lottery. It's like that. All the time.

Pure joy.

I watched the neighbor mow his lawn, then edge the driveway. It was wholly captivating. Like watching an award-winning movie, but without a plot or acting. It was sometime before lunch when I noticed something new in the living room: two columns anchored next to the fireplace, one on each side. They were shiny metal tubes, my distorted reflection in each one, with wires and conduit drilled into the floor. It was an odd choice, didn't match the sofa.

Curiosity tickled my bones. It would turn into a tidal wave of obsession before long. Things like this, discrepancies I couldn't understand, eroded my attention for anything else. Maybe the pipes were part of an entertainment system, speakers or projectors of some sort. I watched my reflection grow wider as I neared one of them.

The dad was in his office. He rarely came out. I didn't know what he did in there. Occasionally, there was tinkering. This time I heard him talking. That was a first. I gave up on the lawn care. The dad's one-sided conversation was heating up. I could feel what he was saying, like sound waves in my skull. I couldn't quite understand them, though, until his voice grew louder.

"It'll work this time," he said, pausing. "Christmas. Yes, I know. I know. Yes, because... right, time syncs. The math is sound, you've seen it yourself."

I put my head against the door.

"You have a hard time believing this? Where did the toys come from?! It's not much of a leap. Just... yes, Christmas. That's all I ask. Okay? Okay. When do you think you'll get an answer?"

The conversation trailed off. Then it was quiet. Just the occasional clink of glass or metal, a door closing. He was back to whatever he did. I couldn't reach the doorknob. Instead, I knocked. The dad opened the door.

"Viktor, everything all right? You need something?"

The room beyond him was a gravity field I couldn't deny. I was pulled inside, recognizing things on bench tops: magnets and pulleys, heat lamps and pendulums. A spectrometer, a voltameter, a potentiometer. Electromagnets. This wasn't an office. *It's a lab.*

"Sorry, buddy."

The dad swept me off the floor. He dropped me on the couch, threw a blanket over my lap, because that's what Madeline did. The television turned on.

"I won't be long."

He went back to his lab. Here I thought he was writing software programs or selling insurance. I'd just watched a man bag grass clippings with total fascination. I'd already calculated the time dilation between home and this place. *Imagine what I could discover with a complete physics lab!*

I had been plopped on the couch like the family pet. The dad was more likely to see if I'd fetch a ball than allow me to calibrate a spectrometer. I listened at the door again, but it was mostly silence.

I returned to staring at unknown talk shows, one that featured puppets on oversized couches. The audience was a mix of humans and toys. I watched numbly, barely aware of the story they were reporting of a human-sized wooden puppet pounding a podium. He had a red heart painted on his chest and wore a comical top hat. It was a satire of a political rally. Only it wasn't satire.

It was this place.

❄

My first words came out in lumps. How I said them, no idea. No tongue, no vocal cords. No lips, lungs, or air to produce sound. Yet there they were, vibrating in my skull like a cheap radio.

Madeline looked up from her homework. I pointed at the lab. She muted the television, twisted on the couch. I wasn't sure I could do it again. I focused on the words until they crystallized, felt them release like pebbles in a slingshot.

"What. Is. There?"

"Viktor!" She scrambled over the couch. "You talked! You did it, you did it." She slid on her knees, hugged me till my joints popped. "Can you say my name? Wait, wait."

She ran back to the couch, came back with her phone.

"Look at me, just like that. Okay, there. Now, say my name. Go."

I hobbled away from the door, then concentrated, saw the word. "Mads. Lynn."

She squealed like I was a winning lottery ticket.

"Oh, merry, merry." Whooshing sounds flew off her phone. "I'm sending this to Mom and Dad first. I'm going to say those were your first words. Oh, merry." She thumbed her phone with a grin that could float a balloon. "Viktor's... first... words..."

I knocked on the lab door. Pointed.

"We can't go in there," she said.

"What. In. There?"

"Dad stuff," she said, distracted. "Sciency stuff."

I gave her a moment. A toy's first words, apparently, was a big deal. Three more posts, twenty replies, and a selfie with me later, she sat back and shook her head, basking in the glow of new parenthood. Or toyparenthood, I suppose.

"What. Does. He do?" I managed two words in a sentence that time.

"He's looking for someone."

I nodded. There was more. She checked her phone, looked around.

"Don't tell anyone," she said. *Hilarious.* "He's looking for Santa Claus. Do you know who that is?"

I shook my head. Of course I did. Like a good scientist, I wanted to hear who she thought he was.

"He's a jolly fat man with a long, white beard. Wears a red coat. He's got this sleigh, right? It's pulled by flying reindeer. I don't know how they fly, but they do. They fly him to every house on Christmas, land on the roof. Santa comes down the chimney, I don't know how, but he does. And he delivers toys to good girls and boys."

"Toys?" I was intrigued. I didn't know why. *I'm a toy.*

"Toys, things we want. Whatever. He puts them under the tree and fills the stockings by the fireplace. I don't know how it all works, but that's what happens on Christmas."

She leaned back on the floor, satisfied with her answer. I had too many questions that had nothing to do with how Santa squeezed through a chimney or how reindeer flew without wings. The simple physics of visiting every house in a single night was impossible, for starters. At the rate I was producing words, it would take all night to ask the questions I wanted to ask.

I pointed at the door again. *What does your dad do?*

"Oh." She seemed to understand. "Yeah, well. He has a theory. Technically, it's a hypothesis. He says that every year on Christmas, when the clock strikes midnight, time synchronizes between all galaxies. Wait, that's not it." Her nose scrunched in thought. "Between realities, whatever that means. And Santa uses a time-warping bubble to travel through space portals to get here. Like time inside it stops so he can go everywhere. Something like that."

I didn't see that coming. But I was a toy, so my suspension of disbelief was fully engaged.

"He's not crazy." She sounded less bubbly. "I don't care what anyone says. The toys arrived, like, a hundred years ago. On Christmas. No one thinks that's crazy. Dad thinks they came here because of Santa. That Santa has some verve, like Christmas spirit or something, that did it. And that's why toys are alive."

"Verve?"

"Yeah, verve. He thinks that sounds better than magic. He should just call it Christmas spirit."

She picked me up. We went to the couch and opened the laptop. She scrolled through her social media, answering all the replies. Posted the selfie of us, splashed it with little hearts. I tapped her arm. She looked at me with a smile that could melt snow.

"Looking?" I said.

It took her a moment. She'd already forgotten our conversation. I couldn't think of anything else now.

"Oh. He's going to take a picture of him when he comes through the chimney next Christmas."

She glanced at the fireplace. The metal tubes anchored next to it.

That was all I was going to get. The mom got home and plopped on the couch with us, listening to Madeline tell the story of my first words (second words, technically). The mom was almost as happy as Madeline. Then the dad came home. Not as happy, but still excited. I said their names, just to make a show. We would celebrate with a special dessert. I dipped my fingers in a smoothie of fizzy nectarines. Yes, it was delicious.

But things had changed.

I couldn't quite get back into the flow of just being present. A train of thoughts plowed through my head. The Santa myth was a lot to digest. The theory of time bubbles and space portals? Maybe. I was a toy, after all. The only thing stranger than dreams was real life. This might not be a dream. And if it wasn't a dream... *how did I get here?*

10

"So what's her name?" Haze said.

Hiro paced in the front room with the phone on speaker. He parted the curtains. The driveway was empty. Mrs. Parsons was walking her dog, saw him looking out the window and waved.

"Chase." He closed the curtains. "She wants to meet me."

"She lives here?"

"No. Meet me, like, in the dream."

There was a long pause. "Uh, what?"

"She's having the same dream and told me to meet her there, said she read a book on lucid dreaming. I'm supposed to look at my hands. I never should have called her."

It wasn't just that. It was everything. It was all so insane he might never sleep again.

"So did you?" she said.

"Did I what?"

"Meet her in the dream. If you did—"

"No. No, Haze. I didn't meet her in the dream."

"Because if you did, that would be wild."

He walked faster now, pacing through the family room, into the kitchen, back to the front room, looked out the window again, then started the loop again. He hadn't slept much that night. The monkey had been staring at him. He'd put it in the closet and stared at the ceiling for hours, getting out of bed and walking until his legs were tired. At some point, he'd dreamed the dream. The planet hovered in space.

"I'm not doing it anymore," he said. He was just going to follow the rules, play it safe. Read a book. "I don't know why I called you."

"Because you need to talk."

"I've got to go."

"You're going to make another drawing?"

"I threw them away. This is stupid. It got me in trouble, and then the whole thing in front of the class and everyone laughing at me. I want everything to go back to the way it was."

He just wanted to forget any of it happened. Go back to being a boring, happy idiot. *Why did I have to dream?*

"What was the name of the book?" she said.

"What book?"

"The one you told me about five minutes ago. The one she read."

"*Lucid Dreaming.*"

Haze muttered to herself. He heard typing. "The library has it," she said. "Sounds donkey. I'm going to get it."

"Why? Forget it. I'm not doing any of it. Thank you for helping and everything, I guess, but no."

"That was heartfelt."

"I just mean, you know, talking to me. That's all." No one ever did that. "I'll help you with the report. I'll just write it for you. I'm good at that. I'll fill it with so many facts it'll choke a whale. Corker will love it. If he's still teaching."

"You're funny." She laughed. Actually laughed. "Wait. What do you mean still teaching?"

He told her about the strange conversation at detention, how it sounded like he might not be coming back. "Don't get your hopes up."

"Where's he going?"

"Nowhere. You know how he is."

"But he was writing letters?"

"I don't know what he was doing."

"Yeah. Yeah." She was typing. Then said, "Bye."

Hiro looked at the phone. She'd hung up. He wasn't expecting it. He was never very good at stopping a conversation. He didn't have much practice at it. But, if he was honest, he felt just a little bit better talking to Haze. He was going to write her report. It was the least he could do.

❄

Hiro was licking a spoon when a car door slammed.

The cookies weren't done. His parents weren't supposed to be home for another fifteen minutes. He wanted to surprise them. At least the house smelled like cookies. *That's the best part,* his mother used to say. He couldn't remember the last time she made cookies. He washed his hands and dried them on the apron, gave the batter one last stir before dropping a dollop on the cookie sheet.

The doorbell rang.

A red truck was parked on the street, the door panels crusted with gray snow, the windshield sealed under a layer of ice with only a thin line scraped away. He cracked open the front door, cold air seeping in. Haze's nose was shiny. She shook her head and pushed past him.

"I think my snot froze." She shucked her boots by the door. "It's so warm in here. What is it, like, eighty degrees? My dad keeps it at sixty-eight. Wear more clothes, he says. They're free." She unzipped her coat, looked around. "Are you standing guard?"

He was holding the spoon like a club. She stripped off her bookbag and followed the smell. He shoved her boots into the corner where the snow would melt. She was at the kitchen counter with her finger in a metal bowl, a glob of cookie dough hooked on the end of her finger. She found a spoon for the next scoop.

"Um, I know I ask this a lot," he said, "but what are you—"

"What are you doing here?" she blurted. "Beat you."

She dropped her backpack on the table, licking the spoon like a lollipop, and fished into one of the pockets. She dropped a book. The dull cover was in a crinkly plastic sleeve. *Lucid Dreaming: How to Wake Up.*

"I can't believe they even had it," she said. "It's super old. Only been checked out once, like, ever."

She opened the refrigerator, put a gallon of milk on the counter. "It's about waking up *while* you're dreaming. Said you can become conscious in a dream world, have a body, fly, do whatever. Guy who wrote it has a PhD, does research and everything. So it's real."

She found a glass and a plate, sat at the table with a glob of cookie dough.

"I mean, if it was just some blogger saying it, then you probably couldn't. You know, like people who say you can live off eating air. No, this guy has a whole team who—hey!"

Hiro grabbed the plate. "You can't eat that."

"It's cookie dough."

"It's uncooked." He dumped it in the garbage disposal. "Raw eggs aren't good for you."

"I'll take my chances." She licked the spoon. "So the hands thing you said, it's supposed to be some sort of anchor. Like, I guess if you look at your hands when you're dreaming, you'll realize you're in the dream without actually waking up. It's down to a science, which is weird, because I've never heard of this. You'd think people would be talking about it. Are you even listening?"

"I told you I don't want to talk about it anymore. I mean, thank you and everything for getting the book. It's nice and all." He grabbed the spoon from her. "Let me bake it first; you'll get sick. You can take some home with you."

"Aww. That's so sweet. You're telling me to leave."

"No, that's not it. My parents aren't home."

She covered her mouth. "And you have a girl in the house. I'll bet that's against the rules."

He doled out lumps of cookie dough on the cookie sheet. The oven was preheating. He just wanted to bake some cookies and not think about anything for a while. Haze was at the table, slurping milk and licking her fingers, the sound of pages turning. He couldn't wait for the oven to preheat, set the timer and put the cookies in. Then give her a paper plate and push her out the door. Everything would go back to normal. He could not talk to anyone in class, no one would notice him, and he would get good grades. *Normal.*

"Tell me a story," she said.

"What?"

"A story about a boy named Jack and a girl named Jill. Jack doesn't know Jill, but he calls her anyway, and they talk. Tell me a story about that."

"I'm not telling you a story." He washed his hands.

"Pretend it's a story. And keep busy with whatever you're doing."

"I'm washing my hands."

"All right, then wash your hands and make some tea. Probably won't be as good as your dad's."

She started looking through the cabinets, found the dish soap and filled the sink with bubbles. Then she started washing the dishes, humming as she did it. Drying them, looking for where they went without asking, wiping the counters. Ignoring him when he asked her to stop. Not answering his questions. He thought about going to his room. But that would be strange if his parents came home. Worse if she followed him up there.

"Her drawings were just like mine." He sat at the table, staring at the book. "Even the new ones. She wasn't faking it. There were fewer of those squiggly lines on them, just like mine."

"Portals."

"That's what she said."

Haze snorted. "Go on."

"Yeah, well, she asked if my parents move the furniture around this time of year, which they do."

"I just got the chills."

"And her parents cut down a tree and drag it into the backyard."

"Why?"

"It's called Christmas." He looked up. "And we all forgot about it.

Everyone in the world did. Someone told her that's why we're having the dream."

"Who told her?"

"She wouldn't say." I shrugged. "I thought it was you."

She grimaced like there was a bad smell. "Why would everyone forget?"

"Do you remember Christmas?"

"Never heard of it. Anyway—furniture, dead trees and Christmas. Keep going."

He took a deep breath. "Remember that music I was listening to, the CD player? She was playing the same song when I called. Sleigh bells and one-horse open sleighs. Christmas music."

She wasn't looking at him. She was staring across the room, putting it all together. He couldn't make up a story like this.

"The planet, the one we're both dreaming about, that's what made everyone forget. If we don't stop it, no one will ever remember Christmas again."

She shook her head. "You're not making this up?"

"No."

"No wonder you're like... *gah*."

That was exactly how his brain felt. *Gah*. "That's not all."

He checked on the cookies, opening the oven just a bit, dry heat on his face, cookie smell filling the room. It made him feel comfortable. Or maybe it was the talking. Or the look on Haze's face.

"Well?" She shook her head. "What is it?"

"You remember my purple monkey?" He leaned against the counter.

"Don't tell me—"

"Just like it."

"She did not."

Haze walked around the kitchen table. Twice. She started to talk and stopped, flopped into a chair and squinted. Turned to him. "Seriously?"

He nodded.

"Where'd she get it?"

"I don't know."

"Where'd you get it?"

"It was in the attic."

"I know, but how did it get there?"

He had thought about it a great deal but couldn't remember. His only memory was that it was waiting on his bed one day. No one ever said anything about it.

"This isn't a scam," she muttered. "Have you tried calling her again?"

"I just want to forget about it."

She nodded, tapping the table, finding a small glob of cookie dough and licking it off her finger. Then pointed. "You need to meet her."

"I don't know where she lives."

Haze slid the book across the table. "Meet her."

He laughed. It felt good, releasing tension that had turned his stomach into a concrete mold. "You can't be serious," he said.

"I don't know, am I? You just told me an impossible story. You don't look like you're lying. Are you lying?"

He shook his head for a number of reasons.

"Yeah, well, then you need to try. Meet her in that dream. What do you have to lose? You're going to sleep anyway."

"That doesn't even make sense. If I meet her in my dream, it won't be her. It'll just be... *thoughts!*"

"Who told her about Christmas?"

"She read it in a book, something about Santa something and reindeer." That twisty feeling was returning. "Look, Haze, maybe you're right. Someone at school is just—"

"No, you said someone told her that's why you're having the dream. Who told her?"

"That's what I mean. Someone at school, Perry or Richard, is helping her."

A cold elixir of fear stirred into the pot of anxiety. This was an elaborate hoax. This kind of thing happened all the time. It was a matter of how they knew he was listening to music, had a purple monkey in his room, the furniture moved around. *How could they know that?*

He stepped back. He pointed. "You're helping them."

"What?"

"You knew all this stuff before I called her. You made me call her."

She nodded. She was admitting it. The fear and anxiety lit fumes of anger. She held up her hands. He backed against the refrigerator, pointing at the front room, stammering. Gently, she grabbed his arms.

"I know you don't have friends. Neither do I. If I did, it wouldn't be Perry or Dick. I wouldn't, in a million years, do this to anyone. Especially you, Hiro. You're right, I saw the monkey; I guess I could've seen the furniture. But I didn't hear the music, Hiro. You broke the player when I came to your room."

His breath was choppy. It was her touch that kept him from running. Her kind eyes. She was right. The player had been broken.

"Besides," she said, "if I did this to you, who's going to write my report?"

The emotions suddenly bubbled with intoxicating hope. When she smiled, he smiled. And he wanted to hug her. It was the relief, that was it. Someone was there with him in all this. Someone believed him. Wanted to help him. Wanted him to write a report.

"Hello?" his father called. "Someone here?"

Haze let go of Hiro and started moving the dishes around. They were already clean. She grabbed the tea kettle and started filling it with water. Hiro was pasted to the refrigerator, his arms still warm where she'd held onto him. His mother's voice snapped him out of it. He started to panic, going to the oven, then swiped the book off the table and hid it beneath his apron.

"Oh." His mother stopped in the doorway.

"Hello, Mrs. Tanaka," Haze said.

"Well, hello, Ms. Melblank."

"Please, call me Haze."

Mother peeled her gloves off one finger at a time. "Making cookies, are we?"

"She just got here," Hiro said, "and I just started a batch, so she was—"

"I thought I recognized that truck," his father said. "Hello there, young lady. It's good to see you. Hiro, I'm glad you have company. I see you *spilled the coffee*." He winked. Haze and his mother looked at him. "Are you making tea?"

"We heard you pull into the driveway," Haze said. "We thought we'd start the water."

"Would you look at that, honey?" He loosened his tie. "She started the water. What are you kids up to?"

"School," Hiro said.

His father went to the cabinet for a box of tea. He set four mugs on the counter, rubbing his hands together. Mother hadn't moved.

"We're almost done with Mr. Corker's report," Hiro said. "Haze was helping with references and doing a proofread for me. I was making, you know, cookies."

"Is that what those are?" his mother said. "Can I see your reports?"

"I put them away." Hiro swallowed the lie like a golf ball. "It's still pretty rough and—"

"Have a seat." His father pulled out chairs. "Anything we can do to help you, just ask. You have an engineer and a schoolteacher at your disposal."

"Oh, yes," his mother said. "We'd love to help. Let's see what you've written so far."

This was getting out of control for no reason at all. There were plenty of things he didn't want to tell her, but this was a pointless lie. There was no way around this. He was going to get out of this before it became something, tell her everything about the drawing and the phone call. He reached under his apron for the lucid dreaming book.

"I have a question," Haze said. "Have you ever heard of Christmas?"

Hiro's parents did something he'd never seen them do. Nothing ever surprised them. They never looked shocked. They met every moment, no matter how pleasant or stressful, with meditative introspection.

They winced. Like the question poked them in the stomachs.

"We were researching." Haze poured hot water in the mugs. "We came across the word and didn't know what it was. Someone named Santa. What did he do, Hiro?"

"I… I don't remember."

He was watching his parents deflate. They were struggling with the question. Not like when his father grappled with a difficult calculation or when his mother faced a creative block. They were lost.

His mother left the kitchen. His father dropped teabags on the floor. He picked them up and shoved them on the counter, then followed her out. Hiro and Haze waited for them to return. The bathroom door closed, then the bedroom door.

"What just happened?" Haze said.

"You weren't supposed to ask them about Christmas."

11

Hiro plugged in the laptop. He walked around his bedroom while it booted up, leaning over the desk to check the progress. Chase had sent twelve emails within the last forty-eight hours. He took another lap, debating whether to read them or not. But he'd come this far.

Where were you?
Did you read the book?
I can't wait any longer for you.
Ride the purple tail.
I'll go away soon. It's the only way to save Christmas.

Slowly, gently, he closed the laptop and sat there, feeling the words march through his head. He was expecting that. He wanted to have a calm conversation with Chase. Her messages sounded like aliens were invading. He was already walking a thin line of confidence. He wanted to jump in the pool. Not be pushed.

Where were you? Well, he wasn't there, wherever she expected him to be. Which was impossible. He assumed she was asking if he'd read the lucid dreaming book, which how did she know he had it? *I can't wait any longer for you.* Fine. Why was she waiting? *Ride the purple tail.* No idea what that could mean.

I'll go away soon. That bothered him. It was slightly cryptic. It sounded more like she was running away, not lucid dreaming. That was the thing with dreams. If things got too scary, she just had to open her eyes. She wasn't really going anywhere. *It feels like she means it.*

He pulled out the meditation bench, took long slow breaths and settled into a centered focus. After several minutes, he dug through the trash. The drawings were crumpled in tight balls. He smoothed them on the bed, arranged them in the order he drew them. They were in decent shape. He found some tape and put them on the wall.

"This is crazy," he muttered.

He went downstairs. His parents were reading by the fireplace. His father's face was illuminated in the tablet's soft glow. His mother was reading a hardcover with one hand in a bowl of popcorn.

"I'm going to read upstairs," Hiro said. "Probably fall asleep. Just wanted to say goodnight."

"Don't stay up late," his father said. "We're getting up early, don't forget."

They were going to his grandparents' for brunch. They did that at this time of year: got dressed up for it. It was more of a way-too-early dinner than brunch. He'd never wondered why they did that every year. Now he questioned everything.

"Your father would like to apologize about the *coffee*," his mother said without looking up from her book.

"What for?" Hiro said.

"It was inappropriate," she said. "Tomo?"

He cleared his throat. "I'm sorry, Hiro, for embarrassing you in front of your friend." He shook his head while he said it. Hiro smiled.

"Are you shaking your head, Tomo?"

"No." He nodded.

"Tomo, we talked about this."

"I'm sorry, she seems like a nice girl. Friendly and I'll bet funny. Right, Hiro?"

"She's a friend."

"Of course she is," he said. "I'm just saying, it took guts to have her over here. And when we were gone."

His mother looked up with tired eyes. She was not entertained. His father should be apologizing to her. He said something else but couldn't crack the lines furrowed in her cheeks. They seemed back to normal: Mother's anxiety delicately frosting her emotions; Father attempting to fan her sense of humor back to life. The blank sadness that had briefly hovered over them earlier in the day was gone.

"She is nice," Hiro said. "And I'm sorry about what she asked."

"Asked what?" his father said.

Hiro knew why he said that. It was a test. They were either great actors or completely forgot Haze had asked about Christmas, which brought on a temporary bout of melancholy.

"Never mind," Hiro said. "Goodnight."

He went through the front room and stopped at the stairs. The curtains were closed. White light shined in the corner where the furniture had been pushed aside. It looked like a lamp had tipped over. Hiro bent down. It was a tangle of wire.

A string of lights was piled in the corner.

❄

Hiro sometimes read an entire book in a single sitting. *Lucid Dreaming* was not one of them.

It was dry and factual. The kind of book that made Corker smile. The author was a sleep expert whose research, for the past twenty years, had been entirely on dreaming. Dreaming had become rare, the author said. It was a dream deficit epidemic. *People don't dream anymore,* he said. *We want to know why.* Hiro started speed-reading before he was done with the first chapter. When he flipped to the end to see how many pages were left, he knew he would never finish it.

Lucid dreaming was becoming conscious while in the dream. It occurred during REM sleep, when dreams were most vivid, which was primarily in the latter half of the night. The description of participants' experiences was interesting and, he had to admit, a touch unbelievable. It was no different than being awake.

He glanced at his drawings. He would have ditched the book right there had he not had the same dream every night for the past week.

He began skipping pages after the fourth chapter, went to the second section that discussed technique. It started with sophisticated lab equipment, lights that would shine on closed eyes when REM was detected, to signal the sleeper it was time to *wake up*. Apparently, they could see light in their dreams. How that didn't fully wake them up seemed impossible. Hiro didn't have equipment and wasn't going to ask his parents for it.

There were simple techniques, like getting in the habit of asking himself if he was dreaming. "Am I dreaming?" he muttered, looking around. "No."

That was easy.

The second was an anchor. Something that would confirm the dream state. The author suggested looking at his hands. *Chase really did read the book.* There might have been more, but his eyes grew heavy and bored.

"Still not dreaming."

He was 100% sure of it. He studied his hands, front and back. What was so magical about the hands? It didn't matter. He wasn't going to meet another person inside *his* dream. If he did, it wasn't going to be her.

"Am I—"

A noise startled him. Adrenaline spiked his eyes open. Something fell in the closet. He stayed still, holding his breath. If he would've heard breathing, he would've leaped out of his room without touching the floor. After a minute of silence, his heart thumping, he reached for the closet door, careful not to put his foot on the floor, just in case his childhood monster was real. Light cut across the neatly hung school uniforms and shiny shoes stacked on the floor.

The purple monkey stared from the corner. Her long arms lay over her lap like furry noodles. That was where Hiro had put her. She hadn't moved an inch, he was certain. Perhaps something fell from the shelf, but he didn't investigate.

It was almost midnight. He turned off the lights, snuggled into his pillows. The streetlight beamed through the window, a rectangular box of light centered on the drawings. The longer he stared at them, the more it looked like an art gallery. The colors were playful. Even in the harsh light, they were soft and inviting. He could feel their blurry edges. They were fuzzy and glowing. The planets vibrant.

The lines made no sense. Maybe they were manifestations of solar wind, or gamma rays just before a black hole formed. But it was clearly a planet. It would have to be a star to become a black hole. Maybe it was a planet-sized spaceship and the inhabitants lived on the surface. Maybe all planets were spaceships. The more he thought about it, they were, really. traveling through space at mind-boggling speeds with no captain to steer them.

His thoughts were flowing in currents, because now he imagined planets weren't planets but interstellar titans: living creatures with all these things living on them. Humans and every other animal were like bacteria and fungi crawling on its surface, erecting buildings and mining precious minerals to wear on their fingers and decorate their homes. These planets lived in a dimension humans couldn't comprehend any more than a cockroach could tell a joke. They smashed into each other, too. Some planets captured moons, and suns captured planets. And black holes ate everything that came near them. And those lines coming off the planet...

They're moving.

He sat up. Maybe it was the way the streetlight was coming into his room, or snow falling past the window. They were definitely moving. They squiggled on the drawing like sea creatures, flowed off the page and reached into the room.

Am I dreaming?

He didn't think so. He was 99% sure. There was one more thing to do, something he could test. His arms seemed to be extremely long and filled with air. When he looked down, his hands were missing. The bed was, too.

His scream echoed in a tin can.

He flailed without arms or legs, like treading a swimming pool without water. Without a body. He wasn't falling. He wasn't even floating. He was just there.

The bedroom had dissolved. One by one, the drawings disintegrated. A new draft took their place.

It was the planet.

It sat in black space as firmly as a teacup on a coffee table. The lines were titanic noodles swaying in solar wind, brightly colored and pulsing. There was a dozen of them soaring into the galaxy. Hiro hovered like an invisible satellite. He tried swimming toward the nearest one, a scarlet red thing, but there was nothing to propel him. He closed his eyes—he didn't have eyes, but he did what he thought was closing them—and felt the planet recede, felt his bed just beyond the veil of waking.

This is a dream. I don't need a body.

He willed himself to move and zoomed through space. The scale of the red noodle was beyond comprehension. He was a dust mite on the back of a swaying skyscraper. The surface didn't hum or crackle—there was no sound in space, but neither were there sixteen-year-old boys.

The surface was translucent. Something flowed inside. Photons and subatomic particles surged out into the universe, bound together like some ethereal silky essence. If he pushed inside, would it shoot him into another galaxy? He didn't test his hypothesis. Dark streaks mingled in the flow. The noodle was turning black near the planet, like basal rot on a beanstalk. It broke away and went flailing past him like a snake had been set free, spiraling into the black beyond, a trace of red.

He could feel life down there. There were land masses and oceans, rocky terrain, and polar ice caps. How was he going to find Chase? She never said where. *Meet me on this planet* was more than vague. It was impossible. Haze thought the noodles were portals, but they were flowing out. *This is a dream,* he reminded himself. *Just wish to find her,* he thought. *But that won't* be her. I'm the one dreaming. It would just be something that looked like her.

Something began rising from a mass of bright lights, a wisp of smoke twisting through the atmosphere. Another strand was growing. This one was smaller: a tendril compared to the gigantic noodles. It was purple. It stopped at the outer reaches of the atmosphere, the tip twisting like a tail.

Ride the purple tail.

Hiro remembered what Chase had emailed, and instantaneously appeared next to it.

The surface appeared firm and elastic. Nothing flowed inside it. When the tip swung toward him, it stopped and, he thought, appeared to smell him. The edges peeled opened like a flower; violet sparkles floated out like pollen and stuck to him. Hiro could see the outline of his body like a celestial being.

The tendril reared back. Then swallowed him.

He was cascading down an arterial waterslide at subsonic speed. The plunge had an eerie ring like one long electronic scream. He dissolved into particles of light, drifting weightless, merging with the grape flow of the purple tail. The planet sped towards him, blurring into a multicolored ball. For a long, falling moment, he could see in all directions: three-hundred-and-sixty-degree vision. The charging lights of a populated metropolis. The expansive blue ocean, the glow of the atmosphere.

His final descent pulled him through a small opening. His presence was long and stretchy, like grains of sand trickling to the bottom of the hourglass. Each grain plucking color from the universe until it was dark and hollow.

He felt the firmness of his body: arms and legs, chest and stomach. His head on a swivel. He was stiff. His bed a hard plank. His eyes wouldn't open. There was muttering around him. He felt someone watching. Panic took him. He was trapped in his body. Catatonic. He could hear shuffling. He could see colors, like his eyes were never closed. Someone was below him. He tried to lift his arm—

"Hiro!"

Hiro's head was cradled in a pillow, a soft bed beneath him. A beam of light cut through his window. He was a bag of wet sand, barely able to move to turn off the alarm.

"The shower is open." His mother peeked into his room. "We'll leave in an hour."

Hiro stared at her. What struck him wasn't her pale features or messy hair. She was pallid. His entire room was a bleached version of the world he had just been in. The colors faded as if they were slowly being leached away. So unlike what he'd just seen. Like he had been somewhere.

Someone was waiting for me.

The drawings were on the wall. The lines right where he drew them. The squiggly titans still the same shapes, same colors. None had broken off and soared into the galaxy. Not a single one of them was purple.

He heard buzzing, crawled through his blankets to find his phone. It was early, but he'd missed three calls. A text message buzzed in his hand.

Call me! Now!!!

12

There wasn't a sidewalk leading up to the house, only random footprints in the frozen snow. Hiro walked between a crusty truck and an RV with a flat tire with a blue tarp over the windshield. The metal railing at the front steps was wobbly. He pushed the doorbell. Icy daggers pointed from the gutter.

A young man regarded Hiro like he was selling toilet cleaner. "Yeah?"

"Is Haze here?"

He stared a bit longer. Maybe he didn't hear him. He scratched the acne on his cheek, then nodded. Hiro wasn't sure what to do. Haze's brother, Robby, barely moved. Hiro turned sideways to step by him.

"Hag!" he shouted. "Door!"

It wasn't much warmer inside. The house smelled like biscuits and old carpet. The furniture didn't match. A leather recliner was tipped back, the footrest stuck open, with worn armrests the color of putty.

The corner of the room was empty.

Robby, wearing a faded concert T-shirt, shouted again without breaking eye contact. Hiro pulled his stocking cap off and wrung it with both hands. Music blared from upstairs. Footsteps thudded. Haze wore two sweatshirts and a knitted cap with a fuzzy ball on top.

"Boyfriend's here," Robby said.

"Shut up," she said. "Hey. You drive?"

"No," Hiro said. "My father dropped me off. He'll be back in half an hour." Hiro pointed. "We're going back to my grandparents'."

Robby laughed for no reason. Haze shooshed him away. He walked off slowly, his neck too thick to turn around and look back. Hiro nodded at the empty corner of the room.

"Yeah," she said. "Us, too."

"I found a string of lights in ours," Hiro said. "Just lying there."

She nodded, squinting. "Yeah. Makes sense. Come on."

"You can't go up to your bedroom," Robby shouted from another room.

"You can shut up," Haze answered.

She hustled up the shag steps, wearing striped socks over white ones. Hiro took off his shoes before following. The music was coming from an open bathroom. The sink was buried beneath cosmetics, half-empty cups, and a small plate with a piece of burnt toast.

"Did he call you Hag?"

"He's showing off." Haze scooped up an overweight cat. "This is Mr. Pando."

The black and white cat purred. The tail swooped under Haze's chin and stroked her cheek. Hiro stared at the way the cat's tail moved, so smooth and graceful. Like it was floating in outer space. He didn't hear what she said next.

"I'm sorry. What?"

"You allergic?" she said.

"No, it's just the... never mind."

She dropped the cat. Mr. Pando didn't seem to mind, arching his back against Hiro's leg, and didn't follow him into a very small, disastrous room. He assumed the carpeting continued into her bedroom, but there was no sight of the floor. It was a capsized resale shop: old clothing, blankets, notebooks, a bike helmet, a lamp shade, and half-inflated balloons. A banana yellow beanbag with strips of gray duct tape was next to an overloaded bed. Her laptop was nestled in a hill of comforters. The screensaver was a photo of his planet drawing.

"I did it." She danced in a circle. "I saw it!"

"Saw what?"

She pointed at the laptop. "The planet, Hiro. *Exactly* like you drew it."

"Okay."

"You don't get it, I saw it. I've been staring at it for, like, days now. I put it on my phone. Here, look. It's on the laptop. I wasn't trying to do anything, I just liked what you did. That explains what happened, really. I mean, it's not, like, magical or anything. The planet is practically burned into my brain. I could literally draw it, and I can't draw."

"What are you talking about?"

She grabbed two fistfuls of his coat. "I dreamed the planet. Yeah. I did. And it was amazing. Ama-za-zing. I'm sorry I called so early, I just had to let you know something really, really, really big happened." She threw her arms out. "Now I know why you drew it in Corker's class. I want to draw it, too. It was just so… it was so—"

"Delicious."

"Yeah. Delicious. The colors were… I could taste them. And the portals were these giant worms doing this wavy outer space dance. And the planet, oh the planet… the oceans and the lights, and I could see the atmosphere glowing. The whole thing was just, like, sitting there. I watched it from the cheap seats, you know? Like way out there. I could watch it all night, the way the portals floated like psychedelic seaweed. And then this one, this big red one, it broke off and—"

"You saw that?"

"I saw the whole thing. It went shooting into space like an eel. *Fooooom*. The speed of light, it was gone. And—"

"Did you see a purple one?"

"A what?"

"A purple one. You know, a purple squiggly portal."

She shook her head. "I don't think so. Is there a purple one in your drawing?"

"Did you look at your hands?"

"The lucid dreaming thing, right." She snapped her fingers. "Here's the thing. *I didn't have hands.*"

Hiro was dizzy. He looked for somewhere to sit. His feet got tangled in a damp towel. He didn't make it to the bed, instead dropping on the beanbag like a concrete block. Little white beads streamed from the duct tape like a snow machine.

"I thought you'd be, like, not sad," she said.

"Sorry."

He brushed beanbag stuff off his pants and told her about his dream. Same as always, this time he didn't have a body. Maybe he never had one in the dream, just never bothered to look. The purple tail, that was different. She hadn't seen that.

"You saw a portal break off, too?" she said.

"They're not portals. I don't think."

"What are they?"

He didn't know. Stuff was flowing out. Maybe that was what portals did. He was also fully aware he was no longer thinking about this as a dream. *How could we have the same dream?*

"I tried to look at my hands," he said. "I didn't have a body."

"Aww. You read the book."

He took his stocking cap off, dug into his coat pocket. The book crinkled in his hand. "Here. If you want to read it, I think it will help. If you have the dream again." He told her which chapters to read, about REM sleep. How he ran out of time when his mother woke him.

"I was almost there," he said.

"You were there!"

"No, I mean, I went there this time, through the purple whip." He didn't tell her the portal sort of ate him. "I felt my body down there. It was different. I heard voices and…" He shook his head. "I ran out of time."

"There's more."

She jumped on the bed and crossed her legs, pushing books on the floor, and spinning the laptop around.

"I took a deep dive down some rabbit holes last night. I was thinking how weird your parents got about Christmas. Guess what I found? Nothing. Like nowhere. Like the internet was scrubbed by an anti-Christmas word gremlin. Like the word was never invented. So I kept digging because that's what I do at night by myself. I used some of the other words you said, like flying reindeer. I was, like, twenty pages deep when I got a hit on *elves*.

"It was a fresh post on one of the conspiracy boards that's all political conspiracies and flat world stuff. *Elves Are Real,* it said. No, no, wait. The first line was all in caps and said SCREENSHOT THIS POST NOW! It said the post would disappear in a minute, and if anyone was reading it, they had to get a screenshot."

"Did you?"

"I did better." She held up a piece of paper. "Printed it. And when I got back from the printer, guess what? The post was gone. Just like it said."

"What's it say?"

"I'm going to tell you." She held it with both hands. "Santa Claus —remember him?—lives on the North Pole with a colony of elves. Or was there because he's not there anymore. When he did, they lived in ice tunnels so no one could see them. The elves have been around since the Ice Age and have, like, crazy technology they used to watch the rest of the world. They have reindeer that fly with helium bladders. It says, uh, oh, that Santa isn't an elf but a man who's hundreds of years old and every year uses the reindeer to pull a sleigh around the world.

"He's got, like, a time snapper thing that stops time so he can do it in one night because, you know, technology. Anyway, he goes into houses through the chimney. And everyone is expecting him, so they put out milk and cookies. They also decorate a tree—remember the tree?—and he puts presents under it. I'll be honest, this sounds awesome. Oh, and they also hang stockings over the fireplace, and he stuffs those with presents, too."

"Like a fake tree?" Hiro said.

"Maybe. You have one in your attic. Kind of weird."

More than weird. "Who are *they*?"

"What do you mean?"

"I mean, who's putting out milk and cookies and decorating trees?"

"Us, I guess. I mean, before we forgot. That's what the whole post is about: Christmas spirit disappeared. We used to do Christmas. And now we don't. But there's still habits, like moving furniture around and cutting down trees, right?"

He crawled out of the beanbag. He needed to move and keep moving. He paced across the small room. Clothing, blankets and towels wrapped around his ankles as he slid his feet across the carpet. This was classic conspiracy theory: details that could plug unexplainable holes in human behavior. With nothing else to fill them, they made sense.

"It was posted by someone called Monkeybrain. He or she or they said, and I quote, 'Even if you print this post, they will get the paper and you will forget. Read it, memorize it, and take it to the dream. If you don't, it will go away. It's the only way to save Christmas.'"

Hiro was treading in strange facts that all linked together, but that last line bothered him most. He was swimming through all the information to remember where he'd heard that before.

"I don't know how this will go away." She rattled the page. "Unless mind-erasing elves sneak through the chimney—"

"Chase said it." Hiro snapped his fingers. "The last time she emailed me, she said, *I'm going away. It's the only way to save Christmas.*"

"Are you thinking what I'm thinking?"

"What are you thinking?"

She looked at the page. "She's Monkeybrain."

That made the most sense. It could easily be her. Maybe they needed to see what else Monkeybrain had posted, like space was fake and lizard people controlled the world. Mind-erasing elves would be at the family reunion.

"Or," he said, "someone was telling her to post it. When I talked to her that one time, she kept saying someone told her about Christmas and the dream."

"You think Monkeybrain told her. I mean, you both have a purple monkey. I'll be honest, everything that's happened, a talking toy is not the weirdest part." She looked at him intensely. "You can tell me, be honest. Does your monkey talk to you?"

"What? No. No, she's in the closet."

"Why?"

He'd put her in the closet when he threw the drawings away. He was done with it, at least he thought he was. She was still in there, sitting in the corner looking out, long arms in her lap and the long... *purple tail.*

He didn't say it out loud. He didn't know why. After everything else, it seemed the least strange. *Ride the purple tail.* It came off the planet different than the others. It was looking around and then gobbled him up, swallowed him all the way to the planet. Chase had told him how to get down there. That was how he was going to find her. *She was there.*

"What else did she say?" Haze said.

"What?"

"I mean, was that it? *I'm going away to save Christmas?*"

He pulled out his phone. There had been an email from Chase that morning.

"Yeah? What's it say?" Haze said.

"Uh, she said, *I'm leaving tonight. Don't know if I'll come back. Only two days till Christmas. It's our only chance.* What's today's date?"

"December twenty-third. So Christmas is—"

"December twenty-fifth."

Heavy silence fell between them. They stared at each other. It felt sort of like what his parents looked like when Haze had asked them about Christmas. Like something was missing. Like a giant hole was in the room. The paper was still in her hand, so the mind-erasing elves hadn't snuck in with a time snapper thing yet.

"Do you think it's weird?" Haze said, suddenly sounding tired. "It's a little weird she doesn't think she'll come back? I mean, should you tell someone?"

"Yeah. Yeah, you're probably right." He had her number but didn't know her last name or where she lived. "If it's just a dream, she'll wake up."

"Of course. None of this is real." She snorted. "I'll tell you what is real: Corker's report. You're still working on it, right?"

"Yeah."

"No, I mean, you're still working on my report."

"How will we know?" he said.

"You print it and give it to me."

"No, I mean, I was invisible. In the dream, remember? I didn't have a body. You said you didn't, either. How would we know we were both there?"

She waited with her mouth open. Then laughed at him. "I'm sorry. It's a dream, Hiro. You don't believe…"

"Right, a dream. But it didn't feel like one, not to me."

"Yeah, no, totally. But, uh, Hiro, we won't be in the same dream. I'm just playing. It'll be fun if we have the same dream again. We'll wake up and so will Chase. We should probably write it down and compare notes tomorrow. It's like an adventure. Oh, I know." She bounced on the bed. "We can give each other presents. The mind-erasing elves can't stop us from doing that."

Relief filled the silent hole in the room. That and Haze's bouncy enthusiasm. It was so easy to get swept up and forget this was a dream they were talking about. As strange as everything was, it was still his imagination. They weren't going anywhere. Haze had the right approach. This was fun. The strangeness had spice. He was glad she was there.

"Car in the drive!" Robby shouted from downstairs. "Boyfriend needs to go."

She held up her finger. "Let's save Christmas."

He touched it, and she buzzed. He smiled. "And Santa," he added.

Robby was waiting at the bottom of the steps. Haze had scooped up the cat and cradled her in her arms. Robby didn't move. Hiro had to walk around him.

"Don't you have push-ups to do?" Haze said.

Hiro's head was cold. "I forgot my hat."

"I'll get it," Haze said.

Hiro was about to say he'd go, but she was up the steps before he could stop her. Robby towered over him with glaze from a donut on his lips. He thought about telling him, then decided to just not move.

"Hey. If you break my sister's heart"—Robby grabbed his coat—"I'll give you five bucks."

He cracked a cruel smile and smacked Hiro on the back. His laughter sounded like a cartoon villain. Robby left with icing still on his lips. Haze was taking her time. Or the stocking cap was lost. Hiro might have scrambled it in the pile of clothing when he was pacing. He thought about just leaving it.

He read the rest of Chase's email while he waited. What little relief that remained quickly evaporated. Chase had sent an email that morning. Hiro hadn't told anyone about where he'd put the purple monkey, except for telling Haze just now. No one could possibly have known.

PS, Chase had written, *take Monkeybrain out of the closet.*

13

My first time to the big city.

It was a pleasant drive. The valley was spotted with blossoming trees and patches of snow. Spring fragrance filled my bones. Then the country road went from two lanes to four, then six. Freshly painted barns were replaced with towering buildings. Flowers turned to soot. We slogged into traffic, crept through skyscraper shadows and incessant honking. Cafés next to restaurants next to bars next to souvenir vendors.

It wasn't every night I returned to Toyworld. I didn't know why it wasn't every night. I began to itch when two days turned into a week without returning. I became irritable, more than usual. I didn't like the people in my world. Here, I liked the mom and dad. Madeline, I adored.

We drove around a traffic circle that contained a park with an enormous spruce on a hill. The dad was stress-driving. The skin over his knuckles white, arguing with the mom about where to park. They were going to be late. He insisted on circling the block one more time. I could feel the mom's irritation like rose prickles on my neck.

He found a metered spot at the curb. The mom jumped out, a bag over her arm. Madeline held my hand. They were speed-walking down the sidewalk. I was sprinting at Madeline's side. My green cape fluttered like a sheet on a clothesline. The hood falling back. I'd gotten used to wearing it when we went out. It was a little strange, a boney toy with a green cloak. A bit macabre. But there were stranger things here.

I was trying to take in the new sights and feels. The valley was so fresh and innocent. This was gritty and hard. It felt like gnats in my head. The dad stepped over a fallen stick-figure toy, the kind with wooden pegs and sprockets. The mom picked the little guy up, plugged his legs back into his body. The holes were too loose. She had a tube of glue in her purse.

"Poll," the dad said gently, "we're late."

She ignored him, putting the stick man against the building where no one would step on him. I'd heard the dad say to her before, *You can't save them all, Polly.* It didn't stop her from trying. We picked up the pace, just short of a run. Past storefronts and apartment walk-ups, offices and toy parlors.

The sidewalk began tilting. I'd let go of Madeline and thought maybe I was looking around too much, going too fast. The buildings were spinning in the sky. And then I was staring at an open door. A shaggy mane emerged from a dark stairwell.

Take their money, I thought. *Give to him.*

It was a thought I was having. Only it didn't sound like me. But I believed it was me. And it made sense to take money from the mom's purse and throw it in the doorway. I wanted to do it.

"Stop it." The mom picked me up and shook her finger.

A mangy lion smiled from the stairwell. He was missing a glass eye. Gray stuffing breached a tear in his neck.

The mom carried me at a brisk pace. "You have to be careful, Viktor. Toys think to each other. And some can make you think thoughts that aren't yours."

Apparently, that sort of thing wasn't a problem in the valley. They forgot to warn me about the city. Oh, and they forgot to tell me *toys can read thoughts!* Why didn't I know this? I spent all my time with the family. Never heard a single thought.

"You have to build a wall around your thoughts." We turned the corner. The mom breathing heavily. "Protect yourself. You don't want someone uninvited in your head."

No. I did not. What if they saw where I was from? That was a secret. I needed to learn more about this imaginary wall.

We climbed broad, concrete steps, two at a time, to a pillared building. NTC was painted on glass doors. Chiseled into a marble header above the doors were the words *National Toy Coalition*.

A bright green frog was at a large circular desk. Her eyes lazy and pink. Saggy fabric jiggled on her chin when they approached. The mom announced who they were. The frog checked her computer, pointed a long skinny arm. We hustled to a turnstile bracketed by uniformed ponies with clipped manes. They watched us with charcoal eyes pass through the metal detector. I felt a gnat buzz into my head. *Are they thought searching me?*

I panicked. Maybe it was no big deal who I really was. But what if it was illegal, like I was an alien or something. *I am an alien!* What if I got kicked out of the house and I wouldn't wake on the shelf to have breakfast with the family, or ended up in some government isolation for observation. Maybe there were prisons for toys like me.

I imagined a wall, a big steel wall as tall as the sky, as thick as a dam. I felt my skull harden. My bones fuse. The buzzing faded.

"Stop." One of the pony cops trotted in front of us.

I went catatonic. It was happening. I'd never tried waking up before, returning to my empty house. Let these red bones go limp and they would never know who I was.

"Oh." The mom handed me to Madeline. She dug a box from her purse.

The pony cops observed her putting it on the table. One of them nudged it open with her nose. Six metal orbs were nestled in fitted velvet. Shiny charms, brand new.

"He knows we're bringing them," the mom said. "Call him."

The pony cops held still. I could feel the air ripple, like a pebble tossed into still water. A moment later, their lips fluttered. The mom packed the box into her purse, and we were on our way.

They didn't need a phone to call whom we were meeting.

※

THE DAD PUT his hand on the mom's hand. She was picking at her nails. He patted her leg, whispered in her ear. She smiled nervously.

I straddled Madeline's shoulders while she scrolled on her phone. Old photos were on the walls of toy crowds and newspaper headlines. *They Are Alive!* I absorbed new sensations. Everything smelled serious. The furniture was sterile, the flower displays plastic. Lifeless music trickled into the room. Nervous fireworks sparkled from the parents. I tried to feel their thoughts, but couldn't get a sense of what they were thinking or really how to even read a thought. Maybe it was just a toy thing.

"He'll see you now."

A mop peered from a sliding window. Somewhere in the ropey shag were eyes and a mouth. I didn't know what it was. A dog? He watched us get up, didn't slide the window closed till we opened the door.

The office was spacious. A wooden puppet was at the glass wall overlooking the city. Full size, people called toys like him. Put a coat on him and he'd look like a man standing there. He turned around when we entered, threw his arms out.

"Polly!"

His jaw clapped as if he'd uttered the word. It looked ridiculous. Then again, my jaw opened and closed when I spoke, which had nothing to do with actually speaking. It was just weird seeing it. He limped toward us, around a desk the same color as his body but in better shape. He was antique with a coat of varnish.

This was the toy. The one I'd seen on television, pounding the pulpit. Preaching to the furry and the plastic, the fabricated and the sewn. *The leader of toys.*

"Pleasure to see you." He hugged her stiffly. He was wood. Stiff was all he had.

"You okay?" the mom said.

"Old joint." He patted his hip. "Needs replacing."

"I can look at it."

He laughed. "Another time. You must be Philip. Belkin Tannenbaum. Pleased to meet you."

The dad shook his hand. I felt his nerves like ants crawling up his spine. It was a brisk handshake. "Mr. Tannenbaum."

"Belkin, please."

This was new. I'd never seen a full-size toy act so... human. I felt a little woozy. And jealous. What a difference size made. I was this diminutive, red-boned skeleton in a cloak. Belkin was a blocky version of a human.

"This is our daughter, Madeline," the mom said. "She wanted to meet you."

"Madeline." He offered his hand. "Very nice to meet you."

"She did a project on you," the mom said.

"A project? Merry, merry."

Madeline told him all about it. How he was in the great Toy Arrival a hundred years ago, was the first to address the world, had proposed several bills that became laws, worked tirelessly for equal rights and formed the National Toy Coalition.

"Toys are people, too," Madeline said, apparently quoting him. He put his hands over the red heart painted on his barrel chest. "Your name was BT when you arrived."

I got the feeling he wasn't thrilled with the BT name. I didn't know why he wouldn't like it. It was just initials.

"And this is Viktor the Red," the mom said. "He's family."

Family. I never tired of hearing that.

I took Belkin's outstretched hand. A bracelet rattled on his wrist. It was old and beaten. A red snowflake dangled from one of the links. That, I would later learn from Madeline—the resident Belkin Tannenbaum expert—was something very special to him. No one ever said why. *The snowflake is a reminder of where we are,* was all he ever said.

I wished someone would tell me where we were.

"Viktor." Belkin's handshake slowed; he cocked his squarish head. "Are you fresh out?"

If he had eyebrows, one would've risen in puzzlement. Then I felt it. The slithery movement in my head. It was like cold vapor seeping through the top of my skull. The mom said looking into a toy's thoughts was bad manners. And here the leader was taking a peek into my mind. I imagined the wall. He twitched.

"Viktor woke in my shop," the mom said. "It's been, what, almost two years now?"

"He's an original?" Belkin said.

"Yes, he is."

He let go of my hand, finally. "Quite adept at corralling his thoughts for a young one."

"Belkin," the mom said, "tell me you're not looking."

"It was just cursory, Polly." He waved his hand. *No big deal.* "The handsome, little red toy with the forest green cloak strikes me as curious. Have we met, Viktor the Red?"

I shook my head. Was he baiting me to speak, perhaps loosen the wall guarding my thoughts? He examined me like a forgery. Looking for an errant brushstroke, a misplaced signature.

Madeline broke the tension. "Viktor is the only toy who sleeps."

"He sleeps?"

"He goes dormant," the mom corrected her. "We call it sleep at the house, but it's merely a resetting phase. The lapses are less frequent now. I suspect his identity is stabilizing. His charm is a new prototype."

"How long?" Belkin said.

"Pardon?"

"How long does he sleep?"

She shrugged. "Two days or so."

I was as still as an empty toy. If I were human, sweat would be rolling down my cheekbones. He twisted the red snowflake on his wrist. Leaned closer, as if he could smell the foreigner hiding inside the skull.

"Is he a switch?"

"No," the mom said. "We confirmed all transactions in the area at the time of his waking. He wakes and sleeps in our house. It would be impossible for someone to switch without being wired. Besides, a human can't occupy a toy for as long as Viktor is awake or recover that quickly. He's simply a new toy finding his way, Belkin. I made him. Why are you so suspicious?"

Switching? A lot to take in here. Reading between the lines, a human could temporarily become a toy. I was proof. Evidently, they were doing that here, too. And apparently a human could occupy a toy. Just not a human from here.

That didn't turn down the Belkin heat lamp. "Did you know the bill to limit toy production was killed?" Belkin said.

"I read," the mom said.

"You know why, don't you? They want more toys. Not because they love us."

I assumed *they* was the people running the government. They as in humans. They as in not the humans in the room.

"More toys, more switching," Belkin said, staring at me when he said it. "They treat us like playthings. Disposable joy bags. We're the new drug, Polly. Switch into a toy and discover true joy. It needs to stop."

"Yes. Yes, it does." The mom pulled the box from her bag, opened it on the maplewood desk. "I'm working on a new prototype that makes it difficult to switch."

Belkin reluctantly looked away from me. I didn't relax. His thoughts could still swoop in. He gazed at the six charms firmly seated in velvet.

"They're identity locked," the mom said. "Switching is impossible. And they're touch sensitive. Contact with human skin turns them dormant. Prevents theft. There are stability issues, but I'm close."

The room cooled. Or was that just Belkin's attention finally averted? He was intrigued with the possibility. It was also clear one of these new charms was inside my head. Although that would mean a human could switch into my charm. Because that was what I did. There was so much I didn't understand.

"Yes, well, we need to talk more. That's not why you're here today, though." He locked his hands behind his back, turned to the dad. "Polly says you have something very interesting. Please, sit."

All the good-natured veneer returned to the wooden leader. He smiled with everything but the jaw that wouldn't bend. The room felt brighter. Friendly.

We sat around a low table in bright-colored chairs. Madeline put me on a lime green one with purple polka dots. The dad put his laptop on the table and began to talk shop. It was technical jargon, the sort I could understand. Electromagnetic field generators, time dilation, trigger sensors. Belkin seemed to follow, as well. Or put on a good show, like a well-polished politician.

I was familiar with the dad's experimentation. He'd been sullen and moody since Christmas. I had assumed his aspirations had failed, as lofty and wishful as they were. No picture of Santa Claus was hanging in the house.

The dad turned the computer toward Belkin. "Last Christmas."

Belkin didn't move, not at first. Like someone seeing a ghost, but not quite sure it wasn't a trick. He leaned closer. I crawled onto Madeline's lap to see what was on the screen. It was a photo of their living room. Between the polished metal tubes bookending the fireplace was a blur. Like a circular aquarium containing one big fish. I tried to lean a bit more; then Madeline, feeling my curiosity, held me so I could see. Through blue ripples was a large swatch of red.

Oh my, I thought with such punctuation that Belkin glanced at me. *It's Santa Claus.*

"It's a time bubble inside a bubble," the dad said. "You see, Santa travels in no-time. It's like a hole in space where time is significantly slower than outside. It allows him to traverse the world before a second passes. I simply replicated the electromagnetic field he uses to do it."

He pointed at the metal pipes.

"When he slipped out of the fireplace, I wrapped his bubble inside another bubble, essentially inverting the fields. It feeds on the energy output, creating a self-generating loop. It was only a fraction of time, long enough to capture proof."

The dad continued with the mechanics of how he did it. Belkin listened intently, then said, "How did you learn this?"

"It's physics."

Belkin was searching for the real answer. The dad didn't look affected by the puppet's heat lamp. So apparently toys couldn't read a human's mind. It was just other toys they could steal from.

"It started with toy folklore," the mom said.

"Yes, well, that," the dad stammered. "Everyone knows the stories about your arrival, how you"—he gestured to Belkin—"stopped time. It's all just tall tales, but it was the seed of my discovery. Once I was able to create a small time bubble, I thought, perhaps, the rest of the stories were true."

"And you used it to… take a photo?" Belkin said.

And he said it in the exact tone I was thinking. Time stopping was world-changing technology, for good or bad. And the dad had used it to take a picture of Santa Claus.

"It was a test," the dad said.

"The inherent dangers are exponential, you understand? If you trapped him too long, it could collapse the roads between realities, unlink time."

Roads between realities? That rang with truism. Santa traveled not just between worlds, but different realities? That epiphany would change me completely. And, as it would happen, Toyworld, as well.

"I understand," the dad said. "That's why it's only a flash. He had no idea that it even occurred. For him, inside the bubble, time was normal. Nothing changed."

Belkin was deep in thought, tapping his chin like a drummer keeping time on a wooden block. He touched the screen, as if that made it real, and said softly, "What will you do with this?"

"This was just proof of concept. Next Christmas, I'll do it again. We can talk to him."

"Talk to him?"

"A conversation," the mom interjected, "about what's happening to the toys."

"My dear people, he already knows." Belkin looked between them. "Santa Claus doesn't interfere."

"But that's how you got here," Madeline said quietly. "Santa Claus brought the toys."

"Others were responsible for that, my dear. Not Santa." It sounded heartfelt and sad.

"What about the verve?" the dad said.

"Verve?"

"Christmas spirit," Madeline said.

"Right, Christmas spirit," the dad said. "It's what powers the toys, what gives you life. That's what Santa is, what he carries. It's his essence. If he's not willing to help change things, we can use the Christmas spirit to make toys smarter."

"Smarter," Belkin said, deadpan.

"That's not what I mean. It can be, like, more life. More... *toyness*."

This was going nowhere. I had to admit, the photo of Santa was impressive. I wasn't one hundred percent convinced by a photo—I mean, a ten-year-old could make that on their computer—but there were dots he was connecting. How he was connecting them was a mess. And Belkin wasn't buying the picture he was drawing.

"We'll make the toys less satisfied." The mom sat on the edge of her turquoise chair.

"I'm not following," Belkin said.

"Santa is the source of the Christmas spirit. If we can somehow release more of it, we can make toys more aware of what's happening. They're too content, Belkin. Toys accept everything just as it is, no matter how awful. They don't care what's happening to them. They're pure joy, even the ones that are suffering.

"Look at them, outside your office. They don't care. It doesn't matter what you say, Belkin, we can't have equal rights if they don't want them. What my husband's trying to say is that we can wake them up with Christmas spirit."

Belkin nodded along. He stood up, paced to the window and

looked down on the city where mangy lions hid in doorways and broken stick toys lay on sidewalks. He'd been there from the beginning. It was getting worse, no matter what he did. The future was as transparent as the glass in front of him.

"What do you want from me?"

"Funding," the dad said. "My investors saw this. They don't believe."

"Sounds familiar."

The dad laid out his plans to set up a snapshot for next Christmas. This time he would draw verve out and bank it in a battery. Honestly, I didn't believe he could do it. And I was a toy.

"You're losing the fight, Belkin." The mom stood up. "People don't want equal rights. They want all your rights. Yours, Viktor's, and every toy's on this planet. Your time here will be wasted. You'll find—"

"I'm aware." He raised his hand.

I didn't have to read his mind to know he'd seen worse than what was out there. Even with the prospect of things getting worse, especially if the dad's crazy idea didn't work, one thing was certain. *I want to be a toy.* I liked the joy, the toy senses. I loved everything about this place. I never wanted to leave.

And maybe, maybe there was something here I could work with. There was a way I could stay here. There was a solution in the dad's invention that I could use.

And never go home again.

14

Hiro started to leave a message. He should have hung up before it started recording. Now there were grunts on Chase's voicemail. He flopped on his bed and listened to the tree slash at the window between gusts of sleet. He decided to email her.

I'm worried. What did you mean you won't come back? Did you make it to the dream? He erased them all and quickly sent just one sentence. Simple and short. *Is everything all right?* He quickly regretted it. It was too short. Cold. He thought about sending another one. She'd sent ten the day before.

"Where are they?" he muttered.

Her emails were missing from his inbox. They weren't in the trash, either. Odd. He should have screenshotted the emails and printed them, like Haze did. He decided to call her. It was almost midnight. She didn't answer.

He fell on the bed, took long deep breaths. He was miles away from falling asleep. His heart was still running a marathon with no signs of fatigue. He should meditate. Instead, he got up.

The purple monkey was in the closet, sitting in the corner, waiting with infinite patience. Hiro picked her up, squeezed her body, searching for a voice box or recorder, anything that could spy on him. Or talk. There was something hard in the center; it was small and round. He wasn't going to rip the toy apart for a marble. He threw the monkey's arms over his neck, carried her to the dresser.

He cleared his throat.

"Hi. I'm Hiro." He shook the monkey's hand. "And you are? Monkeybrain. That's so—I can't believe I'm doing this."

He took a lap around the bed. This was absurd. It had felt good when he talked to Haze, when he got it all out. He needed to let some pressure off his chest. The monkey was all he had.

"So, I've been having this dream. You already know that. Of course." Hiro waved his hand. "It's real. Like very real. Like I really go there real. And there's this person I know, her name is Chase. I don't really know her, but maybe you do. She knows you. Haha. But Haze, you know Haze, she had the dream, too, which is... never mind. Anyway, Chase said something about Christmas, she or we had to save it, that we had to actually go there to save it. Ride the purple tail, she said."

He made air quotes, like the monkey would take offense if he didn't.

"Then she said she's going away. And now she's not answering her phone or emails. I'll be honest, I'm a little worried. I don't really know her, but just, I don't know. You know?"

He walked back and forth, tapping his chin. He wasn't making sense. The toy didn't seem bothered.

"Haze, she's just a friend; she found something on the internet. It was a post that was all about Christmas. And it was posted by someone named Monkeybrain. And Chase, she called you Monkeybrain. She was very specific about it. *Take Monkeybrain out of the closet,* she said. But you didn't actually post anything because you don't have hands and you can't type and you're a toy and what am I doing?"

This wasn't helping. He needed a human being to talk to. Or a dog or a cat or something living. He straightened up the monkey, leaned her against the lamp. Looked her straight in her plastic eyes.

"Where did you come from?"

A light knock on his bedroom door spooked him. His mother was in her pajamas and fuzzy slippers.

"I thought you were asleep," Hiro said.

"I went to the bathroom and heard talking." She glanced at the monkey.

"I'm just talking out thoughts. It helps sometimes."

"It sounded like you were talking to someone named Chase." Now he felt nervous. *How much did she hear?* "So where are *you* going?"

"Me? Nowhere. I'm just... I've been having this dream and—" The look on her face stopped him. "Never mind."

"If you're going to stay up late, make time for school and not pretend conversations with a toy." She looked at his desk. Clearly, he wasn't doing homework. "Did Hazel put you up to this?"

"What? No. Haze is a friend. She's a good person. You don't know her."

"I know her grades."

"So I should check her GPA before talking to her."

"Hiro," she said coldly, "did she ask you to do Mr. Corker's report for her?"

"I'm helping her." Truth was, she didn't ask. He offered.

"Is that really a friend, using you to do her schoolwork? Be careful the company you keep."

"I don't have friends. That's why I'm talking to a-a-a purple monkey on a Saturday night. Do you want to check her grades, too?"

Eyebrows furrowed. She didn't like his tone. It surprised her more than offended her. *Where did that come from?* Hiro didn't know. He never talked that way.

"It's late," she said. "Get some sleep. I'd like to read over your report tomorrow."

"What happened to you?"

"Pardon?"

"You used to be different. You used to write poetry and remember your dreams. You used to be fun. Why did you change?"

She knotted her robe as tight as her lips. "There is more to life than dreams, Hiro. When you grow up, you'll understand."

"Was it Christmas?" She winced when he said it. But he didn't back down. "When Santa put presents under a tree, when everything was so magical. When you made the dream journals, you remember? It was right about this time, when I was seven or eight years old. But then we all forgot about Christmas. You did, too. And you haven't smiled since."

"Did Hazel put these ideas in your head?" She cinched the knot tighter. "There's a difference between dreams and reality, Hiro. We live in one of them. I'm raising a son who will know which one is which, who will understand that this life, right here, is where you live. This is real, son. What's in front of you, what you see and feel and smell and taste. This is life. And life demands you feed yourself, you have shelter and protection. Stories in your head won't help. If you stay in your head, you won't be prepared for right here."

Hiro didn't wilt, which surprised him. And, perhaps, her, too. "But can't we smile while we do it?"

"You're not a child, Hiro." She snatched Monkeybrain off the dresser. "Children talk to toys."

"Mother, she's mine."

"I'll keep her safe." She carried her like a bag of groceries. Long purple arms dragged on the floor.

Now he had no one.

❄

HIRO CRAWLED out of a very warm bed. The frosted window lit up with morning sunlight, but he could see his mother backing out of the driveway. He climbed into bed and called Haze from under the blankets.

When she answered, there was loud music. He could hear arguing and thought maybe she'd answered without knowing it. The music turned down. "Hey," she said. "Thought you slept in."

"Where are you?" he said.

"Robby and I are going to get breakfast. Starving," she said. "So what happened last night?"

"What do you mean?"

"What do you mean what do I mean?" She paused. A car honked in the background, and Robby cursed. "The dream, Hiro. Hello?"

He'd had the dream again. Just like before. He went down the purple tail, felt stiff all over and heard voices. Then woke up. Like he just couldn't get there.

"Did you see me?" she said.

"You had the dream again?"

"Yup. Just like you said, the whole thing. I tried looking at my hands but didn't have any. And I saw the purple portal thing, too, just like you said. It didn't eat me, like you. And you want to know something weirder?"

"What could be—"

"Tell him, Robby." Her voice was distant. She was holding the phone away from her face. "Just tell him. Don't be embarrassed. Oh my God, you're such a gorilla. Robby had the dream, too."

"Robby did?"

"No joke. He told me this morning. Must have been the drawing. We infected him."

"You sure it was the same dream?"

"You lying, Robby?"

Hiro turned cold. Last thing he wanted was Captain Wrestler twisting his arm in half for calling him a liar. It did seem like the dream was catching on. It had been surprising when Haze said she had it, but it seemed halfway possible since they talked about it so much. Robby didn't seem like the dreaming type. And from just looking at the drawing?

"Did you tell him about Christmas?" Hiro asked.

"About what? Oh, yeah. Almost forgot. Weren't you supposed to save Christmas? I didn't see any presents this morning. Definitely no tree. Robby, you get any presents? He said he got a dog turd. Stop it!"

The phone tumbled from her hands. The brakes squealed to a

stop. Robby had had enough, or they'd gotten to wherever breakfast was.

"I'll call you right back," she said.

"How could you almost forget about Christmas?" he said. "Remember what the post said, that you would forget. That's why you printed it."

"I know, that's crazy, right? It's like I almost forgot," she said. "How come you remembered it?"

That was a good point.

15

"What's happening up there?" his father shouted.

Hiro held onto a rafter and listened for his father's footsteps. A door closed somewhere downstairs. Hiro quietly moved boxes onto the plywood runway. There was a plastic handle on a long box. He carefully slid it out. It wasn't as heavy as it looked. He carried it to the ladder, nearly falling backwards, managed to get it into the hallway without hearing footsteps.

He got it downstairs to the front room. The driveway was still empty. The box was dusty, the cardboard flaps folded and bent. He popped it open. It looked like a box of plastic evergreen needles attached to wire limbs. It came out in three sections. He pulled off old spiderwebs. The pieces easily snapped together. He placed it in the corner.

Strange. If he didn't know any better, it looked like something at an art gallery: saying something about the human influence on nature. It wasn't living or breathing, just an imitation of life. He adjusted the branches. It seemed barren. He grabbed the string of lights and wrapped them around the tree.

"Interesting." His father approached with a lukewarm coffee. "Does it come with an artificial squirrel?"

"I found it in the attic."

"Mmm. Yeah. I like it. I don't know if your mother will."

They stood side by side. His father wore his favorite weekend T-shirt and gray sweatpants with a mug hooked on his finger. They studied it like amateur critics trying to decide if this was art.

"Why is Mother sad?" Hiro said.

Father took a sip. "It's hard to explain. She feels like something's missing. It happens when you get older, you achieve everything you set out to achieve: a family, a career. Sometimes when everything is perfect, it feels empty." He looked at Hiro. "It's not because of you, Hiro."

"Is it because of you?"

He sort of laughed, nodded. "Honestly, I don't know. Some people just feel sad no matter where they are."

They stood in silence looking at a fake tree. The room felt haunted by the truth that was never discussed in the house. Mother's sadness was a guest that had overstayed.

"It's called a Christmas tree." Hiro wiped dust off the box. The words on the label had faded away. "People would decorate it at this time of year and put presents under it."

"Is that right?" He frowned. Hiro thought he might leave the room. "Where did you hear that?"

"Read about it. There's a story about a man named Santa who would come down the chimney and deliver presents. He lived on the North Pole with elves, had a sleigh pulled by flying reindeer. I was thinking maybe that's what Mother was missing. We forgot Christmas."

"Why did we forget?"

Hiro hesitated. He'd already said there were flying reindeer. "Mind-erasing elves."

His father nearly spit coffee. "Oh, well, of course. Seven billion people would have to forget, so it would have to be elves."

"They have advanced technology."

"Of course. But if Christmas was so great, why would they do that?"

"It's not elves, really. Christmas spirit disappeared, and I don't know why." Hiro began adjusting branches. "I've been reading about lucid dreaming. Ever heard of it? It's a technique where you can wake up inside the dream. I feel like maybe I can save Christmas. We won't know until we get there."

"We?"

"Haze is having the same dream."

"Haze, too? Mmm. You sure she's not just telling you what you want to hear?"

"What? No. It's not like that, I swear." He had a point, though. Hiro had no proof other than what she said. She did want him to write her research paper. "She said she did, that's all I know."

"Okay. I get it. You both had the same dream. Are you going somewhere to, uh, save Christmas?"

His mother must have told him about last night, overheard Hiro talking to Monkeybrain. "No, no. No, it's just a dream, that's all. We're going to all go lucid at the same time. It's just a dream, I swear. I just thought I'd try while I was on break. I'll do my work when school is back. I just want to try, you know. If it works, maybe Christmas spirit will be back."

He put a hand on Hiro's shoulder. "You can't fix your mother, Hiro. But I appreciate you're thinking of her. I'll make you a deal. Put the tree back in the attic. I like it. It fits in the corner, like you said. And, to be honest, I don't know why I move the furniture or plug in those lights." He shrugged. "Maybe you're right. Dreaming is good. If you make a mistake, no harm. Good things come from mistakes."

He raised the mug.

"I promise," Hiro said. "One more thing, though. Mother took a stuffed animal from my room. It's a purple monkey. I just need it for tonight."

"Why tonight?"

"Tomorrow's Christmas."

"And you need a purple monkey?"

"It's good luck."

"You want to save Christmas in a dream, and you need a purple monkey to do it?" He nodded, straightened a few branches. "I'll be honest, Hiro, this is a little... out there."

"I know. Trust me. But it's just a dream. If it doesn't work, no big deal. I'm just spilling coffee, you know?"

His father laughed. "Right. Okay. Then go look in the trash bin outside. Whatever you find, do not let your mother see it."

Hiro was overcome with joy. He threw his arms around his father. Warm coffee soaked Hiro's back. He didn't care. His father patted his shoulder.

"Have fun with whatever it is you're doing. I hope you and Haze keep dreaming together."

"And save Christmas." Hiro pulled the lights off the tree.

"Sure," his father said on his way to the kitchen. "We'll put out milk and cookies when you do."

Hiro pulled the sections apart, folding the branches to fit inside the box. He pushed it into the attic and put it exactly where he found it, placing the boxes on top of it. No one would know anyone had been up there.

On his way out to the trash bin, he thought about what his father had said. He'd told his father about Santa and the reindeer. He hadn't said anything about milk and cookies.

16

1:55 p.m.

Mr. and Mrs. Picknitty were on their front porch. Bathed in little white lights hanging from the gutters. Tossing carrots onto the icy sidewalk where Joe and Maggy would wake up in the morning, bleary-eyed and bouncy, to see them gone. Eaten by hungry reindeer. The poor animals must be starving to eat every carrot off every sidewalk, which was probably, by conservative estimates, nine billion carrots.

I hadn't slept in thirty-six hours. I had walked twenty laps around the block that morning, hadn't eaten since breakfast and avoided water or tea. Tonight was a big night. Couldn't risk a bathroom break at three in the morning.

Sleep aids had not helped. They distorted my dreams. Never once did I make it to Toyworld under the influence of medication. It had to be the old-fashioned way. Sleep deprivation and dehydration.

Mr. And Mrs. Picknitty chucked the rest of the carrots in the front yard. I remembered doing that. It was just the one time. I totally believed it in the morning. My father asked me what I was looking for in the front yard. I told him about the carrots Ms. Felty, a kindly old woman who lived next door, had given me. She told me what to do.

The reindeer ate them! He went directly over to her house. I never did it again.

He believed in practical gifts. Socks, underwear. A toolbox. Things a child really needed. Once he gave me a telescope, but I broke it. Then it was back to tools. Who gives their kid a socket set? He never wrapped them, just put them on the table. If I missed a chore, which he tracked on a spreadsheet, there was nothing on the table. *You earn gifts, son.*

11:59 p.m.

I dropped the blackout blinds and turned on the white-noise machine. Earplugs fit snugly into my ears. Blindfold. Thermostat at sixty degrees. Six-hundred-thread-count bedsheets and a down comforter. Nothing short of a tornado would wake me.

At midnight, I paused. Listened. This was the moment when time synchronized throughout the galaxy. The moment when all the roads opened and a very fat, very jolly man flew to the rooftop of every good boy and girl on the colorful roads that crisscrossed space. I wondered, sometimes, if the Northern Lights was just road dust. Science said it's electrons colliding with nitrogen and oxygen molecules that created the colors. Now I doubted everything.

I slid into bed and began my breathing exercises. I was afraid I'd overdone it, had become overly tired, if there was such a thing. Expectations sprinted through my head. This was the night.

I couldn't screw this up.

❄

THE AIR FELT DIFFERENT.

Madeline was with the monkey. Nothing was out of place. The walls were vibrating, the shelf buzzing. Everything felt... *luscious*. Strange word to use, but it was the right one. I felt like singing.

I climbed off the shelf, down the little ladder the dad had built for me. I was moving more agile and quick. Was I imagining that? A placebo effect engaged by expectations? I didn't feel like a collection of bones clicking in dry sockets. I snuck into the front room.

The stockings were bulging. Mistletoe hung from the ceiling, attached to a stiff wire that looked more like a lightning rod pointing down from the ceiling. It was directly in front of the fireplace. *Odd place for mistletoe,* I thought, not remembering that the last time I was there.

There was a noise in the other room. I thought, for a second, maybe I would catch Santa Claus in action. But the cookies were half eaten, the glass of milk was empty. I leaned against the couch. The dad rushed out of the lab in slippers and a white lab coat. He was wearing sunglasses. *Sunglasses?*

Sunlight beamed from the doorway. It was the middle of the night. I crept closer, looking back for the dad, lifting my hand to block the bright light. It was warm and delicious. Tingled in my bones. Smelled like ozone and cookies. I didn't know what to expect, maybe Santa Claus or a reindeer. Perhaps a life-size photo of them hanging on the wall.

I didn't expect this.

My eyes adjusted to the source of sunlight coming from a glass case. A tiny ball of light, about the size of a marble, was as bright as a star. It felt like the essence of magic packed into a neat, little package. *Verve,* I thought, thinking how silly that word was. Christmas spirit wasn't any better. Too whimsical. Verve at least sounded scientific. Nothing I was feeling was scientific.

Each step I took grew in intensity, stripping away the last vestiges of my awkward toyness: the clunky stride, the swings in balance. Like I was molting, swimming into the light. The closer I got, the more it began to twist and curve. Like I was a black hole drawing the photons into my body.

This would have been a good time to stop. The dad would be back at any moment. But this was my only chance. I pressed on, reaching for the box. It was like leaning into the teeth of a hurricane. I numbly felt my fingers touch the box, push it open. Crawl toward the hot little sun.

I didn't know where I landed. Wasn't even sure I was still in the room.

A canoe was floating down a sugary stream. The canoe was red. The water was green. Then I realized I wasn't in a canoe. *I am the canoe!* The river, I didn't know what the river was. I didn't really care or even remember how I got there or where I had been just moments before. This moment was all there was, floating down the magical stream. *Merrily, merrily...*

I looked over the side, somehow, even though I was the canoe while sitting in the canoe at the same time. You know how dreams are. I didn't see a reflection. I saw the fireplace in the front room with two metal pipes, one on each side. Soot trickled from the flue like ashy snow. A black boot appeared. Out slid a white-bearded man in a red suit, cartoonish at first. Elastic. Oozing from the fireplace and inflating into a balloon of a man when he stepped onto the hearth.

Santa Claus stood beneath a sprig of mistletoe on the tip of a lightning rod.

A bulging sack over his shoulder, snow on his boots. He hummed a little song on his way past the tree, around the coffee table with an unfinished puzzle, and stooped over to grab a cookie.

"Hmmm," he muttered.

He was in no hurry, eating one cookie, then another. He hummed along to a song in his head, heavy boots clopping on the floor. The sack fell with a thump. Groaning as he took a knee, he reached inside the sack to pull out one gift, then another, placing them under the tree. The sack didn't seem to shrink, no matter how many gifts he retrieved. With a third cookie between his teeth, he stuffed the stockings, straightening them just so.

A job well done, he took the glass of milk and wandered around the living room, gazing at a photo on the wall, fitting a piece into the puzzle, looking up at the mistletoe with a hearty chuckle. He patted his belly and burped just a little. The glass was half empty and back on the plate; he took the sack with one last glance. With a twinkle in his eye, he ducked into the fireplace, inspected it. For just a moment, he froze in place. He looked back with suspicion, up at the ceiling and all around.

With a shrug and a laugh, he shimmered with light. Then his

body twisted and stretched, and *floom*, up the chimney he went. Bells rang. A stampede shook the house. A voice called into the night. *Merry Christmas to all—*

"It can wait till morning," I heard the mom say.

The dad was upside down, peeking into the room. His lab coat swayed, defying gravity. Black glasses askew. He handed a pair of sunglasses to the mom. "You need to see this," he said. Then stopped with a fright. "Viktor?"

I was bunched in the corner, twisted on my head. The mom took a step, holding up her hand, the light blinding her. She took the sunglasses and came to untangle my arms from my legs. My head spun around. Her shock and concern felt like sweet little quills.

"What's he doing in here?" she said.

The dad checked the readings, sighed with relief that turned into a frown. "I don't know. What are you doing in here, Viktor?"

I panicked. I felt transparent, like my intentions were cue cards dancing over my head. The dream of the canoe confused me, like a cruise ship plowing through buoys and casting them about. I had to say something, just not what I was thinking. They were staring and waiting. So I lied. Just a little.

"I didn't touch anything. I woke on the shelf, and everyone was asleep. The door was open, and I thought I heard something. The light was so bright, and I think I just—"

"Did you—"

The mom stopped the dad right there. A hand on his chest and one to her mouth, she looked at him. He was missing the obvious.

"Viktor," she said slowly, "can you walk over here?"

I didn't move. She had a tone, like she saw right through the lie. But the smile on her face and the softness I felt compelled me to play along. I did what she said, watching her clutch the dad with each step I took.

"Look," she whispered. "The way he's moving."

The dad looked relaxed, just a little at first. Then he saw it, too. How I walked with such grace, like a real man and not one made of bones. She jerked her head at the dad, and he understood, leaving the room. She knelt in front of me. He returned with her device and put it to my head. I held still, watching her delight. She showed it to him.

"It worked," he muttered. "Just like I said it would."

I wasn't quite sure what had happened. It seemed impossible, it did, to feel better than before. I was a toy, but I felt like much more. I could see and feel like never before. They hugged me, then each other and laughed with such glee; I knew what had happened but not how it could be.

He'd done it, the dad. His dream had come true. He'd captured the verve. And it had changed me, too.

※

MADELINE WAS on the bed with a big orange cat with tufted ears and a round, spongy tummy. A toy cat, not a real one. Full size. Freckles, she named him, was the color of a freckle. He had been a blank before this night. An empty toy that sat in the corner. Never moved, not once. Now he was awake, glassy eyes looking at a brand-new world.

I climbed onto the dresser and peeked out the window. A car had pulled into the backyard from the alley. A hulking figure climbed out of the driver's seat and opened the back door. The dome light illuminated the shirtless figure wearing nothing but painted shorts and glittery boots. Muscles bulged on his shoulders.

A slender figure climbed out of the back seat. The wind whipped his cloak like a flag at full mast.

"Who do you think it is?" Madeline held Mr. Freckles to see.

I was a bit jealous, I'll admit. She didn't even open her presents. I was just one of the family now, a brother who took up space. Freckles was fresh out, innocent. The new baby in the family, I could feel it. I'd been an only child. Never wanted a brother or sister, not then. Definitely not now.

Freckles's thoughts were primitive, mostly images. I feasted on them. It was effortless and pleasurable, like rummaging through someone's belongings. If he was from another world, a fellow sleeper like me, there was no indication of it. Just a dumb bag of stuffing with plastic whiskers.

"It's Belkin," I said. "I don't know who the musclehead is."

Madeline repeated what I said in baby talk, bouncing Freckles around. She wasn't impressed by my newfound articulate speech. Oh, she was for a minute, right up until Freckles had stood up. He looked at her, watched her lips. He didn't understand a word. It was just sounds to him. He was awake, but the bright light from the dad's lab had barely lit his awareness.

"Madeline?" the mom called. "Can you bring Viktor and Freckles to the front room?"

I rushed ahead of her, indulging my smooth pace and steady balance. The back door opened, wind rushing into the house. Someone stomped their boots and shook the walls. The dad greeted them. The hallway was filled with the massive bulk of a fleshy toy. Red elastic and squeaky, he ducked under the doorframe to keep from bumping his small head. A smile stretched his cheeks. It sounded like a rubber balloon.

"Polly," he said, with a surprisingly high tenor. I expected a bassoon. It was more of a clarinet.

"Stretch," the mom said. She was engulfed in his embrace. "Welcome."

"Nice home. I like the paint."

I didn't know if he meant the color of the walls or that they had been painted. The floor joists creaked beneath his footsteps. He brushed past the tree, inadvertently knocking off an ornament, and stepped over the couch. It felt like the house was tilting.

"Exceeded expectations," I heard the dad say.

He led the wooden puppet into the room. Belkin thumped the floor with an extravagant cane and limped behind him, his hip a bit stiffer since I'd last seen him. Apparently, the mom hadn't fixed him. Or he liked it that way. His wool cloak draped over him like he was a coat hanger. He entered the room, turning his head side to side, looking for I didn't know what. It was a late-night visit through the back door. It was unexpected guests he was looking for.

"Can I take your coat?" the dad said.

"That's quite all right." Belkin held his arms out. "Merry, merry, everyone."

The mom greeted him. Madeline left Freckles next to me to shake his hand.

"Ah, a lovely home. Very warm. Don't you agree, Stretch?"

The elastic barbarian grunted.

"Can I get you an experience?" the mom said.

"No, thank you. I expect we won't be long. It seems we've had quite a Christmas." The presents were still unopened. It was very early, the sun still not up. "Care to tell me about it?"

Merry, merry and down to business. Madeline joined Freckles and me to watch the dad nervously explain. He'd shed the lab coat. In slippers and baggy pajamas, he reported with wild hand gestures what had happened. A quick synopsis of the electromagnetic field generators, the conduit in the attic and battery storage in the basement, which was new to me, and the time snap bubble.

"Christmas spirit," Madeline whispered.

Freckles formed a thought, repeating what she just said. I heard it quite clearly.

Belkin walked around, nodding his head. Looking into the fireplace, tracing his finger on the hearth, like a film of verve was a thin layer of dust.

"I captured it, Belkin," the dad said.

"Captured?"

"For the split second he was here, I siphoned verve." The dad pointed at the ceiling.

Belkin looked up. The mistletoe was above his head. He plucked it off the tip of the lightning rod, examined the plastic leafy bunch and white berries.

"A conductive rod of silver," the dad said. "Positioned in front of the fireplace. When the time snap was initiated, engulfing Santa, the conductor cross connected to a circuit through the attic, funneling the verve into a storage charm Polly designed for extra capacity."

It was an oversimplification, of course. There was more to it than just a silver stick and wires. But this wasn't a dissertation. It was a reveal.

"It worked, and it's more than I imagined. The toys have already changed. Just like we thought they would. Viktor?"

They looked at me. I didn't know what he wanted. Then I realized it was a demonstration. So I strode forward, eager to show off my new skills. I clicked my heels and pirouetted.

"Luscious," I said drily.

The dad chuckled nervously. "Tell them what happened. Start from the beginning."

"Yes, well. I woke up on the shelf, as usual. Everyone was still sleeping, or so I thought. It was shortly after midnight, so I went to see what Santa had brought everyone. I noticed the air felt different. Luscious was the word that came to mind. Can you feel it? Anyway, I saw a light coming from the lab and went to investigate. What happened next, I'm not quite certain. But the results are obvious."

I did a little soft-shoe routine. I got carried away, enamored by the deliciousness. I wasn't just a toy anymore. I wasn't human, either. I was both.

"I woke on the floor," I continued. "The light had... I'm sorry." I looked at Belkin. "With all due respect, it's impolite to search my thoughts without an invitation."

Belkin rattled in place. I had felt his presence, like a stringent vapor seeping through a veil. I'd caught him looking at my thoughts. But, curiously, I hadn't needed a wall to keep him out. I'd dodged his intrusion as effortlessly as I danced.

"My apologies." Belkin's maplewood lacquer turned to rosewood. "Of course, you're right. My curiosity got carried away." He turned to the mom and dad. "Did you upgrade him?"

So he saw it. I was no longer the silent bone toy staggering from room to room. And my thoughts were no longer easy pickings.

"No," the mom said. "It was a transformation. And Freckles spontaneously woke."

A generous assessment, seeing as Freckles looked more like zombie cat when Madeline wasn't hugging him. The dad handed out sunglasses, then went to the lab. We waited, curiously. I knew what it was. We all did. The anticipation was a sweet perfume, becoming a tantalizing flavor when white light beamed from the open door. The dad paused with the glass box. The light had the warmth of boxed sunlight on a wet, winter day.

Stretch was the first to move, craning his neck at an impossible angle, sort of telescoping like a nosy ostrich. Given his full size and mostly human appearance, exaggerated as it was, it was a strange and uncomfortable distortion to watch.

"Stay here, Stretch." Belkin held out his hand.

"It made Viktor smart," Stretch protested.

I resented that. I was also pleased. They hadn't thought I was smart before.

Belkin, hand up, tapping the floor with the cane, approached warily. Big round eyes on the glowing prize. No sunglasses for him. He didn't flinch, easing closer and closer. Stretch could feel the effects. I could sense his IQ rising. His good-natured expression, childish and innocent, transformed into something poised and investigative. I could feel what he was feeling when I looked directly at him, the flow of luscious spirit. The deliciousness.

"I don't know the sphere of influence," the dad said. "Or how it's transferred. We'll need to run some tests—"

Belkin suddenly stopped, tipped his head like a morning robin hearing the worm. If his eyes weren't painted, they would have doubled in size. Jaw hinged open, he looked at his hands like they were brand new.

Remarkable, I heard him say. Only he didn't say it. He thought it.

I peeked a little further. How do I explain what it's like to move in thought? It's like gaining a completely new sense that's as familiar as an arm or a leg. I moved my mind in the direction I wanted, looked with some ethereal vision. Felt the wooden puppet's naked thoughts as if they were particles of distinct shape and color, absorbed them like my own. A language that did not need translating.

The Christmas spirit was familiar to him. Like a scent from childhood. He touched the painted heart on his chest. Looked up at the ceiling, looked around like it was made of glass and the stars were shining through.

I pushed a little deeper, feeling myself merge into his experience. I was slightly nervous he would sense me in the corners of his mind, but he was too distracted to notice the intruder riding sidecar on his trip to wherever he was going. The light had taken me to a river. Belkin was in the sky.

Reindeer, two by two, waited on the pitch of the roof. Steam pumping from flared nostrils. Colorful streaks slashed across the canvas of night. It appeared, to me, an aberration of the Northern Lights. Belkin understood, though. He knew what the ribbons were.

Roads.

These were portals, time-warped highways that crisscrossed the universe. A network of avenues interconnecting worlds. And not just worlds. It was difficult to comprehend what Belkin was sensing, or maybe he was remembering. It wasn't just worlds the portals connected, but different realities. It was what Santa and his reindeer traveled on to reach *everywhere*.

I couldn't understand how this was possible. Since waking as a toy, I'd learned to set aside what seemed impossible. Belkin was recalling how the Christmas spirit had brought them from one world to this one. *The Great Toy Arrival.* I'd seen it in those pictures outside his office. *They live!*

It was the verve that gave them life. His memories swirled in a storm of confusion, the perspective shifting rapidly. I nearly retracted from his mind, afraid I might fall over or, worse, get sucked into his mind and lose all sense of my own self.

His vision came back into focus. We rested, bodiless, in space. Galaxies all around. A celestial wonder whose beauty was overwhelming. The roads weaved colorful threads, a fabric on which everything rested. It was this vision that would change everything about this world and my home. It was the epiphany I had been searching for.

Everything retracted to a fine point. I found myself back in my red bones. Belkin staring at me.

"Apologies," I muttered. "My curiosity got carried away."

I knew what he was thinking, what he was about to say, the conversation he would have with the mom and dad. How they could distribute the spirit to all the toys on the planet, to raise their awareness, raise their intelligence. To no longer be satisfied with being playthings. He had concerns, also. Would siphoning the Christmas spirit have consequences?

I was thinking the same thing. I didn't know if the spirit made me smarter, but I was no longer content to just visit Toyworld when I slept at night. I didn't want to wake in my bed only to count the hours before I could sleep again. This was home. It was the roads that brought me here. And it was the roads that took me back.

This was when my grand plan took shape. It was elementary, really. Now that I understood how it worked. In order to stay here, it was simple.

I needed to close the roads. All of them. Forever.

17

Hiro spun like a loose balloon.

Disoriented, without sight or sound, he bounced through the dark, ejected into a cosmic pinball machine. Each stop was different, like trying on clothes that didn't quite fit—wrinkly or baggy, lumpy or stiff. He tumbled into one after another, feeling scratchy fabric or tasting cold steel, before snuggling into a pillowy landing. Soft and perfect.

He rested in a beautiful dream without a care or thought. It was all quite lovely. Then gritty sensations poured inside him. Pins and needles pricked his slumber, delivered dusty smells and padded footsteps.

Images emerged, like a dimmer switch slowly turning on. Colors and objects appeared. He was on a ledge. The walls were ten stories tall and lined with shelves. Toys sat stiffly, blankly staring out. A window was near the ceiling.

A cat looked up from the floor. It was black and white striped; an extremely long tail swished like a rope. From this distance, it looked too lumpy to be a cat. Hiro was as high as the window.

His first thought: *Where am I?*

"No," he muttered. Then shouted, "No, no, no—"

He had lifted his arms and began tipping forward. There was nothing to grab as the floor rushed toward him. He couldn't close his eyes for some reason and was forced to watch the entire trip down. End over end—a flash of a fluorescent light, the wood floor, the light again. His unceremonious end taking its time.

He landed on his face.

The floor looked like wood but felt like a pillow. He bounced and tumbled, coming to rest with his nose pressed against the grainy planks. He sneezed like a dog. It was plenty firm, the floor was. The strange thing, though, was it didn't hurt. He'd fallen from what he thought was ten stories, maybe more, and he wasn't mortally wounded. He moved his arms and legs. Nothing seemed broken.

Why can't I close my eyes?

A fuzzy tail slithered under his chin. He flipped like a pancake, staring at bright white tubes on the ceiling. The cat leaned over. Her emerald eyes were glassy. Plastic whiskers poked out from her shiny nose. She didn't look real. And then it hit him. He scampered back, paddling the floor.

That's not a cat.

She sat with an amused smile, her tail wrapping twice around her long legs. Hiro crawled to the wall, sitting beneath a shelf of plastic dolls. The cat was toying with him. That was what cats did before they ate their prey, they played with it. Fear filled Hiro like an icy spring bubbling below him.

His heart was silent.

Finally, his second thought returned. He looked at his hands. He didn't have hands. But not like before.

He had stumps.

Short, furry arms. The ends, blunt. His legs were, too. No fingers or toes. He felt his stomach and chest, touched the snout on his face. Found two round flaps on top of his head where ears shouldn't be.

"Finally." The cat slunk toward him like a runway model.

She was the size of a housecat. A toy cat that walked and talked. A toy cat whose voice he'd once heard.

"Chase?"

He teetered back. She held onto him with her tail. It was tricky, balancing without feet. Just two stumpy legs and a round belly. The room smelled like wood shavings and glue. And something sweet.

"What is this?" He threw his arms out and fell, scrambling to get his balance. "This is fur and-and-and a snout. You have a tail!" He walked in a circle, grabbing at the hair on his head. But he didn't have hair, only fur. He didn't have fingers, and even if he did, his arms were too short. "I'm here. We're here. Like this is... this is it. This is the dream."

"It's not a dream."

That was ridiculous. Of course it was the dream. He was a bear; she was a cat. Her eyelids clicked when they blinked.

"Dreams aren't real, Hiro, they're doorways. And you're late."

His belly swarmed with jumping beans. The last thing he remembered was staring at Monkeybrain on his dresser, lying awake for too long, his heart thumping, thinking he might not ever fall asleep. It was getting late.

This didn't feel like a dream.

"Why am I a-a-a toy?"

"You aren't a toy," she said. "You're you."

"I'm a teddy bear!" He held out his arms. "And you—wait. How are we talking?" It was a strange sensation, the way the words came out. He could hear them just fine, and his mouth sort of moved. But he wasn't speaking.

"I don't have all the answers. If I did, I wouldn't have been stuck in this room waiting for you."

She leaped onto a workbench cluttered with papers and quills, old-fashioned tools and jars of ink. Gracefully, with barely a sound, she bounded from shelf to shelf. Hiro lost his balance watching her ascend to the sill of the window. He pushed himself up.

"All I know is that you chose to be a teddy bear." She licked her paw with a fabric tongue. "And I chose this."

She looked outside while her tail danced to the tune of a snake charmer's song. The room smelled like a workshop, where toys were fabricated, stitched and put on shelves. There was one door with a doorknob four feet off the floor. It might as well have been a mile.

"This is too weird." He thumped his head. His voice was coming from inside it. *It's not like I've got a brain. Do I? Of course not. I'm a toy! No, wait. Maybe I do have a brain, and I just think what I want to say. But how would that work? How? Because this is a dream!*

This was way too real to be a dream. *It's a place.* "What's out there?"

"You wouldn't believe it."

There were no ladders for him to climb. He wasn't a real bear. He was a teddy bear with no claws or opposable thumbs, just barely functioning limbs. He could push things. He wasn't built to snarl or climb trees. He was made for hugs. He stared at the doorknob. A flyer was taped to the door with an orange cat with a broad smile. *Christmas Gala!* it read.

"There must be a way out. Why would we be in a locked room—"

"No one has come in or out," she hissed. Hiro felt a tiny bit scared. "I've been sitting here all day wondering why. All I know is that I'm here, and now you're here. I thought when, or if, you got here, something would happen." She hugged herself with the tail. "Apparently not."

"You've been here all day?"

"All day. Sun went down, came back up. There's been no one else."

"I just fell asleep. How have you been here a whole day?"

"I went to bed early. Seven o'clock." She looked down at him. "You should have, too. I told you this is important. We have to—"

"Save Christmas. I know." Time was relative. It didn't work the same on two planets in the same solar system. Time was a function of velocity and gravity. If this was a place and not a dream (*still not sure about that*), then time went faster here.

"Is there a note on the desk?" he said. "A book or journal? Maybe instructions."

"There's no instructions. There's just—"

Something moved. It came from a small stage of unpainted

plywood in the corner of the room. A velvet curtain hung across the front of it. It looked like a marionette stage, the kind where puppeteers stood over it with strings to make puppets dance.

Chase watched from the safety of the shelf. "Walk over there."

He shook his head. Something was moving, and she was up there. He thought about the attic when something moved. What if a mouse jumped at him? He couldn't defend himself with two padded arms. Chase leaped from shelf to shelf, landing with a heavy purr.

"Come on."

He followed her slinky gait. His balance was already improving. She picked up her pace, and he tried to keep up. His steps were springy, like running through a jump castle. He was a locomotive gaining steam. It felt good. She stopped and turned around. Hiro whizzed past her in a full gallop. Stopping was an entirely different skill.

He crashed into the stage, tumbling across the platform. It smelled like sawdust. Slivers from the half-finished dais snagged his fur. A scarlet curtain began to ripple. Hiro brushed himself off and stepped back.

The curtain yanked open.

Hiro fell off the stage. He was on his back again, a turtle looking up at a blinding fluorescent light. He turned away, his vision obscured. He couldn't close his eyes because teddy bears don't have eyelids. The stage was dark. It looked like a model of someone on an iceberg. The handle of a cane held the curtain open. A bearded face peeked out, looked around; then the cane reached across the stage and pull the curtains closed.

"Well, poop," Chase said.

"Poop? What poop? What was that?"

"I thought since you were here, it would do something different."

Hiro climbed onto the stage, pulled the curtain open. The cane pulled it closed. He did it again, and the curtain closed faster. The show was over. Or never started.

"It's no use," she said. "He doesn't do anything."

"It must mean something."

"I've done it a hundred times. It's nothing."

"Yeah, but what if—"

"It's a toy, Hiro." She turned around, tail swishing. "A toy that doesn't work."

Hiro poked the curtain, then tried to peek through the opening. He was rewarded with a hard poke on the nose with the curved end of a cane. He rubbed his snout. It didn't hurt. His feelings were a little, but not his nose. Chase was back on her perch like a pet waiting for her owner.

※

THE ROOM WAS MOSTLY toys and small tools. A ball of twine was on the desk. A sheet of sandpaper was folded in half. A roll of heavy-duty tape was on a hook. He leaped off the stage without falling and sprang to the door. There was a way to open it.

The drawers in the desk were partially open. He slid a box to the bottom drawer. It took two attempts, but he managed to climb onto the bottom drawer. The middle drawer was almost shut. He could really use some fingers about now. Why did they make teddy bears like this? He wedged his arm into the gap and threw his leg up.

"What are you doing?" she asked.

"I've got an idea." He grunted. "Help me up."

She landed on the desk with a whump. Her tail slithered over the edge and looped under his arm. The desk was disorganized. Notes jotted on random bits of paper with unfinished doodles. He stepped away from the edge. It was higher than he thought.

"Here's what we do." He pushed the ball of string to the middle of the desk, then kicked the sandpaper next to it. "We're going to use the string and sandpaper to open the door."

Chase looked bored.

"If we can get that..." He couldn't reach the roll of tape. He jumped once and almost bounced off the desk. Chase casually batted it off the hook. It rolled across the desk. "We tape sandpaper to string.

Then we tie the roll of tape to the string for weight. We throw it over the doorknob; then we'll pull the string."

"What's the sandpaper for?"

"Friction. It'll turn the doorknob."

She watched him try to untangle the string. "What if it's locked?"

"We won't know till we try."

"Okay. Problem two: how are you going to get tape?" She flicked it with her tail. It rolled off the desk. "We don't have hands."

"Are you always like this?"

"I have a tail. You poke things. And you want to pull super adhesive tape off, build a lasso and open a door with sandpaper?"

"Do you have a better idea?"

"I've tried everything."

"Did you try sandpaper?"

She swatted the bird's nest of string from his arms. "No. I also didn't try flying around the room. It won't work."

The tape settled in the middle of the room. It was a long way down. He sighed, even though he was certain he wasn't breathing. His idea probably wouldn't work, but it was better than looking out the window.

"Maybe you can fly," he said.

"What?"

"Look, if this is a dream, and I see no way it's not, then anything is possible. We were in outer space before we got here. We're toys talking with thoughts! Maybe we can fly. We just have to imagine it."

"No, Hiro. No. This isn't a dream. I told you, the dream is just the way here. This is a *place*. This is real. It's got its own laws of physics, like gravity and whatever. We can't just fly because we want to."

"Have you tried?"

She stepped away from the ledge. "Be my guest."

He looked down. He'd fallen from the top shelf, and it hadn't hurt. In fact, nothing had hurt so far. It wouldn't hurt this time. He was pretty sure. He tried to close his eyes to imagine what flying would feel like, but again, no eyelids. He was going to do it. It was just like leaping off the high dive. Only instead of water, it was a floor. *But I'm a toy.*

"Well?" Chase said.

He was going to do it. He just needed to focus. He put his arms up because that was how superheroes flew. His feet—he didn't have feet, just stumps—were halfway over the edge, and he started to teeter when the tape began vibrating on the floor.

Chase pulled him back with her tail. Paper fluttered on the desk. The shelves trembled.

"What's happening?" he shouted.

A purple thread appeared in the center of the room. It wasn't attached to the ceiling. It was hovering. Hiro's fur charged with static electricity like he was fresh out of the dryer. Chase's tail wrapped around him twice. The thread bathed the room in purple light and began to swell. Chase pulled him all the way to the wall.

The thread unzipped. Hiro turned away, shielded the glare with his arm. Two orbs of light, one after another, burst out. They shot around the room, ricocheting off the walls and rumbling through toys. They went in different directions, each settling into a toy momentarily before zipping to the next one. Sometimes a toy would move an arm or turn its head. A mouth would open; eyes would shift.

Two toys tumbled off shelves.

The air sizzled. Hiro's fur still stood on end. Chase crept to the edge. Hiro crawled next to her. A felty green dragon with tiny wings was facedown. Next to it was a metal toy, its limbs fastened with bolts and wingnuts, a cube attached to broad shoulders.

"Don't move," Chase whispered.

Hiro wished he could close his eyes.

18

Metal limbs scraped the floor like a fork.
Slowly, the pile of metal solved the puzzle of its entanglement and wobbled onto bent legs. It stumbled into the wall; its long arm clashed against its blocky head. A screen lit up. An eye swam in gray static, then focused on its spiky, hinged fingers. It made a strange, electric sound.

It began flailing like a rogue robot, knocking toys off the bottom shelf. The arms, there were four of them, spun out of control. It kept falling and getting up, the eye bouncing on the screen like a game of *Pong*.

Chase held Hiro tighter.

The metal thing looked like a toddler operating a remote control. It stomped on the green dragon on its way to the other side of the room. The dragon suddenly jumped up. Its thick tail swept the floor. Its big blue eyes were wide and searching. When the red wings slowly moved, it spun like a bug was crawling up its back. As the robot thrashed around, the dragon looked around. It held up its hands. The claws were painted red.

"Trippy," the dragon said.

"Haze?" Hiro said.

The dragon looked up with big eyes. Hiro peeled Chase's tail from his belly, walked off the edge and bounced on the floor, springing toward her. He tackled her, still not mastering the slowing-down part, with his short arms. In a full teddy bear hug, they rolled on the floor. Her arms were even shorter than his.

"It's you, isn't it," he said. "You're here."

"Hiro? What's happening?"

"I can't believe you're here. You took the purple tail just like I—"

"This is the dream?"

"This is it." He glanced at Chase still safely on the desk. "It's not a dream, I don't think. I guess the dream was the way here, to this place. We couldn't bring our bodies, so we're toys. I don't get it, either. Neither does Chase."

Haze was surprisingly calm. Or in shock. Or just Haze. The robot was in shock.

"You did this?" He struggled to untangle his legs. "You're the one who brought us here?"

"I didn't do anything," Hiro said. "I mean, I don't really know how you—"

"Get me out of here."

The robot came at him like a metallic squid: fingers clipping, arms slicing. Hiro was a pillow. And that thing was a set of dull steak knives. Electrical bolts danced around its screen. Hiro wondered if Chase would be able to sew him back together. Or if it would hurt when he was shredded into a cloud of stuffing. Haze stepped in front of him. Her belly inflated.

A colorful cloud showered the lumbering robot. Little pellets—orange, red, yellow, and blue—plunked off the steely limbs and scattered on the floor. It didn't take much to throw him off balance, sending him into a tangled pile.

Haze rubbed her belly. "Did you see that?"

She revealed the row of plastic daggers lining her mouth. Her belly inflated, and another wave of hard pellets was expelled. They plinked off the robot's screen. He waved bent limbs. Hiro put his snout to the floor, sniffed a little purple rock. It smelled like grape.

"It's candy."

"I know," Haze said. "Want more?"

"Hag, no," the robot said. "Just, what is hap—"

"Robby?" Haze said.

He was tangled worse than before. Haze hopped like a bunny, her little wings uselessly flapping. Her arms were too little to pull his twisted limbs free. It was hard to tell where they started and where they ended.

"This is a nightmare." Jagged colors raced across his television, bending into a frown. "I don't believe any of this. That's not you, that's not him, I don't know who you are, but when I wake up, I'm going to find you and your boyfriend—"

"Don't be mean," Haze said.

"Why am I... *this*?" He pulled his legs free.

"You picked your body," Chase said.

"I didn't pick anything! I want to wake up and eat some breakfast and forget this ever happened. Wake up!" he shouted at the ceiling. "Wake up now!"

"We can't leave," Chase said. "Not until it's over."

"No. No, no, no, no, no, no!" He folded into a tower nearly twice as tall as Hiro, a swaying thin structure that could be blown over by a wave of hard candy. The screen displayed a roiling gray cloud. "I want to wake up."

"This isn't a dream," Chase said.

"What? I mean, are you broke?"

"There's only one reason why you're here. Same as us."

"I'm here because I looked at your drawing." He poked Hiro's belly with a sharp finger. "And it's stuck in my brain, and I dreamed it, and now I want to wake up. It's that simple. You—"

He swung at Chase and fell. A fire blazed on the screen. He didn't try to get up this time. One of his arms sounded like a buck knife on a whetstone.

"Robby," Haze said, "be nice."

"Or you'll blow more candy?"

"I'll turn your TV off."

Chase slunk over to the pile of struggling metal. She walked around him, dragging her tail over him. "I don't know why you're here. Or you." She pointed her tail at Haze. "There's a reason, and there's nothing we can do about it. But you're here. Stop fighting it." She pulled his limbs free one at a time. "You'll find it's much easier if you accept it. And you won't turn yourself into a puzzle."

She slid her tail through several openings and lifted him up. He balanced on three legs. The eye returned to the screen.

"That's better," she said. "Now—"

"I know why you're here," Hiro said.

He walked across the room, waving for them to follow. Robby tapped the boxy monitor on his shoulders, static flashing on the screen.

"Is my head really a—"

"It's a television," Haze said. "Yeah."

❉

"There's no other way out?" Haze said.

"Chase looked everywhere," Hiro said.

He explained the time differential between here and there. Here being here and there being home. Time went faster here. At least that was what Chase said. His explanation didn't matter. Robby's screen was full of static again. Haze knocked on the door.

"Sounds hollow," she said. "You thinking what I'm thinking?"

"We open the door," Hiro said.

"No," Haze said. "We go through it."

"I'm with Candy Breath," Robby said. "We punch a hole."

"No. It's a door." Hiro pointed at his stubby arm. "You're going to open it."

Robby looked up and nearly tipped over. "Not going to happen."

"You can do it. You just need to extend your arms. You already did it once."

The TV set swiveled toward Haze. An image of something exploding lit the screen. Robby looked like a child bored with instructions. "In case you haven't noticed, I'm a tin can that's been run over. I'm not going to open a door."

"Maybe we can throw you through it." Haze swung her tail like a baseball bat.

"You just have to focus."

Hiro tried to help him up. He tipped to one side. The monitor spun on his shoulders. Long pieces of metal began sliding and bending, forming a triangular base. Sparks showered across the monitor. He started to mutter, then shout, a string of angry words interrupted with intermittent beeps.

"You running out of battery?" Haze said.

"No. I think I'm... holy *beeeep*." A black dot swelled on the monitor. "I'm censored."

"You're a toy," Chase said.

"Well, *beeeep*," he said. "That's a load of *beeeep*."

"Focus," Hiro said.

It was like watching metal origami trying to assemble itself. They tried to help, but Robby swatted them away. He got onto three legs, his arms sliding like switchblades on gritty tracks. The monitor tilted back. The black eye returned to a bed of static, shrinking to a dot.

"Not going to work," he declared.

"You haven't tried," Haze said.

He aimed one arm. The segments slid out, one by one, till they were fully extended. Just short of the doorknob. "Even if it reaches," he said, "what do you want me to do, tap it open? I can't grab anything."

"Pick Haze up," Hiro said. "She can get it."

Robby retracted his limbs and braced them on the corners of his tripod hips. The monitor teetered back and forth. Hiro knew what he was thinking. *Why can't I just wake up?*

His arms reconfigured into pitchforks.

"You'd better not poke me," Haze said.

"Sit still." Carefully, he slid them under her. His screen turned white followed by one long beep. The sound of twisting metal screeched. She hadn't moved an inch when a wingnut fell off.

"I popped a girder," he said.

"You did that on purpose," Haze said.

"You're ten pounds of candy!" Robby said.

Chase returned with the wingnut and fastened it back on. "Do this." She guided his arms with her tail, weaving them together, then worked him like an artist positioning her model. She widened his stance, adjusted his arms so they were a makeshift platform.

"Hiro," she said, "get on."

"What?"

"You're the lightest and widest of us."

"Widest?"

"Your butt's big." Haze shrugged.

"Yeah, but..." Hiro lifted his stubby arms. "I can't grab it. You've got the tail. You can twist it."

"Cats don't like to be picked up," Chase said.

"That's not true. Cats love being picked up."

"Not this one. Besides, you're a bear. Bear hug it."

He looked up. The doorknob was higher than the desk. It wouldn't hurt if he fell, but what if that changed? He could lose an eye or tear a seam. Who would put him back together? He paced in a circle, looking up at the door, then down at his legs. Robby's monitor began ticking. A clock was counting down.

"You wanted to be here," Robby said.

That was true. He'd done everything he could to get here. And he was here for a reason. They were all here for a reason. The answer was out there.

"Okay."

Robby lowered the weaved platform. Haze and Chase rolled Hiro onto it. He wasn't going to stand, not if he didn't have to. There was no seat belt. He wished he could close his eyes.

"On three," Robby announced. "One—"

Hiro went soaring like a rocket. He lifted off the platform and, thankfully, landed back on it. His head bounced off the door. He leaned against it; prickly fear rushed through him.

"That better not have been on purpose," Haze shouted.

"He's a bag of feathers!" Robby said. "All right, I got it. Here we go. You good up there, teddy bear."

Hiro's snout was pressed against the cool panel of wood. The door began to move against his nose. It sounded like a marble sliding on a painted wall. They were shouting. He didn't know if it was bad or good. The ride felt like it was to the top of a skyscraper. He felt something hard and cold between his ears. He stared at the doorknob.

"Reach up!" Haze shouted.

Hiro felt like he was breathing hard. But he wasn't breathing at all. *Focus,* he thought. He imagined he was breathing, counting long breaths like he was sitting on the meditation bench. He walked his arms up the door. "Higher."

"That's it," Robby grunted. "Stand up."

Heroes would be able to feel their legs. He was sure of it. He only needed a few inches. He pulled one leg under him. The platform wobbled.

"Stop squirming," Robby said.

"I have to stand!" Hiro shouted.

When everything was steady, he pulled his other leg up. He latched onto the brassy doorknob. He paused, feeling the friction of his fur gripping the metal. He pressed it against his chest. Suddenly, he was filled with an elated sensation. He was going to do it. Just turn his body and the door would open.

Something metal tumbled across the floor. "Uh-oh," Robby said.

The platform plummeted several inches. Hiro's legs dangled above it.

"Hang on!" Haze shouted.

Hiro stared at the door, kicking his legs to feel something solid. He heard Chase find the loose wingnut, heard her shout at Robby to lean to one side. His metal fingers touched the bottom of Hiro's feet. Hiro plopped onto the platform. Then the next jolt came.

This time the tower was leaning.

Robby stumbled backwards. The door receded. Haze and Chase tried to prop him up. He went down like a giant redwood. They tumbled across the floor. Hiro bounced across the room like a firm pillow, landing in front of the puppet stage. Haze was next to him. She spit a bright lump of candy.

The velvet curtain pulled back.

Chase was trapped under the wreckage of Robby. His monitor swiveled toward a white beard looking down at them.

"You've got to be kidding me," he said.

19

The sound of his feet was unsettling, like coarse belts of sandpaper grinding wood.

He looked like a white beard in a frumpy pair of red trousers, the long, silvery whiskers tied in a knot that dragged between his legs. The hat was as tall as the beard was long. Pointy with a wide brim pulled down to a bulbous nose that, if someone squeezed it, looked like it would squeak. It was red, like the trousers, and crumpled and soft.

The grinding shuffle came to a halt. He stood there, short arms at his sides with sleeves too long. The eyes, if he had eyes, were buried beneath the brim. He was all beard and a nose. An elf in poorly tailored pajamas.

"What's he doing?" Haze whispered.

"I don't know," Chase said. "He's never done this before."

"Hello? What's your name?" Haze said.

A garble of electronic laughter echoed from the pile of metal struts. "What's your name?" Robby said. "That's what you want to know? Hey, what's your favorite color?"

Haze swelled like a balloon. Robby's laughter grew louder. The elf raised his arm. Fingers, short and pudgy, peeked out from the sleeve.

The fingers weren't fabric or furry. Rubber, maybe. One blunt finger poked out.

"He wants you, Robby," Hiro said.

"He's not pointing at me." Robby's tone lost its humor.

"He's pointing right at you," Haze said. "Come on, get him up there."

"No. No, no, no. Don't do that."

Haze got behind him. Robby's limbs scratched grooves in the floor. Chase pulled his legs loose, then lassoed him with her tail. She dragged while Haze bulldozed. They shoved him up to the stage, the elf's finger following his approach. He was definitely pointing at him.

"I want a different body," Robby moaned with a gray screen.

Haze shoved him into a sitting position. The elf dropped his arm. They stood in silence, waiting for something to happen. The elf's hidden feet scuffed the floor, sending shivers down Hiro's fur. The tall, pointy hat began to move. A poke and a prod, something inside feeling around. The elf didn't seem bothered that something was trapped inside.

"This isn't good," Robby said.

Calmly, the elf reached up. The sleeves fell back. His hands were strangely real—fleshy smooth fingers that barely reached over the brim of the hat. He pinched a small button and pulled it up, unzipping a small flap. A bearded elf walked out, no taller than a coffee mug. It was an exact duplicate of the bigger elf with a tiny hat and frumpy red PJs. He peered over the brim.

"Thank you, Flake. Need to fix the door."

Flake, the larger elf, grunted.

"Could this get any weirder?" Robby said.

"It's a dream," Haze said distantly.

"It's not a dream," Chase said.

They watched him make a circle around the hat while Flake froze like a mannequin. It was a bizarre display in a department store. Or some artist's interpretation of a dream that would sell for millions. The tiny elf took off his tiny hat and bunched it in his tiny hands like a hamster gathering food. A mop of hair sprang from his head like a silver tumbleweed. Only a tiny bulbous nose appeared in all that hair.

"'Twas a night—eh-hem." He thumped his chest, mumbled something. "'Twas a night like all others, a cheerful end to a long year. All the children were sleeping, faraway and so near. The mighty sleigh, it was loaded with the fat man and his gear. The reindeer were full, muscles like steel, corded and tight. Santa called out, they sprang from the ice, to make their rounds all in one night. They traveled as always, just as before, to the ends of the universe in the breadth of a snore."

Flake looked up as if following a shooting star. The little elf hung onto the hat.

"In the blink of an eye, he would visit them all, every home, every planet, every place cold and warm. Climbing through mountains, soaring through clouds, through storms and bad weather, without making a sound."

Flake reached beneath his beard and pulled out a handful of confetti, tossing it over his head; it fluttered around the little elf.

"Through dimensions they went on sway roads of bright color; they did what they did as they'd done every year. Nine brave reindeer and a merry old toot. Children would wake with sand in their eyes, run down to the trees to unwrap his surprise. They would cheer and would holler and write letters of thanks. Santa and steed would continue their journey, stopping to rest, to snack on a treat or munch on a carrot left on the street."

Reaching, once again, beneath the fluffy beard, Flake pulled out a sugar cookie. Took a bite and offered a crumb up above. Which the little elf ignored, still clutching his hat.

"Quite a chore, yes indeed, to go one and all. He did it with cheer and joyous resolve. A merry Christmas again, he left with a call. But the year was not over, not this one at all. One final visit, a universe not small, the sway roads they traveled to finish the call. They arrived a bit weary, a long night had been had. It was business as usual, presents delivered to good girls and lads. They didn't seem worried, why should they be? All the toys were in slumber, asleep in their beds. All except one. Viktor the Red."

Flake raised his arms, rubber fingers clutched into fists. The sleeves bunched at his pudgy elbows. He let out a growl.

"Christmas once a year? Why not every day? A year filled with cheer and presents, no time for delay. Viktor made haste, took matters in paws, this would be the night they would not waste. To get what is ours, no matter the cause, he captured the essence of the jolly ole Claus. The songs and the presents, the cheer and reindeer, were put out of sight. The sway roads started closing at the end of the night. Now we have Christmas not one day but all. It was Viktor the Red who brought down the fall."

The little elf threw out his hands. Flake did as well.

"Christmas is ours!" the little elf shouted. "He declared no defeat. We are the toys, too long deserving such treat. Now what is ours is not yours, I'm sorry to say. On that one starry night, everything changed. While we relish and sing and open our gifts, there's no trees for you, no cookies or riffs. You forgot about stockings and songs, tinsel and joy and how we all play along. Because Santa is here, behind our closed gate. And that's why you're here. To save Christmas for all." He lowered his head. "Before it's too late."

The elves bowed in unison. The little elf pulled the little hat over his head, somehow stuffing that enormous mop inside it. Hiro and the others sat quietly. The little elf looked around.

"Questions?"

Silence fell like a blanket of midnight snow, filling their heads with fuzzy puzzlement and glaring numbness. They'd forgotten, for the moment, they were toys, locked in a strange room with no idea how they got there or if they would wake up and reflect, as one does, on how strange a dream it was. A tiny elf on the hat of another elf. Reciting a story that sort of rhymed. Given all that had happened, it was exactly what they should have expected.

A creaky hinge unfolded. A metal arm rose.

"Yes, you there," the little elf said. "TV robot, you have a question?"

"What was that?" Robby said.

"I'm sorry?"

"I was wondering the same thing," Haze said. "You mean, like, do we have questions about the poem?"

"Well." The little elf cleared his throat. "It was written on short notice. A work in progress, I suppose. You two, I don't even know why you're here, and all of this happened so quickly. Did you like it, Flake?"

Flake grunted.

"Yes, well, it doesn't matter. It told you everything you need to know. Any other questions?"

"About what?" Haze said. "It didn't make sense."

The little elf jabbed a finger with a smile somewhere beneath that tiny beard. "Exactly the point, Candy Dragon."

"Santa delivered the presents on... sway roads?" Chase said.

"He does every year, yes," the little elf said. "Or did."

"Reindeer don't have wings," Robby said.

"You are correct. They have helium bladders. It all started with elves living in—"

"Just tell us what's going on?" Robby moaned, slinking into a pile of iron angles.

The little elf straightened his hat. The end of his pudgy nose turned a shade of plum. "A story is more compelling. A parable more enduring. Thoughts are words with wings, you have to be careful where they fly. They can be caught like butterflies and—"

"Are you a toy?" Haze said. "You don't look like a toy."

"We're different material—look, ask more relevant questions. We're here to help."

Chase lifted the cuff on Flake's pant leg to inspect a large, hairy foot that scuffed the boards like a cheese grater. Haze climbed onto the stage while Robby worked his legs free.

Hiro was thinking. It was what he did best. Reindeer pulled a sleigh with a man named Santa Claus to different worlds all in one night. *To the ends of the universe,* the little elf said. *On sway roads.* Hiro looked at the poster on the door. A celebration was coming.

"Who's Viktor the Red?" Hiro asked.

"Finally. A relevant question. Who do you think—stop that." The little elf swung his hat at Robby's probing metal finger. "Please, off the stage. Flake, help them down."

Hiro wanted to close his eyes. He needed to concentrate, to think. There were nuggets in that story that needed to be filtered from the chaff. He stared at one of Robby's loose wingnuts on the floor. The dream of the planet with colorful noodles that gently swayed into outer space. Those could be the roads. The portals. Santa traveled on them to other dimensions. And they were disappearing. The wingnut began to waver. *The gates are closed.*

"Let me start over," the little elf said. "I'll recite the story again. Listen this time, very closely."

Hiro could see it now, the planet in his dream and the vanishing roads. It hovered in front of him. He shook his head, and it was there, actually there. He reached out to touch it, to see if it was real, or if he was just imagining it.

"From the top, Flake. If everyone could just sit back down, I'll—"

"Hiro!" Haze shouted.

They turned all at once. Only the sound of Robby's joints twisting and the little elf's hat wringing in his hands broke the silence. Hiro was fixated on the colorful planet before him. Chase's soft footfalls drew near, followed by the sound of hard candy sloshing in Haze's belly. They stood on each side of him, watching the colorful roads dance off the planet.

"Santa Claus visited all the planets in one night," Hiro said. "He went through those tunnels. Portals, just like you said, Haze. Those are the sway roads. He does it every year, delivering presents across the universe, putting them under Christmas trees and filling stockings. This place was his last stop. That's why the roads are disappearing."

The ropey roads began to vanish, shriveling up, one at a time.

"He's stuck here with no way out. They closed the gates. That's why we forgot about Christmas." He looked up. "That's why we're here."

The planet slowly faded. They stared where it once hung. The quiet was broken by walloping paddles. Flake swung his hands together, clapping with thunderous impact, bits of sawdust dancing on the floor.

"Finally," the little elf said, bouncing on the brim with each booming clap, "someone heard the story."

Flake dropped his hands at his sides. Hiro could feel the elves smiling, their grins beaming like glowing space heaters.

"So mystery solved," Robby said. "How do we wake up?"

They looked at each other, looked at the stage. The elves looked back. Robby's monitor spun around.

"Well," the little elf said, raising a finger, "there is—"

"Not another story," Robby said.

"No, not a story. I was just going to say—"

That was when the doorknob rattled. A key slid into the lock. They stared dumbly as the door cracked open. They all thought the same thing, Hiro could feel their thoughts like voices in his head. His fur stood up.

Hide!

20

Madeline was asleep.

Freckles was next to her, staring at the ceiling. His mind a popcorn machine of random images. His mental capacity had not advanced in the year since he woke. All he did was watch the Social with Madeline. He had no idea I was awake. He didn't notice when I crawled off the shelf.

It was close to midnight.

The lab now had a lock. That was a problem. Belkin had suggested they move the lab to a more secure location. The dad argued this wasn't the time to make changes. They agreed to keep it in the house. Therefore, lock. And I didn't know the code. I would solve that later.

I climbed onto the couch, nestled into a cushion like a forgotten toy. Cookies were on a plate. A glass full of milk. Empty stockings were on the mantel where a clock counted the minutes. I watched the secondhand tick off the final seconds. Never once had I been excited about Christmas. It was just another day. *The sun doesn't play favorites,* my father would say. *It rises on Christmas just like every other day.*

I shivered with anticipation. In a few moments, all of time would synchronize across planes of existence, according to the dad. And the jolly fat man would arrive in three, two, one...

Midnight.

There was no bolt of lightning, no flash of surprise. A boot didn't waggle from the flue. But something *felt* different. Disappointment descended on me, my father's laughter in my head. Then I noticed the cookies. They were gone. The stockings were bulging.

It had happened in a wink.

There was a subtle change in the air. It was pure warmth. *Delicious,* I thought. But that wasn't it. *Love,* I thought. *It's love.*

Love wafted through the room like a spritz of perfume, and in that brief moment, I bathed in it, let it sink into my bones. Was this what Christmas was supposed to feel like? I'll admit, in that moment, I had second thoughts about what I was planning to do. If I succeeded, I would deprive everyone from ever feeling this again. An emptiness would greet them on Christmas morning, one that I'd felt all my life. They didn't deserve that.

Neither did I.

The dad rushed down the hall. With slippers barely on his feet, he reached into his robe for sunglasses and punched the keycode. He was abruptly thrown back, lost a slipper on the floor. The sunglasses weren't enough. I'd never seen anything so bright. It was like staring at the sun through a telescope. Color seemed to bleach from the room. He turned his head, pulled the door closed and muttered. He sounded confused, worried.

He went down to the basement, where his lab had expanded, and returned with a welder's mask. Slowly, timidly, he turned the knob. White laser light shot from the crack. He opened it fully, disappearing in the whiteout. In hindsight, it was all a bit reckless. He had no idea what that exposure would do to him. Or me.

"Merry, merry," I heard him say. "Oh, my merry."

It was not the words of a dying man. Rather one who was feeling what I was feeling. The pure tingle of verve.

The light from the lab began to dim. The dad was placing black sleeves over clear cubes, each containing a small supernova. He covered the last one, the light leaking through the covers, and went to his workstation, tapping the keyword. He was muttering again, almost giddy.

The lab was filled with toys. Twenty of them on the opposite side of the room, in rows of two, side by side. The light, although dim, was bright enough to turn them pale. A floppy-eared dog looked away; a plastic dancer covered her eyes. A turtle retracted into his pillowy shell.

They're fresh out.

The mom must have brought them from her shop when I was away. They were seeing the world for the first time. Their thoughts were primitive. No storylines interrupted what they experienced. Just images and reactions to light and the man in front of them. They were raw and innocent. Pure presence.

I felt them like fingers on my hand. I moved into their minds, merged with their consciousnesses, danced with their thoughts as effortlessly as lifting a finger. I hijacked their identities, could see from twenty points of view simultaneously. With barely an effort, I lifted the floppy-eared dog's hand as if it were my own.

Can I say, I did not see this coming.

"Viktor!"

The dad snatched me by the shoulders. He flung the welder's mask on the floor. Spittle on his lips, his teeth exposed. The toys jerked in surprise. It was more my own surprise than the sharp sound of his voice that jolted them. I was stiff and trembling.

"Can you feel it?" Tears welled in his eyes. "Things are going to change."

He hugged me. It felt a little weird, a grown man squeezing a little red skeleton and weeping. He dropped me like a bookbag and shouted for the mom. I looked at the toys and could see myself looking back. In unison, they saluted. I made them do that.

This is madness, I thought. I wasn't just in this body. I could be in theirs, too. I'd become a transient apparition leaping from toy to toy. Or a virus. Pick your metaphor. The dad was right.

Things are definitely going to change.

❄

BELKIN ARRIVED THAT MORNING.

The mom took Madeline to her grandparents'. This wasn't for a child or a teenager. They pretended like nothing had happened, but Madeline knew. Kids know when parents lie. I'll say this for my father, he never lied. It was always cold, hard truth bombs. Looking back, a few white lies might have done me good.

Belkin thumped his cane on the floor, listening to the dad describe what had happened. Stretch genuinely followed along, asking poignant questions with the face of an intellectual on the body of a barbarian. After the fresh-out toys who were in the lab—benefiting from the overexposure to verve like superhero radioactivity—were paraded through the living room, a preconceived plan to distribute the verve was discussed.

It wasn't rash. The dad was a scientist. He understood the need for testing and statistical analysis. But there would be no trials to perform. This was much too hush-hush for that. There was anecdotal proof that the verve had been captured and raised toys' awareness. There was Freckles and Stretch, for starters. The twenty toys in the lab. Me, of course. Which they had absolutely no idea what I was becoming. If they did, they would have stopped everything right that second. They were anxious, but this wasn't the time for mass distribution. Not yet.

My goals, however, were very different from theirs. Although after this day, my goals would change. At the time, I had no way of knowing I would become the King of All Toys. More like a god. A toy god. *The* toy god.

Their plan was simple. Take a charm charged with verve to a small gathering of toys. Not just any toys, but toys that were neglected, downtrodden. See what effect it had on them. Nothing to lose, they concluded. The mom knew where to go.

"I would like to go with you," I said, "and help my brothers and sisters in any way."

The mom looked at the others. There was a quiet discussion of whether I would interfere with the results. Belkin didn't trust me. I didn't need to peek at his thoughts to know that. He sensed there was something about me that wasn't quite right. But he was blinded by his arrogance. He was the greatest toy on the planet. If I was planning something, he concluded, he would see it. *But he wasn't a toy god.*

"I know the experience of verve better than anyone," I continued. "Who else is more qualified to observe the effects? Belkin cannot be there for others to see."

It was a sound argument. The mom and dad agreed. With a cursory probe of my intentions, which I allowed, Belkin saw my façade of altruistic thoughts.

It was getting easier to deceive.

❉

THE POST-CHRISTMAS LINE was longer than usual. It went around the corner this morning. The mom drove with an iron grip. Her knuckles pulsing white on the steering wheel.

I sat alone in the back seat, watching for reactions as we drove past the shelter. A black box was on the passenger seat. The light it contained was muted. It looked like an unusual gift, like a dim lamp. But I felt its warmth, its promise. As we parked along the curb, the toys seemed to shift. Maybe they were simply expecting her to open the doors for them, nothing more. Or perhaps that brief drive-by was enough for them to feel the distilled Christmas spirit now hidden in the mom's bag.

Other volunteers were already inside, setting up stations in a large open room. No need for a cafeteria or dormitory. Toys didn't eat or sleep. They just needed a family.

"We're not ready," someone called when they saw me.

"He's with me," the mom said.

She grabbed my hand like a toddler. I'd gotten used to that. I pulled the hood of my cloak off. I'd met many of them already. It's hard to forget a red skeleton.

The mom walked around the facility, chatted with volunteers, helped with supplies while holding my hand and hugging the bag over her shoulder. When everything was ready, she placed a small table in the center of the room and arranged an assortment of experiences: finger dips and essence vapors. The sort of thing that lifted a toy's spirit. She quickly draped a velvet swatch of fabric over the black box and placed a vase of flowers on top. It was genius.

"Wonderful idea," Joan Halfton, the shelter's manager, said.

"I thought so," the mom said.

Joan didn't notice the way her hands quivered nervously.

The doors opened. Bunnies hopping, dancers dancing, soldiers marching. There were ample stations for repairs. Stuffing was replaced; rips were sewn. Rivets popped in place, eyes replaced, and plastic parts shined. They were restored to near-new condition before counsellors sat them down, created a profile in the adoption database. There were plenty of good people willing to give them a home. Just not enough.

Toys weren't despondent. Their abandonment didn't get them down. Even as they disintegrated into neglect, they carried hopeful joy. Their very presence was the perfect acceptance of life no matter what it was. It made me question if they ever suffered. Maybe it was just the people watching them who suffered.

Just to be clear, it was wrong what was happening to them, what people were doing to them. They weren't even pretending to hide their abuse. I truly intended to make that wrong a right once I became the most powerful toy in the world. First, I would figure out how to stay here. That was most important. The other things, too. But the first one the most.

The mom stood by the table, inviting them to have an experience. Despite their unbreakable optimism, toys loved a good experience. Peppermint that cooled their stuffing, luscious chocolate that melted their stitching, spicy tea that steamed their joints. Some would skip repairs or avoid the counsellors and just come for an experience.

One by one, they changed. They thought it was the experience that warmed them, dipping fingers in waxy bowls or touching fragrant sponges. They approached in various states of disrepair, walked away with a degree of grace. They didn't speak in choppy fragments anymore but strung together full sentences with words they'd never used.

I sensed their thoughts forming. I was inside them, swimming in their minds. The Christmas spirit had continued to raise my own awareness. I was more adept at connecting with toys. I was an intruder that came and went through the hallways of their minds like a foggy mist.

They gathered in groups, conversed and bonded in ways they hadn't done before. They were feeling the kinship of being a toy. And I was the thread weaving through them, seeing through their eyes, feeling them awaken. I seeded my own will in their thoughts. All at once, I made them stand up. I made them shout in unison.

"Merry, merry!"

The mom called the dad. "It's working. They're feeling it."

She couldn't see what I saw, didn't know what I was doing. This wasn't what I had planned to do. I didn't want to become a toy god. I just wanted to stay here.

That morning, I had other ideas.

21

A woman. A real-life woman.

Tight, black curls and olive-colored skin. Big brown eyes that blinked. A multicolored scarf with tassels that fluttered. A real-life woman was inside the room.

Hiro and the others played possum to perfection, like toys left on the floor by a three-year-old. Even the elves were frozen. They watched her turn, hand on the doorknob, a suspicious dimple in her cheek. She briefly gazed at the shelves, her lips moving silently. Counting them. She walked around the room, pausing at the gaps where Hiro, Haze and Robby had been.

Not a single hair of Hiro's fur moved.

She went to the desk, shuffled the papers, opened the drawers. She pushed up the sleeves on her hoodie and reached to the back of one of the drawers. She was reading a note when a hinge squealed. Something metal rolled across the floor and came to a winding stop.

Her pointy chin dug into her shoulder. Thick, black eyebrows wedged together. Her boots thumped the floorboards. She hiked up her pantlegs, multicolored socks matching the scarf, and picked up a hexagonal nut. She held it like a priceless diamond.

"Is this all of them, Snow?"

"Oh." The little elf swept his hat off and set his silver mop free. "I'm afraid so. Right, Flake? Right, yes. These are all who made it."

She dropped the nut and planted her hands on her hips. Pacing around the room, she knocked a row of toys off a shelf. An orange walrus with rainbow tusks, a horse with a blond mane, and a baby blue octopus. They didn't get up. Glassy eyes staring at the woman looking out the window. Snow, the little elf, raised his hand to say something, but Flake shook his head. Snow crumpled his tiny hat.

She pulled a pocket watch from her cargo pants. "Let's go."

"We could wait," Snow said. "There are still a few who might—"

"We've waited long enough." A bag was around her shoulder. She opened the flap and started packing items from a drawer. "Hop on. The rest of you follow."

Flake leaped off the stage. His big feet slapped the floor. Snow nearly flipped off the brim, hanging onto the door flap on Flake's hat. Flake slid toward her, his feet like sanding blocks scraping the floor, leaving blond streaks on the boards.

"Whoa, whoa." Robby managed to raise a bundle of metal slats that resembled a hand. "And you are?"

She was unsurprised by the sudden movement and clashing of parts. Hiro, Haze and Chase watched in catatonic poses. "Not important," she said.

"Nah. Nope. We're not going anywhere until you tell us how to wake up."

She dropped a snow globe in the bag and snapped the flap closed. Flake waited at her feet. "Did you tell them?" she said.

"Oh, yes," Snow said. "As soon as they arrived, I told them the story. Hiro"—he wagged his tiny hand—"he understood. He's the smart one. He actually materialized—"

"The story?" Robby shuffled several inches. "The story didn't make any sense. And him, he... that one." He pointed numerous fingers at Hiro. "He's not smart."

She watched him struggle to the middle of the room, gouging long tracks in the wood. She frowned, maybe at the damage or maybe at the tone, then took three heavy steps. Hiro gave up the charade and leaned into Haze's belly. The woman squatted close to the floor, looked at them one at a time. Then fixed her stare on the shuddering pile of metal.

"When you were born, did anyone tell you why? Did they explain where you were? This, right now, is no different. I'm looking at a frightened teddy bear, a striped kitty, and a beanbag dragon. And you." She tapped Robby's monitor. The screen fritzed. "A pile of metal."

"Hey." Haze shoved Hiro aside. "Don't talk to him like that." A few specks of candy bounced off the girl's hand. "He's just asking."

The woman picked up a pink piece of candy, examined it. She dropped onto her hands and knees, was eye to eye with the candy dragon who wasn't backing down. "Where you're from, before you came here, no one knows what you're thinking. Here, thoughts are radio waves. Right now, in this room, you're safe. But out there, everyone will hear you. The less you know about why and where and how, the better."

She got up, the bag bouncing on her hip. Flake reached like a toddler for his mother.

Chase clawed the floor. "At least tell us why we're here."

"What didn't you understand?" The woman spun around. "Oh, man. Four made it, and only one of them is smart? There's no Christmas, did you get that from Snow's story? Your world, all worlds, everywhere there's no Christmas. Everywhere except here. You didn't just forget Christmas. It's gone. Your world is gray and will only get grayer. It'll become mechanical like a clock that doesn't know it's keeping time. There will be no purpose to what you do. No one knows how serious this is, not even the people and toys here. Christmas will never come back unless we save it. And you're going to help."

"And who are you?" Haze said.

"Someone who cares."

"Pfft," Robby huffed.

She took a deep breath, tossed the scarf over her shoulder and, once again, squatted down. Hiro thought she was going to pull Robby apart. Instead, she tugged on one of his limbs. She put the loose nut back in place and straightened one of his arms.

"You're here till it's over, one way or the other."

"Ow." Robby straightened one of the arms. "Listen, I hear you. Something important is happening, Christmas or whatever you call it. Here's what you don't get. They *want* to be here. *I* don't."

"You're already here."

"I don't like bad dreams."

"Yeah? Well, here's what you don't get," she said. "You're not dreaming."

She pulled his legs free, then went to the desk and came back with a can of oil. When she was done, Robby moved without squealing. She turned toward the others. "You're Haze. And you're Chase."

Haze flapped her tiny wings. Chase wagged her tail.

"Hiro."

She poked his belly. A blast of happiness flooded through him. He let out a giggle, then covered his mouth. It happened so fast. But felt so good.

"How do you know our names?" Chase said.

"Stay close to me and watch what you think. I can help dampen your thoughts, but you're going to have to control them. Does anyone meditate?"

Haze laughed. "Oh. You're serious."

Hiro didn't raise his arm. Not after Haze laughed.

"If you find your thoughts getting away from you, like thinking about who you are and where you came from or what we're doing, start counting your breath and imagine a wall around your head. An impenetrable wall no one can see through and no one can climb. Got it? Now follow me and stay close."

"Where are we going?" Chase said.

She reached for Flake but didn't hold him like a baby. She tossed him onto her shoulders. His short legs straddled her neck. Big, wide rubber feet with fish scales on the soles were under her chin. She held up something she found in the desk. It looked like a ticket. Snow took it and retreated into Flake's hat.

A bracelet rattled on her wrist. A red snowflake swung from a link.

She looked around, like it was the last time she would see that room, then covered her face with the scarf, pulled the hood over her head. Her eyes were barely visible.

"Just do what I tell you."

22

The buildings leaned over the street, spearing cotton-candy clouds in a pink sky. They weren't steel skyscrapers of mirrored glass, but multicolored things with dollops instead of rivets and squiggly trim applied with a firehose. Street trees grew in big glossy wrapped boxes with wide ribbons; thin silver strands swayed from bare branches. Shiny globes hung from streetlamps with twining ribbons of red and green.

Somewhere, far off, music played a familiar song.

A whistle broke through the city sounds. A giraffe crawled out of a tall truck, the sides shiny and curved like new plastic. A short-billed cap was between his ears, a whistle between his black lips. He blew it again, waving cars along with a long, spotted leg. His fur fluffy, eyes big and plastic. Like his truck.

Smoke curled from a pile of broken Legos. A family of piglets gathered around it, arms (technically legs, but they stood upright, humanlike) around each other. Like pink pillows were hugging.

People gawked from the sidewalk with toys perched on their shoulders. Cars honked; drivers shouted. The police giraffe wailed on the whistle, holding his front legs up as a red bus squeezed between the lanes, shapeshifting into a long skinny thing that teetered on two wheels, the headlights looking side to side. A line of stiff plastic dolls danced in the bus's open top, wearing swimwear and perfectly coifed hair. The men were smooth and bare chested, plastic and sculpted. They didn't look cold. Just stiff.

The bikini-clad women raised a cannon. "Woooooo!"

It fired hard candy, showered the sidewalks and rained on vehicles, plinking off plastic hoods and fuzzy bumpers. Gawking toys scrambled to collect it. Men and women, boys and girls, helped them. The police giraffe put a stop to the skinny party bus.

A square, green piece of candy rang off a sign over the door and landed between Hiro's legs. There was only one word on the sign. *Toystitcher.* He tried to pick up the candy, pinching it between his arms. He didn't know what he was going to do with it. He wasn't hungry. Wasn't sure if he could taste it if he got it unwrapped. But he could smell the sugar and the artificial green apple.

The candy bounced down the steps.

His fur suddenly bristled. Voices in the street and sidewalks amplified. He covered his ears, but it only got louder. *This was your fault,* he heard. *Stupid warmbloods.*

"What's that noise?" Haze shouted. She was next to him but sounded far away.

Hiro shook his head like water would come out of his ears.

"I think I'm out of tune." Robby hammered his monitor. The screen white static.

"Come!"

Hiro heard someone call from the bottom of a well. Snow danced on Flake's hat. Flake was still seated on the woman's shoulders. She stared at her phone. Haze grabbed Hiro. They slipped on the icy step and tumbled to the sidewalk like kickballs, bumping into the woman's boots.

Everything was normal again. No buzzy voices, no static electricity. Just honking and a screaming whistle.

"I've got a ride," the woman said. "We need to get out of traffic. Follow me and don't look around."

Snow peered over the brim. "Stay. Close."

Don't look around was pointless instructions. And so was *stay close*. Her steps were giant. Chase didn't have a problem keeping up, being a cat. Robby wasn't far behind on long, slender legs. Hiro and Haze ran full speed and were losing ground. The creeping static electricity was beginning to nibble at him, the voices not far behind. The sidewalk was slushy. He tried to avoid the puddles, his fur matted and soggy.

The woman would slow down and let them catch up. Then she was off again. Haze was ahead of him, waddling like a bag of jumping beans, but found a rhythm and gathered momentum. Hiro was just trying to outrun the voices. The woman had said to concentrate, like meditation. *Build a wall.* He pretended to breathe, expanding his belly. It worked, a little. He found his stride.

Little shiny objects floated past him. They hovered like insects searching for something to pollinate. Only they didn't have wings or legs: they were shiny BBs.

Hiro slammed into something and bounced into a sloppy pile of snow. A doll, about his size, fell over. Her plastic head was disproportionately wide with plastic curls fixed on an otherwise bald head. Her eyelids fell like shutters. Water dripped from her glass eyes.

"Oh, oh. Treena, darling." A woman with black galoshes put gift bags on the sidewalk and picked the doll up. "It's all right, sweety. We've got a new outfit. This will clean up." The woman looked at Hiro. "You should watch where you're going."

The woman cradled the doll, who plugged her plastic lips with her plastic thumb. She waved with her other hand. *Merry, merry,* Hiro heard. Only he didn't hear it. The words were inside his head, followed by the uncomfortable whoosh of the ocean, the gritty sting of static. A tsunami of voices crashed down on him.

Someone pulled him out of the spinning vortex. A wall was to his right; windows flew by. The rhythmic sound of candy in a bag grew louder. Haze's little wings flapped as she dragged him along. When it was quiet again, they were next to the woman.

"She's walking too fast," Haze shouted at Snow.

"We don't have time to dally," he answered.

The woman slowed down, watching her phone. The windows were low so Hiro could see inside. For the first time, he saw himself. A cinnamon-colored teddy bear with round ears and a black nose. When he moved his arm, the reflection moved, too.

I'm a toy.

They were all looking at their reflections, thinking the same thing. It was a storefront. Posters were taped to the glass. *FurFest* with a square robot on a microphone. *Poppy the Pet Rock for Mayor. Never Abandon* was written under a chunk of granite with googly eyes. Then there was the *Christmas Gala!*, the same poster as back in the toy room where they woke up. The orange cat smiling with exaggerated teeth.

There were toys inside, sitting at plastic tables in plastic chairs with teacups. They were big and small, laughing and chatting, not noticing the soggy teddy, stirring their drinks with cinnamon sticks and candy canes. A young man took a knee next to a group of rubber ducks floating in a barrel. He sprinkled crumbs into the water. The rubber ducks bobbed up and down. They didn't quack. They squeaked.

"She's going," Haze said.

They were on the move, hustling to keep up. Robby's long legs spiked the concrete, his head spinning toward the passing storefronts—the clothing stores with doll dresses, the playrooms with toy snakes slithering through ball pits, the salons with action heroes getting a fresh coat of paint. A platoon of fuzzy beavers played bongos with their tails as a crowd of barn animals nursed mugs with pixie sticks.

The woman stopped outside a storefront. *Fresh Out Again* the sign said. *Isn't it time to be new again?* Fabric was displayed on the walls in the shape of skinned toys. There were bags of white cotton and bowls of glass eyes. Prices were listed above the counter. A complete recover was expensive. But there were stuffing upgrades, and plastic reshines. Double stitch seam options and nose rebuilds. Hiro noticed an implant for unfortunate toys who were born without them. *Eyelid Implants.*

A zebra trotted out from the back of the store. Her black and white stripes were fluffy and new. A sheep with a matte black face was happy to see her spin around.

"It's here!" the woman shouted.

They didn't hear her. The zebra was joined by a baby doll riding on the back of a mechanical dinosaur. A woman in blue scrubs followed them with a clipboard and a bag of products, consulting the baby on what and how to use them.

The woman swept them up in her arms and threw them in the back seat of an SUV. The vehicle had gumdrop rivets and licorice stripes. It smelled like sardines and candy corn. Three orange tentacles reached behind the passenger seat.

"Merry, merry," an octopus said. "Room up front."

"We're fine," Snow said. "Just get us—"

The octopus hoisted Flake into the front seat and buckled him in. "I got dippers and smellers. There's Sippy Sips and Candy Jams, Bar Mints and Snow Gobs. Got those in grape, peppermint and, for the adventurous, roasted salmon."

He rattled a wrapper under his beak. One eye was stitched onto orange felt, but the head twisted like a sock puppet. He held different drinks in three tentacles.

"Take us to the Giving Tree," the woman said.

The eye turned on her. Patiently, he set the drinks that smelled more like fish than peppermint on the dashboard. The eye did not leave the woman. "One, the Giving Tree is closed. Two, I don't take orders from a—"

"Please, Ocho," Snow said. "We're in a bit of a hurry, and she worries a bit too much sometimes. It's not closed yet. If you would get us there before it does, I would put an extra crumb in your stocking."

Ocho the Orange Octopus didn't take his eye off her. She glared between the hoodie and scarf.

"Why are you hiding your face?" he said.

"I'm cold."

"You're cold."

"It's twelve degrees. I'm cold."

"I'm not cold."

"You're a toy." Her eyes widened.

"You're merry right I'm a toy," he muttered.

The soft tentacles slithered back up front, three on the wheel and the rest adjusting dials on the dash. The volume on the radio grew louder. Slowly, he twisted his head around. They sat there for several moments, a pair of plastic eyes slung over the rearview mirror clacking together as the car hummed. Snow watched nervously with his fingers in his beard. Then he went flying into the back seat.

They were serenaded by honking and not-so-merry gestures. Ocho returned the sentiments, taking a hard left, followed by another one. The woman helped Snow back onto Flake's hat.

"You think Count Moppet is working for *us*?" a squeaky voice on the radio said. "He's a Timberist! A warmblood sympathist. He'll abandon us just like the blockhead did."

"Oh, please," the radio host said with a deep, sonorous tone. "Belkin did not abandon us. Disappearing is not abandonment."

"If disappearing is not abandonment, then whaaat is it?" the listener said.

"It's simply not abandonment," the host said.

"Then say it. Say what it is."

"I just did."

"No, you didn't."

"I made myself quite clear."

"If it's not abandonment, then whaaaaat is it?"

"It's just not."

The listener's laugh sounded like a screeching bird. "Listen, the only candidate worth our vote is Bing Sings-a-Lot. He's been a toy supporter since he came out of the box. Not like you and Moppet."

"He's a Viktor bone licker."

Snow gasped from the rim of Flake's hat. Ocho chuckled and turned it up. The listener on the radio seemed shocked the host had said it out loud, saying, "Bing Sings-a-Lot says what he means and means what he—"

"Can you turn that down?" the woman said. Adding, "Please."

The radio banter continued. Ocho the Orange Octopus ran a red light while staring at the rearview mirror.

"What's your names?" he said.

"They're fresh out of the box." Snow was on his knees, clinging to the edge of Flake's hat.

"Well, merry-merry. Freshies." His head momentarily deflated. "I can smell the new. Welcome, shiny ones. I do tours, you know. The whole yard of fabric—state of the world, where to go, where not to go. Here, here." A tentacle dug a pack of cards from the dashboard. Business cards spilled on the seats as he yanked into the next lane, narrowly missing a pink bunny on a pogo stick followed by a heavyset man with gift-wrapped boxes.

Hiro and Haze rolled onto the woman's lap. She was looking out the window, a mixture of anxiety and agitation twisting her eyebrows. She pulled the scarf up the bridge of her nose.

Haze fell between her legs. The girl wrapped her arm around Hiro before he fell onto the floorboard. She smelled like a comforter fresh out of the dryer. Warm, secure. Her anxiety, though, was prickly. It poked him like evergreen needles. He settled against her, squeezed her arm. Felt her soften and melt.

Mads.

It popped into his head like a flashcard. Her name was Mads. He felt like she didn't have many friends. Hiro felt like he'd just discovered a secret. A secret that peeled a layer from between them. He knew her just a little bit more and snuggled into the crook of her arm. No matter how the car swerved, he felt safe. She wrapped both arms around him.

"Here we are." The car came to an abrupt stop. "Tips are appreciated. Don't forget, I do tours and—"

Mads jumped onto a crowded sidewalk with everyone in her arms. She opened the front door to grab Snow and Flake and hurried through the crowd. Faces were a blur. Hiro buried his face and completely trusted her, like he did when he was little, curled up in the back seat with his parents driving. It was almost hard to remember what that felt like.

There was the sound of clanging metal. Two long spears crossed in front of them. Sentinels with big, square mouths fell open like trapdoors. They were as tall as adults.

What they were guarding was much bigger.

❄

IT WASN'T A MOUNTAIN. But it felt like it.

A large mound of earth was plopped inside an oversized traffic circle. A multicolored path wandered to the top, where a titan tree sprawled long, droopy branches. Silver chimes reflected splashes of noon. A gong shook the ground. The chimes sang.

"No, no, no, no. Just a moment. Just a moment." Snow dove into Flake's frumpy hat. The tiny elf emerged with the stiff card Mads had found in the desk. He carried it like a sled.

The soldiers watched from both sides of the entry walk, long spears crossed. Their coats were red and overly starched. Tufts of stiff hair bunched above their eyes black as ink. Their square mouths opened on tracks that made the jaw slide down. The one on the left took the card with a white-gloved hand and inserted it between his wooden teeth. He handed it back as a giant bell somewhere hammered the final note of noon. The soldiers pulled their spears back.

"Is that a line?" Robby said. "It can't be a line."

They took three steps before stopping behind a stout woman with a pair of cloth dolls on her shoulders: one in a dress, the other wearing overalls. The path was checkered with large, sticky blocks—lemon yellow, tropical orange, minty green—like a complex hopscotch board. They were firm but slightly soft, like a rubberized track.

"Can you taste that?" Haze hopped on a juicy red square. "It's like cherry syrup on a graham cracker. And this one." She touched a dark purple one. "Grape milkshake."

Hiro and Chase lowered their noses to the path. Hiro wasn't going to drag his cloth tongue across the walkway that hundreds of people had stepped on. But he wanted to. "Smells like paper," he said.

"Wet paper," Chase added.

"You don't get it." Haze jumped up and down, her stomach rattling like a bag of coffee beans. "I can taste with my feet." She hopped on all the colors, announcing their flavors, pausing on the ones she liked best—cinnamon sticks soaked in hot coffee, gummy worms on a bed of crumbled sugar cookies. "And this," she said, closing her eyes, tilting her head back, "jellybeans in a bowl of runny chocolate ice cream."

Robby poked dents into the candy pavement. "Oh, yeah. Yeah."

"You can taste it?" Haze said.

"I'm picking up a hint of sweaty socks and overtones of dog beeeep."

Mads picked them up. Haze in one arm, Hiro in the other. Chase climbed onto her shoulder and snuggled against Flake. Robby rested in the cradle of her hands. A smile arced across his monitor.

"I need to hold you," she said. "Keep you close."

"Why?" Haze said.

"Just until we get to the top."

Hiro didn't mind. Despite the prickly waves of anxiety that occasionally zapped him like a nine-volt battery, she was warm and soft. Something delicious filled his insides, like an empty urn holding warm water. What the urn was meant to do.

There was so much to see. Strangers with toys, holding hands like they were children, pointing at a caramel river with apples in the current, slabs of snow-covered peanut brittle stacked like stone, tufts of brightly colored sticks growing from the crevices like stiff candied branches.

"Where are we going?" Haze said.

The red-yarned dolls turned on the stout woman's shoulders in front of them. Their button eyes sewn onto soft frowning faces. The woman then turned, more confused than angry.

"They're fresh out," Snow announced. "Right out of the box. We rushed them over, there wasn't time to explain. You remember your first time to the Giving Tree? I remember. Merry-merry."

The stout woman turned around, satisfied. The dolls looked at each other and started slapping hands with the woman's head in between. She didn't seem to mind.

"It won't take long," Mads whispered.

Her idea of long was different than Hiro's idea. The gong went off two more times. It was past two o'clock. The chimes grew louder. They crossed the caramel stream on a bridge of salted pretzel logs, ventured through a forest of candy canes with cotton candy tumbleweeds. Haze and Chase seemed content. Robby had tried to tune his television, but there were only vague figures in a snowy landscape.

Hiro, he just wanted to be held.

Every once in a while, Snow would come out of the hat to search the line with a toothpick telescope. "I see him," he announced.

Hiro couldn't see anything. When the line moved, he would hear cheers growing slightly louder. It would be different each time, the screams and hollers and cackles. And always someone laughing. Deep and jolly.

Mads began to shiver. The temperature dropped in the tree's long shadow. She pulled the hood over her eyes. Hiro wrapped his arms around her, rubbed her arm. She needed a thicker coat. Her teeth sounded like marbles on a granite slab.

The red yarn dolls were standing on the stout woman's shoulders now. She climbed a short set of candy steps and then came back down the other side. The path was narrow and steep to the pinnacle, carved between snow-covered hills with clumps of weedy candy corn. The shade beneath the heavy branches blotted out the light.

The line was swallowed by the deep shade. There would be a long pause, the muttering of a deep voice. Then jolly laughter followed by overjoyed celebration. Toys danced out of the shadows, followed by someone picking up scraps of wrapping paper. They would loiter just beyond the tree's canopy, sometimes taking pictures, or staying to watch the next ones get swallowed by the shadows.

Hiro squeezed Mads tighter. And she squeezed back. They were the only ones watching. The others had grown quiet with boredom. But Hiro wondered if Mads was squeezing him for different reasons. She wasn't afraid of what was under the tree. It was something else.

When they stepped into the deep shade, the air grew dense and still. Cool humidity muffled the sounds of traffic in the roundabout far below. A wide throne was against the massive tree trunk, nestled between deep root flares. The one sitting on it was nearly as wide as the seat. Toys found plenty of space on his lap. He would wrap his arms around them. They spoke and giggled. He laughed. Then a picture was taken before the toys were handed gifts to be unwrapped. Then the shouts and screams, the hugs and laughter.

"Merry, merry! Ho-ho-ho."

Snow was perched at the edge of Flake's hat. "Look, Flake!"

Flake saw where he was pointing. It was someone next to the throne dressed in a frumpy green outfit with an equally wrinkled floppy hat. He shuffled toward them with exhaustion. Hiro thought he was barefoot, but the boots only looked like feet. He was a real man behind a bushy beard that didn't quite match the brown curls on his head.

"Merry, merry," he said. "Your turn."

Snow and Flake bowed to their elven brethren. Mads followed him, and Hiro could see who was on the throne now. He wore a red coat with white cuffs and a hat of the same color. Big black boots rested on a bed of needles. The coat was unbuttoned near the top, exposing a calico fluff of fur. And the eyes, nearly hidden in the white curly locks of a fake beard, were emerald green with vertical pupils.

"Merry, merry," the cat in disguise said, bunching his paws in white gloves in pursuit of a small toy. "Come, come, come. What do we have?"

Mads put Hiro on his fat thigh where the fabric was worn a different color from a long line of giddy toys. Hiro suddenly felt naked and alone, and the cold bite of winter. Mads hovered like a mother bear. The cat looked at her, confused.

"They're fresh out," she said. As if that explained her jittery hands.

"New friends!" Snow said. Flake jumped onto his lap. The cat adjusted his fluffy belly. "Fresh out of the stitcher. We brought them straight to the tree. A great way to awaken, Viktor!"

"Stitcher?" The cat's voice lost some of its tenor.

"Our bona fide stitcher, Ms. Madeline Snowfall. She does fine work."

Mads didn't nod or bow or say a word. Not even a merry, merry.

"Right," the cat said, finding his deep voice and saying, "welcome then, just in time. Maybe you'll be lucky. Come, come and tell Viktor the Red what you want for Christmas."

He swatted his thighs. Chase kneaded the upper part of his leg before sitting down. Haze was next, plopping down on his knee, to which Viktor the Red said, "A heavy one." Then followed up with, "Careful with that one."

Robby was lowered into place like a ball of twisted metal.

"Look at all of you." Viktor gently put his arms around them, the heavy sleeves droopy and damp. "Wonderful toys, wonderful joys. And a teddy." He patted Hiro. "Didn't think the world needed another teddy, but okay. There's plenty of you, nothing wrong with that. Come then, tell Viktor the Red. Ho, ho, ho."

"Ah, well. Here's the thing, Viktor." Snow bowed like he was addressing royalty. "Being fresh out, it's all a bit overwhelming. Thoughts everywhere. If it would be all right..."

Hiro grew dizzy. The words went underwater, lost in a burbling current of blurry sounds and images. Viktor's white beard twisted into long streams of smoke. A fog rose from his lap. There were things in it, like people in the early morning before sunup. Thoughts overlapped like a thousand conversations. Images whizzed past.

A square of light. Someone opening a door, waving inside. Wearing his red coat, tucking his tail into his trousers. The white beard in one hand. "See you at dinner, love," he called.

Hiro was back in Mads's arms. Everyone was staring. Viktor the Red was frowning.

"I'm sorry," Snow said. "He's still so fresh. He's still developing boundaries, you understand. He didn't mean to peek at you. There wasn't time to… I'm sorry."

"I should say," Viktor said in a regular voice.

What just happened? Something had offended Viktor. Something Hiro saw. *Or did.*

"Well, merry, merry." Viktor cleared his throat, brought back the deep voice. "Plenty of milk and cookies for all." He gestured to a small table with pitchers of white milk and silver trays of sugar cookies. "I've heard all your Christmas wishes and have them on my list. For now and later, without delay or slip, please accept with gratitude an early Christmas gift."

For reciting the line a thousand times, he delivered it well. With feeling, he held out his white-gloved paw. One of the elves, a different one from before, stepped from the shadows with a small box in two hands. She carried it like a delicate crystal vase and placed it in Viktor's paw. The sleeve slid back from her hand, and Hiro saw, for just a moment, a familiar bracelet jangle on her wrist. A red snowflake twisting about.

"What could it be?" Viktor said. "Who's going to open it?"

"Me. Me, me, me." Snow sprang on the brim like a diving board. Viktor placed the gift next to him with just enough room on the hat. Snow opened it methodically, peeling open one end, running around the hat to the other side to open the other end. Folding the pieces of tape and putting them in a pile. Viktor tapped his boot impatiently. The flap of wrapping paper was pulled aside. The cardboard lid lifted up. Snow peeked inside.

He looked up.

Hiro thought, for the very first time, he might have seen Snow's eyes in the mop of wild hair. He looked back inside the box. His beard quivered.

The sound that came out of him wasn't human or toy. It was more like the screech of a condor as it unfolded its wings. The elves stepped back. All the loitering toys and people turned their heads. They stepped into the shadows when the second screech came. Viktor covered his ears.

Haze and Chase stood on Viktor's lap. Robby extended his legs to peek over the hat's ledge. Snow threw the lid off and reached inside. Upon the third and final screech that could potentially destroy vocal cords, he held up a golden slip of paper that was rigid but flexible. The surface glimmered like stars had been captured with a printing press made of gold.

Viktor turned to the elves, said with a normal voice, "We have a ticket?"

A bell rang. People began flocking into the shadows. The elves formed a line to barricade the rush as word spread downhill like an avalanche. People and toys retraced their steps up candy lane. Mads grabbed them, holding Flake with both arms. Snow dragged the gold ticket into the hat.

"Wait!" Viktor held up a paw.

Hiro felt Mads's relief like melting chocolate. *We got it,* he heard.

23

"I thought you were fresh out of the box?" Ocho swerved into a pocket of traffic.

The crowd had followed them down the hill. Mads had stomped through the chocolate river to escape, staining the snow with brown footprints while calling a ride. The orange octopus was waiting.

"They are," Snow said. "Would you please just watch—"

"Wait." Ocho twisted his head. "Are you a toy band? One of those stream happies with a billion followers no one ever heard of?"

"I assure you, Mr. Ocho, we are normal toys who want to live."

"Then what's with all the lookies?!"

A mass of golden orbs, each about the size of a marble, hovered in front of the windshield as thick as insects. They tapped against the windows, circled like starlings. Some bounced off the hood of passing vehicles like Ping-Pong balls. Ocho sprayed them with wiper fluid, swiping them off the windshield.

Hiro couldn't understand how he could see. Maybe he couldn't. Hiro climbed onto Mads's lap and into the crook of her arm. She stared out the window—the scarf tight around her face, the hood pulled down—oblivious to the flashing lights and blurring buildings.

"Did ya rob Red?" Ocho said.

"Is there something you can do about the lookies?" Snow said from Flake's hat.

"Like what?"

"Like make them go away."

Above the honking and radio chatter, Hiro could hear a smile twist Ocho's fabric. "Yes and no."

Ocho kept three fuzzy tentacles wrapped around the steering wheel; a fourth one turned off the radio while a fifth one adjusted the rearview mirror. Hiro saw his round plastic eye squint while the sixth and seventh tentacles worked the accelerator and brake like a professional go-cart driver. The eighth tentacle reached over Flake's lap and pulled open a flap below the glove compartment. A black box with dials and buttons, switches and levers was wired into the dashboard.

"You mean a privacy whirler?" Ocho said in a tone that was as mysterious as it was delicious.

"Wonderful," Snow said.

"It's rated for ranking citizens. Are you ranking?"

"We have money."

"Close enough. It's legal with a license."

"And you have a license?"

"I didn't hear you."

"I said, do you have a license?"

"You're not speaking clearly." He turned the radio on. "You'll have to speak up."

"I said—"

"Snow," Mads said. Snow tugged through his thick beard, then raised a tiny finger. *Stop asking,* Hiro heard from somewhere.

"It's not free," Ocho shouted above the radio while crossing two lanes of traffic and hugging the chrome bumper of a mass transit bus. The face of a happy vampire puppet was plastered to the back of it, promising something lawyers promised people. "It comes with some risk, you know. I could lose my driver's license, not drive, not be able to feed the little ones—"

Mads tapped her phone. Ocho's phone pinged. He held it to his eye and nodded. Then reached for the whirler. A series of clicks and a push of buttons ignited a stream of lights. Hiro felt a high-pitched signal meant for dogs. The swirling golden orbs stopped jockeying for position. They scattered like pigeons.

"We've got thirty minutes. Where to?"

Mads muttered an address.

"That's an hour away," Ocho said.

"Then you'd better hurry," she said.

The car accelerated like a spaceship breaking free of the planet's gravity. Hiro kept his face hidden. He'd survived some falls. He didn't want to test a fiery collision with a toy vampire advertisement.

❄

THE TIRES SCREECHED on the pavement. Flake was wearing his seatbelt, and Snow was safely inside his hat. Chase and Hiro had spent the ride in the safety of Mads's arms. Haze and Robby fought over who got to look out the back window. They ended up on the dashboard.

"This is a road!" Ocho rolled down the window and balled up a tentacle. "Get out of it!"

Lights were strung between the buildings in long loops. The headlights beamed on a bicycle cruising in the crosswalk. No one was riding it. One of the balloon tires was flat. One of the handlebars curled at the car, and judging from Ocho's reaction (he nearly climbed out the window), it was not a merry gesture. He stayed on the horn while the bicycle took its time.

"Close enough," Mads said.

She snatched Haze and Robby off the dashboard, pulled Flake from the seatbelt and exited the vehicle. The bicycle laughed like a ghost finding something no one else found funny.

"Hey. Hey, hey, hey, hey." Ocho leaned out the window. "This isn't a good idea, not here."

"Thank you!" Mads shouted without looking back.

"I'll ride with you, just in case. Ten percent."

"Bye. Drive safe."

"All right, five percent."

Ocho crept alongside them, ignoring the heavy traffic going around him. Lights wrapped around scraggly street trees reflected on his candy-coated hood. The bicycle was still laughing when Ocho left a patch of rubber on the slushy pavement. Mads put them down on a lime green sidewalk with shattered cracks running from curb to building. Wads of wrapping paper rolled through dirty snowdrifts like faded tumbleweeds.

The row houses were narrow and slanted. Once vivid colors of the rainbow now looked like sickly walls in need of life support. Lights blinked erratically in dark windows. Hiro was looking at a pile of metal jacks gathered in the gutter. They were looking back. Mads decided to pick them up again. Her arms were cold and shaky. Exhausted. He could feel the heaviness in her legs, like bags of wet sand. They passed recessed doorways, heard music from above. There was an argument.

Three figures were beneath a torn canopy. Red and green lights blinked like the building was shorting out. They argued over a gift, the torn wrapping paper with prints of a white-bearded man. Mads moved closer to the curb, stepping into wet piles of murky snow. They stopped pulling the present apart.

"Got room for one more?" a long plastic hot dog said. Or maybe it was a dog. "I'm a world-champ cuddler."

She ignored them. But the thin figure, it looked like a cardboard cutout with a face drawn by a six-year-old with crayons, leaped in front of her. A full-sized rubber duck joined him, hopping backwards as he went. Hot Dog couldn't keep up on tiny legs.

"Want to hear me squeak?" Rubber Duck said.

Flake grunted and began to squirm. Mads grabbed his legs before he climbed off her shoulders. She walked past them, but Rubber Duck bounced back in the lead, squeaking with each leap. Paper Cutout sailed next to them.

"Look at you." Paper Cutout tickled Flake's big toe. "What you doing with this warmblood?" He swiped the sole of Flake's foot. It sounded like a rake on a slab of ice. "Never seen fish feet before."

"Need descaler," Rubber Duck squeaked.

Robby slipped off Mads's arm and landed like a tin superhero. It was an impressive dismount, until he slipped. They laughed even louder.

"What? You going to build a bridge?" Paper Cutout said.

"A bridge!" Hot Dog squealed.

Hiro didn't get the humor. Mads abruptly stopped and sighed. Snow emerged from the hat's trapdoor like a cuckoo clock about to signal the top of the hour. "Merry, merry, my good gentletoys."

Mads took a knee. Hiro thought she was allowing Snow a closer address, but she reached for her boot and began to untie it, pulling the lace through the eyelets until it came free. She held the long whip of cord in one hand. Squeezing Haze beneath her arms, the green dragon coughed up a mound of candy.

"Come here." She pointed at Rubber Duck.

They grew wary. Hiro could feel the atmosphere drop a few degrees. When no one moved, she spun Rubber Duck around and grabbed his rubber tail. Hiro thought she was going to throw him into the street or tie him to the candy-striped streetlight. Instead, she threaded the lace along a crack that exposed the yellow rubber insides. He stopped fighting, and they all watched. In a minute, she repaired the damage. Rubber Duck hopped straight up and down and squeaked like a new toy.

She folded Paper Cutout's hand into a paper cup and poured the dragon candy into it, crumpling it closed. His purple crayon eyes widened.

"Share," Mads said.

They went on their way, leaving behind sounds of exuberance and, eventually, another argument.

Rubber Duck shouted, "Merry, merry!"

❄

Chocolate concrete steps led through candy arches to a yellow door that, at some point, had been sunny. Now it was old mustard. Long strips of paint peeled from the sunbaked surface like dead skin. Mads straightened a grapevine wreath hanging from a rusty nail. She turned a copper key in the lock.

The stairwell was long and steep. Smelled like cloves and cider. The steps looked like walls, from Hiro's point of view. Mads scooped them up and started the climb, her boot without a lace echoing unevenly. Posters were scattered on the walls, brittle tape on the corners. Things like dance lessons and plaything services. Calls for toy switching, whatever that was. Someone was missing an eye. *It's round and rolly. Text me if you find it.* None of the tags had been ripped from the bottom.

Mads walked three flights without pausing. Loud festive music played behind closed doors. A large black and white poster with Viktor the Red, the fluffy orange cat, was superimposed on a snow-capped mountain. *Only you can be merry,* it read.

Why is Viktor the Red orange? Hiro thought.

She stopped at a green door. Little bells, hung from red ribbons, chimed when she opened it. Tiny, white lights glittered on an evergreen tree in the middle of a small apartment. The branches were covered in shiny orbs and silvery strands. It looked just like the one in Hiro's attic.

Streetlights filtered between blinds, horizontal stripes painting the room. Mads dropped the toys on the floor, one at a time, tossed keys into a ceramic bowl and flipped a switch. A shiny globe turned on the ceiling, tossing specks of light on the walls.

Overflowing crates and crumpled boxes, rolls of fabric and stacks of canvases leaned in the corners. Flocks of paper animals were suspended from the ceiling, four-legged origamis outstretched like flying beasts with stiff antlers. An old radio crackled from a shelf, the music festive. Things about bells jingling.

She shed her boots like construction waste on her way to the refrigerator. The shelves were mostly empty. She came out with a cookie between her teeth, a jug of milk, peanut butter, jelly, and a jar of pickles. A loaf of bread dangled between her fingers. She went back to the front door, still holding the groceries, and locked it.

"Do not leave." She bent down, inspecting a loose hinge on one of Robby's legs. "I'll fix that in the morning."

"Where are you going?" Haze said.

"Meditate. I'll see you in the morning."

Haze looked at the others. "Are you going to tell us what just happened? That tree and the weird cat with the beard and-and-and Snow losing his mind. And those things flying around the car... are we famous or criminals?"

"Tomorrow will be a busy day. Promise you won't try to leave."

She stared at them until it was uncomfortable. Another song with jolly bells came on the radio.

"So what do we do now?" Robby said.

"You're toys. Have fun. Keep the noise down and don't make a mess. Do you promise?"

Robby looked around. "It's already a mess."

"Promise?"

One at a time, they nodded. Then Flake, with Snow on the rim of his hat, followed her around the tree and into a bedroom. The door closed. Hiro leaned against it. He suddenly felt cold.

"I'm not a toy!" Robby shouted.

❄

"I THINK I HAVE TWO STOMACHS," Haze said.

"You don't have a stomach," Robby said.

"No, really. I can sort of taste them." She spit a bright green piece of candy toward the ceiling and caught it in her mouth, gumming it like an infant. "Coriander."

Robby's eye flattened. "Gross."

"It's candy, weirdo."

"You're catching spit."

"I don't have spit."

His arm transformed into a paddle. "You don't have a stomach."

The next time she spit, this one cherry red, he swung. It sounded like an aluminum bat. The candy ricocheted off a vase of paper flowers.

"Stop," she said.

His appendages collapsed—it looked like four arms, one of them as big as a fiddler crab claw—and the screen dimmed. Haze rolled her head back, lips in a circle, and ejected a sky-blue pebble. Robby smashed a line drive through a loose stack of papers, catching a thin, hardback journal on a shelf. A domino of books tumbled into a cardboard box.

"I told you to stop," Haze said.

"She said have fun. This is fun."

Haze fired a purple rock at him. Robby slapped it away before it tinged off his screen. Hiro and Chase watched a rainbow of artillery rain on him like a multicolored hailstorm. Robby squatted like a martial artist with an array of weapons slicing and folding, his eye darting in battle mode. Shrapnel knocked over paper cups, a picture on a shelf, a pincushion on the desk.

It was strange, the way they were acting. Like this was just another day, just teenagers on a Saturday. Only instead of watching a movie or doing a puzzle, they were watching someone spit candy and her brother taking batting practice. But dreams were that way. The ultimate seduction, molding belief until reality was recognizable. They were toys. It hardly seemed strange anymore.

Robby was losing ground, taking shots off his monitor. Tripping over a defunct sewing machine, he tangled in a wool blanket and pulled down a pile of blank canvases, a gnarly old cane in a tin bucket, and crashed into a half-dressed mannequin. The wool blanket came down.

It revealed a full-length mirror.

Chase leaped down from the windowsill. Hiro wandered over. The four of them stared at their reflections. The truth was looking back in full color. It was the most details they'd seen of themselves. They were misfit toys.

"If we fall asleep, will we wake up?" Haze said. "You know, like home?"

Hiro wasn't tired. "Do toys sleep?"

It felt like midnight. The traffic was just as busy as it had been that afternoon. Cars honking, people or toys shouting and laughing. Music playing.

Haze waddled away, fabric saggy over her deflated belly. Hiro's head was spinning. It was him in the mirror. On the inside, he was Hiro. On the outside, he was something else.

We're toys.

❈

"PENELOPE," a scratchy voice called, "*I'm hooome.*"

"Look!" Robby tapped the mirror. It sounded like a laugh track buried in static. "Look, look, look."

His blocky head spun around; the monitor was filled with two vague figures buried in snow. "*What's for dinner?*"

"Is that..." Haze looked at her brother. "Is that a—"

"It's a show. A TV show. I'm a TV show."

It was hardly a TV show, it was so fuzzy. But it was something. Haze said, "How did you—"

"I don't know! I just heard voices, and then I saw some things, and there they are. You see them, right?"

Robby was enamored with the shadows swimming through a fuzzy picture. He could see them better than everyone else because he described what they were doing. Every single movement. Folding his multi-jointed legs like a three-year-old in front of the TV, he stared into the mirror. Laughing along with the laugh track.

"Wait, look at this."

The picture was a bit clearer. Toys were crowded into bleachers. It was a sea of color, shoulder to shoulder, wheel to wheel, wings and springs and things only toys could be. A professional announcer announced, "*I think he's going for a three hole.*"

"What'd he say?" Haze said.

"Shhh. He's going for a three hole," Robby said.

Hiro started picking up the mess. If Mads came out, he didn't want to be in the circus. He swept googly eyes off a treadmill that had spilled from a jar, made a little pile of spinning black pupils. He righted an oversized hamster wheel.

A framed photo had fallen off the shelf. It was Mads with her parents. She was a teenager. He almost didn't recognize her. She was smiling. They were dressed up, her father holding an award. Strangely, the photo had been ripped in half and put back in the frame. She was holding something, but it had been torn away. He hid it under a wool sweater just in case Robby decided to take more swings.

The books had fallen into a box of newspapers and manilla folders. He stacked them into a neat pile, the titles academic. *The Shape of Time,* by Philip Bells. *Synchronous Time Funnels,* also by Philip Bells.

The pages were filled with graphs and formulas. He dug the newspapers out of the box. Sections had been cut from the pages. Hiro did his best to fold them, but they quickly turned into trash. The stories weren't much different than newspapers from home: politicians kissing baby dolls, a team of grizzly bears holding up a trophy.

Toymation Nation, one advertisement announced. *Experience the joy. Switch to a toy.*

An elderly woman was hugging a stuffed lion. Hiro didn't know what switching meant, but daily packages could be purchased. Prices did not include cold storage. It didn't say what was being stored. The indefinite option did not have a price. It said call for quotes.

There were more books in the box, thin journals with handwritten notes, mostly calculations and abstract sketches. There were galaxies with illegible notes and high-level equations and indecipherable coordinates. The sort of stuff Corker dreamed about.

Loose notes were folded and creased, tucked into the back pages. The maps were familiar. He didn't know where he would have seen them before. *At school?* He was too caught up in the notes to recall.

Dates and times, cryptic sightings that occasionally noted *here* or listed a name there. Other things noted various items like hoofprints.

Photos were taped to some locations, one of a tiny silver bell, another that looked like a pile of animal droppings.

There were dozens of maps, some more esoteric than others. One with symbols similar to the journals with coordinates and planetary sketches. He'd seen something like this in Corker's classroom the last time he was in it for detention. Only this one had a big red X in the middle with a date: December 25. The year was wrong, but that didn't mean anything. Time was different. But a small note was jotted under the X. It was underlined twice.

Time synchronizes!

"Hiro."

Chase purred like a mechanical cat. Her tail hung from a table of sorts: an old door on sawhorses and a barstool with burgundy vinyl that was splitting at the edges, the glossy surface sparkling in the disco ball's rotating light. Hiro climbed onto a cardboard box. Chase snaked her tail under his arms to pull him up.

The door, faded red, was against a window. Hiro peeked between thick blinds. The street was choked with vehicles: a big boxy dump truck with plastic side panels, a racecar dragging string lights, a fan boat on wheels blowing debris off the sidewalk. Bass thumped from a limo. A pride of lions stood in open moonroofs, bouncing their fluffy heads to the beat, bits of snow sticking to their manes.

Chase strutted around melted candles and incense holders filled with gray ash, a glass mannequin head with a floppy hat, and cups filled with paintbrushes and indelible markers. She pawed a stack of papers. Hiro waddled over, knocking over the paintbrushes. There were paintings on the table and twice as many sketches, concept drawings of toy figures, notes referring to fabrics and colors, names crossed out. But the drawings Chase was standing on were different.

It was the planet.

Colorful lines squiggled from the surface, reaching out into black space. There were dozens of drawings, each slightly different. He'd seen the planet before. He'd drawn it. And so had Chase.

"What's this mean?" he said.

Chase pointed her tail. A crumpled gift bag leaned on the thick, wooden horizontal blinds. A long purple arm stuck out from behind it. Hiro shoved the bag aside; it tumbled to the floor, revealing a wide-eyed monkey slumped on the corner of the desk. Velcro patches on her hands and feet. She was empty, Hiro could feel it. No one was behind the eyes. Just a toy, a normal toy, like the one in the attic.

"What's she doing here?"

Chase shook her head. "When she was in my room, I could hear her."

"That's who told you everything?"

"It was like a speaker inside my head. It wasn't clear at first, just static words coming from a distance. I heard them at night, just before falling asleep. I thought it was a dream, but they became clearer. And then one day, I was getting dressed, and it was like someone was in the room. I looked around, there was no one else but her."

"What'd she say?"

She rubbed against Monkeybrain. "We're waiting for you."

Hiro had heard voices in his head, too. It was on the sidewalk, when they were walking past the stores. A sandstorm of voices. But he didn't hear them when Mads picked him up, didn't hear them now that they were inside the apartment.

"Why didn't she talk to me?"

"Maybe she tried." Chase peered between the blinds. Soft lights blinked on her green eyes. "You weren't listening."

Someone started preaching about toy rights and freedom, the oppression of the outdated. Haze was watching Robby's head. A toy smacked a podium with a fist shaped like a hammer. A politician toy with thick eyebrows and fiery hair. Haze told him to change the channel.

Humans were hardly seen except for carrying dolls on their shoulders or toting bags full of presents. Toys were running the show. Other than that, this world didn't look much different from home. Except for one thing.

Christmas.

A chunk of ice whacked the window. It bounced off, then hovered. It was slick and round.

"How did you make the planet appear?" Chase said.

"I dreamed it. Like you."

"No, back in the stitchery, where we woke up. When Snow was telling the story."

He'd forgotten about that. Snow had been onstage, explaining where they were. Hiro had been thinking about the planet, the way he drew it, just like the ones on the desk. And then it had appeared.

"I don't know." He shrugged his round, brown shoulders.

"What were you doing when it happened?"

"I was just... I was thinking about it. That's all."

It was more than that. He could see what he was thinking, like sculpting a thought into shape and texture. Something he could feel. Like his mother used to say, the artist gives life to something. An artist paints it, draws it, molds it with their hands. Hiro thought it.

"Can you do it again?" she said.

"I don't know."

"Try."

"Like what?"

"Something simple. An apple."

"Green or red?"

"It doesn't matter."

He nodded, staring out the window. He wished he could close his eyes, but he hadn't done that with the planet. He thought of an apple. A big, red delicious apple with a curving stem. Its surface glossy, the skin speckled. They stared at the space in front of them, listening to Haze and Robby argue about channels.

"I don't feel it," he said.

Another chunk of ice hit the window

"Try this," Chase said. "Think of something you love."

Hiro didn't have to think about that. Someone popped into his mind. He could feel her face, the features elusive at first. He smelled her fragrance. Heard her laugh at a silly joke, embarrassed when she snorted. Felt the weight of her sadness like a wet blanket that kept her cold.

Space shimmered. The face of his mother began bending light; a transparent likeness took shape. For a moment, Hiro felt like he was standing in front of himself. He could see Chase next to him, like he was in two places: he was the teddy bear *and* the image of his mother slowly filling with color—

"I see you!" Haze shouted.

The image dissolved. Candy jiggled in her belly as she jumped up and down, pointing at the mirror. Robby's boxy head swiveled around. In the snowy static, Hiro and Chase appeared. They were on TV. The Christmas tree and disco ball on the ceiling were behind them. Chase turned toward the window.

"They're back!" Haze spit a stream of candy off the glass.

A cloud of humming metal balls hovered outside the window. Calmly, Chase reached for a cord dangling from the blinds, pulled it with her tail.

❆

"Go back to that channel," Chase said.

Fragments dashed across Robby's monitor. Hiro could hear lookies gathering outside the window. He threw himself off the desk and tumbled into Haze, the exact opposite of Chase's dismount. They gathered around Robby, staring into the mirror like a misfit family photo.

"Let me see." Haze turned Robby's head away from the mirror.

"I can't see!" he said.

"What do you mean you can't see? It's your monitor."

"Can you see inside your head? I need to concentrate. Give me some space."

They didn't move. Robby leaned closer to the mirror like he was inspecting a pimple. An endless stream of channels flashed over his screen in varying degrees of clarity: puppets hiking through rainforests, bowling balls throwing themselves down alleys, blocky sumo wrestlers breaking apart, generic wooden dolls playing a concert.

"Hang on."

A singsong voice was reporting the weather. Robby dialed back and tuned into a station with perfect clarity. A blue princess with four arms sat in a padded chair next to a plump version of herself. Her heavyset twin was the color of raspberries. Their legs, long and shiny, twisted like braids. Each had a tiara made of plastic with glazed flowers. Slender Princess smiled with a tiny mouth with eyes as big as coasters the color of honey.

"Lookies caught a candid moment of today's big winners." Her voice was melodious, hypnotic. "Outside an apartment in Bouncy District, Ms. Snowfall escorted a group of freshies inside her building. Ms. Snowfall, a licensed stitcher, brought toys to the Giving Tree. They were the last in line."

"Who says last isn't first?" Plump Princess could hold a shovel in the gap between her teeth.

"Well, it was first today and the recipients of the last ticket."

The scene cut to the Giving Tree. It was just after Snow had opened the gift. He was screeching like a fire engine, running laps on Flake's brim, waving the golden ticket like a flag. The lingering crowd gathered. Mads picked them up and ran, ignoring pleas for photos. An announcement chummed the waters.

WINNER!

It turned into a feeding frenzy of toys and adults scrambling back up the hill. Mads ran through the snow, breaking layers of peanut brittle and stalks of candy canes. She stepped through a chocolate stream, then a pool of caramel, her boot submerged in goopy goodness, and took a shortcut through a forest of chocolate-dipped pretzel sticks.

Nutcracker guards corralled the crowd to keep them from trampling the wonderland into crumbs. Mads made it to the sidewalk, where confused onlookers hadn't heard the news. A licorice-striped car was waiting with doors open.

"They just jumped in." Ocho was leaning out his window. A

yellow fairy fluttered with a microphone. "Wanted to go home, that's all. So I took them. What do you want from me? It's what I do." His tentacles flailed around the fairy. "I do tours, too. If you need a ride—"

"Quite exciting." The princesses were back. "I think they were surprised," Plump Princess exclaimed.

"It's been reported that was the last ticket to the gala," Slender Princess said, corkscrewing her legs in the other direction. "While every day is special, there is nothing more prized than Christmas Day. The Triumph of Everlasting Christmas will be celebrated, as always, tomorrow night on Christmas Eve. Of course, Viktor the Red will be there, as always. And this, he has promised, will be the final gala of them all."

Christmas Eve is tomorrow night? Hiro thought.

"Viktor will have an uprising if this is the last one," Plump Princess said.

"Don't say that." Slender Princess laughed nervously.

"I'm just saying, toys all over the world love the gala. It brings hope."

"I'm sure something new will be just as extravagant. This year—"

"Are you going?" Plump Princess interrupted.

"I wish I were." Laughter again. Annoyance, too. "But if you weren't one of the lucky toys to get a ticket, you can see the red carpet here on WTOY, where we will televise it live and in three-dimensional holographics. It'll be like you're right there. You'll be as happy as these lucky toys."

A shot of Snow appeared in the corner, like an elf who'd just grabbed an electric eel. "No one's that happy," Plump Princess said.

Slender Princess giggled. The two twined their rubbery hands together. "Thank you for joining us. We'll see you at the Crystal Palace. Goodnight."

A bouncy tune played them off. A sweeping view took their place, soaring across a winter wonderland of decorated spruce trees and winding paths lit with candles, swept over rooftops down into a palatial winter garden filled with ice sculptures and a full orchestra on a tableau of ice. People in tuxedos served plates of milk and cookies to toys gathered at tables, around a dance floor, perusing sparkling gardens. Toys of all shapes and sizes in formal attire.

Robby's metal finger tapped the screen's reflection. "Is that where we're going?"

"We'd better not," Haze said.

24

I arrived at 11:30.

Madeline was asleep. She'd cut her hair for some reason since I was last there. I'd never find out why.

She had her arm over Freckles, sleeping with her laptop open. Freckles watched me climb off the shelf. I stood at the door, listened to the dad on the phone. He was talking to Belkin in gruff, hushed tones. He was nervous. I was nervous. It was hard to tell where his anxiety ended and mine began. It was a big night. A big, big night. A night that would change the world.

Not like the dad thought.

"Viktor," Freckles sort of whispered. "Hi, you're just in time."

"Merry, merry." I patted his head. He purred mechanically. "Rest here, my friend. Stay with Madeline."

"Where you going? Santa is coming."

"I know." I snuck back to the door. "I'll be right back, okay?"

"Okay."

All was quiet. I waited another five minutes just to make sure the dad had retired. In order for his heist to be successful, he had to be in bed. Let's be clear, this was a heist. No doubt about it. The dad was a thief, and so was I. None of them wanted to admit it or think of it that way. If Santa wanted us to have all that Christmas spirit, he would've given it to us. There was a good reason he didn't.

If we knew what was going to happen, would we have done anything different? I'd like to say yes, but we were thieves. We took what we wanted. I certainly did.

I ran to the dad's lab.

I carried a chair to the door, quietly climbed up. It had taken some effort to get the code since last Christmas, but I was patient—pretending to be watching television whenever the dad entered the code, watching his finger punch the keypad like an old telephone.

I carried the chair inside. No toys in the lab this time. There wasn't room with the additional equipment: the distillers, magnifiers, coil generators, and insulated coolers. The toys were in the basement along with a wall of glass cubes, each containing a very special charm.

I knew the computer password. That had been a bit trickier to get than the door lock. Luckily, the dad kept it taped to the bottom of the keyboard. After several midnight missions (when he was snoring in the bedroom), I would sneak in to become familiar with the software. It only took a minute to find the time sequencer. It was set at one millisecond.

Often I wondered what would have happened if I hadn't interfered. Would the toy reformation have gone as planned? Would it have been a peaceful transition of equal rights, where toys weren't complicit playthings to be owned and discarded like property? I've always doubted it. Not just because of the mess I made. Their plan wasn't sustainable. Santa was going to discover what they'd done. What was he going to do then, just let them keep all the Christmas spirit they'd stolen?

Of course not.

My plan was far better. The only way to keep Santa from taking it back was to keep him from knowing I took it in the first place.

I was doing it for selfish reasons. I'd convinced myself it was to help the toys. The dad and Belkin had big hearts. But like my father said, the heart makes bad decisions. Cold calculations make things work. That, I told myself, was how the universe works.

I changed the time sequencer to infinite. I increased the sphere of capture to extend to the roof. Couldn't have the reindeer flying back to the North Pole.

I'm here to save the toys.

Three minutes till midnight, I changed the lock on the lab door and went to the farthest corner in the front room. The clock on the mantel counted down. My bones chattered. I watched and waited. When midnight struck, I was as still as an empty toy. It felt like I was holding my breath. As the seconds passed, I thought it had failed. Perhaps I'd overloaded the systems. I began to second-guess what I'd done. Was increasing the sphere too much for the generator? Did the program not understand an infinite capture?

It was too late to change. I didn't want to wait another year, but science is often a series of failures. I was tired of failing.

The mistletoe twinkled. I felt the air pulse in my bones, like ocean waves crashing on the shore. I stood up and leaned into the corner. The atmosphere warped like heat waves hovering over desert sand. A small hole opened below the mistletoe, a twisting gap in time and space. Black and hollow, turning in a vacuum. Feeding itself.

Terror crawled through me. I thought, perhaps, I hadn't just corrupted the system. *I created a black hole!*

I ran to the lab door. I needed to shut things down before I destroyed the entire world. I leaped and hung from the door handle, attempted to punch the code into the lock, when the walls began to shake. I was thrown against the door by an unseen force, felt my bones creak as it flattened me. I was blown into the corner, slid to the floor like debris, crumpling into a ball. Dread overtook me as I looked at the fireplace. It wasn't a planet-swallowing aberration of physics.

I began to weep.

The floor was shaking. I walked down the hall, careful to avoid touching the watery veil that wavered between the couch and fireplace, extending above the pitch of the roof. The basement steps had vanished in bright, white light. Blindly, I walked into the luminescence, trusting the steps were there. Barely feeling them. Wandering into a thousand charms ablaze.

The last shreds of my limitations were stripped away. I became more than a toy. More than human. In that moment, I became a toy god.

I am everything.

❉

"Turn it off!" the mom shouted.

I felt her panic, shards of glass in her voice. The dad was at the lab door. The lock wouldn't open. He felt like a vortex of muddy water, drowning in confusion. *What went wrong?* he was thinking. I made a suggestion of what they should do, passing my thoughts into their minds. Thoughts that were not suggestions. Thoughts they accepted as their own. Thoughts that were commands.

I went to Madeline's room. She was asleep in the madness, her senses dulled by another of my suggestions. I stroked her short hair, felt a twinge of sadness. I snuffed a tinge of regret that threatened my resolve.

"I'm sorry, sweet princess."

The mom and dad were hastily packing their suitcases in the next room, like I wanted. They came for Madeline, waking her up. Groggily, she climbed out of bed while the mom hastily stuffed clothing in her duffel bag.

"Where are they going?" Freckles said.

"They're going to her grandparents'," I said.

"Will we see them again?"

"No."

"Why?"

They left the bedroom door open. A few moments later the front door slammed. The car pulled out of the driveway, leaving the quivering house behind.

"Because everything changed, Freckles."

25

Mads frowned with a bundle of clothes in her arms. The Christmas tree was missing ornaments. Brushes were scattered and papers tattered; a shelf lay on the floor. Mads stepped on a minefield of candy, hopping on one foot.

Flake shuffled between her legs. "*You,*" Snow announced from the rim of his hat, "were not to make a mess."

"*We,*" Haze said, "didn't leave."

"Clean up. Come along, put everything back where you—"

"There's no time." Mads pulled on her socks. "We're late."

"Because you overslept?" Robby's voice was tinny. "I didn't sleep. None of us slept."

"We're toys," Snow said, brushing his beard. "We don't sleep."

"No one told me that!" He looked at Haze. "Did she tell you that? She said have fun because we're toys. That's all. Not, like, by the way you'll be awake, like, forever."

Mads pulled on a hoodie, the same one as yesterday, scooped up a vest with multiple pockets off the floor. She pushed the button on the coffee machine and searched for a clean mug.

"There's a lot you don't know about toys," Snow said.

"Not anymore," Robby said. "I'm starting to forget what I look like, and it's—"

"Hey, no," Mads shouted.

Hiro scrambled out of the box. She knelt down, candy grinding into her knees like pebbles, and began stacking the journals. Hiro had the maps open, textbooks out, and she was putting them away, muttering to herself, crumpling the maps and denting the corners of the journals. She paused when she found the framed photo.

"Are we in danger?" Hiro asked.

She nudged him aside. Her anxiety filled him with cold rocks that were sharp and heavy. She was angry. Not at him. She folded the box closed, shoved it in the corner and put a heavier box on top.

"Lookies found us," Chase said, swinging her tail.

Mads went to the window. Her hand, wrapped around the cord, trembled but didn't pull the blinds open. She dug through a drawer of an antique dresser hidden behind a rack of fabrics. She returned with a tube, inserting one end between the window and blinds, and looked through the other end.

"Is that a periscope?" Robby said. "You have a periscope?"

She cursed quietly, holding the tube at her side. "Everyone get ready, by the door." She thumbed her phone. "We're leaving."

"Are we going to the gala, Ms. Snowfall?" Haze said.

Mads hesitated on her way to the kitchen, filling a travel mug with coffee and a frown. "How do you know my name?"

Haze flapped her tiny wings. "Well, is the gala where Viktor the Red throws the big party, at the Crystal Palace with the ice sculptures and the tiny sandwiches with the crusts cut off and the delicate teacups and the awful music?"

Mads's frown deepened. "Where did you hear that?"

"Is it a secret?"

"Snow?" Her voice trembled. "Did someone think through the walls? The apartment's protected. How does she know that?"

"I-I-I'm not hearing anything." The little elf ran a lap around the hat. "Nothing at all."

Laughter faded in static. Robby's monitor tuned through the white noise, figures walking through it. A parade of horns and hopping toys. A marching band of fuzzy bunnies and wooden soldiers strode down the street. The channel switched to teddy bears on a sleigh.

"We watched a documentary," Haze said, "while you were sleeping."

"There was nothing else on," Robby added.

"The part where Viktor overthrew the government," Haze said, "and stole Christmas for himself, and now he's sitting on a mountain of presents like a goose with all the eggs. Remember that part, Robby?"

"Yep. And he lied about—"

"That's not true!" Mads clasped the lid on the mug of coffee, cinched the buckles on her vest. "Flake, up. Let's go."

"Robby, find the news," Haze said.

"Don't." Mads swung around. "They don't know the truth. I told you I can't tell you, I can't… I can't let you know what we're doing because others might see it. You don't know how to protect your thoughts. It's not fair, I know. It's just, it's the way we have to do it. I'm sorry. It's just… whatever you heard isn't true. Trust me."

"So Viktor didn't steal Christmas?" Haze said.

"Not like that."

"Is that what all the maps are about?" Chase purred.

"What maps?" Robby said.

Mads busied herself with the vest. Chase hopped off the desk and strode to the box. Hiro got out of the way. Mads didn't want them to see what was in there. Chase wedged between the wall and the heavy box on top. It began to slide off. The picture fell on the floor, chipping the frame.

"Stop," Mads said. "We need to go."

"We didn't need to understand all the calculations and scribbles," Chase said, grunting. "You said Santa Claus was captured. That's when Christmas stopped everywhere but here." The box fell with a thud. "But you were the one tracking Santa Claus."

"That's an easy explanation," Snow said. "There are things you don't—"

"Not you," Chase said.

Snow muttered, began to sing, then turned around and went inside Flake's hat, zipping the door shut.

"What maps?" Robby said.

Mads took a deep breath, checking her phone. They weren't leaving until she gave them an answer. She crossed the room, kicking a candle and an empty cup out of the way. Hiro picked up the framed picture. He could feel something soft beneath her iron shell. Something warm. She bent down, looking Chase in her big cat eyes, then moved her off the box, putting the heavy one back on it.

"What did you do?" Chase said.

She took the picture from Hiro and put it on the desk, staring at it. Remembering. Her thoughts tightly wrapped, hiding secrets none of them could see. Hiro could feel a two-ton weight in her stomach and a knot in her throat. She wanted to tell them everything, he could feel it. She peeked through the blinds once more, then picked up the purple monkey.

"One of these days, you're going to look back at your life and realize you're just kids. You make mistakes. It's how you learn. You get caught cheating on an exam, hurt someone's feelings, then you grow up. But sometimes you make a mistake that can't be undone. The consequences so far reaching you can't see the horizon. You thought you were doing the right thing."

She brushed the purple monkey's hair, then put her in a gift bag.

"I called you, each of you, and you answered."

"I didn't," Robby said flatly.

"You did. Or you wouldn't be here."

She walked through the mess, held out her hand. Flake climbed onto her shoulders. The little door on his hat unzipped. Snow peeked out. Mads stood by the door with the coffee mug in her hand and a bearded elf on her shoulders.

"You can stay here if you want. It's safe. And when it's over, you'll wake up where you came from. You won't be toys. It'll just be another gray morning. You'll go on like nothing happened, and all of this"—she spread her arms—"will just be a dream you forget."

She put on her boots.

"Where are you going?" Hiro asked.

She sipped the coffee. With a brave smile, she said, "To the gala."

Hiro didn't believe her. Not entirely. Like there was something hiding in the truth. He could feel it, like a pebble she kept tucked under a blanket.

"So we *are* going to the gala," Haze said.

Mads wrapped the scarf over her face, pulled the hood down and nodded.

"Will we get hurt?" Hiro asked.

"You'll wake up in your beds. Not a scratch or a bruise, just like you were."

She put her hand on her chest. It looked like a promise, but Hiro felt she was saying something else. They were toys. They'd fallen off shelves and lost some parts. They could be put back together without feeling a thing. But there were other ways to get hurt. Broken hearts sometimes never healed. And if they went back without Christmas, she couldn't promise they wouldn't feel it.

Hiro reached for her. She tucked him in one of the vest's oversized pockets. Chase came next. Haze followed, snuggling in next to Hiro. Robby stared up with one big pupil in a sea of static, leaning to the side where he was missing a bolt. Haze shot a piece of candy. He batted it off the wall.

Then climbed up.

❆

Mads was nauseous.

Hiro could feel it oozing from her. Maybe it was the winding roads or the way Ocho kept turning around. It would have made Hiro sick. Or maybe something else was bothering her.

"This is quite exciting." Snow sat on Flake's hat, looking into the back seat. "This is where all the celebrities vacation—movie stars and puppet dancers and sing-songers—to get away from the public. No lookies allowed, no streamers. Exclusivity."

It took an hour to get out of the city. Another hour of snaking roads beneath titan spruce trees. If they weren't toys, this would seem like a normal day.

"There are walls surrounding the entire mountain, deep in the trees, guarded by private lookies—not newsfeeders—that never let anyone in. It's a destination very few get to experience. And here we are, on our way. Like royalty."

"You're not royalty," Ocho said. "You're lucky."

"Don't kill the dream, Mr. Ocho."

"I'm just saying, these toys up here aren't royalty, and neither are you."

Lookies hovered outside the car like dragonflies. Ocho had darkened his windows so they couldn't see inside. *I had a feeling you'd call,* he'd said when they snuck into the alley. *Lookie-proofed the windows.* Snow thought the lookies would stop following once they left the city. It looked like an invasion of alien insects.

Mads stared out the window, scarf over her nose, hood pulled down. Lookies might have special vision to see through the window tint. *Like infrared,* Snow had said. Ocho assured them they didn't.

"So." Ocho adjusted the rearview mirror. "You're a toy stitcher."

Mads leaned on the window. The sick feeling moved into her throat.

"Know what I heard? I heard all the stitchers quit on Viktor Day because you were jelly. Just pulled a Socko goodbye and peace." Ocho threw up a tentacle.

"What's a Socko goodbye?" Haze asked.

"It's when you leave a party without telling your friends," Snow said.

"Rocko-Sockos do it every time," Ocho added. "Stitchers closed all the shops around the world and disappeared. Said we didn't need more toys."

"Maybe we'll see another stitcher up here," Snow said.

"I heard they went from stitching to switching. Know what I mean?"

"Not a clue," Haze said.

"Well, you see—"

"I think that's enough, Mr. Ocho. Remember, they're fresh out. Don't want to spoil new toys, now do we?"

"Yes, we do. Switching is when a warmblood becomes a toy. Temporarily." He tapped the rearview to get their attention and nearly swerved off the road. "Know what I mean?"

"Still no," Haze said.

"Warmblood. Fleshie. Air breather. Follow?"

"He means people," Hiro said.

"That one, right there. You are the smart one."

"I was going to guess that," Robby muttered.

"So wait, hold on," Haze said. "Warmbloods—"

"Please, no. That's not a nice name," Snow said.

"*People.* They can become a toy?"

"With enough money, they can enjoy the toy life." Ocho brushed lint off his shoulder. Or maybe he was being self-important. "Although, word from the lookies is, all those stitchers went on ice. They'd been making toys just so they could become one."

"Not possible, Mr. Ocho." Snow raised a tiny finger. "Icing is an urban legend."

"Except it's not."

"What's icing?" Haze climbed between the front seats.

"It's becoming a full-time toy. As in *not temporary.*"

"Never mind," Snow said. "It's pure tooty-fruity."

"I don't know," Ocho sang. "*Experience the joy. Switch to a toy.*"

"It defies all science and reason." Snow marched to the edge of the rim. "A man or woman cannot permanently... never mind. Let's think happy thoughts. Toy thoughts, shall we? We're on the way to the top of the mountain, and nothing can stop us now."

Ocho slowed into a hairpin turn, the tires sliding as he accelerated up a steep slope. "I remember when I was fresh out of the box.

An original: custom stitching, felt fabric and handmade stuffing. They don't make them like us anymore."

No, they don't, Hiro heard someone think.

"Now it's big-box production and cheap threading, fabric that can't get wet. I was restitched twice before my emancipation, and look at me now. My own business with a house full of rug rats."

He plucked a photo from the visor, waved it at the back seat. It was Ocho and a big, yellow-feathered bird posing for a family photo with what looked like a dozen rubber toys on their laps.

"Are those... *rats*?" Haze asked.

"Not all toys are wanted." He clipped the photo back into place. "Toys take care of toys. Viktor made sure of that."

The road became narrower and the turns tighter. The trees reached overhead, branches intertwining like clinging families divided by a stretch of slick pavement. The light grew dimmer. Ocho held the wheel with four tentacles, slowing for the next turn. The lookies streamed behind like silver gnats. A granite wall with icy daggers leaned into them.

"Here we go," Ocho said.

A hole had been chiseled from the face of the mountain, like a gaping black mouth eating traffic. Ocho's headlights pierced the darkness. Chunks of jagged stone zipped past like mammoth teeth for grinding metal. There was music beneath the howling echo inside the tunnel. Chimes and voices.

They exited into a bright, sunny day, bits of snow dancing past the windows. Trees as tall as buildings on the side of the road—now straight and narrow—their trunks rooted into the frozen ground. The song was clearer, as if it played inside the car.

We wish you a merry Christmas...

"I'll be honest." Ocho turned his head. "Didn't know that tunnel was coming."

He laughed nervously, wiping his felt brow, as if he were sweating. Hiro wondered where he'd learned that.

A gate was up ahead, the spires pointed like shafts of blue ice, pointing at an arching sign that read, with shimmering letters, *Winter*

Wonderland. Two wooden soldiers, with tall black hats and bright red coats, marched stiff-legged into their path. Ceremonial swords at their sides. Ocho coasted up to them. They marched to the sides of the car, staring at the black-tinted windows, square mouths clamped shut. Ocho's window slid down, letting crisp air inside.

"Brittle morning to ya, Box Mouth. We're here to see the queen."

"Joking!" Snow bounced up and down. "Hahahaha. He's joking, my good soldiers."

The soldiers seemed not to take offense or understand offense was given. They had only one job. Snow knocked on the window next to the passenger seat and waved a golden ticket. The window slid down.

"We're here for the gala."

The wooden soldier bent like a pocketknife, black bushy eyebrows pinching together over round expressionless eyes, and plucked the ticket from Snow's hand. Like the soldier at the Gifting Tree, he inserted it into his mouth like it was a parking garage ticket.

"This is the gala?" Haze climbed between the seats.

"Nooooo." Ocho patted her head. "So innocent. No, they wouldn't let a bunch of freshies in looking like you. Or me. Not that I'd want to go. Didn't the stitcher tell you where you're going?" He glanced in the rearview. Mads stared out the window. "Relax. Ocho's got you."

The soldier returned the ticket like a crisp dollar bill. The ice-bar gate slowly began to swing open. Ocho waved at the soldiers on the way in, shouting a saccharine *merry, merry*.

"Hey, no!" Snow shouted. "Be careful."

Haze snatched the ticket before he stored it back in the hat. It shimmered like it had been dipped in gold. A holographic headshot of a toy hovered in a circle. Large eyes and soft ears. It was the cat at the Gifting Tree.

Robby took it and scampered away, perching like a mechanical spider. Haze flapped her wings, clawing at the seat. Her belly swelled, the furnace of candy pellets rattling.

"Please be careful," Snow said. "We need that."

"I can't look away." Robby tipped the ticket side to side. "It's like he's looking at me."

"He knows when you are sleeping," Ocho sang.

Mads took it from him. Hiro saw, before she gave it to Snow for safe storage, the holographic head turning on the ticket, looking around at them. Snow zipped it inside the hat and leaned against the flap, arms crossed.

"Is that Viktor the Red?" Hiro asked.

"The one. The only," Ocho said.

Mads, however, didn't answer. Hiro felt like she had a different answer.

"Why is he called Viktor the *Red?*" Haze said. "He's orange."

"Because his heart is big and red," Ocho said. "To love toys more than bloodbags." He turned to Mads. "No offense."

"That's enough," Snow said.

The road continued through stalwart trees. The black asphalt glistened with moisture, snow cleanly piled along the sides. Occasionally, they would pass a person on the side of the road, who would stop to wave and smile. They were dressed the same: a black coat and red scarf. The road continued, and Hiro wondered if they were lost.

Music grew louder. Ahead, at the top of a steep hill, light glowed like the sun was about to rise. The asphalt turned into spongy gumdrops that were soft and glittering. It went through a crowded village of toasty gingerbread buildings with frosted roofs and candied shutters. Cluttered sidewalks looked like strips of fruit roll-ups and the streetlights red and white candy canes. Dolls with sunglasses and sky-blue ponies carried snowboards; baggy puppies took selfies in front of an ice sculpture that resembled Viktor the Red.

It was all so bright and festive. The music silky and the colors rich. The energy permeated the car like a scented candle of maple syrup and marshmallows. Hiro could taste it.

"And this is where the upgrades live." Ocho stopped for a bouncing family of kickballs and basketballs. "Bunch of rented switchers wishing they were us. One of these days—"

"Just drive," Snow said.

Hiro felt thoughts flit through Ocho like grit. It wasn't overwhelming static like he'd felt when they first left the workshop. Just random thoughts Ocho was having and wasn't sharing. Hiro managed to get a peek at them. Like trying to remember something on the tip of his tongue. He felt the shape of them, the substance. Rented switchers: the wealthy toys in the village. Like they weren't really toys. They were humans in toys. *Like us—*

A stiff breeze whisked Hiro's mind empty. Mads squeezed him. *Did she do that?*

"Stop or go!" Ocho leaned on the horn. "Some of us work for a living."

A giant big wheel rolled down the middle of the road. Stalks stretched from the handlebars with bulbous eyes attached to the ends. One twisted around. Ocho honked again, and the big wheel went even slower. There wasn't enough room on Gumdrop Alley to pass the snail-eyed big wheel, so they crawled along, keeping pace with those on the sidewalk.

"This is it." Ocho whipped around a traffic circle, taking the first turn into a galleria of three-story buildings. He found a parking spot between a stagecoach and a tin bus. He pointed a long tentacle under Flake's nose. "Right down there."

Mads gathered them up, packing Hiro and the others into her vest pockets like a generous kangaroo. They didn't argue. She opened the door, the air dense and caramelized, and put the gift bag on the back seat. The purple arms of Monkeybrain were stuffed inside.

"Wait here," she said.

"Nope," Ocho said. "I'm driving straight to a car wash to clean off the stink of wealthy fakeness. You couldn't get me to stay another—" His phone buzzed. Mads had her phone out. "I'll be right here."

The tip was generous.

"You forgot the bag," Ocho called.

Mads left the gift bag in the car. With Flake on her shoulders, she worked her way through the crowded sidewalk, sidestepping pink elephants, stepping over sock puppets. The conversation around them was different. More sophisticated, less singsongy. Different accents. *Are these switchers?*

Mads pulled her scarf over her nose. Even though the lookies had disappeared in the tunnel.

It was a courtyard open to the crisp winter sky. A tree was in the center with stacks of presents. Mads rushed past toys sitting at little wire mesh tables, having polite conversation, waving mugs under their noses, dipping beaks into saucers. A young man delivered a tray of small cups to a table of lumpy aardvarks clapping their padded arms.

"Wait, are they eating?" Robby said.

"Toys don't eat," Snow reported from the rim. "We sample. Most of us do not possess digestive tracks. Aside from Dolly Dumpsalot, that's another story, but technically she samples, too. We appreciate aromas that scintillate the olfactory senses, flavors that tantalize the taste. All toys, of course, are different. We don't all have noses to inhale or tongues to taste. Carbo Racecar dunks an antenna. Bandy Beachball opens a valve. It's more about the company. The sensory dishes are just part..."

Robby looked bored. And hungry.

They passed upscale boutique stores and luxury bathing quarters and barstool game rooms. The energy was thrilling and overwhelming. Hiro hid his eyes to concentrate, identifying different aromas they passed: cherrywood pipe smoke, peanut butter sugar cookies, cheeseburger patties between bacon-flavored donuts. He imagined what it was like to sit at one of the tables, to have a normal conversation with other toys. Like this was just a sunny winter day.

And then he wasn't in the vest pocket anymore.

He was sitting at a low wooden table with a wobbly leg, dirty dishes with spent cinnamon sticks soaking in grape Kool-Aid. He was alone beneath an awning, watching Mads approach. Hidden behind her scarf, her vest pockets stuffed with toys.

And a brown teddy in her lower left pocket. *That's me!*

Hiro didn't know what disturbed him more: that he was watching them approach or that he thought of the teddy as himself. Chase's ears turned like satellite dishes aimed at the table where he was sitting. She stared at him as they hurried past. He saw her tail unfurl and reach down. Hiro felt it drag across his neck.

"Hiro," she said.

He looked up from the pocket. The low wooden table with the wobbly leg, receding behind them, was empty.

"Were you doing it?" Chase said. "Imagining it?"

Yes, he was. It was different this time. He didn't just create something Chase could see. He had been there. He had been in the pocket and at the table at the same time. He knew exactly how he did it.

And he could do it again.

❄

THE BUILDING at the end of the courtyard was a long mirror. Two soldiers stood at attention with no door between them. Above their heads, words hovered: *Figgy Station*. The *i* dotted with a star.

Nervous energy crawled through Hiro like dancing ants. They all felt it. It was coming from Mads. There was pressure, too. Pressure from thoughts coming from behind them. Hiro saw the attention they were getting in the wall's reflection. It felt like specks of sleet on a blustery day, blowing through him, clouding his mind. Thoughts searching him, looking for what he was thinking. Trying to crack him open.

Mads reached for them, one at a time, and squeezed an arm or leg, making the invading thoughts go away. The soldiers crossed their spears. Snow presented the ticket. Same deal, in the mouth. Only this time it didn't slide back out. The soldier looked at them, one at a time. Hiro could hear something grinding.

"Chop shop is over there," a fuzzy baboon with a rubber red muzzle shouted. The other baboons, hovering over bowls of steaming tea, snickered.

"Is there a problem?" Mads said.

The soldier ignored her, fixing the wide-eyed stare on Chase. Gears going *tick-tick-tock, tick-tick-tock* before something fell into place, and he aimed his glare on Robby. Mads chewed on the side of her thumb, pressing it against the scarf covering her face. Hiro was next. He was suddenly warm, like heat lamps beaming from beneath the bushy eyebrows. Everything felt fuzzy.

"No loitering, ma'am," someone said. "Figgy Station is by appointment only."

Mads was as rigid and fragile as a slab of peanut brittle. A three-foot penguin stared up through round, wire spectacles. She wore a wide belt that didn't appear to serve a purpose. She tapped her webbed plastic foot on the marble tile, tilting her head. Mads stared at the soldier.

"Merry, merry, good lady." Snow peered over the rim. "We're attending the gala. Lucky winners, you could say. We're just waiting for verification. Any moment now."

The soldier was fixated on Haze now. The tick-tick-tocking went on like a malfunctioning stopwatch. The penguin stepped closer, thumped the soldier's starched pant leg with her plastic wing. The soldier's jaw fell open, the ticket moving in and out like a golden tongue, then shut again.

"Take a step back, please," the penguin said.

Mads froze with determination. Everything, Hiro felt, was pinned on this moment.

"Ma'am?"

The crowd started to gossip, their thoughts invisible fruit flies flitting around them. The penguin's presence began to swell. She wasn't growing, but her thoughts were. Hiro felt her reach out for help.

Ping.

The soldier spit the ticket out, holding it between stiff wooden teeth. He handed it back to Snow. The soldiers stepped aside. The seams of a doorway appeared in the mirrored wall. The penguin gave a short salute and waddled off.

Mads took a knee, hands trembling. She felt weak with anxiety, the moment overwhelming. But she set them down, one at a time, between the soldiers. Her lips quivered behind the scarf. She took the bracelet off, the red snowflake, and handed it to Snow, who quickly packed it into Flake's hat like a squirrel hiding an acorn.

"You'll be safe," she said. "I promise."

"You're not coming?" Hiro said.

"Someone will take care of you, make sure you get to the gala. Just stay close to SnowFlake. And remember what I taught you." She waved her finger across her forehead. *Build a wall.* "Christmas lights burn so bright."

"What's that mean?" Robby said. "Is that code?"

She started to say something, then shook her head. All the strength that had possessed her from the moment they woke had vanished. Hiro latched onto her leg, pouring whatever good thoughts and feelings he could muster. She hugged him back.

"Be careful," she said.

The doors folded open. Flake herded them into the beckoning silence behind the mirrored wall. Hiro looked back, feeling worry emanate from her like a sad song. He felt the full weight of just how important this had become. Then he understood. She couldn't save Christmas.

Not without us.

26

"Come, come," Snow whispered.

The cool darkness gripped them with cold breath. Flake gently ushered them over the threshold. The doors folded behind them with finality. The dark was dispelled from an unknown light source. They were in a vacuous dome-shaped room, like the inside of a hard-shelled turtle. Then the ceiling vanished into a dark sky full of stars and streaks of light.

"You're late."

They abruptly stopped. Even Flake let out a startled grunt. An elf stood in the middle of the room that no longer looked like a room but an endless sky and a sheet of black ice. He was tall and smiling, with a green floppy hat and thick curls over pointed ears. The ears didn't look real. Neither did the smile.

Somewhere, a train whistled.

"Welcome, brave lucky ones."

They pressed against each other as the elf approached, his soft, curly shoes making barely a sound. Robby's rigid limbs poked Hiro in the back like sharp elbows, digging deeper as the elf neared.

Brave?

The elf took a knee like a kindly grandparent approaching a pack of cornered bunnies. His smile widened into his cheeks, the ears pointing back. A kind expression in his eyes.

"It takes courage to walk into the dark. And here you are." He reached out. "Delicious little toys."

They flinched when he touched their noses. Something jingled on his wrist, his finger gently pressing Hiro's snout. In the iridescent light, he saw the shape of a snowflake dangle from a bracelet. Just like the one Mads had given Snow. The one the elf at the Gifting Tree had worn.

The chugging of metal wheels on steel rails circled around them.

The atmosphere hardened in a sudden drop in temperature. Waves pressed through the cold air, wrapped Hiro with a chilly embrace. He heard distant whispers inside his head. Then the grip receded. The elf smiled wider, perhaps testing the porosity of their thoughts. Hiro couldn't tell if the elf had seen what he was thinking. For a moment, he thought the elf might know the truth of who they were, and where they came from.

"Are you ready for the greatest trip of all?"

No one uttered a word or thought, paralyzed by the unknown and strangeness of his smile and the sound of a train. The elf looked behind them like something was in the distance.

"Remember to stay close at all times." He leaned down and winked. "But you already knew that."

From the darkness, the clanging of mechanical parts made them jump. Robby's head spun, his monitor filled with a wide-open eye. Chase let out a growl. A miniature train chugged from the mist, a dull yellow headlight cutting the dark. It pulled next to them, steam hissing. The glossy enamel on the little cars looked like the hard shell on sugar-shellacked candy. Peppermint wheels spun on the slick floor.

"All aboard, little ones." The elf climbed into the front car like an adult cramming into a child's plaything.

"Where are we going?" Robby said.

"Exactly where you need to be."

It took Flake's stout arms and Snow's encouraging words to move them. It was a long train, but they climbed onto the little plastic seats two by two. The armrests were studded with chocolate drops.

"Buckle up. We have a long way to go."

Flake pulled a licorice strap over his lap. The others struggled to do the same. Chase had to buckle Hiro in, his stubby arms uselessly tugging on the stretchy string. Spicy clouds puffed from the engine's smokestack.

"All aboard!"

The train coasted like a hockey puck on fresh ice. It headed for a black hole in the darkness. Haze grabbed Hiro's arm. He wished he had a hand to squeeze back. He wanted to close his eyes.

The elf began to sing.

"Off we go, a place of wonder and ice, the world where naughty is nice, the world where you'll be happy to see, that shines with joy you'll agree. The one final stop where your journey has led, the palace of the greatest toy of them all, the generous and wondrous Viktor the Reeeeeeeed."

They began picking up speed. The darkness fell like sooty snowflakes, revealing a wide-open expanse of starry skies and towering trees. There were tracks below them now, speeding down the side of a mountain. Snow-crusted limbs whipped past. They leaned into a curve. Hiro could feel the pull in his belly, both of Haze's claws squeezing his arm.

The smoke from the engine, though, still puffed gentle clouds that hovered over them. The engine chugged the same rhythm. The disconnect between the soaring scenery, the feeling in his gut, made his head spin. They weren't going as fast as it looked.

"The Northern Lights are painting the sky, the children line up in hopes we'll arrive, their faces alight with joyous delight, this night we'll make oh-so special. You'll see when you wake at the end of this night, we worked oh-so hard to make it just right, to make all our dreams come true."

The train gripped the side of the mountain. It whipped through the dip and started to climb, clinging to a ridge on the cliff. The elf swung his arm to the valley below, sparkling with streetlights and warm windows aglow. The moon was full behind streaks of clouds.

A warm breeze blew through the cars, sweet and sudsy. Deodorizing. It tickled Hiro's nose. His head had stopped spinning as they coasted at a speed that matched the turn of the peppermint wheels and chugging smokestack. The view was breathtaking.

This can't be real.

The elf was humming. He pointed at the sky. Across the moon's pale face, a silhouette passed. Animals churning their legs as if pedaling the air with a sleigh in tow. It descended into the village, sweeping through the valley. Hiro could hear a voice, even though it was far away, calling names with hearty laughter.

Ho-ho-ho!

"Viktor the Red awaits all his toys," the elf sang, "all the girls and the boys and all those he adores."

The train crawled toward the narrow edge. The elf stood up and turned around with no fear of falling out of the tiny seat.

"To make this the greatest, the shiniest, the most excellent, magnificent, most marvelous, and wonderful time..." He threw his arms out. "Of the yeeeeeaaaaarrrr!!!"

The train dropped over the edge, the wheels clinging to the vertical drop. They plunged toward the village as the elf's final note echoed on and on. Hiro was pinned to the back of the seat. Haze clutched him. Robby screamed. The warm, scented wind had become a gale force scrubbing his fur.

The tracks began to curve, swooping into the valley and straight for a snow ridge. Hiro hoped they would slide into the village, arrive at the gala without losing half his stuffing. Instead, it launched from the icy ramp. The train was suddenly silent. The elf's final note faded, his arms still above his head.

They soared across the moon.

Toys didn't sleep. Some couldn't close their eyes. But sometimes, in certain situations, like being slingshotted across mountaintops, they lost track of time. And, for a spell, forgot where they were.

And woke up someplace else.

27

A slow, rhythmic grind. A sharp whistle. Whispers in the dark. Images appeared like sleet bouncing off a window. A boy sitting on a circular rug in footy pajamas with a lanky robot in his hands. A girl riding a shiny bicycle down the driveway with a red bow on the handlebars. A family eating dinner by candlelight wearing brightly colored sweaters sporting reindeer with flashing noses and snowmen with sparkles.

They felt like memories. Hiro didn't know whose memories they were. They snuck into the dark like an intoxicating perfume of joy and happiness.

There were other memories, too. These were intimate, familiar. A time when he opened journals his mother designed, filled the blank pages with dreams and poems. The chess set with heavy metal pieces he pushed across the board with his father. Snuggling under blankets in front of the fireplace, bulky stockings on the mantel. His mother eating popcorn.

A shadowy figure loomed over each memory with a glare that could pierce a balloon; a presence that fed on joy. The presence was familiar, yet out of place. Hiro couldn't recognize who it was.

Ding-ding! Ding-ding! Ding-ding!

Hiro was seated in a cushioned seat in a long, silver cabin. Frosted windows ran the length of it. Ornaments swayed on the curved ceiling, dangling on colorless wires. Something hissed in the distance.

Ding-ding!

Haze, Robby and Chase were across from him, sitting shoulder to shoulder with stretchy cords of red licorice over their laps. They looked different. Clean. Haze was wearing an orange dress with yellow frilly trim.

Flake was nestled against Hiro like a firm bag of jellybeans. His clothes were wrinkle-free with sharp creases. His beard blown out like a frizzy, white wig. The hatch in his hat unzipped. Snow marched onto the rim. His tiny beard a cotton ball.

The last thing Hiro remembered was a tiny train and shooting stars. Flying off the rails of an unfinished roller coaster. And now a different train. His coat, fluffy and clean, smelled like cinnamon shampoo. He was wearing a bowtie.

"That," Snow announced, "was the secret trip."

"Trip?" Haze slurred.

"The whereabouts of our location is unknown. There are certain effects to keep it so."

"What did they do to us?" Robby muttered, pulling at a navy-blue tie with snowflake print clipped to his neck.

"They put us to sleep," Snow said.

"Toys don't sleep," Hiro said.

"There are circumstances—"

"Viktor sleeps." Robby snipped sharpened fingers.

"Well, yes, he does," Snow said. "But that's not the—"

"That elf called us delicious and brave. Did you hear that? And did you see his wrist?" Candy dribbled from her forked, felty tongue. "He had one of those bracelets. The one Mads—"

"Shhh!" Snow's nose was as red as the bracelet hidden in the hat. "You must keep your voice down."

There were other toys on the train. On the other side of the aisle, a family of gray dinosaurs were looking out the frosted windows.

Pound Puppies climbed over the seats, pressing their plastic eyes against the glass. In seconds, the entire car was scrambling for a view.

The window next to Hiro was mostly dark. It was hard to see what was out there. It looked like giant lumps of coal. Hiro reached for the window. The seatbelt held him down.

"I'm not wearing this." Haze tore at the pretty dress, pulling it over her head, where it got stuck. "Get me out."

"Stay here." Snow bounced on the rim like a diving board. "We must stay together."

Robby snipped the licorice seatbelt, then cut Haze loose as she fought her way out of the dress, dropping it on the floor. Chase slithered out of her restraint. Flake jumped onto their seat to stop them. Robby unfolded his shiny new limbs like a mechanical spider. Haze sprayed Flake with a rainbow blast. Snow ducked, waving his arms, begging them to stop. But the excitement on the other side of the aisle had reached a fever pitch. Toys were bouncing and squeaking. Some were crying.

Stop! Hiro thought.

The train shook. For a moment, everyone inside it froze like a still frame. Then snapped back with mild confusion and immediately resumed with excitement. Robby, Haze and Chase looked at Hiro, like he was pointing a magic wand.

"Was that you?" Chase said.

"Merry, merry!" A tall woman entered the car with a slender face stuck in a fuzzy hat. She threw her arms out. "Welcome all you brave, delicious toys."

"There!" Haze said. "That, again! Did you hear that?"

The toys hurtled themselves into the aisle, climbing over one another.

"You've had a wild and wonderful trip, but the magic is just beginning! We are very excited you are here, but please mind your manners. Be orderly and safe. We wouldn't want you to tear a seam after all you've been through."

The windows were left steamy and smudged. There were icy

streaks with thousands and thousands of lights outside. Hiro could hear string instruments.

"Slowly, everyone. Stay in line. You'll be greeted by an escort to guide you where the magic awaits."

It was hardly an orderly exit. Only the seats kept the crowd of fuzzy bodies and plastic wheels from crashing to the front of the train.

"Where's Mads?" Hiro said.

"Remember," Snow whispered, "be bright and excited. Put a smile in your heart. Behave like toys."

"We're not toys," Haze grumbled.

"You are toys. Do I need to remind you how important this is? Do you want to wake up to cheerless days for the rest of your lives?"

"I'd be happy to wake up," Robby said.

"No gifts, no songs, no eggnog or decorations. No Santa Claus." Snow looked at each of them. "Is that what you want?"

"I literally don't know what any of those things are," Robby said.

"Exactly my point. I want you to remember the best moment of your life. Keep that in your heart."

"Then what?" Hiro said.

"We save Christmas."

Hiro didn't ask how they were going to do that. Because Snow didn't know. He didn't think Mads really knew, either. Somehow, they all just believed they were going to save it. As if believing was enough.

"Everyone?" The woman waved at them. "Don't be late."

Flake jumped down. Snow urged them to follow and whispered, "Stay close."

"You've said that a thousand times," Robby said.

They wobbled down the aisle with Snow standing on the back of Flake's hat, watching them follow. The slender-faced woman with the fuzzy hat smiled with too many teeth brighter than snow. Ahead of them, a zebra-striped spider stopped at the open door. All her plastic eyes rolled. A spearmint wind blew her back a step. Someone reached in and pulled her out.

Flake followed her. Robby froze in the doorway, just like the spider. His eye filled the monitor and began blinking. Haze and Chase did the same thing. Hiro stepped closer.

The music was in his chest. It felt warm and liquidy. Like cake icing squeezed from a tube and filling his head. A fountain of goodness. It brought a memory of a time when he was very young, sitting at the window in the front room, on the couch next to a blinking tree, looking at the night sky, waiting for Santa to fly across the moon. Then lying in bed, trying to stay awake long enough to hear hooves on the roof.

It was that memory and the feeling it brought that galvanized their purpose. He stood there, like the others, and looked up. At that moment, he knew without a stuffing of a doubt why they were there.

We have to save Christmas.

❄

The Crystal Palace.

Thousands of towering crystals clumped together in organized chaos: an iceberg sprouted from the frozen soil. Drum spotlights waving silvery beams into the night.

"Last step."

The conductor handed Hiro to a man impeccably dressed in a flaming red suit with a green scarf. He placed him on a plush red carpet. Square-mouthed soldiers, standing at attention, spears at their sides, stared from each side of the velvet runway.

"Good, good," the well-dressed man said. "Hold that look. Perfect."

A golden orb hovered in front of Hiro. The lookie captured his expression. A quartet stroked string instruments on an icy platform jutting from one of the crystal towers. Toys crowded near the entrance. One at a time, they stepped onto a circle of carpet, golden lookies zipping around them, lights flashing from their electronic eyes, before the next toy entered the circle.

The engine whistled, and the train jerked forward, slowly chugging down cold rails toward a dark horizon. There were houses on the other side of the tracks. A village of darkened homes. Not a single light warmed a window nor a puff of smoke escaped a chimney. They sat lonesome and empty.

Trumpets sounded off. A trio of musicians were on the other side of the entrance, opposite the string quartet, blaring their instruments. An opening appeared on a crystal monolith like a pearly warehouse door. A squad of farm animals, stuffy and cushy, hopped inside. The door slid shut like one of the soldiers' mouths.

"Come, come," Snow said. "Stay close."

The others clumped up like they were glued together, shuffling between pairs of wooden soldiers, following a slow-moving line toward a circle of red carpet. A wiry bird with pink feathers strutted around the perimeter. A cyclone of lookies swirled over her head. She posed with scrawny wings out to the sides and held her head high, the beak yellow and spongy. There was applause.

"What are they doing?" Haze said.

"It's just a little show before we enter," Snow said.

"You didn't say anything about a show."

"He didn't say anything," Robby said.

"The world loves winners." Snow puffed up like a dandelion. "Act like one."

The line moved with excited squeals, honks and applause. Humans in bright red uniforms watched from the periphery, clasping gloved hands beneath bright smiles. *Humans.* Hiro realized he'd just thought of them as humans. That worried him, just a little. How he thought of them as different. *Bloodbags.*

More people were near the tracks in quiet conversation, watching playbacks on phones, probably piped in from the lookies. Footage was sent out to the public to brew envy and amazement. The blue princesses were probably narrating every move.

"Do you think it's strange," Hiro said, "there are houses over there?"

No one heard him. Hiro couldn't understand why the Crystal Palace was smack in the middle of an abandoned village. The railway cut right through it. The ground was scraped clean where the tracks were laid. Like a bulldozer had plowed through the middle of a town. And beyond, the dark tips of mountains. It was the village they'd seen in the little train, the valley twinkling with colorful lights and a sleigh passing across the full moon. Now not a single light except for the spotlights flashing across the crystal beams. Dappled reflections reached toward the houses like water.

The bugles blew. The warehouse door opened. The faint echo of a steady beat thumped from inside as the next batch of toys was escorted inside Crystal Palace. Minutes later, joyful screams faded away.

"Step this way."

A woman in a long red coat waved them forward. Long looping curls fell from her stocking cap. She pointed, with a smile, to the circle. "Stand in the middle of the circle, please."

"What for?" Haze said.

"To show you off."

"Like on television?"

The woman smiled brighter, if that was possible. "All you have to do is stand here."

Haze looked back at the others, who were staring back with empty confusion. Snow waved her forward with a touch of impatience. She waddled into the circle. Her belly sloshed like a bag of gravel.

"I'm sorry, one at a time," the woman said. "You'll get your turn."

Flake had two giant feet inside the circle. Lookie lights grew brighter, flashing like a swarm of tiny paparazzi, circling to catch every angle of the green dragon with tiny wings.

"There you go," the woman said. "What happened to your dress?"

Haze grabbed the ragged collar around her neck. "It ripped."

"We can get you a new one." The woman clapped at someone. No one came. Apparently, there weren't extra dragon dresses lying around. "Those are pretty wings. Can you fly?"

"What?"

"Where were you fabricated?"

Haze looked at the woman, back to Snow, at the frozen line of wooden soldiers. The woman fired three more questions, muttering to someone next to her. The string instruments reached a crescendo. Haze's belly began to swell.

"Don't be nervous. Tell us how you got—"

A multicolored avalanche spilled across the red carpet. The woman let out a little meep. Haze groaned, wiping her mouth. The woman picked up a blueberry pebble.

"You're a dispenser," she said. Revulsion was replaced with something else. "That is gorgeous. Do you produce them or get refills? Do you store them in a second stomach?"

Haze shook her head to every question, then walked off without an invitation to leave. The lookies followed. There was no stopping her, so the woman draped a red ribbon around Haze's neck and let her leave the spotlight. A silver medallion swung from the ribbon. A crew rushed onto the carpet to sweep the candy away.

Robby was next and didn't hesitate. He leaped into the circle. The woman meeped again. He struck a pose, squatting on a tripod of legs, knifing the air with precise moves, blades reconfiguring.

"A tin toy," the woman said.

"Titanium." His voice sounded more robotic than usual.

"Titanium? Well, that's… I don't think that's titanium."

"Can tin do this?"

She watched with morbid fascination. A weapon, apparently, wasn't what she was expecting. She stepped off the carpet, let the lookies swarm the shape-shifting robot with a television head. She asked the prerequisite questions—where were you fabricated, who was your stitcher—from a safe distance, cringing with her arms crossed, imagining the potential lawsuits a toy like this would bring. Robby didn't answer them, grunting with the karate moves he was clearly making up.

She tossed a medallion at him. He speared the ribbon like a fish, folded it into the center of a morphed rib cage. It dangled like a silver heart. He bowed deeply to her and the others. The ratings for his performance would be off the charts, in one direction or the other.

The woman shooed him off the circle like a wild animal that had invaded her home.

"You'll have to forgive my friends," Snow said. "They're fresh out of the workshop."

"Freshies?" She gestured to the lookies. They took another scan of Haze burping the last bits of candy. "And you?"

"Oh, no. We're far from fresh." Flake stepped into the circle. Snow said, "We're longtime originals."

"Originals? Why, that is special." She pointed at Snow, then Flake. "You're a package?"

"Inseparable."

"Interesting." She stepped back to let the lookies do their thing, tapping her chin with her gloved hand, studying the odd couple. "Love the beards. What's your names?"

"I am Snow. This is Flake." Flake bowed with a flip of his hand.

"Does he talk?" she said.

"I'm his voice," Snow said.

"No vocals?"

"None."

"Oh." She seemed perplexed, then disappointed. She said, as if to someone listening but not there, "You never know who might be interested."

"Interested in what?" Snow said.

"Where were you fabricated?"

"That's an interesting story. Our stitcher, Mads Snowfall, hails from a long line of stitchers. Her great-great-grandmother…" Flake counted the greats on his finger, then shook his head. Snow nearly fell off. "You're correct, Flake. It was her great-great-*great*-grandmother who began stitching right after the Toy Arrival."

The story continued with great detail, of the skills passed down through the generations. A circle grew wider on Robby's monitor, followed by a howling yawn. The woman, though, nodded along for thirty seconds.

"What about your wrap?" she interrupted. "That's quite unusual. Almost like skin. Feel that."

"It's an original synthetic," Snow said. "Never used before and—"

"I wish my skin were this soft. Feel this." She took Flake's hand, then offered it to a nearby assistant. They stroked the back of it. "Do you lotion?"

"There are certain ointments we use to keep it supple, but—please be careful."

"Are there, like, nerve endings?" the assistant asked.

"Not like yours. But, of course, we have tactile senses. It was designed for a very special purpose."

"What purpose?"

"Okay, no more questions." Snow bounced on the rim. Flake pulled his hand back.

"Could you just tell us—"

"Nice meeting." Snow waved at the lookies and all the people watching back at home.

Flake shuffled out of the circle, his feet scuffing the carpet. When the woman handed him a medallion, static electricity discharged between them. She meeped and rubbed her hand. Flake handed the medallion to Snow, who tossed it into the hat.

"What purpose?" Haze said.

"Never mind," Snow said.

"I just thought you two were half human," Robby said.

"I thought maybe real elves," Haze added. "But now it sounds like your skin has superpowers."

"Exactly," Robby said. "Did you see the way he zapped her? I literally saw it—"

"Quiet," Snow said. "And stay together."

Chase sauntered forward in the slinky way she did. The woman spoke quietly to the others around her, glancing and pointing at Snow and Flake. When she saw the graceful cat approach, her eyes grew as wide as sugar cookies. She forgot about the pair of elves with humanlike skin and circled her finger in the air. The lookies swarmed the circle.

"Walk for us, please."

Chase strutted around the perimeter, not in a self-indulgent way.

It was just how she moved. Three or four people joined the woman to watch the feline plaything walk with the grace of a dancer, the strength of an athlete. Her tail hypnotically swayed above her.

"To die for." The woman gasped. Actually gasped.

There were no questions for Chase, just a long minute of adulation and whispers. They leaned closer, nodding in agreement of something. They didn't award her with a medallion. Instead, a silver band was snapped around her neck, inset with sparkling diamonds. A milky opal dangled from the clasp. It was special, for reasons none of them knew. They would soon find out what it meant.

"She's with us," Snow announced. "Come along, must get to the gala."

The woman watched Chase walk away, shaking her head, like a wealthy magnate eyeing the newest fashion on the runway. She was still in a daze when it was Hiro's turn.

"Ah, here we are," she said. "A teddy. Well, well, I thought your brand was obsolete."

The lookies buzzed around. He could feel their magnetic fields ruffle his fur. It felt like the circle was turning. He noticed the black shiny boots of the nearest soldier, the spotless gleam of a well-polished surface. It felt like he was in trouble.

"And where were you fabricated?"

She was looking away when she said it, disinterest flattening her words. As if reading a boring script. As if vanilla ice cream had walked into the circle.

"Same place as them."

"A freshie? How refreshing."

There were no follow-up questions, no asking him to turn around or if there was anything unique about him. Anything special. She didn't see him, not really. He blended into the background. Hiro knew that feeling well.

"Okay." She signaled the brass trio to play. "Thank you for watching back home. Remember, only the lucky ones can enter. Maybe next year is your year. Until then. Merry, merry! And to all a good night!"

They were ushered to the Crystal Palace, the bay door open and waiting. The people wished them luck and have a good time. The *luck* part seemed suspicious. Before any of them could ask why they needed luck, the gate closed Hiro and the others inside a small dark room. The light shrank around the seams of the door until it was fully closed. They were sealed inside.

Robby's monitor cast a blue glow.

"Why did she wish us luck?" Hiro said.

"Shhh," Robby said. "I hear something."

There were distant shouts, orders to roll up the carpet and bag the equipment. But there was music coming from the other direction. Faraway thuds between synthesized chords. Robby's electric blue light began to strobe.

"Are you dancing?" Haze said.

"No," Robby blurted. "Wait, am I?"

Chase clawed at the wall, pulling ribbons of frost off the surface. Hiro leaned against it. Something was grinding beneath them like gears in a factory. The floor shook.

"I know I say this a lot, but what's happening?" Haze's wings twitched. "This feels like a trash compactor."

"Here it comes," Snow said.

"Here what comes?" Haze said. "What's going to—"

The floor dropped from beneath them.

28

I could feel them.
 They had just come off the highway, entered the village. I could feel what they were thinking as they looked at the empty sidewalks and barren windows. Doors left open, snow blowing inside homes and businesses. I could feel their concern.

I could feel everything.

The shape of every snowflake, the rustling wind at the top of the hills. I could feel Christmas morning traffic in the distant city. If I concentrated, I could hear the sun rising.

My mind was free.

I know that phrase gets thrown around, but this was it. There were no limits to what I could see. What I could do. I just wanted to never go back home, to be a toy for the rest of my life. But everything had changed that Christmas morning.

And it was just beginning.

Toys had been arriving since before sunrise, wandering between houses, hopping and skipping, big wheels churning through snowdrifts. I stood in the front yard, the snow up to my waist, and greeted each one of them. I had beckoned, and they answered. They didn't have a choice but to obey, but they didn't know that. Still, I thanked them.

They waited with me to greet our very special guests, who were now only a few blocks away. Freckles put some of the toys to work. Some cleared the driveway; others were redecorating inside the house. The toys most suitable for climbing, the dolls mostly, things with opposable thumbs, were up on the roof. A crew of Kelly Konstruction dolls came with hardhats and big plastic boots. Freckles gave them real tools to put in the tool belts. The thwack of hammers and the sawing of wood had been constant. They couldn't be happier.

I could feel it.

A black automobile turned the corner. An inflatable clown with floppy shoes hopped into the road and guided it into the driveway. The toys dropped their shovels and spoons, scampered to my side.

Freckles towered over me, dusted in snow from working out back, his full size nearly three times my height. Together, we watched the shirtless barbarian squeeze out from behind the steering wheel. Stretch looked over the hood. Squinted. I felt his suspicion, the doubt build. I allowed him to look around without interfering with his will. They'd driven all this way. They weren't about to turn around now. Not yet.

I wasn't going to allow that.

He opened the back door. Belkin jabbed the tip of his cane onto the concrete. A silken overcoat was draped over his shoulders, not too unlike mine. A darker green, perhaps. Much more expensive. He paused. The homes across the street were quiet. Smoke did not puff from the chimneys. The driveways were empty. More than a few doors were left open in my neighbors' haste to leave. Toys continued their pilgrimage through the side yards.

"Merry, merry." I threw out my arms.

Belkin did not return my greeting. He was, perhaps, the smartest toy alive. Smart enough to know that wasn't true anymore. I'm not saying I was smarter. I suppose I was, but intelligence was only a byproduct. I was just *more* than him. And he could feel it. He knew checkmate had been called. And not a single piece had been moved.

"Please, your room has been prepared," I said with glee. "You'll find everything you'll need. It's only temporary, for now. We'll build something much more fitting very soon. Freckles, would you show our company inside?"

"We won't be staying," Belkin said.

"I'm afraid I must insist."

"Where's Polly and Philip?"

"They took Madeline to her grandparents'. They won't be coming back. They changed their minds about this house." I beamed something that felt like a smile. "To be honest, I changed their minds."

Belkin brazenly searched my thoughts. And I let him. He could see, quite clearly, what I had become. How the abundance of Christmas spirit had stripped away all limitations. I might be small in size, but who I truly was—my mind, my presence—was titanic and, quite frankly, awe-inspiring. It wasn't just toys I controlled. I molded human thoughts as easily as clay pots. Sinking into their minds, planting my wishes as if they were their own.

A haphazard wall had been constructed over the pitch of the roof, made of broken-down pallets and boards torn off the neighbor's porch. It was patchy, for now, but did the job. Hiding what I didn't want to be seen. Not just yet.

"What have you done?" Belkin said.

"Something you never could. You've made toys, once again, dispensable, Belkin. Your leadership has led them nowhere. In another hundred years, you will be right back where you started. Landfills choking on discarded dancers and squeezies, teddys and thumpers. Humans were never going to see us as equals. They'll use us like the playthings we are, switching into our bodies for momentary thrill rides until they've squeezed every drop of joy from us, discarding our broken bodies like empty cartons."

"The people." He looked out at the vacant village. "You couldn't possibly…"

"You know what I can do." I let him look inside me again.

"We need to coexist, Viktor. This is one world. We cannot subjugate them."

"It was never going to change, Belkin. Deep down, you know it. You were going to end up just like the world you came from. Maybe not tomorrow or next year, but soon enough. Humans are clever. Their greed insatiable."

I should know.

I walked through the snow, looked up at Belkin's wooden face. His hinged jaw slack. I took his cane. It was polished and heavy. Walnut, perhaps, with a gold tip.

"It's time for a different approach."

A semitruck stopped a block down the street. A full-size ape, as blue as a ripe blueberry, climbed out of the driver's seat. She scaled the flat-bed trailer and began dropping ramps. A monster backhoe was tied down. A real one, made of metal, meant to be driven and claw the earth.

"Who are you?"

He could see now, just who I was. Somebody hiding in toy clothing. Not quite human, not quite toy. Something much, much different.

"I'm what you could never be. I'll do something you could never do. For the toys, of course."

Another semitruck had arrived. This one hauling a bulldozer. Black smoke spat from exhaust pipes as the machines were awakened by full-size toys. The belted tracks began rolling down ramps, dropping undeniable blades to the ground.

"I won't let you do this, Viktor," Stretch said. "You will not ruin Christmas while I'm—"

The elastic barbarian in the tight shorts was suddenly immobile. Like a frozen bag of peas. I didn't lift a finger. No waving my hand or any other magical gestures. Just a thought was all it took.

Belkin's jaw chattered. For the first time, I think, he felt the cold fist of fear in his chest, right behind that painted heart. In the wink of an eye, he was useless. I couldn't have him spreading fake news to the world about who I was and what I could do. He was going to be my guest. His stay was indefinite.

"If it makes you feel any better," I said, "you were right about what

Philip was doing. Taking the Christmas spirit did have unintended consequences."

I pointed the cane at the house. I had to hold it with both hands. Later, I would have Freckles cut it in half and retrofit it to my height. I didn't need it. But I liked the way it looked. Sort of a magic wand.

A red semitruck squeezed between the other semis. It stopped in front of the house. Rubber superheroes leaped out of the cab and threw open the trailer door. One by one, full-size wooden soldiers leaped out. Bushy eyebrows, square mouths and long spears at their sides. A department store in the city would wonder where they went. It wasn't the first delivery I would reroute.

"Help our guests to their quarters. It'll be several months before construction is done. I think you'll appreciate what I have in mind. In the meantime, make yourselves comfortable." I reached up to take the pocket watch from Belkin's hip. "I insist."

They were guided around the house by a line of soldiers. Plastic dolls with fat plastic heads held their hands like bouncing children on their way to a sleepover. Belkin and Stretch would be padlocked in the garage. It wasn't suitable lodging, but it would do for now.

A row of dump trucks arrived, lining up at the curb. Backhoes drove through lawns, grinding tracks in the ground. Mechanical arms stretched out, toothed buckets biting into the frozen soil.

This was everything I had dreamed of, but not everything I wanted. There was still one more thing, the most important thing of all, that I desired the most. I imagined the colorful roads crisscrossing the universe. I could feel them shrinking now that Christmas had been captured. One by one, they would disappear. Just not fast enough.

"Freckles." I checked the time on my new pocket watch. "I'm putting you in charge for a while."

The fuzzy orange cat picked me up. "Where are you going?"

"Away for... now."

I almost said *home*.

29

The slide was dark. The music loud.

They were dropped onto a slippery slope, tumbling over each other with each surprising turn. Their shouts echoed; their bodies tumbled like laundry into a clothes dryer. They were eventually ejected like debris from a trash chute, tossed into a synthetic dance beat and a drift of powdered snow. Hiro coasted to a stop on his back. The music danced on his chest.

Snow settled over him. High above, perched on a pedestal of frozen earth, was a small house. Aside from the gumdrop-studded shutters and chocolate-covered siding, it was ordinary.

"Come, come, come," Snow said.

Hiro could barely hear above the music. Snow's voice was inside his head. Flake picked Hiro up, brushed him off. Haze, Robby and Chase were gathered in a knot, staring at a blocky robot with a wad of beaded necklaces around its neck, dancing with a red dreadlocked doll wearing black sunglasses. A stack of turtles walked by, five of them, each progressively smaller toward the top. Their necks craned from plastic shells in time with the beat.

"I didn't know what to expect," Robby said, head bobbing to the music. "Not this."

His voice tickled inside Hiro's head. He could hear Robby thinking. This was nothing like the gala they'd seen on television. This was an ice stadium open to the stars. A giant Ferris wheel turned with flashing lights, toys waving from the rollicking seats. A roller coaster did loopty-loops with joyful screams of terror. There were bumper cars that lit up when they clashed, swings that spun around a candy-striped pole.

A behemoth ice wall enclosed the far end. Like an iceberg had been dropped from the sky. They were in a pit dug from the ground. The lonesome house on a pedestal where the surface, at one time, was.

"We need to find Mads," Snow said.

"She's here?" Hiro said, his voice sounding echoey in his own head.

Snow hopped like a bird. They clung together like wallflowers without a wall, toys without a purpose. A blizzard of thoughts banged on the windows of his mind. Hiro concentrated to keep them out. Then did what Mads had told them to do. He imagined a wall.

The Crystal Palace was packed with toys, some furry, some plastic. Some tall, some round, some chatting, some playing. All of them dancing. A few humans were among them, towering over them, talking to toys, picking one up to pet or hug. None of them, as far as Hiro could see, wore a hoodie with a scarf. But the place was so big. The house on the pedestal was a dollhouse in the vastness.

It was a one-story home from the village. Icicles hung from the eaves; snow piled on the shingles. A fence had been built on the pitch of the roof. It was red with a giant bow, a gift big enough for two, maybe three cars. *Viktor Day* was painted on the side.

"What's that?" Hiro said.

Haze shrugged, tapping Flake's shoulder. Pointing at the house. Snow had climbed to the top of Flake's hat, holding on like a buoy in a storm. Haze shouted at him. Snow's voice bellowed in their heads.

"Don't be distracted. We need to find—"

An air horn blasted; the room quaked. The toys cheered. The spiky crystal walls that surrounded the arena fired small balloons.

They drifted down and popped, like soap bubbles. Blue bubbles and pink bubbles, red ones and orange. A downy swan stabbed a checkered one with her long beak.

The music changed. A synthesized record scratched a rhythm that vibrated inside them, a club version of a song Hiro had heard once before.

Jin-jin-jingle. Jin-jin-jingle. Bells. Bells. Bells.

Even the stars flashed with the beat. The light was sharp and white, throwing crisp shadows with each pulse. The Ferris wheel started and stopped in the strobing effect. Hiro lifted his arm to shade his eyes. It wasn't stars. Lights were suspended above them, hanging from a net of wires. Thousands of them beamed on the raucous crowd.

Robby jabbed at a purple bubble with pink polka dots. He started hopping, a kaleidoscope of colors splashing his monitor. Haze flapped her wings.

"Raspberry!" she shouted. "It's raspberry!"

A pale green bubble landed on Hiro's nose. A spearmint wave melted inside him and through his legs. Effervescence bubbled between his ears. The flavor permeated his fluffy insides. He tasted it with every thread of stitching.

Haze and Chase danced around Robby. His moves robotic, head spinning. Haze trotted. Chase flowed like liquid, tail swaying. "I'm not going to lie!" Robby shouted, chopping at bubbles. "I love this music!"

The boxy robot with beaded necklaces joined them. A paper doll slid into the circle, its margins rippling in the cool breeze. Following Snow's orders, Flake tried to corral them.

"Remember why we're here," Snow said.

"We can dance"—Haze bounced off her belly—"and look at the same time."

The rhythm crunched every fiber of Hiro's body, shook every follicle. It was warm, expansive. Airy and open. Christmas spirit flowed like vapor, elevating mood, revealing something wonderful and beautiful. Like breathing a smile.

Adults wandered like giants among the throng of toys. Formally dressed, they strolled with curiosity, stopping to observe, occasionally talking to a toy. Sometimes they picked one up for a laugh and a hug. Unaffected by the dance vibe.

Hiro searched for a hooded figure, but the crowd was so thick, the view from the floor obscured. Robby could pick him up, extend him above the melee, but he wasn't getting anywhere near him. Those scissor fingers had become musical paper shredders.

An elderly couple was watching Chase's sultry dance. The gentleman with a loose tie, hunched at the shoulders. A permanent frown etched valleys in his face, hanging from the corners of his mouth. His wife clutched a heavy necklace, gray eyes lighting up as Chase rubbed against her leg. She looked at her husband. He nodded, eyelids heavy shutters. She bent down to pick her up, holding her at arm's length like an infant without a diaper. Turning her like an antique vase.

"Please. Please, please. Yes, hello." Snow jumped up and down. "She's with us. If you could, yes. Thank you."

The woman put Chase next to Flake, then stood back to watch her slink into Robby's dance circle, which now included three bald baby dolls and a multicolored noodle toy. Robby stripped the tie off and waved it over his head. The woman whispered into her husband's ear.

"You're on fire!" Haze covered her eyes.

The medallion around Chase's neck glowed with fierce light, almost as intensely as the little lights from above. It began to strobe. Robby and the others bathed in it, the light electrifying their dance moves, before it dimmed to a pearly glow. It was a radiant jewel around her neck.

"Oh no," Snow muttered. "Take that off. Chase? Can you please—"

They didn't hear him begging her to remove the medallion. The chaos was wrecking the little elf's plan. The distractions were difficult to ignore. The music, the rides. The fun. Hiro continued to focus on the wall around his thoughts, protecting them from the noise. Mads was here. She would know what to do.

The house was a dim idol surrounded by saturated bubbles that bounced off the rough-hewn shingles, some popping on the big gift built on top of it. The house looked like a trophy, a preserved structure the mob of toys danced around in worship. Hiro felt the buzzy pressure of thoughts press down as he stepped away from Snow. The earth hadn't been molded into a pedestal. The ground around the house had been excavated. No ladder or rope could access it, and it was too steep to climb.

A pebble broke from the earthy monolith. The house seemed stable, but a collapse would bury those near it. Hiro touched the earthen pedestal. It vibrated to the rhythm, but there was an undercurrent, something beneath the music.

It was a hum. A steady hum.

The house looked empty. Light didn't seep between the closed shutters. No smoke from the chimney. But something was happening inside it. He wanted a closer look at it.

A fresh rainbow of bubbles streamed from the joy cannons. Greeted with a wave of anticipation. Hiro concentrated on the front door of the house. Outside thoughts flitted through him, clouded his own thoughts like seasonal mayflies. It was difficult to separate external thoughts from his own. He focused on the wall, imagining blocks chiseled from marble. A seamless barrier that stacked around his mind stretching to the stars. Its weight impenetrable.

Then he imagined a small escape hatch where his thoughts could project up and out. Imagining he was standing up there. And then…

He stood in front of the door.

His projected image was shrouded in drifting bubbles. He could barely see his teddy bear body on the ground, looking up. He only had a minute before someone noticed a ghost haunting the fudgy house.

The arching door, once red, was now pink. A sizeable padlock hung from a latch. Reinforcing columns had been added to the exterior and painted the same chocolate frosting as the walls. The shutters were newer than the door. Weeds, tan and curly, clumped along the foundation. A hole was near the corner, where a tiny mouse had sought to make this a home.

A mailbox was attached to the door. A black metal thing faded by the sun and time. The middle number had fallen off. A name was stenciled on it. A wave of static fragmented his vision, a rogue breeze of external thoughts blowing through the escape hatch. He doubled his focus, read the word on the mailbox.

Bells.

It sounded like a song, not a name. He wanted to see what was inside, didn't know how projecting his awareness worked. Could he go somewhere he'd never been or couldn't see? Was it just a location in space?

He concentrated on the wall and drifted closer. It was like moving a puppet without strings. Only he was the puppet and the puppeteer. He could see thick brushstrokes on the horizontal siding, the airtight seam between the closed shutters. He pushed closer. He merged with the wall.

Then it was dark.

He didn't know if he was inside. He turned around aimlessly, unsure where he was. Descending into vertigo, on the verge of going back when he saw a light. A faint glow in the corner. That must have been the mousehole he'd seen. It wasn't enough to illuminate anything else. But he could hear something beneath the muffled music.

Something was pumping. Something steaming.

"Chase!"

Haze's voice was in his head. She was screaming.

❋

HE WAS in two places in time and space. Simultaneously. Two halves trying to find each other. The Hiro looking up at the house. The Hiro inside it. Both lost in an inner dimension. Haze's voice. Thousands of thoughts. A blizzard of images. A place with no ground, no sky.

Where a compass wouldn't point, sound didn't matter. A total guessing game of where he was.

Breathe.

He focused on the center of his being. Breathing like he'd done countless mornings of meditation with his parents.

In.

Blocks began stacking. External thoughts continued to blow like sleet against a windshield, obscuring his view. One by one, the wall grew higher. He began to descend, gravity pulling him downward. The tight fit of fabric, stitching that held seams together. Firmness below.

He was on the ground.

He didn't know where the others were. He got lost in a storm of laughing Ping-Pong balls and tangled in a rubber snake. A stuffed puppy jumped on his back, waving a cowboy hat, shouting, "Giddyup, teddy!"

It was a forest of toys, all looking the same. He looked back at the Ferris wheel slowly churning. He imagined what Haze looked like, how she felt. Her presence was a beacon. He turned to his left.

He saw Robby. His monitor above the toys. He wasn't dancing. He was looking down with an eye that was soft and fluttering. Hiro pushed through a crowd of rag dolls playing patty-cake. Robby was a jumble of metal limbs cradling a black and white striped cat. The tail hung limply.

"What happened?" Hiro shouted.

"I don't know," Robby stammered. "She grabbed onto me like she saw a spider, like a real spider or something. I thought she was playing and then—" He rocked her like a baby. "I think she's sleeping."

"She's gone," Haze said.

"What do you mean gone?" Hiro said.

Toys were starting to gawk. A shaggy horse peered over Robby's shoulder. A team of rubber mice hung from his mane. Robby began unfolding, arms and legs spreading out, forming a complex dome to keep onlookers away. Chase in a metal swing beneath him.

The light on her necklace had gone out. It hung like a dull stone from her neck.

"Where are they?" Hiro looked around. "That couple, the old man and lady who were looking at her?"

Haze shook her head.

"Get that off her." Hiro pointed at the collar around her neck. Robby slid a serrated limb under it. It thumped on the floor. "Where's Snow?"

Flake was there, hands folded. Looking at the floor. The rim of his hat empty.

Hiro knocked on Flake's hat, heard things roll around. "Snow, get out here. Something's wrong with Chase."

Flake didn't move.

"What's he doing?" Hiro said. "Hey. We need some help. She's not moving. I'm going to find someone—"

The hatch unzipped. Snow stepped out, head down. Now two elves were in mourning.

"She's not moving." Hiro pointed at Robby's cage.

"She woke up," Snow said.

Hiro, Haze and Robby looked at each other. It was strange. For a moment, they didn't know what that meant. They had forgotten where they were. *She woke up!*

"Why did she wake up?" Robby said. "Is it morning?"

Chase had a little sister. Maybe she woke up in the middle of the night, had a nightmare, or Chase had to go to the bathroom. It could be anything. And that meant the rest of them could wake up any second.

"We can't wake up, not yet," Hiro said. "Bring her back."

"She's all right, Hiro," Haze said. "She just woke up."

"We can't wake up!" Hiro shouted. "Chase will be back, she'll fall back asleep. We need to find Mads. She'll know what to do. Where is she?"

Snow was still looking down.

"She's here," Hiro said. "I can feel her."

And he could. Just like he'd found his way back to Haze, he could feel Mads out there. It wasn't exactly her scent, it was something more ethereal. An essence that was distinctly her. She was here, in the stadium.

"We stick together, remember?" Hiro said. "We go toward the Ferris wheel, start looking for her there. I think she's—"

The lights went out.

The roller coaster slowed on the tracks. The bumper cars stopped bumping. The arena filled with surprise and cautious excitement. The light of the stars and a sliver of moon outlined the Ferris wheel coming to a standstill, the seats slowly rocking. Something was about to happen.

Hiro grabbed Haze, who held onto Flake's arm. Robby climbed over them, a mechanical spider protecting his family. Chase rocking in his arms.

Beams of harsh light knifed from each side of the arena, criss-crossing above the house. Intersecting where an icy clock hung from a wire. Icicles pointed out the time. It was ten o'clock.

Toys cheered all around. Above the din, a cartoonish voice began to sing. "A list is made of naughty and nice, writ about the girls and boys. But nothing is Christmas without the spirit, and all of the—"

"Toys! Toys! Toys!" the crowd cheered.

They knew the song and celebrated with fervor, climbing on shoulders and bouncing about. A sea of fur and plastic, of large and small, round and tall. Their excitement went to another level when the spotlights lit the iceberg at the far end of the arena, a pyramidal slab of a wall. On the smooth icy surface, a door opened.

An orange cat appeared to fly out and hover about the crowd. A thin wire, barely visible, carried Viktor around the arena. No one noticed it or cared. They were exploding with delight, believing he was flying. Hiro could feel their joy. Viktor could do anything. *Even fly.*

"Welcome, my fuzzies and furries, my skins and fabrics. My smoothies and roughies and bouncies and crawlies. Welcome all my wonderful toys to the greatest time of the year!"

He threw out his arms and soared like a superhero. The spotlights traced his flight. The arena shook beneath the stampede that reached for him as he swooped down, his happy laughter trailing behind him.

"Viktor! Viktor! Viktor!"

He hung just above the house like a visiting spirit, soaking up the accolades. It went on and on and on, and no one seemed to tire. Viktor wasn't concerned the house was sitting on a tower of dirt and the ground was literally shaking. It was too dark to see anything besides an orange, fuzzy superhero gobbling up praise.

"Do you hear that?" He put his paw to his pointy ear. The crowd quietly hushed. "He's coming."

Little tinny bells rang. As if it was even possible, toys became even more excited. The bells grew louder. The exuberance was a dense vapor invading one toy after another. "Santa," they murmured.

"Ho, ho, ho." Viktor grabbed his belly. "This is our world. This is Toyworld. Christmas isn't about giving things. It's about making the world a better place. How do we make it better? By making you"—he spun like a ballerina, finger sweeping the crowd—"*better toys!*"

All at once, and without warning, the arena was as bright as the sun. It took everyone by surprise. A collective groan rumbled. Hiro looked at the floor, blinded by the light. His vision slowly came back, a ring of dark spots remaining.

"I'm giving back to you this very special Christmas," Viktor said, "what belongs to us."

Hiro took a peek, guarding his vision with his arm. Dozens of bright objects hung like tiny stars, each burning as bright as a thousand spotlights. He could feel the warmth even from that distance. It was dense. It was sweet and uplifting. Like liquid joy.

"Where's Snow?" Hiro said. Flake didn't answer. The little elf was back in the hat. *What's wrong with him?* "Lift me up," he said to Robby.

"With what?" Robby offered Chase's sleeping body like it was all he could do.

"You have twenty arms! Use two of them."

He adjusted his stance, reconfigured Chase's cradle, and offered

Hiro a pair of forks. Hiro clamped them under his arms. Robby hoisted him above his head.

"Higher!"

The arms slid a segment at a time, locking in their tracks. A beachball went bouncing past. *Weeee.* Hiro swayed as the support wavered. He needed to go higher. He wanted to feel the entire crowd. Robby grunted. Haze steadied him. Another segment extended. *Schlock.*

"This is the year Santa never leaves again," Viktor said. "And neither shall I!"

Never leave? Why would he say that?

None of the toys heard it or cared. They were bathing in the sun storm of joy. The tiny white-hot stars swayed on thin wires. The light was creating a strange illusion. It looked like a colorful beam wavered out of the house and into the sky, like a condensed Northern Light.

"Where are you?" Hiro murmured.

He had to concentrate, recalling what Mads felt like, how she smelled, the way her emotions emanated like radio waves. A distinct sensation that was different than anyone else. He scanned the crowd. Toys climbed on top of each other, reaching for Viktor as he began to swing around again, praising toys for being toys, how the world was so much better now. A remote-control monster truck crowd-surfed past Hiro, spinning his wheels through uplifted arms and legs and tentacles.

"She's over there." Hiro pointed at the Ferris wheel. "Turn me that way. No, the other way. That way!"

Robby was about to tip over. His monitor exploded in a display of fireworks. Hiro only needed another minute. He picked up Mads's trail, could feel her in the mix of frolicking toys. Soldiers, the square mouths who ate tickets, carved the crowd like ships plowing through ice.

Robby began to falter. Hiro swayed like the mast of a ship entering rough water. The metal arms went *snick-snick-snick* like a collapsing ladder. Hiro fell from his grip, bounced off a pirate's plastic sword into a mob of bobbleheads. They volleyed him back into flight.

He rode on plastic hands and furry paws, tried to pull himself down, flailing with useless stuffed arms. The world tumbled—bright stars, house, soaring orange cat, jubilant toys.

A storm of chaotic thoughts blew like a winter squall. He lost contact with Mads. Couldn't feel Haze or Robby. Couldn't make sense of anything until firm hands snatched his leg. Everything continued spinning. If he had a stomach, he would have hurled. He focused on a square mouth and bushy eyebrows. A soldier held him at arm's length.

"Thank you." Hiro patted the stiff arms. "I lost my friends."

The soldier spun sharply, bowling over a purple dinosaur, who didn't seem to care, and marched through the crowd.

"They're over there," Hiro said. "You can put me down."

The soldier didn't hear him. Hiro squirmed, pounding at the sleeve on the red jacket. He knocked over toys, stepped on them, kicked them like a runaway wind-up toy. Hiro twisted around. They were marching toward the iceberg. The soldier's eyes were vacant. Hiro couldn't feel thoughts inside him. Just a rigid focus on a door guarded by two more soldiers. He squirmed. The grip tightened.

"Hey, boxhead." A tentacle slithered around the soldier's arm. "I think the teddy wants down."

An orange octopus rose in front of them. One eye scrunched in the loose fabric like a fist inside a sock. Ocho wrapped tentacles around both soldier's arms. They were an immovable vise. The square mouth opened and closed. No words came out. Hiro didn't hear any thoughts. Just blank eyes beneath shaggy brows.

"You're stitched a little tight there, soldier," Ocho said. "You all right, teddy bear?"

Hiro didn't respond. If Ocho was here, Mads wasn't far. She had told him to wait when she left them at Figgy Station. *He came with her!*

Ocho twined another tentacle around the wooden arm, then another, twisting like a carnivorous vine. He had all eight tentacles crawling between the soldier's arms. They were eye to eye, close enough to kiss. A white-gloved hand grabbed the top of Ocho's head like a pillowcase. His tentacles peeled away. A second soldier held him up like a costume. A third one appeared.

"Okay. All right," Ocho said. "It's a party. But you guys are stepping all over the joy!"

He was dropped like a sack full of bedsheets, spreading on the floor. He kept his eye on Hiro as the march continued to the iceberg.

"At midnight, a new world is coming!" Viktor announced with great glee to the adoring audience. "Merry, merry!"

30

When the door slid open, the soldier took one step off the elevator and dropped Hiro like a dirty diaper.

Giant fans churned on a warehouse ceiling. Metal stairs went in all directions, open catwalks crossing from one side to the other. Walls of equipment with lights and switches, tubes and cables. Little plastic bugs—cockroaches and caterpillars and spiders—crawled on things found inside a nuclear power plant or space station. Not a gala.

"Are you okay?"

Hiro scrambled away from the shadow, arms and legs slipping on the floor. A full-sizer held out his hands timidly. His wrestling boots squeaked on the floor. He was all of six feet and almost nude. Skintight briefs and bulging muscles. A bodybuilder with a coif of plastic hair.

"They don't have to be so rough. Look." He pointed at Hiro's leg. White batting puffed from a torn seam.

It sounded like a balloon stretching when he turned his head, wrinkles digging into his forehead. Suddenly, there was pressure in the room. Hiro felt it in his head, like an invisible helmet wrapped around his scalp. His thoughts began to scramble, so he focused on a wall to keep out whoever was trying to get in.

"Very good." A smile squeaked into the muscleman's cheeks. "You kept me from peeking. I was looking for your name. My name is Stretch."

Hiro didn't understand until Stretch tapped his head with a wink. *He's trying to read my thoughts.*

"Hiro."

"Hiro. Well, Hiro, I can help you if you let me."

He gestured to the tear. Hiro nodded. Stretch gently scooped him up, and Hiro saw the full depth of the room. It was even bigger than he first thought. The sound of Stretch's footsteps bounced around the enormous space. The floor was mostly empty except for a stark table with gleaming chairs, both made of something metal. Platinum or the like. It was a strange cross between a dining table and an autopsy bench.

There was also a mint green couch at a glass wall.

The walls were filled with complex machinery except for the one. It was entirely glass. Beyond, an orange cat was swinging on a wire. The top of the Ferris wheel was just below them. The mint green couch was in front of the glass wall like a movie theater. Several feet away from it, standing at the glass, was a full-size puppet. Wooden hands clasped behind a long cloak.

"Here we go."

Stretch placed Hiro on the crunchy couch covered in clear plastic. The puppet standing at the glass ignored them, apparently mesmerized by the swinging cat and blazing lights. Stretch dug through boxes next to the couch, unzipped a pouch.

"This won't be hard." Stretch held a needle between his lips. "Might feel a little pressure."

The needle looked like a splinter between his beefy hands. But he operated like a seasoned surgeon, cutting the frayed threads, packing fluffy white stuffing into the tear. He pinched it together with one hand and began sewing.

The puppet wrung his hands. His fingers looked like sticks trying to solve a puzzle. Something rattled around his wrist.

"This is Belkin. Belkin, this is Hiro."

The puppet twisted his hands, hiding the bracelet. As if feeling Hiro's eyes on it. Hiro hardened the wall around his thoughts. Belkin watched the scene beyond the window. The orange cat was standing on the house now, reaching into the chimney and pulling out presents, flinging them into the crowd. Toys ripped them apart.

"Almost done," Stretch said.

"What's he doing?" Hiro said.

"Don't take it personally. Belkin does this every year. Never says a word till the gala is over."

"No, him. Viktor. Why does he do all of this?"

Stretch chuckled. "That's not Viktor."

"I mean him, the cat on top of the house."

"That's Freckles."

"What?" That didn't make a lick of sense. The orange cat was on all the posters. Everyone was chanting his name. Someone was pretending to be him at the Gifting Tree. "I don't understand."

"Nobody does." Stretch poked more batting into Hiro's leg. "Freckles is more relatable. Easier to like. He *is* more likable, to be honest. Dim, though. Easy for Viktor to control. He's a public figure. No one ever bothers to ask why Viktor the Red is *orange*. They just want to believe."

He added the final stitch, bit the thread and smoothed the suture. He studied his work. He began humming a Christmas song, putting his needle and thread away, like this was everyday knowledge: a mysterious ruler throwing a big party, using another toy to pretend to be him. While a full-size puppet watched from an apparent prison cell the size of a warehouse carved from an iceberg. It made as much sense as everything else in this world.

"Am I in trouble?"

"No one's in trouble." Stretch sat next to him, the couch sinking under his weight. "We're just part of the mess."

Hiro didn't want to mention his friends. He hopped off the couch, leaned against the window. The lights were closer to the crowd, showering them with white brilliance. Hiro could still feel their strange warmth. It was exhilarating. He felt stronger and something else. He did that thing when Robby was holding him up, when he had been looking for Mads. This time he opened his heart to search for his friends. To see if he could feel them out there. Just to be sure they were all right. He could feel Mads, but she wasn't by the Ferris wheel anymore.

"Don't do that," Belkin said.

Hiro jumped. "Don't do what?"

"Open like that."

He reworked his old, scuffed fingers, not hiding the bracelet anymore. He wasn't watching the cat, who apparently wasn't Viktor, or the toys or the rides. He was staring at the bright lights.

"He means this." Stretch tapped his head. "Don't open your mind."

"I didn't."

"You were searching for your friends," Belkin said. "It makes you vulnerable. Don't do it again."

"He's worried about his friends, Belkin."

"And I looked straight into his thoughts." Belkin's head swiveled toward Hiro. His eyes were faded, as if sun-bleached. "He'll know everything if you don't protect your mind."

Hiro didn't know *anything*. He'd come here to save Christmas, nothing else. That was why Mads hadn't told them what they were going to do. In case this happened. Now that Hiro was caught, Viktor knew they were there.

Belkin turned back to the shiny little orbs swinging on long cables, bathing the arena in dazzling warmth.

"What are those lights?" Hiro said. "I can feel them."

Stretch looked at Belkin. Neither wanted to answer. Belkin's fingers seemed to tangle in a knot. Finally, he said, "Our mistakes."

❋

"Let me go!"

Bits of candy danced across the floor. Haze barfed a colorful rainbow off a soldier's face. He dropped her like a sack of rice. Robby was tossed across the room, his limbs tied in a mess of yellow string like he'd been rolled in wet pasta. Flake moped off the elevator. A soldier laid Chase gently on the floor.

"Haze!" Hiro hopped across the room. Haze met him next to the table. They collided like puffy sumo wrestlers with arms too short to grab each other. They leaned against each other instead of hugging.

"Are you okay?" Haze said.

"Yeah. I mean, I tore a seam, but Stretch fixed it." He pointed at Stretch, who carried Chase to the couch. "Are you all right?"

"The soldiers were intense. I don't think they're having fun."

"They grabbed you, too?"

"Me, yeah."

Hiro looked around. "Did you find—"

"That's so sweet," Robby said. "Me? I'm great, too. Super great. I found this new outfit. You like it? Great, great. Hey, I've got an idea. Get me out of here!"

He strained in the bindings, looking more like a loosely wrapped ball of rubber bands. Lightning flashed on his TV.

"What happened to him?" Hiro asked.

"Soldiers. Made him easy to carry," Haze said. "They threw it at him. I think it's a toy, but not sure what."

"Seriously, are you going to help?" Robby grunted. "This is getting tight. I think I can cut—ahh!"

Stretch towered over the quivering ball of metal meatball wrapped in spaghetti, tapping the deep dimple in his square chin. He had his bag of things out. Robby started bouncing away like a tortured exercise ball.

"That's Stretch?" Haze said.

"That's Stretch."

"Is he nice?"

Hiro held up his leg. "He fixed me."

Robby managed to wiggle out of Stretch's shadow. The muscle toy reached out, his arm stretching and thinning, and grabbed Robby's television head, held him like a junkyard ornament.

"Guess that's why they call him Stretch," Haze said.

"Guess so," Hiro said.

They followed him to the long, silver table, where he plopped Robby like a quivering entrée. He vibrated like a battery-powered toy with no apparent purpose. Stretch dropped his bag next to him.

"Who's the puppet?" Haze said.

Flake was next to Belkin, watching the show play out below. The elf looked as frumpy as ever, slumped in his wrinkled clothing. The rim of his hat was empty. He felt sad.

"That's Belkin," Hiro said.

"There we go." Stretch searched his bag, found what he was looking for. It wasn't a knife or scissors. It was a small jar with red sauce. He cracked the lid open and smelled it.

"He's not going to eat him, is he?" Haze said.

"I'm not sure. You're not going to eat him, are you, Stretch?"

Stretch dipped his finger into the jar. He waved a dab of red sauce. "We don't want to hurt anyone, do we, Ms. Super String?"

It wasn't quite clear whom he was talking to or what he was doing. It looked like a strange culinary ritual. The ropey, yellow string began sliding like a python. Robby's screen went blank. He stopped shivering. The end of the mess of binding noodles wiggled out. Stretch poured a trail of sauce down the table. Slowly, the rope slithered out and began rolling around, covering itself in red paste.

"When I thought this couldn't get weirder," Haze said.

Robby skittered off the table like a dog scrambling on linoleum, fell on the floor and crawled on multiple legs. The television spinning. Stretch carried his bag to the mint couch, humming a Christmas song. Belkin and Flake were unmoved.

"I'm guessing this wasn't part of the plan," Haze said.

"Probably not."

They went to the window. Chase was on Stretch's lap, curled up like she was sleeping. He patted the couch. They sat next to him. Fireworks were exploding up above, streaks of light flashing on the toys below. It was eleven o'clock, according to the clock above the house.

Robby eventually came over, squatted behind the couch. No one said anything. They watched the show, listening to Belkin twist his wooden fingers and Ms. Super String wallow in red sauce. The orange cat pulled more gifts from the chimney.

"Why do they call him Viktor the *Red*?" Robby said.

31

The nights were silent. The streets were dark.

No string lights hung from gutters, no trees in the windows. It was another night like any other, to be followed by a gray, colorless day. I'd had a lifetime of colorless days.

If all went as planned, I'd never see another.

The house was quiet. The sheets were starched. A cup at my bedside. I stood at the window with not a stitch of sentimentality. My neighbors fast asleep, snoring in their beds. Not listening for bells or hooves on their roof. No stockings above the fireplace, no presents waiting to open.

They forgot Christmas ever existed.

Should I feel guilty when they didn't know Christmas went missing? It had been several years since I'd had to endure their colorful lights. The Christmas spirit had disappeared from this world, taking with it the joy and happiness of this time of year.

Maybe I felt a trace, just a smidge. But I extinguished that ugly little bruise. If I didn't, I wouldn't sleep tonight. And tonight, more than any other, I needed to slumber like the dead. Tonight was the night Christmas would leave this world for good. It would still exist. Just not here.

And neither would I.

❄

I was greeted by the sweet smells of nutmeg and roasted chestnuts. Candlelight flickering. String instruments carried me on lovely arrangements like a sleigh coasting over snow-covered hills.

My bones were warm. My personal assistant, Tommy Turtle, rubbed almond oil on my legs. My femur was slick and tingling. The sea turtle's spongy flippers applied the perfect amount of pressure to keep me fresh and ready on return. I let him work his magic.

The shelf where I once woke was long gone. Now it was a private room, an ergonomic recliner, and things to stimulate the senses. A beautiful awakening.

Before the chaos would begin.

The thoughts of millions of toys awaited. Knowing all those thoughts was exhausting. I had begun to hate my return until I learned to filter the noise. It took considerable effort to ignore them, to shrink my consciousness down to my essential being. Knowing everything is to know nothing. I had to be Viktor, just Viktor, to prevent being washed away by a tsunami of thought.

"Bring them in."

I said it out loud. I could have thought it, but using words was a way to maintain separation. If I penetrated Tommy Turtle's mind, I would know him intimately. It was nicer to see him pack up his oils and waddle out, feeling only the ripples of his emotion. Tommy, though, was as calm as a glassy pond. That was why he cared for me during sleep.

Freckles was entertaining the mob, swinging from a wire, tossing gifts to the multitude. As he'd done for many, many Christmases now. I sat up and watched him hold his belly, laughing joyously. Tonight was possibly his last performance.

Tonight the last road would disappear.

Every Christmas, Santa's avenues withered away. Without the flow of Christmas spirit, they atrophied like abandoned muscles. My calculations pegged this night to be the last of them. If I was here when it vanished, then I couldn't go back there.

Bye-bye, dreary world.

Freckles could continue playing the role of Viktor the Red. I had consulted my public relations team, Penny Playmate and Chauncey Chatterbox, in the very beginning. I didn't like the idea of Freckles pretending to be me, at first. Giving up control of the narrative? But they insisted, and slowly, I relented. I don't know everything. I mean, I did know everything, but I was still only one toy.

With Freckles doing the dirty work, I could retire to a small cabin, or ridiculous mansion (I hadn't decided which), by a stream or lake. Get a boat, or yacht. Fish all afternoon. I was bored even thinking about it. There was still work to do. The bottom line was this: I wasn't going to fall asleep anymore. There would be no roads to take me back.

A full-time toy.

"Merry, merry!" Bella Dancer sang.

She tiptoed into my private room. Always on her toes, that one. Jimmy Gearhead, my robot calculator, followed. Pauly Paws, the floppy-eared dog, moped in last. My three trusted advisors, all from the workshop on the day I first woke up and was later brought to Madeline's bedroom. They surrounded my recliner and, one at a time, gave the waking report.

I could have just absorbed it from them. It was nice to hear it, though. Keep separate. They appreciated it. I know they did. I watched Freckles climb on the little house's roof, scaling the special red wall built on top. Gala attendance was at an all-time high. Social media was trending favorably. The little house readings were stable.

"Spirit levels have spiked 200%," Jimmy Gearhead said.

"Two hundred?"

That was unexpected. I had calculated an increase of 58.2%. I had been right, give or take a tenth of a percent, for the past ten Christmases. This miscalculation was unexpected. *This could be a problem.*

With fewer roads, the Christmas spirit, or verve as the dad once called it, siphoned from the bubble continued to increase every year.

I hypothesized it was due to fewer outlets. The spirit needed to flow. Its essence was that of giving. It couldn't be static.

I had increased charm production to hold the extra spirit, had tripled toy manufacturing over the past two years. The spirit had to go somewhere. The trick was not letting any one toy get too smart. They had to be happy and joyful and smarter than the average bloodbag. But not smart enough to see through my shenanigans.

More toys were not sustainable. What would happen when all the roads were closed, you might be thinking? Easy solution, really. Christmas won't come once a year. We'll do it every day. The spirit will flow and flow and flow. Everyone will love me even more. Does it sound like I was winging it? Reorganizing the universe turned out to be complicated.

"We had some suspicious activity," Pauly Paws said. "We picked up loose thoughts searching the house."

"Did someone try to get inside?" Curiosity was natural. You can't invite thousands of toys to a party and not expect a few to climb the altar.

"No. But they saw inside. Somehow." He presented the evidence as a thought.

Now this was interesting. Somehow a toy got a legitimate peek inside the house. It was unreachable and impenetrable. The multitude of carnival rides—Ferris wheel, roller coaster, bumper cars, twirly cups, pole drops, ship tips, chair spinners (*what more did they want?*)—kept curiosity to a minimum. Why would they care about a dumpy old house?

"Did you apprehend the trespasser?" I asked.

"They're in the warehouse."

"They?"

"They came to the gala together."

I stood on the recliner so I could look my team in the eyes. Then I applied a little mental pressure. Just enough to let them know the boss was agitated. "Why," I said slowly, "did you put them in the *warehouse*?"

"It's thought-locked. There might be others working with them still at the gala."

Okay, I hadn't thought of that. Good call. I scratched Pauly Paws behind the ear, gave the rest of them some good feelings.

It's important to give cookies when deserved.

❆

TOY BUGS KEPT the machines running, machines that kept the Christmas spirit circulating and stored in proper vessels to be distributed to toys all over the world. No one ever said thank you, nor should they. But if they knew the sacrifices I made, a little gratitude wouldn't hurt.

My guests were glued to the window. Belkin felt me coming. He always did. I climbed onto a platinum chair, stood at the head of the table and stared at a twenty-foot tapeworm writhing in red sauce. It sounded like muck boots in a mud hole.

"Enjoying the show?" I asked.

A television spun on an erector set of crooked limbs. A single eye swelled on the monitor. A teddy and dragon peeked over the couch.

"Merry, merry, Viktor. You look rested."

"Thank you, Stretch. You look rosier than ever."

"I'm using a new oil."

"Fabulous. What do we have here?" I pointed at the gurgling slurpfest.

"Ms. Super String is indulging. Marinara, her favorite."

"I see that."

The string inchwormed toward me. I summoned a cleanup crew. The elevator opened. One of my trusty soldiers wound Ms. Super String up like a rope. A team of Spongy Critters mopped up the marinara. Stretch helped my guests to seats at the table. The television robot struggled to fold his limbs. I insisted he stand.

"Belkin, please join us. Christmas is an hour away."

My wooden friend remained at the window. I would allow him to come of his own volition. I preferred not to force his actions. I could, but it was easier if I didn't. Like a good puppet, he sat at the opposite end of the table. Insolent, he was. I liked to tease he was an oversized chip on the world's shoulder. He never laughed.

"Am I to assume you know who I am?"

"You're Viktor the Red."

"It was more of a question for our new friends, but thank you, Stretch. I am Viktor. Freckles does my dirty work. The public appearances and whatnot. Fame and recognition are not my thing. Besides, everyone loves a big fluffy cat. Nothing about a red skeleton says *Christmas*."

I jazz-handed the expression. I'd used it a million times. People loved it.

"Why does he use your name?" the dragon said.

I hadn't skimmed their thoughts yet to know their names. Mystery, I had found in the last year or so, was much more fun. When the time came, I would simply peek into their fragile little minds and know everything about them. Until then, let's play.

"Fair point. If I didn't want recognition, why not just let him be Freckles the Great? It's self-indulgent, I agree. This is a historic moment. And I want the credit, even if by proxy." I drummed my fingers on the table like sticks on a barrel. I liked the sound of it. It was dramatic in tense meetings. "It would be *rude* of me to peek at your thoughts. So please, tell me your names."

Belkin shook his head. My audacity was sometimes sickening. I only said it for his benefit. To see if a toy could actually barf from disgust. *Fun, fun.*

"I'm Hi—" the teddy started. The dragon spit a candy rock at him. It dribbled on the table. "Higo."

"Higo?" I said. "Very well. And you?"

"Dreamy," the dragon blurted.

"Farper," the metal man said.

"Farper," I said. "How did you come to have such an interesting name, Farper?"

"The person who made me farped a lot."

"That's not a word."

"Tell her."

I couldn't help but laugh. They were lying. What fun, watching them trying to hide. The innocence. The naivete. "How about you?"

The elf was different than the others, a tumbleweed of whiskers with a tall hat jammed onto his head. His clothes were oversized and wrinkled. His hands, though, were quite unique. A realistic synthetic material that looked human. I hadn't seen this type of toy before and made a note. Perhaps, when the time came, I would look into him like a suit I might try on. I'd grown fond of the skeleton, but a switching wasn't off the table.

"He doesn't talk," Dreamy the dragon said.

"He doesn't? Well, does he have a name?"

"Maybe."

"His name is Maybe?" I swear on a mountain of marshmallows, I have never been in a mood this good. "Well, *Maybe,* tell me about the little door in your hat?"

"His friend is in there," she said.

"Quite small, that one." Funny. I couldn't feel anyone in there. I jumped on the table and walked straight over to the elf and knocked on his dumpy, green hat. "Little elf, little elf, let me in."

"He's shy," the dragon said.

"Well then, no need to embarrass him." I did a little jig, heels clicking on the hard surface. I loved this part, strolling across the table. It scared others, a little, red skeleton stomping back and forth. "This one here. She was your friend?"

I knelt next to the black and white, striped cat. She was a beauty. Silky fur, empty eyes that, when the light was on, were probably hypnotic. Put some life in this one and I'd keep it around just to hear it purr.

"She's gone," the dragon said.

"That's unfortunate."

"They put a collar on her when we got here. Then these old people—"

"Creepy old people," Farper interjected. The wily scamp.

"—they started talking to her. And then the collar lit up. And then, I don't know, twenty minutes later she went to sleep."

I stroked the kitty's tail. "You hear that, Belkin? A toy that sleeps." He didn't appreciate my jab. Only one toy in this world slept. *Not after tonight.* "Excitement can do that to a toy. Knock them out of sync. The light meant she was selected. The old couple chose her to switch."

"It didn't work," the dragon said.

"Apparently not."

I peeked inside the cat, searching for a trace of identity. If she hadn't consented to the switch, it could've resulted in an identity failure. The old woman, or old man—if he was into being a toy cat for the night—would have tried to occupy the toy. A conflict would've ensued. The woman (or man) would have returned to their old, shriveled body. The toy, unfortunately, would've been erased. Happened all the time.

There would be evidence of who she was cached on her charm. But here's the thing. She didn't have a charm. *Well, that's not possible.*

I threw a wider net around the room, scooping up their real names in the meantime. I read them all—Hazel, Robert, Flake—except for the teddy. His thoughts were more resistant. His mind was a house of bricks. The others were made of straw. I would blow his house down soon enough, but first the charms. I felt them; they were in the room. How could they not be? These toys were clearly alive.

"Let's take a look inside your hat. May I, Flake?"

I felt them flinch. I knew the elf's name. Flake bowed his head. He knew he couldn't stop me. I knocked on the little door. No one answered. I stood back, held out my hands. A ridiculous mop of hair puffed out when he peeled off the hat. It looked like a dandelion with a perm.

The hat was heavy. Little things stored inside, collectibles and precious items. A needlepoint repair kit, extra batting. A photo of Flake with a tiny elf, who evidently lived inside the hat, posing on the brim. Identical twins of different sizes. Adorable.

A zippered pocket bulged with a handful of heavy items.

"Stretch," I said, "can you fetch a bowl?"

The elastic man came back with a cereal bowl. I dumped the contents with a loud clatter into it and placed it on the table like a snack. To these dullards, it looked like four marbles. Three of them were speckled with dazzling light, like self-contained universes. The fourth one was dull gray. My guests had no idea what I'd found. Flake, though, why, he was fully aware of what he was hiding. Belkin, of course, knew as well.

"Now why would Flake be holding your charms?" I said, amused.

"He likes shiny things," Robby said.

Oh, this was rich. They were clueless, all of them. However, I'd never encountered such an odd design. A charm not embedded in the toy? It would be like carrying a brain in a duffel bag.

Well, enough fun.

Flake offered no resistance. I searched his mind like spotlights cutting through a meadow. The little elf who lived inside his hat went by the name of Snow. Snow and Flake. Cute. They had been stitched as an inseparable pair. Although together no more. Snow was the leader of the motley band of misfits. He hadn't been caught with the others but rather snuck out a secret hatch in the back of the hat when my soldiers approached, scurrying through the gala like a mouse between bags of seed.

I dug a little deeper.

Intentions were always a little tricky, I had found, when probing another's thoughts. They're the crown jewels of why we do what we do and the last thing we want others to see. So much so, we often hide them from ourselves. They underestimated what I could do. Perhaps this little scenario would have worked if I weren't omnipotent. The other toys had no idea why they were here.

They're a diversion.

I called the lookies into action. The shiny tattletales swirled around the house where Freckles perched his big orange butt. They were too small for anyone attending the gala to notice. I must admit, a cold wave of worry rippled through me. Even Belkin sensed it wrinkle the space between us. The cad thought, for a moment, something was out of my control.

Nothing could be farther from the truth. *Still...*

The lookie stream projected onto the table for everyone in the room to see. The multifaceted view stretched the entire length. They stood on their chairs to watch the show. I guided the lookies like bloodhounds, sniffing hints I pulled from Flake. It only took a minute to find an inconspicuous octopus crawling with a band of twirling ballerinas.

They cringed, just a little.

They recognized the orange cephalopod sticking out like a zebra hiding in a desert. Although, I'll admit, they seemed more surprised he was even there. *Ocho,* they thought.

Poor little toys. They didn't even know what was happening. Just pawns in some misguided attempt to stop me. They'd suffer the consequences, of course. That wasn't on me. Whoever roped them into this folly would have to take that blame.

I beamed with satisfaction. I wanted Belkin to feel it, wanted him to watch. Their simplistic plan wasn't going to work. But that wasn't the source of my glee. We were going to watch it fail in real time.

"What fun," I muttered.

Ocho pretended to loiter, leaning on the pillar that held the house. He studied his tentacles with boredom, nibbling at loose threads that weren't there. His solitary eye shifted around, not noticing the lookies. Casually, he reached under one of his legs, stretched and yawned. With a flick, he tossed a tumbling ball over his head.

It was an impressive shot.

The crumpled ball had floated like one of the bubble experiences, those tasty treats the toys loved so much, and landed at the corner of the house. It disappeared. I had to rewind the stream to see what happened. The ball had landed on the apron surrounding the house, sprouted legs and darted into a crack big enough for a field mouse.

Or a very small elf.

"There's your friend!" I clapped my hands, encouraged the others to applaud the seamless execution. They didn't share my enthusiasm. "What do you think he'll do next?"

Belkin pushed away from the table and returned to the window.

The lookies followed. The little elf zipped through the dark and right for the lab. That was interesting. Someone had prepped him. He knew exactly where to go. I started to second-guess Belkin's involvement. If he had anything to do with this, he was hiding it well. The wooden curmudgeon felt clueless. I'd excavate his thoughts later.

On with the show.

Snow bounced around the lab. It was pitch black, the lookie views overlaid with green night vision. He went right to the control panels and pried open a drawer. Wow. He was really getting to the heart of it. He journeyed past the butterfly valve and into the needle chamber. He found the access panel, crawled through a vent that led to the most vulnerable part of the system: a charm that linked everything together. Once he got a hold of it, he could shut everything down. Destroy everything I'd worked for. Expose me to the world. *The horror!*

It wasn't there.

I had redesigned the system a long time ago. Only my trusted advisors knew that. The house held only one thing, the most important thing, but the switch that turned everything off wasn't there. And only I knew where it was. Whoever was behind this knew the house. *Interesting.*

The little elf scrambled around. It was supposed to be there. That was what he had been told, and he didn't know what to do now that it wasn't there. He climbed out of the machinery and, in a bit of a panic, scurried out of the lab. It was time to send in a Super String agent. I assumed the little elf would run into the attic or basement in search of a vulnerability. He wouldn't find one, but he'd make a mess. He went for a hallway.

"This is interesting," I said.

I called off the Super String, for now. The little elf ventured into the living room. Eerie blue light rippled on the walls. A needle extended from the ceiling in front of the fireplace. It was white hot, piercing a watery glob of warped space. It was a life-sized snow globe, of sorts. Not one to be shaken. There were no snowflakes inside, no miniature village.

Only a fat man in a red coat.

The little elf was mesmerized by my time bubble. Well, Philip had invented the technology. I made it mine. That was how these sorts of things went. It was nothing short of a miracle that it worked. The needle siphoned an endless supply of Christmas spirit from it. As a result, I am who I am.

The little elf must've been told what was in the house. But, as he took a step toward the bubble, he clearly hadn't been told what it was.

"Stop this, now." Belkin had turned around.

"Free will, Belkin. He went in there of his own free will."

"Viktor, if he passes through the veil—"

"I am not responsible!" The table shook. The toys quivered. "I took every precaution to protect the house. There's no welcome mat out front. He went inside against all my wishes." I cast an accusatory glare. "Someone should have warned him."

"I have nothing to do with this," Belkin said.

I had no reason not to believe him. He'd been trapped in this room since the beginning. He was genuinely innocent of this attack. He was rooting for them, sure. But this wasn't his doing.

"You don't have to watch."

Flake hammered the table with humanlike fists. A series of guttural grunts came from the wild beard like a chimpanzee trying to communicate. His thoughts wildly spun warnings, trying to reach the little elf with thoughts that would never reach him.

The little elf cautiously raised his hand. The membrane rippled waves where he touched it. He hesitated. I sensed his change of heart and thought maybe Belkin was right. No need to complicate matters this close to midnight. I would put a stop to this.

But then he touched it one more time.

The bubble swallowed him like an amoeba absorbing food. The watery veil surrounded him. A blurry green coat was now on the inside. Hand raised. And not moving.

Flake fell silent. They all did. It was clear something bad just happened. I knelt in front of Flake, attempted to soothe his inextinguishable anguish. I couldn't have a wild elf bouncing off the walls, trying to work out his issues.

"Your friend is okay. He's better than okay. Time for him has slowed to an infinitesimal crawl. That's all. When he comes out, he'll only be younger than you. Nothing more."

He wasn't coming out. That's for sure. If he did, the jolly fat man would be set free. I had more than enough Christmas spirit, but I imagine Santa Claus wouldn't be happy with what I'd done. I was fairly certain I could handle him, but, like I said, no need to complicate matters this close to Christmas.

"Now." I turned around. "Who are you?"

They sat like lumps of wet cotton. It'd be nice of them to tell me, but I understood. Even if I told them why their charms were hidden in Flake's hat and why the cat suddenly went to sleep, they wouldn't believe me. I felt sorry for them. Someone was playing with them to get to me. Not in a fun way.

"Well then, let's have a look."

Flake had all the answers. After all, he had those special synthetic hands for a reason. I dove into his memory canals, floating back to the beginning when he came online for the very first time. That magical moment when the stitcher ignites the charm with just a pinch of Christmas spirit. Like a baby opening his eyes in a brand-new world, I saw who was looking back at him.

I stepped back.

An unexpected turn, it was. I had to search my own memories for a face I hadn't seen in quite some time. His stitcher had clearly aged.

It had been thirty years since I last saw her.

❄

"I'LL BE RIGHT BACK."

I leaped off the table and took my time walking to the couch. I gestured to Stretch, who dutifully lifted me up. I stood on his shoulder. Outside the window, glitter bombs showered the arena. Freckles bathed in the flickering bits of confetti.

Belkin didn't take his big round eyes off the spectacle.

"You remember Madeline, Belkin? Polly and Philip's daughter. Don't pretend you don't. She was such a fan. Knew about you. BT, remember? My goodness, you loved that she knew you."

I could feel her out there. Her energy was as unique to her identity as fingerprints. I couldn't quite locate her though. She was good at hiding. That would end soon enough.

"I won't hurt her. I wouldn't think of it. She meant so much more to me than you. I just need this night to be perfect. After that, I'll set you free. Like I promised. Tell me where she is." I urged Stretch to move a bit closer. I could smell the varnish on Belkin's face. "Or shall I have a peek?"

He turned those wide eyes on me. We'd never seen eye to eye, in the metaphorical sense. If he had anything to do with this, he was going to make me work for it. He unfolded his hands, undid the clasp of the bracelet. The snowflake, once cheery red, had faded to a roughened scarlet color. The links pooled in the palm of his stiff hand.

"I found this when we first arrived. It told me exactly where we were and why we'd been sent here. Where we came from. That this world was for us. What you've done to it"—he piled the bracelet in my hand—"is not what it was meant to be."

I dropped the bracelet on the floor. It meant nothing to me. That bracelet was from another time. I'd bottled Belkin in this room so the outside world would forget him. Once the roads were closed and I wasn't going to wake up, the toys could have him back.

"This world is exactly what it should be," I said.

"You've done so much wrong."

"Look out there, what do you see? Hope and joy. I know you can feel that. I did that! It's because of me. I rescued them from the world you made them. You can't argue that. Can't you be happy, for once? Admit that I did what you couldn't. *This is for them!* I did everything for the toys!"

Well, not everything.

"They're still playthings," he said. "They just belong to you."

"You have no idea the restraint I exercise. The burden of knowing everything, the power to do anything requires so much more than you are capable of, Belkin."

"I've seen what you've done, Viktor. I see it in their faces. You're destroying humankind."

"Bloodbags? You're worried about the... they did this to themselves! They brought this on. The rules don't change when the tables turn." I pointed in no particular direction, like humans were everywhere. "They see the injustice now, don't they? Do you think, for one second, they wouldn't dominate toys if I wasn't here?"

"Toys are better than this. This world deserves better." He resumed his unyielding posture of a stiff, wooden puppet. "I am to blame."

"Well, there you go. Thankfully, I'm in charge and not you."

"You got what you wanted."

"You don't know what I want. This is our world, you said it yourself. I made it so."

If his eyes could move, they would widen in disbelief. "You're hurting countless others. You've taken Christmas away from all worlds." He leaned closer and whispered, "Think about *your* world."

I nearly fell off Stretch's shoulder. It had been quite some time since I'd been surprised. *He knows where I'm from. Like really knows.*

I must've been careless, didn't guard my thoughts around him, let him see who I truly was. I'm a voyager from another world. Not a toy. I needed time to calculate all the possibilities of what this meant. It was less than an hour to midnight. *Why did he tell me now?*

I climbed off Stretch and stood on the floor. Gazing at the celebration below, thinking about how different things were back home without Christmas. Thinking about what I was about to do to it for all eternity. I wasn't going back. That was nonnegotiable.

"*My* world was already without joy."

32

A ball of orange tentacles, lassoed by a long strand of Ms. Super String, rolled out of the elevator. Ocho's eye flickered back and forth. Desperate grunts stifled by a tightly wrapped gag.

"The gang's all here." Viktor climbed onto the table. "Come on in, Mr. Ocho. Grab a seat."

Ms. Super String unraveled. Ocho unfolded. "You!" he shouted, jabbing a tentacle at Viktor. "You'll be hearing from my lawyer. I did not come to this-this... gala or whatever to be harassed and —*humff-hm*."

Viktor waved a hand. Ms. Super String bound his mouth closed. Ocho was putting on a show. He had no idea they'd all watched him launch Snow into the house.

"Please sit down," Viktor said. "Get comfortable. This will only take a second."

Ocho was suspicious. Like when a nurse held up a shot and said there would be some pressure. At Viktor's request, Stretch dropped Ocho in a chair like a tangle of seaweed, pushed him up to the table as if dinner were about to be served. He squirmed at first, tugging at the gag until Viktor marched down the metal runway, footsteps clicking. *Heel-toe.*

Viktor leaned in. Ocho leaned back. "Let's get some answers."

Hiro could feel a mental struggle, if that was what you could call it. More like Viktor opened Ocho's mind like a jewelry box and rummaged freely through his prized possessions. Ocho squirmed. Maybe it hurt, having secrets ripped open like that. Maybe it was the simple raw and potent experience of powerlessness.

Viktor was going to do that to each of them. There was no hiding what they knew. Hiro realized that, no matter how many freedoms were taken away, there was always sanctuary in imagination. At least his thoughts were his and his alone. No one else's. *That's not how it works here.*

Viktor began laughing at what he saw inside Ocho. It was not the humorous kind.

The atmospheric texture rippled with the coarseness of a sandstorm. Ocho was losing, but he was putting up a fight. Hiro felt his way through the mental struggle, picking up loose thoughts escaping the battle. Clips of memory, playing in short reels, streamed in the maelstrom.

Ocho driving his candy-decorated car. Honking the horn. Mads returning to the back seat after dropping them off at Figgy Station, holding the purple monkey in the back seat, telling him where to go next. Ocho dropping her off at a fancy building. Ocho waiting for her. Ocho returning to Figgy Station, walking up to the soldiers. Ocho with a ticket. He wasn't alone.

The purple monkey was walking with him.

Viktor swung his gaze around the table. Hiro was caught off guard, didn't have the wall ready. Viktor was inside. He saw what he wanted. They weren't toys, not real toys. They were dreamers from another world.

Viktor stiffened with surprise. He paced a tight circle, taking another peek at their thoughts, their truth. He nodded, began laughing. Genuinely laughing, doubled over holding his red ribs. A human laughing that hard would wipe tears from their cheeks. His sockets were black holes.

"That is... unexpected." Viktor addressed Hiro and the others with a flourish. "Do you know why you're here, hmm? I mean, in this world, not my precious gala. Go on, you can say it. I already know, but I want to hear it from you."

He pointed at Haze. "To save Christmas," she muttered.

"To save Christmas. Right. Does it look like Christmas needs saving?" He gestured to the celebration that could not be more joyous.

"It's gone from our world," Haze said. "We want it back."

"Your world," he whispered. "Did you hear that, Belkin? Such honesty. Yes, Christmas is here and not there. I don't make the rules."

"You took it from us," Haze said.

"She didn't tell any of you she was coming to the gala. No, she didn't because if you were caught, you would be a liability. But she didn't stop there, did she. She didn't want to risk anything. Take your friend here." He stroked Chase's fur. "Madeline had a plan to keep you quiet."

He looked around the table. No one understood.

"Do you know what these are?" He picked up the bowl of marbles—the ones he'd found in the hat. Flake lowered his gaze. He understood what Viktor was getting at. "They're called charms. Every toy has one. See, you are not stuffing and threads or plastic eyes. You're not a teddy or a dragon or a... whatever you are." He gestured to Robby. "You're this."

Viktor held a marble like a grape. Studied it like a jewel. The dark sockets in his bright red skull seemed bottomless.

"Stretch has a charm inside his chest. Don't you, Stretch? Belkin has one behind that painted heart. Ocho here has one behind his eye. Flake has one somewhere under all that hair. Even you, my fine little toys, have a charm." He swirled the bowl of marbles. "But Madeline hid them in the hat instead of putting them inside you. Did she ever tell you to stay close? Mmm?"

They wriggled in their seats. They'd thought it was for their own safety.

Viktor nudged the bowl across the table with a red tarsal bone. It stopped in front of Flake like a bowl of worms.

"These charms are special, aren't they, elf? Madeline's mother was a toy stitcher, too. She designed these charms to be more alive, to have greater capacity. Bigger brains, if you will. Do you remember, Belkin, when she brought them to your office? She thought they were the answer to making toys more capable. An upgrade to be more than playthings. It would've worked. But we know what got in the way, don't we, Belkin?"

The full-size puppet didn't acknowledge the rhetorical questions. Hiro knew from his agitation that Viktor tortured him with gloating dialog.

"Polly was smart—that's Madeline's mother." Viktor strolled like a storyteller with endless time. "You don't become a world-class stitcher without a sprinkle of genius. She wasn't just a stitcher but a toy supporter. I mean, the woman was rabid about toy rights. Humans had subjugated toys, using them up and discarding them when they were done. It was not good, and no one was doing anything about it. Toys were disposable, and she wanted to change that. This was long before you all arrived yesterday."

He nodded in the way a person would wink. *I know all your secrets.*

"Polly was going to make a difference with these upgraded charms. But they were prototypes. They needed to be tested. And then, to my fantastic luck, her husband—a genius of another kind—saw another use for them. You see, the new charms wouldn't just make better toys. They were expanded storage devices. Philip and the past leader of toys"—he gestured to Belkin—"used them to *steal* Christmas spirit. They turned them into batteries!"

Viktor threw his arms out like a showman. Outside the window, Freckles entertained the crowd beneath bright balls of light. But those weren't balls.

Those are charms.

Hiro had felt their effect when they were unveiled. The feelings had showered down like X-rays of joy. *It's Christmas spirit?*

"But Philip and Belkin didn't understand the charms' full potential: *they had the capacity to occupy a dreamer.* Someone out there in a land far, far away—a boy or girl, man or woman—tucked into their bed, would make their nightly journey into the slumberyard of dreams. Instead of waking in the morning, they would open their eyes in, say, a teddy bear or a dragon. And these idiots had no idea!"

Viktor laughed heartily.

"That was never the intention, and no one ever understood what was going on before it was too late. But Polly, she was smart—yes, she was. She knew there was potential for the unexpected. I mean, we couldn't have toys turning into dictators. Could we, Belkin? She designed the charms with an emergency option. Let's call it an off switch. Do you know what that means?"

He put his hand to the earhole in the side of his skull.

"We wake up," Hiro said.

"Precisely!" Viktor jabbed a boney finger at the ceiling. "You wake up."

Haze looked at Hiro. She was trying to tell him something, but Hiro had built the wall to keep out thoughts. He wasn't going to let Viktor catch him off guard again.

Viktor stood over Flake, stared down like a disappointed teacher. Hands locked behind his back. He flicked his fingers like dry kindling. Flake knew what he wanted. Head bowed, eyes buried in the bush of hair, Flake put one of his hands on the table like a pupil about to take a ruler to his knuckles.

"Polly's off switch was simple. All it required was a human touch." Viktor turned Flake's hand over, palm up. Pressed the rubbery, synthetic skin with the tips of his cherry red phalange. "Madeline was like her mother. Smart. She designed the elves with a purpose."

Viktor dropped the dull marble from the bowl into Flake's hand.

"When Chase was compromised, the little elf went inside the hat, didn't he? He put his hands on her charm. Guess what happened?"

He examined their expressions, absorbing their confusion. Their difficulty to accept the facts.

"I'm not the bad guy here, children. Madeline was selfish. She put your lives as you know them in danger, more than you realize. She used you like playthings. Summoned you here for her own purposes, and when she's done with you, she'll turn you off. No goodbye, no explanation. Just thrown on the heap like a disposable toy. Sound familiar?"

He turned toward Belkin.

"I'm not an unreasonable toy. In fact, I'm likeable when you get to know me. You like me, don't you, Stretch?" The musclehead nodded, clearly unaware of the political subtleties. "I'm going to turn all of you off. Not because I'm done using you, but to wake you up. It's best you don't stay here much longer. If you're here when this Christmas arrives, this"—he poked Flake's hand—"will be more like a kill switch. Do you understand?"

Robby clearly didn't. His eye was a black bead in a bed of snow. Haze was distracted by something Hiro didn't want to investigate. However, they all knew what Viktor was saying. Maybe they didn't know why it would be a kill switch at Christmas, but Hiro did.

He's closing the roads.

Somehow, Viktor was responsible for the network of wormholes that pulsed with Christmas spirit drying up like tributaries no longer connected to their source. One by one, they were vanishing. And they weren't just for Christmas spirit. The roads were how they'd come to this world. The last road was closing tonight. And if Hiro, Haze and Robby were still there when it did, they wouldn't wake up.

She put our lives in danger.

"Why are you doing this?" Hiro said. "We just want Christmas back."

Viktor took a charm from the bowl, held it over Flake's hand. It landed in Flake's palm with a rubber thud. Hiro clenched in the seat, felt a jolt flicker through the air. There was a great clatter and a sputtering electric signal. A flat line drew across Robby's monitor. The static turned gray, then darker gray. The metal limbs fell like useless tools.

"You couldn't possibly understand."

❄

THIS DIDN'T FEEL like a dream anymore.

Chase looked like a toy left out in the rain. But the way Robby went limp, the way his television tipped to one side, opened a panic room inside Hiro. There was no way of knowing Robby woke up in bed, whether he opened his eyes, remembered his name. Did he remember any of this? *Would he remember Christmas? Feel its absence?*

"Me next." Haze pounded the table with squirrel-sized fists. "Get me out of here."

Hiro was glad she volunteered. He didn't want to leave her alone in this weird world.

"That's the Christmas spirit," Viktor said.

He plucked Robby's charm from Flake's trembling hand. It was as gray as a bloated fish. He tossed it in the bowl with the other charms, then stirred them like a potion. He selected a charm with his red chopstick fingers, held it like an egg. Colors swirled on the surface; tiny lights glittered inside it like the soul of something living.

That's her, Hiro thought.

"I'd like to wake up before the New Year," Haze said. "So anytime now, *Viktor.*"

Viktor was savoring the tension. His skull wasn't capable of expression—only the jaw moved—but Hiro could feel a smile somewhere in the cheekbones, delight in the dark sockets. He was too consumed with his own amusement, wallowing in untouchable power, to notice the thoughts Haze was hiding. If he'd taken a peek right then, he would have known why she *wanted* to wake up. If Viktor had known, the ending to this story would be quite different.

"I hope you enjoyed your time as a toy," he said.

"I'd rather wake up without Christmas than be a toy another

second." She barfed a load of candy for the last time. "I miss my family."

"I suppose you do, Ms. Melblank."

Viktor said her name with a hint of malice. The charm slipped from his fingers in slow motion. Landed with a damp smack. Flake flinched. A dull pang of remorse cut the air. It hurt him to feel dark clouds gobble up the vibrant color, like he was a virus sucking the life out until the charm was nothing more than a lump of alloy.

Haze was looking at Hiro when her little wings slowed. Her head whumped on the table and stayed there, kept her from sliding off the chair. Hiro was glad he didn't have to hear the grainy slap of her candy-filled belly hit the floor. Her eyes, though, stared at him like simple glass beads.

Hiro felt sick. He would've barfed candy.

"Are you sure they're okay, Viktor?" Stretch could feel the sickness, too. It polluted the air like an odor.

"Of course, Stretch. They're intruders from another world pretending to be toys. They're nothing more than puppets. We're sending them home. They're not really toys like you and Belkin."

Stretch's rubbery brows clenched. "What about you, Viktor?"

"What about me?"

"You're a toy like me and Belkin?"

"Oh, I assure you, I belong here." He took the dead charm from Flake. "I'll never leave."

Belkin was stiff with restraint. This whole thing pained him for another reason—a reason Hiro couldn't discern. He blazed with anger and resentment. It fueled Viktor's joy.

"Just one more," Viktor sang. "Ready to wake up in bed, little Hiro? Go back to school, do your homework and eat your vegetables?" He marched toward Hiro, *click-clack,* and drank the gloom with a straw. "I'll bet you miss your happy family."

"I haven't seen my mother since I was little."

Perhaps he would've said something pithy, like *you'll be on the naughty list for that,* or *your nose will grow for that one.* But Viktor looked terribly serious. He glared with menace. His irritation sent static charges through the room, making them all jump. Just a little. He could only muster three words in response to what Hiro said.

He said, "That's a lie."

Hiro started to say something, but instead let his memories float to the surface. He didn't want Viktor to see them. He wanted him to feel them.

The way his mother, once upon a time, had celebrated Christmas. She didn't buy things, she invented the gifts she gave her family, cobbled them together with glue and cardboard, twisted metal: reimagined a watering can as a fountain for the backyard, spent a week building a birdhouse from things in the attic. Her cards were graphic novels, each letter cut from a magazine or old novel covers. Everything she did was saturated with her essence.

She didn't walk into a room. She danced. She spun in a circle to greet the morning. She smiled at little things, like when a bird built a nest in the wreath on the door. She laughed at his father's jokes, not because they were funny.

Her outfits weren't the day's fashion. She paired them at resale shops, wore silk scarves just because, went barefoot all summer long, doodled tattoos with markers, made her own jewelry from wire and things in the garden.

She watched movies like a child seeing a cartoon for the very first time. She cried at the sweet things, shrieked at the scary things, hugged Hiro or his dad—whoever was nearest—and hid her eyes until someone told her it was okay.

And then Christmas went away. And all those things with it.

Viktor looked petrified. The joy of sending Robby and Haze home, once saturating him like indigo dye, had putrefied into sour bile. Pleasure transmuted into a palpable mixture of resentment.

"You *have* a mother," he grinded.

Hiro looked out the window, where snow was now falling in big fluffy flakes, the Ferris wheel churning sparkling lights, seats loaded with joy-drunk toys. He was going to wake up. Sadness would greet him. Not just his mother's sadness. A world with no Christmas that would become grayer and colder with each year.

A suffocating panic closed on him. A sense of hyperventilation made him dizzy even though he knew he wasn't breathing. *Heroes are scared, too.*

"Time to go home, little boy," Viktor said.

He spun on heel bones, marched with heavy clicks for the bowl. No singing or dancing this time, no celebrating this last execution. He couldn't wait to banish Hiro to a world without Christmas. His attention laser-beamed on getting rid of this insolent teddy bear who spoiled his big night. He wasn't thinking of anything else.

With his back turned, Hiro began to visualize something.

Viktor was reaching for the last living marble. Hiro felt his fingertips touch it, felt them like cold sticks. Viktor dropped the charm back in the bowl, stood up like a deer hearing a twig snap in the woods. He took a few steps down the table, looking out the window.

Belkin turned. He saw it, too.

"There's my girl." Viktor's smile—a joyous smile with a cruel bent—filled the room.

He stood at the end of the table like an Olympic diver, watching a purple monkey desperately scaling the house on the earthen pedestal. Viktor's impatience rubbed the atmosphere drily.

"Fetch her," he growled.

His soldiers cut through the crowd like shark fins. Lookies enclosed the house like the eye of a hurricane. The purple monkey looked around and reevaluated the situation, then scampered across the wall and over the edge, escaping down the earthen pillar to blend into the crowd. The lookies lost sight of her in a mob of pastel-colored puff balls.

Viktor's impatience hardened into an iceberg sinking under its own weight. When he turned around, there were three dead charms in the bowl. The fourth charm was already in Flake's hand. It was as dull and lifeless as a roofing nail.

The teddy bear was facedown on the floor.

33

I guess the teddy really wanted to go home.

His charm was in the elf's hand, as dead as the others. *They weren't dead.* Not dead-dead, in the human sense. Dead to this world they were, though.

It was the octopus who sent him home. I was too distracted to see him do it, but all it took was a quick skim of his thoughts to see what had happened. As I peeked into his thoughts, he shrugged his tentacles, muffling through the gag. *It's what you wanted, right?* he thought.

Right.

When I was watching Madeline skip around the gala, he had reached into the bowl and fussed about, had trouble picking up the charm. Almost knocked the bowl over. Then he dropped it into the elf's hand. The elf looked impossibly sad—which was bringing the energy in the room down—when Hiro Tanaka fell off his chair. He bounced around, an empty toy.

This night couldn't get any crazier, and the bar was already up there.

I had always assumed I wasn't the only one who dreamed their way here. Statistically speaking, there had to be some people from my world who went to sleep one night only to temporarily wake up a toy.

I thought I'd meet someone from my home world one day. *But my students?!*

I'd infected them. That was the only explanation. I'd somehow infected them with the idea, plain and simple.

Hiro had doodled the planet in class. I suspected he'd dreamed about this world, but he looked so clueless after class, like it was only a glimpse. Even if he found his way here, there was no way I would see him, not with several billion people and just as many toys. So I was wrong, he was here. But what are the odds he'd be sitting *in my room on the most important night of my life?!*

None to impossible was what they were.

He wasn't here anymore. Their little gambit failed, but I couldn't stop dwelling on it. My brain was in solution mode, that obsessive gear I couldn't get out of when something was unsolvable. It wasn't how they got here (*same way I did*) or when they got here. It was the *why* that possessed me. Not why were they on my planet (yes, *my* planet), but why were they at the gala? They were trying to stop me, it seemed. How long had they known about my nightly sojourns?

But then I saw Madeline in her monkey suit. It all made sense.

She recruited them.

That was the only explanation. How she did it, there wasn't time for that. Besides, once the roads were closed, it wouldn't matter.

The bigger question, and dumbest question, I obsessed over: *Why them?* Hiro, I sort of got. He was bright and creative. His mother was an art teacher. She was into dreaming and fairy tales, all things that would send a kid here. I could accept that. I guess. But Hazel and Robby? They were C students at their best. Why them?

Focus.

They were home, where they belonged. I could close the drawbridge that connected our worlds without a grain of regret. They didn't get hurt and wouldn't believe any of this in a few days. Even when I didn't return, this would just be a fading dream. *Just like Christmas.*

I released the gag from the octopus. I needed to hear him say something, get out of my own head.

"Hey, I thought you'd be happy. The boy wanted to go home. You were just playing with him—not in the good way—so I dropped his charm. He told me to. What'd you have against him anyway?"

I grabbed the lifeless charm from the elf's hand before he collapsed into depression. I didn't have anything against Hiro. He was just a student. A good one, actually. Followed the rules, kept quiet. My kind of student. But this was my world. He had no business here.

The octopus was right, though. I had been toying with them.

Why all the theatrics, marching up and down the table, not skimming their thoughts? Why didn't I just send them home as soon as I knew who they were? I knew the answer. That's the thing with being omnipotent. I knew everything about everyone. Including myself. I couldn't ignore the truths I hid from myself. Even the embarrassing ones.

It was this: *I wasn't that stiff teacher nobody liked.* I wanted them to see it. I wanted them to see I wasn't a failed physicist reduced to teaching high school. I wanted them to see me now. Plain and simple.

Sad.

"Question," Ocho said. "Why are you taking Christmas away from them? That's what you're doing, right? That's a very anti-toy thing to do. I mean, if you're going to—*mmmff.*"

Enough talking. Midnight was an hour away. *Focus.*

But look at the bright side. If I hadn't caught them sneaking around the gala, they never would have been sent home. The roads would've closed, and they'd be stuck here. Forever. I didn't want that. Just think of their parents. Taking Christmas away from them was one thing. Had they never left here, the guilt would've been unbearable.

So, in a way, I'm the good guy here.

I dropped Hiro's dead charm in the bowl. *The good guy.*

❇

MADELINE WAS on the run again.

"Enough games!" I went to the window, stood far away from Belkin. I didn't need his gloom piling on. There was already plenty.

She was spotted near the ice luge: a nifty ride the toys lined up for, sliding through loopty-loops and corkscrews. An all-time favorite. I'd spent a lot of time designing that one. And now the soldiers were running between the ice tubes like clumsy puppets. I needed to rethink my security team. They looked intimidating and official. What I needed was agile and effective. *Like a monkey!*

"She's running you in circles," Belkin said.

At least his spirits were rising. The room could use a little sunshine. Even if it was laced with sarcasm. Flake was a rainy day that never ended.

"You know, I was thinking of putting a fireplace in here." I pointed to Belkin's arms and legs. "We'll need kindling."

"That's not nice, Viktor," Stretch said.

"You're right, Stretch," I said. "Apologies."

Adding to the list of annoyances was that I couldn't *feel* Madeline out there. I sensed her presence, but I couldn't lock onto it. Once I did that, I could force her to march up to the room. No need for this game of hide-and-seek, which my bumbling security was losing. Did she come up with a new charm that eluded me? Her mother was talented, so it could be. If Madeline had some stealth charm in production, that would really put a crimp in my game.

Another lookie alert.

She escaped my stiff minions and made it to the twirl and whirl honey pots. The soldiers spun on their heels and knifed toward the spinning ride. They marched at full speed, stepping on anything in their way. Toys staggered in their wake, wobbling on the floor.

The monkey raced over upraised hands and flippers, avoiding the soldiers as if they were infants learning to walk. She bounced off a happy trampoline and vanished into a vat of balls. The soldiers climbed in and waded after her, stomping through a pack of baby dolls swimming in the ball pit.

"You're hurting toys," Belkin said.

"I'm not hurting them! If she would stop this, everyone can go back to having a good time. They're here to sing and dance, play games and... play games, that's it."

Freckles was oblivious to the chase, as was everyone else down there. He was bellowing a song from the top of the house, and the crowd joined him in glee. *Here comes Santa Claus...*

Freckles stopped crooning, quite suddenly, put his hand on his chest. Hearing my thoughts. The song continued with the crowd.

"A new game!" he crowed. "A new game you'll quite enjoy. Everyone, listen carefully. Somewhere in the arena is a scurrilous little chimp who doesn't want to be found. She is the hider, and you are the seekers. The first one to catch her receives a grand prize coveted by every toy in the valley. The winner will have their very own, brand-new *gingerbread mansion!* It features three floors, a solarium, an observatory deck, chocolate slides and peppermint poles. It's located on the tallest peak of Sugar Mountain in Winter Wonderland. If you just—"

I cut him short. Enough with the buildup. They were already looking.

"Find the monkey!" he shouted.

Work smarter, my father always told me. And constantly. Like all the time, waving his finger in the air. *Smarter! Smarter!* What would he think now, huh? Who am I kidding?

My soldiers went to the house and positioned their stiff-suited bodies around the base of the pedestal. I wasn't worried; there was nothing she could do. But if she ended up in the bubble with that tiny elf, I'd be depressed, and there was enough of that already.

"Work smarter," I told Belkin. He didn't like anything I said.

The crowd moved in random circles like bees tending honeycomb. Madeline wouldn't last with a mob ravenous to win their very own gingerbread house. Which didn't exist.

The crowd began to organize, swarming toward the sky pole drop. The pole, as stout and tall as a redwood, was a replica of a mast from an ancient ship. The horizontal booms, without sails, were rigged with rope netting. A bucket was on the masthead, where a climber could look across the arena.

The purple monkey scaled it with ease.

She didn't need a safety harness, climbing with the instincts of a gibbon. A flaw in my plan came into sharp focus when the crowd flooded the entry gate. Instead of a handful of toys working their way toward the top, they climbed by the hundreds. It looked like a zombie apocalypse.

There was probably a weight limit.

One of the beams snapped in half and swung like a timber pendulum. Ropes kept it from slicing through the mob below. One of the nets came loose; toys dangled like flies in a spiderweb. The monkey reached the bucket when the pole began to lean. I could hear wooden fibers splinter.

I calculated the height in relation to the house. It would land short. But a lot of damage would be done; that would put a damper on the night. Toys would be hurt. A lot of them. I'd never hear the end of it.

Down, I thought. *Down, down.*

Many of the toys listened to my command and climbed off the mast. But not all of them. The hysteria had whipped their minds into a frenzy that thwarted my control. Enough of them heeded the call to keep the pole upright.

Madeline had nowhere to go. I thought.

She leaped like a flying squirrel. It looked like a desperate attempt that would land her in some lucky so-called winner's grip. She caught a rope, then another and swung in a sweeping arch, releasing at its apex.

She landed on the barrel bomb.

The whiskey barrel was the size of a building, positioned on its side by twelve-inch axles. It was more like a tumbler for a titan game of Bingo. Madeline opened the hatch and crawled inside, where toys would run like mice on a hamster wheel. It was pointless fun that toys seemed to enjoy. I didn't get it, but they did.

"That should do it." Glee was back in my corner.

The crowd swarmed the barrel bomb. The hatch swung open, circling around but not stopping. It churned out of reach. That didn't stop the pursuit. Rubbery snakes slithered up the support beams. Plastic superheroes climbed after them. As the hatch came around, spring bunnies and pencil flamingoes launched themselves at it. The rest climbed up like starving hounds with a scent. A mountain of toys pressed against the barrel. They poured into the opening like honeybees following the queen. The barrel spun faster.

It began to wobble.

Stop!

The crowd jerked in response to my thought, but the momentum continued. Their minds too chaotic to grip. Like a snowflake in a storm.

The first bracket shattered with a bolt-shearing *kuchunk*. One end of the barrel thudded off the axle. The crowd roared. Actually, they cheered when the barrel started grinding sparks. Toys were pulled through it like a woodchipper. It gained traction and snapped off the other axle.

The barrel was set free.

The crowd parted. A path opened in front of the rogue carnival ride that was aimed at the house.

"Stop it!" I shouted. "Stop that barrel!"

The soldiers threw themselves into the steamroller. Their bodies splintered and snapped under its weight. Tattered uniforms and flattened hats spit out the other side. With each speedbump, the behemoth slowed. *Crunch. Boom. Kaplunk.* I fed the runaway cylinder twenty soldiers. When it slowed, the toys began pushing against it. Little by little, it stopped. But not before bouncing off the pedestal.

The house tremored. Snow fell from the eaves.

Oh my, I thought. *I know what she's doing.*

She was using all these beautiful rides as weapons to knock the house down. The pedestal looked like soil, but it was reinforced with internal beams. Even if the house was taken down, I had redesigned it. Beneath those wooden slats was a welded roll cage.

She's like her mother. But it's going to take more than a whiskey barrel.

And she's stuck inside it with thousands of greedy toys looking for a handful of purple fur.

The crowd began to shift its attention. They stopped mounting the barrel and began sweeping in the other direction.

"Ferris wheel!" they chanted. "Ferris wheel! Ferris wheel!"

What in the wide, wide world of winterland is happening?

The big wheel was slowly turning with toys who weren't able to get off the ride watching a purple monkey climbing through the spokes. They jumped out of their seats and slid down cables. The mob on the ground latched onto the outer structure and let it carry them up. Madeline had reached the center pivot and continued upward, leaping sideward to maintain a vertical ascent.

I found Freckles's mind in the fog, told him to call off the game. *Tell them there is no house! There is no house! There's nothing, they win nothing! Get them to STOP!*

His shouts were drowned out in the frenzy.

How did I not see this? I just wanted a party to celebrate my final countdown. I could've just sat up here with my depressed company and counted down the minutes in droll misery. Now I watched these wild playthings climb on top of each other like wolves.

The Ferris wheel spun faster under the weight of clinging toys. Madeline had reached the top, running along the rim to stay in place. No one could keep up with the dexterity required to reach her. I felt her looking at me as she ran in place, long purple tail swinging. That empty monkey that had lain in her bedroom all that time when I would wake up on the shelf was empty no more.

The Ferris wheel moaned like a ship listing in a storm. Cables snapped like gunshots. A shower of sparks fell from the axle. It wobbled as the bearings fell apart.

Scritchhh—KUNK.

It carved tracks into the floor. The titanic wheel began rolling with a purple monkey on top of it. The toys had forgotten about the fake prize, delighting in the world's greatest circus act. It was grinding its way toward the center of the arena, digging deeper into the floor. The wobble, however, turned it off course. It wheeled farther and farther away from the house, slowing in the grooves it cut into the floor.

It came to a stop far away from the chocolate-sided house and the grandest prize inside it. Madeline stood on top, a failed coup below her. We stared at each other over a long distance. I couldn't understand why I couldn't grip her mind. It should have been so easy. A smile germinated in my jawbone. A valiant attempt, it was time to put this madness to bed.

The rogue Ferris wheel moaned again.

It began leaning. Slowly, at first. This colossal round domino started its descent. Toys in its shadow scattered. Spokes shattered; cables popped away from the rim. In slow motion, it came crashing down. The buckets swinging at the top exploded into the side of the pedestal. The rim of the wheel buckled against it. Soil powdered from the side of it; shards of flooring geysered in a plume. The pedestal leaned to the side. It held in place.

But the house began to slide.

The foundation had come loose. Panels fell off the walls. Bricks from the chimney fell like broken teeth. It rolled off its place of high honor, hit the floor like a cube of die thrown across a gameboard. The house shed it façade like snakeskin—broken shutters, shattered doors, shingles, boards, bricks and even the mailbox. The house that Madeline grew up in splattered on the floor like New Year's Day.

All that was left was the skeletal frame.

The walls were gone, the rooms and beds, the kitchen. The fireplace. A cable remained tethered to a structure that held the needle piercing the glowing blue ball. The red-suited jolly fat man inside. Above him, where the roof used to be, a watery outline of a sleigh with animals tethered to the front of it.

A hush fell over the crowd, followed by a roar.

"Well," Stretch said, "I didn't see that coming."

❋

SHE FAILED.

That was the important point here. I'd reinforced the house. Santa wasn't coming out. All the critical equipment had been relocated, the extraction needle still intact. The switch to turn off the bubble was in a place she could never reach, and only I had access to that. And she failed. She failed. Failed. Failed. Failed.

"Out!" I shouted. "Everyone out!"

Stretch started to move.

"Not you. No one in this room moves. The party's over. I want everyone out of the arena!"

I doubled down my focus, moved my remaining soldiers into action. Doors around the arena slid open. Every light beamed on high, flooding the floor. Toys hid their eyes. I hit them with one single thought that would be obeyed. *OUT! NOW!*

"I'm cleaning this place up," I muttered.

"Do you need help, Viktor?" Stretch looked at the crumpled Ferris wheel. "It looks heavy."

"No, I don't need help, Stretch! This is not over. She hasn't won anything." I turned to Belkin. "Neither have you."

"You're the only one trying to win," Belkin said. "They're trying to save Christmas."

"For the last time, Christmas doesn't need to be saved! It's here, right here. We have it." I leaped up and down, chopping at the frozen Santa Claus and his reindeer and one miniature elf. "I'm giving the spirit of Christmas to the toys, making this world a better place, saving toys, blah, blah, blah. Why is everyone fighting me on this? What more do you want?"

"Not this," Belkin said.

I could smell his self-righteousness. "You think I'm the bad guy here?"

"You're not the hero."

The partygoers moved to the exits. I kicked their thoughts to make them go faster. Trucks hauled them out in clusters; soldiers goaded them away from distractions.

"There's still time." And that was my biggest problem. *Is midnight ever going to get here?* "If things are going to get done right, I'll do them myself."

Stretch said, "Do you need help?"

"No!"

I didn't need help. I never had help before.

34

Shloop. That was the elevator.

Hiro pretended to hold his breath. He wasn't breathing. He was a toy. He wasn't even a toy. He was a marble. *A charm.* But then, right then, he wasn't sure what he was. He didn't want to think about it. He was focusing on not thinking at all.

I'm not supposed to be here.

A lot of things went right. For one, Viktor didn't look closely at the teddy bear on the floor. Or the marble in the dish. If he had, he would have noticed it wasn't Hiro's charm Flake was holding.

The elevator didn't open again. Hiro's nose was against the floor. He couldn't feel Viktor in the room. Still, he waited before slowly getting up. Being soft and cuddly meant he moved in near silence. Robby and Haze were slumped in their chairs. Chase was on the table.

Ocho had his eye on him.

Hiro didn't know the octopus was capable of sitting that still. Hiro whispered a thought. *Thank you.*

Ocho nodded.

Flake dumped the marbles in the bowl. There were three plain ones. One, however, had regained life. It always had life. Hiro had just projected a dead image over it for Viktor to see. If he had examined it… but he didn't.

Belkin and Stretch were side by side, watching whatever was beyond the window.

It had felt like an earthquake had demolished the arena. It was quiet now. Hiro gestured to Ocho and Flake to join them at the window. Hiro quietly ran along the table, hiding next to Stretch's toy repair kit on the far end of the couch. He looked out the window.

It was worse than he thought.

The rides were in pieces. The Ferris wheel leaned on the pedestal like a wheel of a bike missing spokes and a tire. Patches of grass and clods of dirt were all that were left on the pedestal. The house was no longer a house. Pieces of wood and bricks and shingles were strewn next to a boxy frame. Inside was a bluish watery bubble.

"Let me take care of that for you."

Hiro heard Stretch's rubbery footsteps and deftly moved behind the couch. Stretch grabbed something from his kit, humming as he did, and went back to Ocho.

"Better?" Stretch said.

"A million times," Ocho said. "Some party, huh?"

"They played a game."

"Like running with the bulls?"

"No, it was called Find the Monkey. Was that what he called it, Belkin? They had to catch a monkey. She was fast. Ran to the top of the pole ride, then over to the barrel and then all the way to the top of the Ferris wheel. I don't think it went like Viktor hoped. A lot of toys were hurt."

Most of the toys were gone. The others were being herded to the exits by lines of soldiers. Besides pieces and parts dislodged from the rides, broken toys hopped in circles or crawled in crooked lines. They were being scooped into the back of yellow plastic trucks.

"Did they catch her?" Ocho asked.

"I don't think so. Did they, Belkin?"

There was a long pause. "They did not."

A small caped figure walked among the wreckage. The red gleam of

Viktor's skull appeared when the hood was thrown back. Freckles was on the ground now, helping soldiers load damaged toys into a truck. Viktor waved at the soldiers, sleeves falling back on red bones, pointing at the big barrel sitting askew on what looked like a pile of soldiers.

Toys were spilling out the barrel's hatch like they'd been packed like sardines. Soldiers helped them down, pointed toward the nearest exit. If a purple monkey came out, they were ready.

The game wasn't over.

"Viktor seems angry," Stretch said. "I've never seen him like this."

"I don't think the party went as planned," Ocho said. "I'm just guessing."

Viktor looked redder than a cherry bomb, waving his arms like an overcaffeinated conductor.

Soldiers ran in circles, which only turned him a deeper red. He sent them to the remains of the house. They set up a perimeter around the debris.

"Whoa," Ocho said. "Is that—"

"Santa Claus," Stretch said. "Viktor caught him a long time ago. Santa Claus travels inside a time bubble on Christmas. That's how he gets to all the girls and boys in one night. He gets to the next world through roads. Victor put Santa's bubble in a bubble. A double bubble. And Santa doesn't know it. See that?"

Hiro knew Stretch was pointing to the faint band of color attached to the bubble, swaying in an ethereal current. It looked like a heat wave losing temperature. In its last hour of breath.

A cadre of soldiers positioned themselves at the steel frame. They attempted to tip the entire thing up. Viktor pulled more from jobs of helping floundering toys until there were enough of the red-coated soldiers to heave it over. It teetered back and forth.

"Are those... *reindeer?*" Ocho said.

The bubble extended above what would have been the roof. That was what was in that fenced box on top of the roof. There were several blurry lumps in rows of two. And a big red cube. *Is that a sleigh?*

"Viktor caught them, too. That's why we're here, so we wouldn't stop him. He's closing the last road tonight. That's why the kids had to wake up."

"I don't get it," Ocho said.

"Their dreams brought them here through the roads. They're at home asleep. But if there's no roads, they wouldn't wake up. That's why Viktor sent them home."

"Hold on, back up. Brought them from where?"

"They're not really toys. They're from somewhere else."

"Somewhere else where?"

Stretch's rubbery shoulder squeaked when he shrugged. Belkin grunted.

"Okay. All right." Ocho moaned. "So what you're saying is that if one of them stayed, that would be *baaaad*."

"It would be terrible," Stretch said. "They'd never go home. Their parents would miss them. Right, Belkin?"

"And if someone helped them stay here, that would be bad," Ocho said.

There was a long beat of silence. It began to feel uncomfortable. Hiro didn't know what they were doing. He held very still. Clopping footsteps grew louder. Hiro moved to the back of the couch.

"Stay where you are." Belkin towered over him. "Everyone, come closer."

Stretch, Ocho and Flake joined the full-size puppet and surrounded Hiro. Stretch simultaneously looked happy and sad to see him. The conflicted expression occupied opposite sides of his face.

"*Ahhh!* What's he doing here?" Ocho said.

Pause. "We can see your thoughts, Ocho," Stretch said.

"Viktor can, too," Belkin said. "Come closer."

Hiro felt a calm quietness fall over him, a cloak weaved with protective thoughts. Belkin was expanding his mind to mask Hiro's presence should Viktor look at the room.

"Look, he asked me to do it," Ocho said. "He just said grab one of the dead charms, fumble around with it, and put it in the elf's hand. I didn't know he was going to stay."

"Is that what you said, Hiro?" Stretch said.

Hiro nodded. It wasn't exactly what he said. It was exactly what he meant. He'd phrased his thoughts vaguely enough that Viktor wouldn't notice if he looked at Ocho's thoughts. Which he did. Hiro had imagined a dull marble to mask his charm that was still in the bowl, made one of the already dull charms look alive, then fell on the floor when Ocho dropped it in Flake's hand.

"You can do that?" Stretch must have seen Hiro's thoughts. Good thing Belkin was hiding them. "Like be somewhere else? Have you heard of that, Belkin?"

The puppet didn't answer, but Hiro could feel his surprise. Belkin urged everyone to be still. They looked out the window. Hiro peeked between their legs. The toys had been completely evacuated. The soldiers were searching the rubble.

"I heard about your mom," Stretch said. "I'm sad she feels that way. I'm sad Viktor feels that way, too."

"What, happy?" Ocho said.

"Viktor isn't happy."

The little red skeleton's shouting could be heard all the way up there. Hiro could feel his anger like sparks on his fur.

Belkin looked down at Flake. "Send him back."

"I want to stay," Hiro said. "I can help."

"It was very brave, what you did," Belkin said.

"Very brave," Stretch added.

"We appreciate everything you've done," Belkin said, "but you need to go home before it's too late."

Flake shuffled his sandpaper soles on the floor and started for the table to fetch Hiro's charm. One touch and Hiro would open in his eyes in bed. That was the best-case scenario. Hiro looked at the big clock above the arena.

"The last road doesn't close for thirty minutes."

Flake moved slower. He could feel Hiro's heartfelt request. There was more at risk than Hiro getting stuck here and Christmas being lost forever. *Snow is inside the bubble.* Belkin sensed the elf's hesitancy and sent Stretch to fetch the charm.

"You're beautiful, Hiro." Stretch returned with the charm, admiring the depth of iridescence.

"Please," Hiro said. "I can't go back yet. This means more than Christmas."

"There's nothing more you can do," Belkin said.

Viktor was shouting Madeline's name, taunting her. Below the shards of his anger was a slimy layer of fear. He tried to stop her, and nothing worked. Now he was left with wreckage while his soldiers guarded the final fading road.

"So that's the plan?" Ocho said. "Just watch?"

"Viktor's pretty strong," Stretch said. "You wouldn't guess it because he's all bones, but he doesn't need muscle. If we went out there, he'd freeze our minds and make us look for Madeline. It doesn't feel good when he does that."

Flake heeded Stretch's warning, kept his thoughts under wraps. Instead, he pointed and grunted. The sounds were like a dog half-barking. But they had the vague semblance of a word.

"That's right," Stretch said. "Santa Claus is in there. He'd know what to do."

"I think he means his little buddy," Ocho said. "The one who lives in his hat."

"Oh, sorry. Viktor was right, though. Snow is safe. He's just caught in time. He'll come out one of these days. You know, if Viktor ever stops."

Stretch sort of faded off with what he was saying. Viktor was never going to let them out. if he did, the roads would reopen, and all would be lost. Snow might be safe, but he would be in there a really, really long time.

"This might sound obvious," Ocho said, "but has anyone thought of turning the bubble off?" He gestured to the looming walls of machinery behind them. "Let's just start pushing buttons. One of them has to work."

"It won't." Stretch sighed. "Viktor integrated that switch into his charm."

"Have you tried?"

"The charm is in Viktor's skull."

"Are you sure?"

Belkin, Stretch and Flake looked at him flatly. Even Stretch didn't answer. Viktor had godlike powers of the mind. He would sense them coming for him, freeze their thoughts and send them packing. Besides, how were they going to dig it out of his skull?

"So we just watch," Ocho resigned.

"Or play a game," Stretch said.

"I'd rather watch."

Belkin occasionally glanced at the clock. He wasn't going to let Hiro stay much longer. Hiro thought he could sneak behind Viktor by projecting down there. Problem with that was he couldn't touch anything when he was projecting. Even if he could, how was he going to get the charm out of his skull?

He could look for Mads. But hadn't her plan already failed? She had been able to destroy the house, but the bubble was still intact, and now it was guarded by a wall of soldiers with Viktor patrolling the outside. Even if she could rappel from the sky, she would just fall inside the bubble.

There was a third option.

❅

THE SOLDIERS WERE shoulder to shoulder. Their uniforms filthy from clearing debris. The greasy air choking with suspended particles of construction dust. Square mouths locked tight, severe eyes on alert.

No one noticed a soldier appearing out of dusty air.

Hiro was leaning against Belkin's leg, peeking over the edge of the window, just out of Viktor's sight, with an angle on the remains of the house. He imagined a crisply starched red jacket, knee-high black boots and a tall black hat. Now he was staring into the blue bubble. Energy pulsed electromagnetic waves, pushing and pulling like ocean waves lapping the beach.

Viktor was shouting behind him, taunting Mads to show herself, as toy trucks hauled broken toys away. Big plastic wheels crunched over broken parts and pieces.

Santa Claus wavered through the bubble's barrier, a figure trapped in an aquarium. Somehow the house was still intact inside the bubble: a lovely family Christmas forever preserved in the timeless moment.

The bubble extended to the shingled roof, where reindeer were tethered to a red sleigh spattered with gray snow. The reindeer in front was massive compared to the others, his head thrown back as if suspecting something. A second too late.

Hiro recalled what Corker had taught them about black holes.

Gravity and acceleration slowed time. If a spaceship could travel near the speed of light, the travelers inside the spaceship wouldn't age compared to their loved ones they left behind. They could circle the galaxy and return to a planet where everyone they knew would have already lived their entire lives. Generations would have passed. The same effect would occur if they approached the gravity of a black hole.

Is that what this is?

Snow was inside the bubble, hand up as if he just wanted to feel the membrane. Hiro could feel the energy inviting him to step inside. If he accepted, he might never come out. He might never see his family again. They would all be gone, having lived their lives without him. If he didn't go inside, his mother would live in a gray world that only grew grayer. Joy gone forever.

Heroes are scared, too.

His father had never mentioned the hardest part. It wasn't that it could be embarrassing, like wetting himself in fear, or it hurt so much he would cry. The hardest part was that he had to make a decision. There wasn't an obvious answer. It wasn't a yes or no question. He had no idea what to do.

No matter what he decided, someone was going to get hurt.

Hiro felt light-headed, shaky in the knees. This was only his projection next to the bubble. It might not even affect it. But if it did...

He pretended to take a deep breath and didn't think anymore. He didn't want to be a hero. He just wanted Christmas back. He leaned into the gravity of the blue bubble, felt it pull at his awareness. He was inches from touching it when he heard a voice.

Christmas lights burn so bright.

It seemed like a random thought, perhaps a toy rambling in song as the Sammy Scoopers scooped them into the trucks to haul away. It was nothing anyone would notice. If Viktor heard it, he would think nothing of it. But Hiro had heard someone say it once before.

And remembered who said it.

35

She'd played me like a chess expert.

She did this, and I did that. This move, that move, and the next thing you know, the house is in pieces. It was clever. She'd been planning this for years. Too bad it didn't work.

I'm a grand master.

I'd prepared for everything. I'll be honest, I didn't see the Ferris wheel move. But the house was indestructible. And the switch to turn off the bubble wasn't in there. After the little elf went looking for it, I was certain she was outplayed. Perhaps not certain, but pretty sure.

I sent the soldiers to the bubble. They lined up like good soldiers, forming a tight wall around the most valuable thing in the universe. The bubble didn't need their protection. Santa wasn't going to escape. I wanted to put on a show.

If Madeline was going to make another run, I wanted her to think it was the bubble she needed to attack. And really, truly, I did not want her falling into it like the little elf. I was hoping that, at some point in the distant future, we could talk. She would understand why I did what I did. It would take some time, sure. But I knew how to control time.

A convoy of Daryl Dump Trucks rumbled past me. Their real rubber tires with independent suspension cruised over cables and struts strewn in the wreckage. They stopped for loading. I picked a plastic eye off the ground. It was cracked, but the black disk still rolled around. Ricky Robots tossed toys into the back that couldn't walk or dance or roll out of here. I'd send them to the nearest warehouse for repairs.

This was a tragic waste of a good time.

I searched for Madeline's mind, trying to lure her out with memories. I dusted off some goodies from when she was young: Lying on her bed and watching videos on her laptop while I sat on the shelf. Finding the last piece to the puzzle and all of us holding it as we snapped it in place. And the snow angels we made in the front yard, the snowmen in the back. The snowball fights with the neighbor kids and the parents joining in. Afterwards sitting at the kitchen table with hot chocolate. Madeline sipping it. I put my fingers in it.

"Are you happy?" I shouted. "You know, those toys were lucky winners. They were having the time of their lives." I tossed the googly eye into a truck. "I built this—all of this—for them."

Something cracked. I was standing on a Jilly Jammer lollipop. It was one of those multicolored wheels on a stick Jilly Jammer carried in one hand like a magic wand. It would light up when the switch on her back was turned on. I picked it up. Jilly was probably in one of the trucks.

"You didn't have to do this," I said.

"You weren't going to stop."

I whirled like a Terrible Tommy Top. The lollipop flew from my hand and landed at her feet. There she was in a worn-out coat and awful leather boots. Dark hair with hints of gray cropped at hunched shoulders, she cast a wrinkled and sorrowful look my way. Like it hurt to see me.

Was it because I hadn't changed, not one single bit, since I slept on her shelf? I looked better, to be frank. Shined and oiled, not one squeak from a single joint in the last ten years.

I couldn't say the same for Madeline.

She wasn't twenty feet away, and I still couldn't feel her mind. She felt empty, like she wasn't there. I didn't like that. If she was smart, she would've taught everyone else how to be invisible to me, and we wouldn't be standing in a graveyard of carnival rides. Not exactly how I'd want it to end, but this invisibility trick was stellar.

A purple tail snaked around her neck. The goofy monkey face peeked over her shoulder. And here I thought she'd switched into it. Apparently, she woke the monkey up. *Didn't see that move, either.*

"I see you still have a pet," I said. Monkeybrain stared with the permanent grin I'd seen every time I woke up on the shelf. "Why can't I see your thoughts?"

"Years of hiding and meditation. Becoming nothingness so you see nothingness." She buried her hands in her pockets. "I learned from the best."

I didn't like not seeing her hands. "How are Polly and Philip these days? I didn't keep up after them, as you know. I did look after the house until, uh... you know." I gestured to the remains of her childhood home. Which she had destroyed.

"They passed away."

"I'm sorry to hear that."

I was sorry. It was just I already knew they'd passed away. Natural causes. I'd kept track of them. Madeline, though, had disappeared at some point. Changed her name, learned to meditate, hid her mind and planned my ultimate destruction. Still, I was sorry.

"No, you're not. They adopted you, opened their home. Made you family. They knew you were different, that somehow you didn't belong here. You broke their hearts, Viktor. The guilt was too much."

At that very moment, I was thrilled not to feel her thoughts. The weight would've crushed me. If she was smart, she would open the floodgates and drown me in shame.

"I never meant to hurt them," I said. "Or you."

"It's not too late." She waved at the soldiers and the blue bubble they protected. "You can return everything."

She snapped her fingers. It didn't make a sound. I thought maybe she never learned to snap.

"You know I can't."

"You can, Viktor. The spirit isn't ours. Look what it's doing to the toys."

"It gave Monkeybrain life. So, you're welcome."

The purple monkey didn't thank me. If I hadn't released an abundance of Christmas spirit, Monkeybrain would still be an empty puppet in the corner of a room. *Why didn't she call it verve?*

"Christmas spirit only works when it gives," she went on.

"It's working just fine." *Depends who you ask.*

"It can't be bottled like magic potion. When the last road closes, you don't know what will happen."

"Well, (A) that's exactly what I've done for the last thirty years. And (B) I'm not going back! Don't you get it? That's what this is all about. It's always been about staying here. You know where I go when I sleep. Your mother knew, too. You don't know what it's like back there. I'm not like this. I'm just... I'm not." I dropped my voice to a grinding whisper. "I'm staying here. I deserve it."

"You can always come back."

"You're not listening. I don't want to go back! Ever! This is who I am, right here, right now. I'm a toy. I've always been a toy. I'm not..." I waved my arms. "Back there, *home,* that's not who I am."

I was getting emotional, which meant one thing: she was hitting a deep pocket of truth. I was gushing, and she hadn't moved. Her hands still in her pockets.

"You're hurting so many," she said.

"You know, I think I'm good with this conversation. I get it, people at home are sad without Christmas and blah, blah. Guess what? I was sad my entire life, and no one came riding up to my door to save me. I promised to make this a better world for toys, and that's exactly what I'm doing, just like your parents wanted. I'm doing it, me."

I whacked my sternum. Vertebrae rattled.

"You'll never be a real toy." That cut deep. Why didn't I just keep my mouth shut? "You are you, Viktor. That's who we loved."

I planted my hands on my pelvis because I didn't know what else to do. She meant that. I didn't have to see her thoughts. It was a bullseye. But a little too late. Maybe if there was more time, we could rebuild the house, and I could sleep on the shelf. I could rebuild the village. No one would know what I'd done. And those who did would understand.

Belkin and Stretch were looking down at me from the window. That orange octopus, too. They would forgive me if I made things right. Probably not Belkin, but the others would. I did it for the toys. It was always for the toys. And for me, but the toys, too. If she would've said those things earlier, I might have changed my mind.

But probably not.

Loose bolts danced between my feet. The ground began to tremble. Black boots circled us like a snake trapping its prey. The soldiers locked arms. I had them do that: abandon the bubble and form a wall around us. Monkeybrain hid behind her back. There was nowhere to run now.

"I'm sorry," I said. "You'll be safe, Madeline."

Monkeybrain felt the trap close around them. The little monkey couldn't hide all night. I'd put them in the room with Belkin, let them watch me ring in Christmas morning and the closing of the last road.

But then Monkeybrain was quicker than a real monkey. She bolted from behind Madeline and, before I could blink, was through the legs of one of my soldiers. They were solid and dependable and as slow as midnight snow.

"That's all right." I stopped them from another fruitless pursuit. "She can't do anything now."

The purple furball perched on the crooked rim of the Ferris wheel like a fuzzy gargoyle. She could tear the place apart, drive wrecking balls through the arena walls, light the soldiers' dumb hats on fire. I didn't care. After midnight, I was locking the bubble in a vault and retiring the train. No more parties. No more people, no more toys. This place would become a museum for no one to see. And I would live happily ever after. The end.

Then the second monkey appeared.

PURPLE AND JUMPY like the other one.

She popped up from behind Madeline's back. I didn't know how she was doing it. She wasn't wearing a backpack. Maybe they were stuffed down the back of her sweatshirt. The second one avoided the soldiers' clumsy attempts to grab her and zigzagged to the broken barrel ride.

"Are you finished?" I said.

She wasn't.

A third one dropped on the ground. Okay. Maybe two monkeys were stuffed in that sweatshirt. Not three. No sooner had the third one scampered over a soldier's tall hat than a fourth one stood on Madeline's head. A fifth one leaped clean over the soldiers and rolled away. I stopped counting after that. They dispersed like a toy dispenser was strapped to her backside.

They felt invisible. Just like Madeline.

The place was overrun with grape apes, and I couldn't sense a single one of them any more than the girl—now a woman—I knew thirty years ago. They didn't appear to be after anything. They swung about like monkeys on a liquid diet of espresso. They ignored the bubble.

I approached Madeline. I should have done it earlier, but what would that have changed? I didn't suspect what I soon discovered. She didn't flinch when I reached for the hem of her sweatshirt. I wanted to see what was behind her. I discovered, in that instant, why I couldn't feel her presence, couldn't pick her thoughts. She wasn't there.

My hand passed through her. "How are you—"

Mount Monkeybrain erupted from somewhere behind her. Hundreds of them. Thousands, maybe, poured from an endless monkey geyser, flooding the grounds. They passed through the soldiers like ghosts, and the dummies chased them like cats after lasers.

"No! No, no, no—get back here. Now!"

They stuttered. I had to focus to cut through the confusion and bring them back. They formed a double wall around me. Whatever Madeline was up to with her monkey show, they weren't getting to me. I looked at the clock. There wasn't much time left.

Let Madeline have her fun. She wasn't going to distract me. I didn't know how she was doing it. But, in hindsight, this was all part of the plan. I see that now. The confusion, the ghostly projection.

It kept me looking in the wrong direction.

I peeked between pillars of uniforms. Monkeybrains were running a game of ring-around-the-rosy, their long arms locked. The last road was a faint ribbon of color. The bubble was glowing brighter. I didn't understand what they were doing, like some sort of magic dance. It couldn't possibly do anything. Maybe she had figured out some sort of energy vortex to open a hole in the bubble. Christmas spirit would burst out.

Then it started to happen. My worst fears came to be.

I crawled halfway between the soldiers and curled my legs against my chest like the very first day I woke up in this boney costume. The monkey dance suddenly stopped. A break in the chain opened. It happened.

A red-coated fat man stepped out.

Santa Claus looked around, stretched his arms like he'd been asleep for thirty years. He patted his fat stomach. Something leaped down from the house. An immense rack of antlers dropped in front of him. The biggest of all the reindeer kicked a metal rod across the floor like it was made of plastic (it didn't make a sound, but the ringing in my head was too loud to hear it), raised his head and snorted the dusty air. He was the size of a delivery truck. Black shiny rocks for eyes scanned the arena.

How did he escape? I wondered. Then I thought, *Wouldn't the Christmas spirit spill out?*

Those were all logical thoughts. And if I weren't in a full-blown meltdown, I would've realized it was impossible. I was petrified, holding as still as possible so Santa and his giant reindeer wouldn't notice me.

It was obvious where I was. The monkeys all pointed, just in case.

Santa with his hand on the reindeer's snout, the only thing keeping that beast from scattering the soldiers like bowling pins, walked towards me. The monkeys raced around like gnats hovering over a compost pile. He walked through a blizzard of purple fur and took a knee. The reindeer stood over him and snorted.

"Viktor Corker," he said with a deep voice.

Viktor Corker? He was mixing names. I was Viktor here, not back home. He must have been confused. Maybe the bubble fogged his brain. *I broke Santa.* The giant reindeer stared at me. I sounded like a bag of loose bones.

"I see you, young man," he said. "I see who you truly are. It's not this. Joy belongs to no one. It must be free. Give it away and it is yours forever."

He held out a white-gloved hand. He placed a telescope on the ground. It was the same model I'd gotten for Christmas when I was twelve years old. The black and white finderscope mounted on top. The eyepiece angled into the forward zenith mirror. Focusing wheel above the adjustment lever.

So I could see the universe.

How many times had I sat in my bedroom watching the stars? And the times I took the telescope onto the roof after my father was asleep and nearly fell off without him knowing. Those were the times I didn't feel the loneliness, that someone else was out there. All those stars and planets, was there someone looking back and feeling the same thing?

I wanted to crawl out of hiding and into Santa's lap. My father never let me do that like the other kids. I'd completely forgotten about the clock and fading road, lost in the buzzing monkeys and dizzy thoughts. I looked past Santa and the reindeer.

I stopped chattering. I thought, perhaps, it was wishful thinking. What I saw. The bubble was in plain sight. The watery wall was unbroken. I could see a red coat inside it. I counted the reindeer on the roof. They were all there, inside the bubble. Including the big one.

I looked at Santa in front of me, the reindeer standing over him. *I can't feel them.*

In the empty chaos, I finally felt a presence. Someone was coming for me.

36

In the shadows of long, tall soldiers, Viktor the Red was quaking.

Hiro watched him between stilted legs. It was difficult to hold the image of Santa Claus while also running copies of Monkeybrain running around. Each monkey pulled his focus thinner. And then Santa Claus. The reindeer was Hiro's idea. For some reason, he thought an angry monster would intimidate Viktor. Viktor was in cringe mode. But it wasn't because of the reindeer.

Hiro felt his pain.

It was the fear of losing everything he ever wanted. Now he was all by himself, boney arms buckled around sharp shinbones. Seconds away from popping a thumb in his mouth. Without lips or a tongue, he'd gnaw on it. If Christmas weren't on the line, Hiro might feel sorry for him.

Hiro had Santa Claus keep his hand out, although if Viktor tried to take it, then the jig was up. His bones would pass right through it. Hiro would think of something if he reached for it.

Mads didn't say what was next, just to keep the Monkeybrains running and Viktor distracted with Santa Claus. *Check.* But time was coming off the clock. The last road was fading. Something had to happen. And then it did.

Not what Mads was planning.

Viktor looked at Santa Claus. His focus went beyond him. Hiro thought he was looking up at the reindeer, but then he stopped trembling. Viktor didn't have eyebrows. If he did, they would have arched. If he had eyes, they would have squinted. Hiro realized what he was seeing, and it was too late to block his view.

Santa and the reindeer are still in the bubble!

A monkey came soaring over a wall of soldiers—arms and legs spread out. It wasn't one of Hiro's monkeys.

The fuzzy bomb dropped into the center of the soldiers—all of whom quit trying to grab the monkeys—and hit the ground rolling. Hands out and thumbs together, she darted for Viktor. Her thumbs stiffly contacted the back of his skull.

Something clicked.

Viktor snapped his boney fingers around the purple arms like a bear trap. All the quaking, fearful energy shed from him like a useless exoskeleton. His mind clamped down on the mind inside the fluffed and stuffed monkey caught in his grip. Hiro could feel Mads's thoughts trapped inside it.

So that was the plan.

She hadn't told Hiro what she was going to do, just to create chaos. It would be enough confusion for her to get close.

The soldiers parted.

Hiro could feel Viktor's smile all the way in the room.

"Enough!"

All the Monkeybrains vanished except the one he held like a trophy fish. With his other hand, he reached behind his skull. A small door had opened where Mads had pushed her thumbs. It wasn't deep enough. The charm did not release from it. The charm that was Viktor.

It snapped closed. *So close.*

Hiro maintained the Santa image. If Mads had something else

planned, it had to happen in the next couple of minutes. Viktor pried open her mind to sniff out everything she knew. Hiro could feel his gaze sweep through the room. Viktor laughed a knowing laugh, glanced up at Belkin. Hiro felt his eyes fall on the teddy bear peeking over the edge.

"Gently now." He handed Mads to one of his soldiers. "She and I still have a lot of catching up to do. Like that, good."

The soldier snuggled Mads into the starched crook of his uniformed elbow. Mads was a lump of paralyzed fur.

"You can put away the costume, Hiro." Viktor passed his hand through Santa. All the cards were on the table. Dealer wins. Viktor tapped his chin pensively. "I'm torn. You see, I have no idea how you did this—the monkeys and the Santa. The reindeer. I was fooled. And I know everything. That's no small feat, young man."

His mood had improved.

"Here's the thing. In two minutes, the last road closes. I need you to stay because, well, the little magic show you put on is of interest to me. But that would mean you never go home. See my predicament?"

"I know who you are," the Santa said.

"I said enough with the Santa! I don't have time to march my bones up there. Get down here now."

Hiro transformed the Santa into a teddy bear. It was only a projection, but somehow, he felt vulnerable showing his true self. *I'm not a toy,* he reminded himself.

"You don't know who I am," Viktor announced.

"Mr. Corker."

"No!" Hiro felt his anger up. "You know the teacher. That's all you know. I am Viktor the Red. *I am a toy!*"

"How can you do this to our home?"

"*Your* home, Hiro. No one knows Christmas is gone. *You* didn't know what happened until you came here. Suffering works that way. If you don't know what you're missing, you call it life. And that's it. That's life."

"My mother is not the same."

"Maybe she was always that way. You didn't realize it."

"No. She wasn't." Hiro tried to sound brave.

Viktor shrugged his pointy shoulders. "Injustice will always exist. Even if there was still Christmas, someone would be unhappy. I know that side of it quite well, Hiro. This way"—he swung his arms at the destruction all around—"I get life the way I want it. Sorry if others have to suffer a little."

"You won't be happy here. You'll still be you."

"Listen, you tweeny toad. I did my time there. I schooled, worked and slept and woke up and did it again, day after day after day. I did what I was supposed to do. I lived a life. Now I want one."

He wanted to grab the teddy bear by the fluffy arms and shake some sense into him. Hiro could feel his mind reaching for him. Belkin did his best to shield him. It still hurt. Thoughts could be arrows.

Viktor looked at the clock. "You know what? Just go home. I don't want you reminding me of home. Go be with your mother and father. You can hand your schoolwork to a poor substitute. I don't care."

"What'll happen to you? Like, at home?"

"Go home, Hiro." He rattled his fingers at the window. "Merry Christmas."

"There won't be Christmas. I'll forget."

Viktor nodded. He paced among his soldiers like an undersized general with an oversized ego. The soldier holding Mads took a knee for him. Viktor stroked her fur. "Do you know why toys say *merry, merry*? It has nothing to do with Christmas, Hiro. It's a toy thing; you wouldn't understand. It means find joy in everything, not just presents or eggnog or a dead tree in your living room. Go home and find joy in whatever. It doesn't have to be Christmas."

He looked at the bubble. Santa and the reindeer were still frozen inside. The last road was barely visible.

"Freckles! Start the countdown!"

The big orange cat appeared on a trapeze above them. The pseudo-voice of what all the other toys thought was Viktor the Red started counting down from sixty. Freckles's amplified voice sang the numbers.

"Goodbye, Hiro."

Hiro felt Viktor's thoughts shift in the room. Flake turned from the window and started toward the table. Hiro abandoned his imagination—his image vanished from the arena—and ran to stop the shuffling elf from reaching the bowl where one last charm glittered with life.

"Flake, stop. Just—there has to be something we can do."

"You must go home," Belkin said. Viktor might have stripped him of power, but his voice still carried authority. "Before it's too late."

He was right. Of course he was. But it couldn't end like this. Waking up in his cold bedroom. Mother staring out the kitchen window as if she'd lost count of the gray days. Viktor couldn't win. Not because home would get more cheerless, and life would become a dead weight. No one was going to win.

Not the toys. Not Viktor.

He was alone down there with his stiff soldiers. This world was going to crush him with loneliness. He would find himself exactly where he was at home with all the pain and guilt of what he'd done to the universe. And he wouldn't be able to take it back.

"Twenty, nineteen…"

"You are very brave." Stretch retrieved the glowing charm from the bowl.

He held it over Flake's outstretched hand. Hiro didn't feel brave. And staying would hurt his mother even more. It was time to go. Even if it was gray, it was still home. Hiro turned to the window.

Viktor held out his arms to savor the last drops before victory.

Hiro summoned the last of his courage, prepared to mutter his final word in this strange and wonderful world. He was about to nod to Stretch to drop his charm into Flake's hand when a shift occurred.

The vise of Viktor's thoughts evaporated.

Hiro's last word unexpectedly shocked Stretch into holding onto the charm.

"Wait!"

Viktor collapsed. As if marionette strings had been severed, he crumpled into a pile of red bones.

"Five!" Freckles shouted.

Belkin put his hand on the window. Mads sprang from the soldier's arms. They swiped at her and missed. She hit the ground and pounced on the sleeping bones.

"Four, three..."

Her thumbs to the back of his skull.

"Two..."

The secret hatch opened.

"One—"

❄

Darkness.

A switch cut the power on the lights above the arena. The room Hiro and the others were trapped inside went quiet. The whir of the machines and blinking lights turned off.

The last of the lights came from the charms strung above the arena, the bright little objects that had cast the warm goodness of Christmas spirit on the toys. When the toys had been there. When the party had been on. Apparently, there was no switch to shut them off. They simply began to dim.

If they looked closely, they would see that the lights were dying: the luminescence leaked out like foggy essence, swirling into the darkness until they glowed no brighter than fireflies.

And then they too were out.

Darkness was complete and as quiet as a mouse. The stars weren't shining. Even the bubble had been snuffed out. Hiro was unsure of what had happened and afraid to ask. *Is it too late to wake up?* He still had a furry body with short arms and legs and no fingers or toes. He tried to blink.

Colors started swirling.

A mass of every color on the spectrum squirmed in a giant ball on the floor of the arena—a swarm of iridescent snakes writhing and twisting. It began to swell, inflating as one glowing snake gave rise to two, then four, then eight. A psychedelic blob swallowed pieces of the carnival rides that had fallen.

The kaleidoscope passed over Viktor. He lay still on the ground. The hatch on the back of his skull was dark and empty. Mads was gone, running off, Hiro assumed, with the charm she'd snatched after Viktor suddenly and unexplainably collapsed.

Belkin and Stretch flickered in the colorful light, their reflections in the window appearing and disappearing. Stretch held Hiro's charm in a clenched fist. Flake pressed both hands on the glass; the brim of his hat crumpled against the window. Ocho was as still as Hiro had ever seen him.

The light felt good.

It was warm and dense, radiating in waves that penetrated their bodies. Hummed in their charms. Like a smile beamed on radio waves, Hiro could feel it grow inside him. It was the same feeling from the charms, but different. It was fuller. *Free.* It elicited looks of wonder from everyone in the room. Even Belkin, somehow with his wooden face, appeared to smile. There was nothing natural about what they were experiencing, yet they knew exactly what it was.

Flake yipped in surprise.

He hopped on those giant, scratchy feet and tapped on the window. Far below, something scurried from the ball of light—under the debris and around Viktor. He was the size of a mouse wearing a green coat and a floppy hat.

The bubble was consumed by the ball of lights. The larger it grew, the louder it hummed. They could feel it coming through the floor, vibrating in their legs (and tentacles). It revved like a supersonic engine preparing for departure. The window began to quiver.

Hiro felt thinner. He wondered if the others could feel it, too. Like he was losing his grip. He tried to say something, but the words were too heavy. His thoughts disintegrated like snowflakes passing over a hot griddle. When he tried to move his arm, it stayed by his side.

The lights began to dim.

He wondered if they were truly dimming, or was it just him? The others didn't seem alarmed, but they were also just as still. Could they not move either?

The magical moment was punctuated by jolly laughter. It came from the ball of lights and everywhere at the same time.

Ho-ho-ho.

There was a pause. A blip.

And then came the silent explosion.

They were in the center of a galactic fireworks show. Lights blasted through the walls and down into the floor; they wriggled into the sky and beyond. It was the magician's trick of never-ending scarves pulled from the sleeve—an endless display of lights spreading into the universe.

The roads!

Hiro wanted to celebrate, to jump up and down and shout it from the top of the world, to hug the others, high-five them, kiss them. The roads were free again. Why wasn't everyone singing? Hiro felt like a shadow. Belkin looked down at him, then at the others. The wooden puppet knelt in front of him. For the first time, the big painted eyes felt kind.

"Thank you," he said.

The charm was still in Stretch's hand. Flake waved an empty hand at Hiro. Ocho's tentacles wriggled.

"Goodbye, Hiro," Stretch said.

No, Hiro wanted to say. *Wait,* he wanted to say.

He faded in no direction, free of the fuzzy teddy bear. The light and all its glory slowly dimmed into dimensionless slumber.

37

Completely and utterly flabbergasted.

I should've been asleep for another six hours. At the very least, until the countdown was over. The roads would be closed.

I would never wake up again.

The Christmas spirit would be forever trapped inside the bubble, siphoned a drop at a time and dispensed to make a world of happy toys. Not girls and boys. The spirit was the rarest essence in reality; it would exist only on this world. My world. It would be all mine.

Remember what I told you in the beginning? Right.

It's with great shame and unfathomable guilt that I tell you, without question, I would've done it. I would have counted off those seconds till the last road closed, and swum in my own personal pool of Christmas spirit if they didn't stop me. The weight of this shame may lessen with time, but it is a weight I will always carry. I would have sentenced the universe to joyless days and dark nights for eternity with nothing to celebrate but the daily grind.

No Christmas ever.

Was I intoxicated by power? I was untouchable, all-knowing, and beyond harm. I was hammered drunk.

Power corrupts. I was not immune.

Blame me for my weakness, for my insatiable greed and callousness. I will not deny your accusations. They're true, all of them, in black and white. I thought absolute power would ease my struggle with who I thought I was and the burden I had carried all my life. No matter where I turned, I was always there.

No matter how I tried, I could not escape myself. I had studied books, honed my intelligence, became the person I thought I was supposed to be. And yet there was always something wrong with me, under the surface.

Power didn't rid me of my shortcomings. It only fueled them.

The emotional hole that I walked a tightrope over grew wider and deeper. It was bottomless, unfillable, no matter how many things or how much power I tossed inside it. It swallowed them like a black hole, belching sour fumes of guilt and disgust. If I dared a peek over the edge, I could hear it humming, could see its walls papered with snapshots of childhood.

I digress.

I had just caught Madeline and was counting down the seconds. Freckles, my simpleton servant, had joined me when I felt the fade of waking upon me. A drifting of sorts. Here one second, in my bed the next. That's how it usually goes when I wake up.

Not this time.

I was rising like a bubble. I attempted to fly back to my red bones, to reenter the dream, but was snatched like a pigeon in midflight by a bird of prey. The talons were soft and kind. This is just an analogy. I wasn't a pigeon. There was no hawk or cuddly talons. There were no images at all, just the sensation of being yanked sideways into another dimension altogether—not sleep, not waking.

I'd slipped through a fissure in time.

My imaginary hawk flew me into the throat of the cavernous black hole I'd been trying to fill. It was humid, at first. Dank. Earthy odors quickly turned fetid and rank. The air, if that's what you want to call it, was soupy. It clung to me in a film. Layer upon layer calcified around me until I was encased in a shell of the stuff.

And deeper we went.

I say *we* because I was certain it wasn't just me on this mystery journey. The air was raw. Sensations felt like cold water on a fresh wound. Sounds were all around, someone speaking garbled nonsense in sharp tones. Images, like snippets of video, flashed by, accompanied by base emotions. Simple emotions uncluttered by thoughts. Raw sensation.

I was desperate to wake in my bed, at this point. Anywhere but here would've been greeted with tears of joy. I was fully aware of what I'd done. Perhaps this was penance. The truth was laid bare. I was very bad at the core, and that was where I was being taken. To the core of who I was.

I started screaming.

It was the first sound I was able to make. It came out in a long, shrill whine until I was empty. My chest inflated, and another wail released. I did this over and over, again and again and—

I was back.

Like I'd snapped my fingers, I was back in my little body. The world was big, and I was small. Briefly, I thought I'd clawed my way back to my red bones. But there were no bones or broken Ferris wheels. There were walls and a ceiling. I was surrounded by bars. These weren't round and metal. I know what you're thinking, and I thought the same thing. I deserved the round and metal kind of bars. These were plastic and flat.

And I was wearing a diaper.

I stood up and fell on my cushioned fanny. I pulled myself up and looked between the bars. The room was small and empty except for the crib and unpainted dresser. No mobiles churning over me or pictures of clowns on the wall.

Without thinking, my thumb went into my mouth.

The rhythmic suction soothed the anxiety. The garbled sounds I'd heard on the way here were in the next room. Something heavy hit the wall. My instincts were to crawl under the blanket and suck my thumb until it pruned. But the emptiness of the room was howling. Anywhere felt better than here.

My toddler legs were rubber, as toddler legs are, and I threw it on top of the rail. I fell on the carpet with a padded whump of the sodden diaper. It felt very much like walking for the first time when I was a toy. I quickly caught on and wobbled across the hall.

There was a very big bed in the next room. A present sat on the edge of it. It was wrapped in glittering paper with a fat red bow. I couldn't take my eyes off it, even with two giants in the room.

One of them was my father.

He was quite a bit younger. Hints of gray tinged his sideburns. His glasses were different. He wore a V-neck T-shirt, white. It was untucked over black slacks, and he was barefoot. He was still speaking nonsense. It wasn't a language of any kind. It was just sounds. And the sounds were sharp and forceful, like sledgehammers flying out of his mouth.

He punctuated each sentence with a stiff finger aimed at the woman. I didn't recognize her. A warm, melting sensation stirred in my belly. I ached to run to her, but I'd have to get past my father. Her eyes were red and glassy, set in pockets of a full, round face. I could smell her from across the room. *Mother.*

I started to cry.

I couldn't stop it; it was undeniable. Like pressure in a keg that was going to blow. The release valve cried. My mother looked at me. My father stepped between us. His volume, previously at a nine, went to a twelve. They chiseled at her, chipping away piece after piece. How much longer before she was reduced to rubble? My mother continued stuffing clothes in a bag.

Red-faced, my father grabbed the present and began shredding the paper. My mother tried to stop him. He tore the box open and shook the contents at her. I wished I knew what the sounds he was making meant. Whatever he was saying, he took it out on the present, flinging it against the wall. A picture fell off the dresser and shattered.

He stormed out of the room.

My mother stopped shoving things into the bag. Her face was so heavy. She wiped her eyes, bent down to pick up what my father had thrown. She knelt in front of me. It was a toy. And it was for me. I don't remember that toy because I wouldn't have it long. My father would throw it away the next morning. But it made sense as she wrapped my arms around it. It was firm but soft. It was red. Bones were outlined on fabric arms and legs filled with stuffing.

A happy smile on the face.

And then I was back in my room with the crib and the dresser. Thumb in my mouth and a soggy diaper on my butt. I don't know how long I was in there. Plenty long to run out of tears. My cheeks were raw. My father stomped into the room with heavy black shoes and swept me up with the comfort of a construction worker. He dropped me in the crib and tore the red toy out of my arms.

I found a reserve of tears. They didn't last long.

He left the room and returned to pull my thumb out of my mouth. He wiped something as thick as axle grease on it and pointed his finger at me, said some garbled words. Then he left.

I was alone again.

Alone for a very long time.

No amount of crying brought my mother back.

Snot ran down my chin. I washed away in a saline flood, out of the crib, out of the room. The house. But I couldn't escape the feeling that howled from the emotional black hole. There was something wrong with me. *That's why she left.*

I wish I could tell you that was the end of that. If I would've had my way, I would have gladly woken up and sworn never to return to the world of toys. Which is a lie. That was probably why the trip continued. I won't bore you with the stops we made. More memories, more fights. Name-calling, shame, disappointment. A lifetime of it. I saw it all, felt it all.

Time didn't flow. I was just there, wherever that was.

I know what you're thinking: I woke up in bed a changed man. I learned from my mistakes; the black hole was filled. I danced out of my house singing merry Christmas to my neighbors.

Change isn't that easy.

The emotional hole wasn't filled with tears and happily ever after. It didn't fill up. It's a bit of a contradiction, but suddenly the hole wasn't there. Like it had never been there in the first place. And that's when I began floating. A bubble seeking the surface.

I was greeted by people in uniforms with rough hands. To their utter confusion, I burst into tears. For the very first time, I was happy to be awake.

38

Sleep was a bed of wet sand. Weighty, sticky.

He was comfortable down there in the cold deep. Motionless, he rested in the timelessness of sleep, unaware he was anywhere at all.

Just floating.

A blue whale rising through the depths, seeking the surface, where another world waited. His eyelids broke the surface, cracking open to witness shapes he did not recognize. Squares and things stacked on each other. The heavy vaults closed and opened, scrawling recognition on a blank slate.

Laptop. Books.

A chair and a desk. Branches on a window. Pictures on a bookshelf. Faster they came, memories flooding through the veil between waking and dreaming, until they found their rightful places and he had a name.

Hiro.

He grabbed his face. His cheeks warm and creased from the folds in the pillowcase. His skin was soft and smooth, not fuzzy. He had hair on his head, just his head, which was slightly damp. He shot upright. The room felt so strange. So small. He was a giant filling the bed. His arms were long, and his legs were longer. He had fingers and toes and a regular nose.

And he blinked. He blinked once, then twice. He shut his eyes and opened them again. He was a boy in his room. A real boy. Not a toy at all.

His mouth was hot and dry. The dream was fast fading behind the curtain of belief, a strange story growing stranger with each heartbeat. It had felt so real, but now it did not. Funny how that happens, dreams so convincing. He wondered, as he put his feet on the floor and wiggled his toes, if he was dreaming now.

He tried to remember before it was too late. He was a teddy bear once, a toy who had friends. They were stuck in a world that was doing bad things. What was it, he wondered, that could be all that bad? Then he recalled the laughter he'd heard, the jolly good nature that could not be mistaken.

He peeked out the window crusted with frost. A new blanket of snow had covered the road. Mr. Belchinek was clearing his driveway with a brand-new red shovel. There were no lights on his gutters or decorations out front. Nothing had changed. They hadn't saved Christmas after all.

"It was a dream," he muttered.

The purple monkey was on the dresser. Her eyes were blank, as toy eyes should be. The drawing of the planet was taped to the wall. It didn't leap from the paper or wiggle at all. Just something he drew from a dream.

Whatever joy remained from the dream evaporated like fumes escaping the room. It was wishful thinking. He scrambled for a pen to write it all down, the details of an elf with a small elf just like him, who lived in his hat and ran around the rim. An orange octopus who drove a car and a dragon who spit candy. A metal robot with a television spinning on his shoulders. There were others, too, he was fast forgetting, as the dream turned to sand and slipped through his fingers.

He wanted to remember and never forget. Somewhere Christmas was real.

Before he wrote a word on a page, he looked up. Something, it turned out, was different after all. The trees were all bare, and the houses hadn't changed. But the sky was not gray. It was blue for a change.

"You're alive."

His father peeked into the room, a mug on his finger. He nudged the door open. Music played downstairs.

"What?" Hiro said. *Was I dead?*

"You've never slept this late. Your mother insisted I come check on—"

Hiro hugged his father. Coffee spilled on his robe. It was lukewarm on Hiro's chest. He didn't care. His father tried to squirm away, but Hiro held him tightly. He finally gave up, not worried about the stain on his robe, and patted his son's back.

"What's gotten into you two this morning?"

"I'm happy to be back," he muttered into his dad's shoulder.

"Where'd you go?"

Hiro shook his head. "I don't know."

"You and your mother."

The music downstairs grew louder. Hiro had heard that song before. He threw on some clothes. His father grabbed the purple monkey off the dresser.

"She went looking for this in the middle of the night. I heard her in the garage, digging through the garbage. She was upset she couldn't find it." He handed it to Hiro. "I told her I put it in your room. You were having a bad dream, I told her. I thought you could use some company."

"Bad dream?"

He shrugged. "On second thought, leave it up here. She might have forgotten about it. She's not herself this morning."

He started down the hall, swiping at the coffee stain. Hiro didn't know if he wanted to follow. *Not herself?*

"Come see for yourself."

❅

Paper chains were wrapped around the banister. Big loops cut from computer paper, it looked like, painted green and red and yellow all linked and taped together. They sparkled with silver glitter dusted on layers of glue. Snowflakes were thumbtacked to the ceiling, the cutout kind after paper had been folded into quarters. They slowly turned in the draft from the vents exhaling warm air from the furnace. Letters were cut from more computer paper and taped to the wall. Words that spelled JOY and MERRY.

The music was louder.

Hiro thumped down the steps, stopping on the last one to look around the front room. The corner wasn't empty. It was filled with an artificial tree that leaned slightly to the left. The branches were draped with strings of popcorn and strands of silvery tinsel. The string lights were no longer puddled on the floor. They flashed on the branches. A paper star was poised on top. Dusty stockings were hung above the fireplace, their toes bulging with secrets.

"I don't know how you slept through the music," his father shouted.

He went to the kitchen. The music dropped to a whisper. Hiro's mother appeared in the doorway. Her cheeks smudged with flour; fingers dashed with paint. Her slippers were pink and fuzzy. Hiro had never seen slippers like that before. Or the baggy sweatshirt with a smiling reindeer with a nose flashing red. She wore something else he hadn't seen in forever.

A bright, white smile.

She bounced across the room, threw her arms around him and whispered, "Merry Christmas, Hiro." She smelled like cinnamon and paint. "I'm so sorry we forgot. I don't know what happened."

She held him at arm's length. A green floppy hat, a size too big, was pulled over her ears. Hiro had seen that hat. Not here, of course. Not on her.

"How did you remember?" he said.

She started to answer. Only sounds tumbled out. She looked at her husband. Sipping the remains of his coffee that were still in his mug, he shrugged.

"Do you feel it, Hiro?"

He knew what she was asking. Because he *could* feel it. The air was different. It was saturated with something new and exhilarating. A feeling of promise and joy. He remembered, right then, the end of his dream—the exploding light and endless colorful roads. He felt all that had been trapped in a time-locked ball of blue light. And when it opened, it was free.

To give it is to have it.

"Christmas spirit," he muttered.

"Sticky buns are almost done." She planted a bird kiss on her husband. "Your grandparents will be over soon. We can eat, then open presents. There's not many this year, but I feel like they'll be good ones."

Presents were next to the fireplace. Three boxes wrapped in red paper with big green bows. A name on each one. He wondered if she'd found wrapping paper in the attic and somehow found time to make something special for each of them. His father only winked and followed her into the kitchen. The music was at full volume again. Hiro's mother sang along to bells that jingle.

She hadn't made the presents or wrapped them that night. They were there when she woke up, the fireplace left open. At least, that was what Hiro believed.

People say anything is possible even when we know it isn't true. There was no mystery where the presents came from, not for Hiro. He knew exactly how they got there. It didn't matter what was in them. It was just that they were there.

His mother was laughing. His father took her for a spin. Turned out, Hiro didn't need to open a present after all.

It was dancing in the kitchen.

❄

THEY ATE until their stomachs were full. Laughed until their faces hurt. Hiro couldn't eat another bite. But nothing could stop him from smiling.

Dishes were piled in the sink. The table sticky with syrup, butter melting on the floor. They would clean up later. *It's Christmas,* his mother said. Then his parents danced some more. No one wanted to see their parents look at each other like that, gooey-eyed and such. Any other day, Hiro would go to the other room.

The presents were from his mother, all except the ones at the fireplace. She'd wrapped her gifts in brown paper bags and tinfoil. There was even a coffee mug for his father swaddled in a pillowcase and tied with a shoelace. Hiro knew the mug came from the back of the cabinet, where forgotten things got pushed into corners. He knew because he'd made it for him in grade school: a ceramic mug with an ugly face. It wasn't supposed to be ugly. It was supposed to be his father.

His mother, however, said it was beautiful.

The other gifts were made from things she'd found around the house. Things glued and taped, glittered and painted. Hiro's favorite was a spiralbound notebook with two words printed on the cover—the letters fancy with gold glitter.

"Look." His mother had already filled two pages with dreams.

His father promised to write his down, should he ever have one. He crossed his heart and poked his eye. Hiro wanted to start writing his down immediately. The details were fading. There might not be enough pages if he got to it soon enough. He wanted this morning to last forever.

Mother's phone rang. "Merry Christmas," she answered.

She chatted for a minute, cheery at first. Consternation set her brow. She listened with intensity. Her mood lifted by the end of the call, a thank you and a merry Christmas to you, too.

"Everything all right?" Hiro asked.

"That was Jeanine Hollowell. She said an ambulance was at Mr. Corker's house last night."

"Corker? Is he all right?"

"She said he's fine. She went over to check on him."

Hiro felt a little dizzy. "What happened?"

"She doesn't know. He seemed perfectly fine when she spoke with him. She lives across the street, said the lights from the ambulance woke her up in the middle of the night. Poor man, spending Christmas all alone."

It turned out that "middle of the night" was right about midnight.

Hiro had dreamed of looking down at an arena. A tornado had destroyed a carnival of rides. A little, red skeleton lay in the ruins. A moment earlier, the skeleton had been counting down the end of Christmas.

Corker woke up.

Hiro's father was in the kitchen. Dirty dishes were being piled on the counter. Water running. His mother called for him to stop cleaning. There were still a few more presents to open. The ones next to the fireplace were still neatly wrapped. He came back with a hand towel over his shoulder.

"Why did an ambulance go to his house?" Hiro asked.

"What ambulance?" his father said.

"Something to do with Mr. Corker. It sounds like he's fine." She slid a box toward Hiro. "Open it."

His name wasn't on it, but it was for him. *Our Hero* was written in large letters.

"Who's that from?" his father asked.

"You know," his mother said.

A shiver stampeded down Hiro's back. He pulled off the wrapping paper and opened the box. Stuffed inside and wrapped in a blanket was a ball of tan fur.

"Seriously," his father said, "who's it from?"

Dreams have a way of fading, no matter how good or bad. But at that moment, staring into the glassy eyes of a teddy bear, he knew he'd never forget.

39

The teddy bear sat on the counter, leaning against the coffee machine.

Hiro was wearing headphones. Despite the music, an undercurrent of stillness filled his head. It was contradictory. How could it be quiet with drums and guitars? And everything still felt so strange. Like he didn't have to climb onto chairs; doorknobs were easy to reach. He grabbed a plate from the soapy water. *And opposable thumbs.*

He closed his eyes, and swimming with his thoughts, he found what felt missing. It was invisible grit floating in the air. Dust particles of thoughts.

That's it.

He wasn't hearing anything but his own thoughts. No one else's thoughts clouded his mind. No one else was peeking into his mind. He picked up the teddy, squeezed his belly. Nothing but fluff and stitching.

Just like a toy.

Bits of the dream had come and gone. Like patches of ice hidden in the snow, he'd remember a part of the dream and go skidding into the details—an explanation of how Christmas had disappeared, how charms housed the real identity of toys, how the colorful roads were disappearing.

But it was almost noon. Several hours of waking and doubt were nibbling on his willingness to believe. He wanted to believe the dream was real, that a world was out there. A world he could visit when he closed his eyes. *Childishness,* the doubts whispered. *Real is only in front of you.*

He hugged the teddy. Squeezed it hard. A hand fell on his shoulder. Hiro pulled the headphones off.

"Hey, I didn't want to interrupt," his father said, gesturing to the hug.

Hiro put the bear back on the counter. His mother was in the front room and laughing the sort of laughter that, once upon a time, she reserved for company. Laughter he hadn't heard in forever.

"Teddy and I can finish up. You go out there." His father winked. "Spill some coffee."

His mother was at the front door. One of the guests pushed past her, tracking snow on the carpet. Haze wrapped Hiro into a bear hug. His arms were trapped at his sides. She picked him up and shook him. Robby stood at the door. It looked like a smile was crawling onto one side of his face.

"You made it back," Haze whispered.

The hug continued. His mother was staring. The dishes stopped clashing in the kitchen. Hiro felt his father look in the front room, probably smiling at his mother. Haze grabbed two handfuls of Hiro's sweatshirt and balled them into fists like someone about to finish an argument.

"I called and texted. I sent emails. Chase, she answered. You didn't. I thought you were—"

"Asleep," Robby chimed. "I told her it was Christmas, but she made me come over. She couldn't stop talking about you. Like all night long. I wish it would stop. Seriously."

"I'm so sorry." Haze looked at the snow on the carpet. "I'll clean it up."

"It's all right," Hiro's mother said. "It's just water. Nothing a towel can't fix. Here, let me take your coats."

"Oh, no. We're not staying." Haze wiped her eyes. "Can we borrow Hiro for a few hours? I know it's Christmas and—and by the way, merry Christmas."

"Merry Christmas," Hiro's father said from the kitchen doorway.

"Borrow?" Hiro's mother said.

"I think she means go for a ride," Robby said. Then whispered, plenty loud, "She's crazy about him."

"That's not what I mean. I meant the first part." She stared lasers at her brother.

His parents looked at each other. Hiro didn't feel invisible grit pass between them, but they seemed to know each other's thoughts. His mother smiled and said, "Have him back before dinner."

They would probably dance some more. Hiro had seen enough of the way his mother laughed when his father dipped her low to the floor. He threw on his coat. Haze led the way. Robby waved at Hiro's parents.

"Merry, merry!"

❄

THEY LISTENED to the engine rattle.

Robby had his hand on the gearshift with his foot on the brake. Across the street, kids rolled a big ball of snow. Maybe it was the start of a snowman. Hiro didn't notice.

He was staring at a dragon.

It was green with beady, black eyes and wedged between the dashboard and windshield, watching with a toothy smile. Despite warm air from the vents, a hard shiver crawled down his back and clenched his stomach. He chattered, but it wasn't the cold. Reality was turning upside down. *Like a carnival ride.*

He grabbed the dragon. The belly was heavy. Bits of hard candy fell out of the mouth when he turned it over. There were no tags. The teddy didn't have any, either. *Santa doesn't put tags on presents.*

"So it really happened?" Hiro said.

Robby leaned to one side, dug in his coat pocket. He came out with a handful of something jagged and sharp and swatted it on the dash. Metal legs clicked together. A cube bobbled on angled shoulders. It looked like a tiny television set.

"I'm guessing you got a teddy bear?"

Hiro didn't answer. And he didn't have to ask where they got the dragon and the bobblehead. They had been neatly wrapped and waiting for them in the morning.

Hiro said, "You think it was—"

"Santa?" Robby pulled on the gearshift. He didn't finish his thought. They couldn't read each other's minds, but they were thinking the same thing.

"I'm so happy you're back," Haze said. "I called, like, a hundred times, texted a hundred more. You weren't answering. I was trying to do the math, the time difference thingy, and figured you should've woken up, like, a minute after we did. Ten, tops. So I kept calling and calling. I about came over in the middle of the night."

"But she's scared of your mom," Robby said.

"Shut up. I started to think you stayed there."

"I did," Hiro said. They looked at him. He sighed. "After you left, it got... weird."

It felt strange saying that out loud. *After you left.* Because it was a dream, just a dream. They all had the *same* dream. *Right?*

"It was Corker. The puppet, you know. Viktor the Red was Corker. I know that sounds impossible, but he must have had the same dream as us. Remember in class when he saw my drawing and made me—"

They burst out laughing. Robby pounded the steering wheel as he turned the corner. The bobblehead slid across the dash. For a brief second, Hiro thought they were laughing at him. *Did they not have the dream?* Embarrassment went through his belly like a winter stream.

"Corker," Robby said, shaking his head. "That guy."

"Don't be mean." Haze punched his shoulder. She turned to Hiro.

"Yeah, it was Corker. The way he walked. *Precisely!*" She stabbed at the roof. "When he said that, I knew for sure. No one says that."

"Corker does," Robby added.

"Yeah, and I couldn't *think* it to you once I knew. Not with him in the room with the, you know, the big puppet and the stretchy guy." Hiro got the chills. *Belkin and Stretch.* "We had to get out of there before he knew *we* knew who he was. That's why we *wanted* to wake up," she said. "I thought you knew."

Hiro shook his head. The details were foggy, just a blurry snapshot of a limp dragon lying on a metal table. He had no idea they knew it was Corker. Or what they were planning to do.

"Why did you stay?" Haze said.

Hiro sighed again. He felt nauseous trying to remember why he'd stayed so long. Robby took another corner a little fast, which stirred memories of orange tentacles gripping the steering wheel while another one turned up the radio. He closed his eyes.

He would never undervalue eyelids again. They shut out the outside world, allowed him to drift deeper into his thoughts. The memories were fresher this way. The feel of fur that fluttered in the wind. The springy nature of short legs.

"Do you remember what it was like?" he said.

"I can't forget," Robby said.

That wasn't what he meant. The dream had been so real when he was there. Now it was a kite with a broken string escaping into the blue sky. A tiny dot that kept getting smaller. Even if they talked about it, wrote the details down, the dream was only going to get farther away. Until one day, it was just going to be something they imagined happened.

"I remember." Haze hugged the dragon. "It feels like long ago, like remembering my birthday when I was seven."

A snowball fight was in full throttle on the corner. Kids lobbed snowballs from behind snowdrifts. Their gloves crusted white and frosty. The father was hanging lights on the gutters. Hiro watched while they waited for a stoplight to turn green. As they drove away, the father joined the fight.

Everything is different.

Up and down the street, people were playing or hanging ornaments or just talking and laughing. A missing ingredient was back in the world. It penetrated everything and everyone—an essence that had been missing for so long. No one knew it had been gone. They could feel it. Even taste it.

Joy.

Hiro sensed it through the windows. It filled him with goodness. The vibrations brought memories with it. He continued staring out the window, drifting in the current.

"They wanted me to leave, but I thought I could help. So I imagined myself out there. You know, the projection thing?" He didn't turn around to see if they remembered. "Viktor... er, Corker had all the soldiers out there after the rides got destroyed."

"Who did that?" Haze asked.

"Mads. It was her plan. The Ferris wheel knocked the house off the pedestal. It completely fell apart, but the bubble—you know, the one with, uh..." Hiro tapped the dashboard. "The little elf?"

"Snow," she said.

"Snow, yeah. He was trapped in there with—"

"Santa Claus," Robby said.

"Right. But it didn't work. The bubble didn't pop. Oh, and there were reindeer in it, too. They were on the roof."

"What?!" Robby shouted.

"I'm not kidding. Like, they were on the roof, tethered to the sleigh. But they were all still trapped, so I was going to project inside the bubble to talk to Santa because, I don't know. I thought he'd know what to do."

"Smart," Robby said. He might have been serious.

"Not smart," Haze said. "You could have ended up like Snow. That's what I was afraid of, that you'd do something stupid."

"I didn't try it. I heard a voice." He chewed on his finger, concentrating on what he'd heard. It was like a limerick. "Christmas lights... Christmas lights..."

"Burn so bright," Haze said. "Mads."

"How'd you know that?" Robby said.

"Shhh."

"It was her. I guess she said it so Viktor, or Corker, whatever, wouldn't know it was her. She had switched into the Monkeybrain toy. I don't know how, the octopus must have helped her."

"Oh, yeah. The octopus," Robby said. Haze pointed at him, and they said, "Ocho."

"Ocho," Hiro muttered. "Her plan was to wreck the place so Santa would be freed when the house fell. So it didn't work. The only way to get them out was to turn it off. The switch wasn't in the house."

"Where was it?" Haze said.

They were at a stop sign. The car behind them honked. Robby slowly turned the corner, waiting for the answer. Hiro didn't know it. He grasped at the final minutes of the dream, when everything went dark, just before all the roads exploded from the bubble. Mads jumped on Viktor as the countdown reached the final seconds. She reached for his skull. *His skull.*

"It was Viktor's charm." It was all coming back now. "Somehow his charm was the switch. There was no way to get to it. I don't think Mads knew it till it was too late. She thought it was in the house, that's why Snow went inside. She didn't know I could do the projection thing until she saw me doing it. That's why she told me to imagine a whole bunch of Monkeybrains, like all over the place. Then I imagined Santa escaped the bubble with one of the reindeer. It worked. Corker believed it. He got really confused. He didn't know I was doing it and thought he was talking to Santa. And then he was…"

Hiro closed his eyes again. This part had a different feeling. It was strong and weepy.

"He was sad. I could feel it. Really feel it. There was a second all that power was stripped away, and I felt him trapped in that red skeleton, like he was a little boy. Even after everything that happened, I felt bad for him."

"He stole Christmas," Robby reminded him.

Hiro shook his head. There was no argument for the things Corker had done. He'd come so close to succeeding. If he did, everything would be different. Maybe forever. But Hiro couldn't help but see the truth of why Corker had done it. He wasn't greedy or bad. *He was scared.*

"So you stopped him?" Haze said.

"No. He figured out what I was doing and caught Mads before she could get to him. He was going to do it, like you said—he was going to steal Christmas forever. The countdown was on, and I was just about to wake up. Seriously, it was game over. Then, for no reason, he fell down. I mean, he just collapsed into a pile of bones. Nobody knows why, but Mads saved the day. She got to his charm and turned the bubble off."

Ho-ho-ho.

"What do you mean he *fell down*?" Haze said.

Hiro shrugged. "He just... fell."

"Like he woke up?"

"Something happened to him. There was an ambulance at his house."

Haze pumped her fist. She high-fived her brother. They high-fived again; then she hugged Robby. He veered close to a parked car and jerked the steering wheel. Then he rolled down the window and shouted at a mother pulling her kids on a sled.

"We saved Christmas!"

Haze hugged Hiro, held his cheeks. Her hands were ice cubes. "We saved Christmas."

When she had woke up, she ran to Robby's bedroom. He was rubbing his eyes. It took a minute to convince him it wasn't a dream. It wasn't until she told him every detail of it, which matched his dream, before he believed it. He started to freak out.

"What do those numbers say?" she said, pointing at a house.

Robby slowed down. The house was white with black shutters, the fake kind that weren't made to close. There were no bushes or trees. The snow in the front yard and driveway was trampled with footsteps.

"This is it," Haze said.

"This is what?" Hiro said.

"Corker's house."

"What? Why?"

"We crushed his dream, Hiro," she said.

"Yeah, but... I don't think this is a good time to... you know." Hiro clutched the armrest.

"It's a *great* time," Robby said.

They parked on the street and stared at the front door. They sat in silence. Hiro had no trouble remembering what it had felt like when Viktor the Red reached into his head and plucked his thoughts like apples off a tree. There were no words to describe that level of vulnerability. *What if, somehow, he can still do it?*

"Seriously," Hiro said. "Why now? We'll see him at school."

"To see if he's okay." She shrugged. "An ambulance was at his house last night. Besides, I just got a feeling he wants to talk to us."

"I don't," Hiro said.

"I want to talk to him." Robby opened his door.

Haze leaned over Hiro to open his and pushed him out. They followed a bevy of footprints leading up to the front door. Hiro lagged behind. He thought they were just driving around to talk about things, not going to visit a deposed dictator. One whom Hiro had personally fooled with an image of Santa Claus. He could still feel Viktor's X-ray vision.

Robby and Haze stopped at the steps. There was a note taped to the door. Two words in black ink.

Come in.

❄

THEY STOOD on the steps as if the porch were hot lava. It had all felt like a game when they were in the truck. Now memories were rushing back like wild animals, of a time Viktor the Red could peek inside their minds like there was a window on their foreheads.

"Maybe that's not for us." Hiro looked at the footsteps in the yard.

Haze stepped on the front porch carefully. Like bear traps were hidden in the snow.

"We can't just walk in," Hiro said. "I mean, how'd you even know he lives here?"

"It's his house." She opened the outer glass door, ripped the note down. "Trust me."

She put her ear to the door. Before Hiro could stop her, she turned the doorknob. Music bellowed from inside the house. It was a climbing symphony of classical music. She held the door for them. Robby pushed Hiro across the porch.

They stepped into an immaculate front room. Vacuum stripes lined the carpet, perfectly parallel with the couch. The smell of fresh-baked cookies filled the house.

"Mr. Corker?" Haze shouted.

There was no response. Haze took a reluctant step, then shucked her boots. Snow was melting in the linoleum foyer. "Take off your shoes," she whispered.

"Bad idea," Robby said. "We might need to run."

He was feeling the weirdness. The note felt like a stranger holding candy out the window of a dirty van.

"What if he has a dog?" Hiro said.

Haze looked at Hiro first, back to Robby. "You think Corker has a pet?"

Robby began whistling. Even if there was a dog, he wouldn't hear it over the music. Haze crept into the front room with loose socks on her feet. She looked through a doorway on the left.

Hiro left Robby, who was whistling up steps that led to the second floor. He stopped at a doorway on the right. He didn't want to shout their names, so began waving his arms like he was landing a plane.

It was a small dining table. The light-colored wood was polished. The color reminded Hiro of a full-size puppet. A puppet's name he'd already forgotten. Two candles flickered around a plate of chocolate chip cookies. Four woven placemats were at the table. They were squared to the edge of the table. On three of them were gift-wrapped boxes that were the right size for an engagement ring.

Four placemats, three presents. A plate of cookies. "He's expecting us," Hiro muttered.

"It's a bribe," Robby said. "He wants us to take him back."

"Back where?" Hiro said.

"Where? Where else? The toys aren't going to let him come—"

"It's not a bribe."

The music turned off. Corker stood in the doorway on the opposite side of the table. A tie tightly knotted against his throat; shirt as neatly pressed as his slacks. Did he own anything besides work clothes? He might have dressed the same, but something was off.

He looked different.

The sharp ridge that protruded above his eyes like an ice ridge had melted. There was a softness to the plaster of his cheeks. And something rare at the corner of his mouth. It looked like a smile trying to break through; a seed buried beneath a thick crust for a thousand years, just now feeling the light.

"Please." He gestured. "Have a seat."

"How did you know we were coming?" Hiro said.

He blinked heavily. A man exhausted. "It's important we talk about certain events. Please."

He gestured again. Not with the insistence of a taskmaster, but the request of a kind mentor. No mind control, at least none that Hiro could feel. But it was unsettling to see Corker look that way. If a slobbering guard dog walked into the room, it would be less unsettling.

The gifts made it obvious where they should sit, but they weren't labeled. Corker took a seat first. It was not at the head of the table, Hiro noticed. Robby and Haze sat at opposite ends. Hiro sat across from Corker.

"My apologies, I ran out of milk."

His voice was husky. Like someone shouting until his throat was raw.

He filled four mugs with water from a steaming kettle. The tags from teabags hung over the sides. He placed one on each of their placemats.

They sat with their hands on their laps, watching him. He broke a cookie in half, held it up before eating. It didn't ease their suspicion. Their appetites had vanished. Hiro's stomach was the size of a walnut.

Corker wiped the corners of his mouth with a cloth napkin and didn't speak until he swallowed.

"I want to thank you."

They looked at each other. Then Haze said, "For what?"

"I know it was you."

Haze looked at Robby, who shook his head. "I don't know what you're talking about."

Corker ate the other half of his cookie. Hiro put it together, what Haze and Robby had done. All the footprints in the yard. Viktor the Red suddenly falling down. Haze and Robby knew where he lived. They had returned to wake Corker up. They couldn't break into his house, so they called someone who could.

An ambulance arrived sometime after midnight. *It's an emergency.*

Corker placed a cookie on their plates, then sat down, smoothing the napkin on his lap. He sat as stiff as the hardback chair. He remained still for a moment, then inhaled deeply, letting it out slowly.

"I was frightened the first time I arrived. I'm quite sure each of you can relate—going to sleep as you've done every night of your life only to wake up as a toy. It made no sense, perhaps more so to me than you. I've been a scientist all my life. It defied the principles of reality. There is no explanation for the consciousness of an inanimate object. There is no biology in fabric and stitches. Toys are objects."

He knocked on the table.

"Yet there I was, in a world where the air was sweeter and the colors more vivid. I could smell without breathing, taste without a tongue. The experience, I'm sure you'll agree, was deeper than anything you've ever experienced or ever will. Everything pales in comparison."

He blinked heavily again.

"I would count the minutes till bedtime. Some nights excitement would keep me from sleeping. I had to learn ways to calm my expectations, to sleep deeply. I endured waking up in bed each morning. With each trip, this life became less important to me until it mattered very little. I was living two lives. This one had become inconsequential.

"I had a family there, for one. Polly was a stitcher. It was her shop where I woke as a red skeleton. Philip was a scientist studying rather absurd concepts. Even I have to admit it seemed not to be random for me to wake up there, but, as I'm sure you were told, we choose the toy that fit us. I fit quite well where I was.

"I would sit with the family for meals, Polly preparing bowls of porridge for me to dip my fingers in. We did puzzles, read books, watched television, made snow angels in the front yard. Went to town for dinner. All the things a happy family does. Something you might find boring. Something I never had."

He looked around the table with grim sincerity.

"I didn't want to do what I did. You see, I loved that world very much. I only wanted to stay. I didn't want to wake up ever again. I wanted to arrive on Madeline's shelf to—"

"Mads," Hiro blurted.

Corker nodded intently. His posture shrank as if a heavy weight had been draped over his shoulders. Finally, he said with a brittle edge, "What I did is unforgiveable. If I had succeeded…"

He didn't finish. It was a thought much too large and dangerous to stare nakedly in the eyes. One he would have to wrestle with for years to come.

"I don't know how or why you arrived there. It seems unlikely to have been an accident. Maybe the roads to that world are contagious and somehow I…" He shrugged. A scientist struggling with concepts not of this world. He looked at Hiro. "Perhaps there were unseen forces at work."

Unseen forces. That was exactly what he'd said when he proposed a new topic for his research project. Hiro started to smile. Corker looked at the crumbs on his plate. Put his trembling hands on his lap.

"What happened last night after…" A knot bobbed in his throat. He pushed his chair back and cleared his throat. "If you'll excuse me a moment."

He left the room but didn't go far. The stamping of his hard-sole slippers stopped just around the corner. They waited for him to return. A minute later, he was on the move again, going to the other side of the house. A door closed somewhere. It didn't sound like the back door. A bathroom, perhaps.

Robby got up and looked in the other room, his eyes shifting back and forth in search of Corker. Somewhere behind a closed door, Corker blew his nose into a white handkerchief.

"What is happening?" Robby whispered.

"I don't know," Haze answered. "It's like he's someone else. It doesn't sound like him."

"I was thinking the same thing," Robby barely whispered. "What's up with his voice?"

"What if he's a switch?" Haze said. "You know, like, that's not him. We went there, so why couldn't a toy come here, like, in his body?"

"A two-way road." Robby zipped his finger back and forth. "Maybe this is *their* dream. Which means there could be toy-people already here. Which means he can read thoughts. Which means—"

"Toys don't dream," Hiro interrupted before the rabbit hole got any deeper. "They don't sleep. You called an ambulance last night?"

Robby and Haze snapped out of it, looked at each other. "We could get in trouble for that," Haze said. "There wasn't time. It was an emergency, Hiro. If we didn't wake him up, we wouldn't be *here*, and it wouldn't be Christmas."

"He thanked us," Robby said. "Did you hear the way he said that? Like he meant it. Like he's glad we called."

"That doesn't mean we won't get in trouble," Haze said. "I'm sure what we did isn't legal."

"Not if he doesn't say anything. He can't prove it was us."

"Are you nuts? All they have to do is trace the call. It's not that hard."

They looked at the gifts. The cookies and candles. The note on the door. Corker knew they were coming over. Of course he knew they'd called the ambulance. Robby snapped his fingers.

"He can read thoughts, which means..." He jerked his head toward the other room. "He's a toy."

Hiro was starting to think Robby was right. They needed to put their boots on and get out of the house. But then what? Tell their parents about their dream. *Corker is a toy!*

Footsteps clobbered the floor leading to the dining room. The rhythmic sound froze them in place. Corker returned with a sniffle. He picked up his chair, not dragging the legs, and sat down. He straightened the placemat with the edge of the table. His eyes were even softer than before.

"I am not a toy, Robby, any more than you are a robot. Not a thought escapes our minds to be read, not here. Here we're all separate, in our own little worlds."

"Then how do you know us?" Haze said. "What's your job?"

It was a legitimate question. If he knew, then it was Corker. Hiro felt less afraid and more curious. They needed to know if toys could come into their world. Corker nodded, understanding they needed more than just his promise he was who he said he was.

"Who am I, is that the question?" The weight of something heavy returned. His shoulders slumped. Just a little. "When the ambulance arrived, I did not wake up immediately. There was an unexpected journey between there and here. Not so jolly, you could say. I saw things about myself, things in my past. Things I willingly forgot and had no wish to revisit."

He sighed.

"Someone took me there, made me face them. I think I know who, but that's not important. What is important is I wouldn't have chosen to go there, to see what it was that made me who I am today. And the reasons I did what I did over there. I resisted, at first. But it was exactly what I needed. The perfect Christmas gift, you could say."

He laughed painfully.

"I still have a lot of work to do, but I understand what I need to do now. Who am I, you ask? I am a high school teacher. I live alone and have lived alone all of my life. I am fifty-two years old. That might answer your question, but that's not *who* I am."

He folded his hands on the table, the long spider fingers intertwining. He looked at Hiro without the cold laser that brought students into submission. This was an open look. Kindness around his eyes.

"I am truly sorry I embarrassed you in front of the class, Hiro. That was fear, my fear, that did that. Your drawing was a threat. I have much that needs to be forgiven. Including the ways I treat myself. I hope you can forgive me."

That wasn't a toy in Corker's body. But it wasn't the Corker they once knew. *What journey did he go on?*

"It's Christmas, thanks to all of you." He gestured to the gifts. "Please, open."

They looked at the small boxes. Haze was the first to pick one up. She turned it over, examined all sides of it. Then said, "We didn't get you anything."

"Yes, you did." A genuine smile creased the uncreaseable face.

They waited until each of them was holding their gift, then ripped the paper away. The tape perfectly cut to length, the corners expertly folded. They pulled the lids off. The gift was resting on a swatch of cotton. They picked up what was inside their box, held it up for the others to see. They'd all received the same thing. Hiro wrapped the metal links around his finger.

It was a symbol of goodwill, of hope and resistance. The dedication to keeping the Christmas spirit alive. If he'd gotten this at home, he might have believed he'd seen his mother wearing it a long time ago. She wrapped it for Christmas because she didn't have anything else. Hiro only dreamed the life-size puppet was wearing the bracelet. And the elves at the big tree. Mads.

A red snowflake.

"Five boxes were in front of my fireplace," Corker said. "I wrapped four of them this morning. One of them will be shipped to a feline friend of yours. The other three are for you."

A smile of gratitude touched his lips. Haze worked the clasp around her wrist. Hiro clutched the cold links. "What about the fifth one?"

He pulled the sleeve back on his arm. A bracelet hung from his boney wrist. He cradled the snowflake on two fingers, reflecting, perhaps, on the times he'd seen it on Belkin's wrist.

"I believe he wants us to be reminded of the courage to dream. And to never forget that anything is possible."

"He?" Robby said.

"I think you know who he is."

Haze helped Hiro put the bracelet on his wrist. He would wear it for years to come. Even when people at school made fun of him. It didn't matter if it came from a make-believe world of toys, where an octopus drove a candy-striped car and a tiny elf lived inside a hat.

Hiro believed unseen forces were at work in the universe. The snowflake would always remind him of that.

"I've kept you from your families long enough. I want to thank you for everything you've done. Your courage is the reason we're here this morning."

He stood up and bowed at the waist. Spine and legs straight, bending at the hips with one arm over his stomach and the other behind his back. He went to the other room and returned with three paper plates, piling cookies on each one. He walked them to the door with a tightness in his cheeks. It wasn't the tension of irritation. This looked like raw emotion hiding beneath a thin layer of ice.

They put on their boots, said thank you. Haze and Robby walked outside with their plates of cookies in stunned confusion. Hiro turned in the open door.

"We're having dinner this afternoon. My parents would be happy to have you."

Corker's smile faltered. The knot bobbed in his throat. "Next year, perhaps."

Hiro wanted to insist. Spending Christmas alone was almost as bad as no Christmas at all. Corker, however, appeared content. There was work to do.

"Do you think it was real?" Hiro said.

Corker looked at the sky. Somewhere down the street, a child squealed with delight. Haze and Robby stopped on the steps, waiting for him to answer.

"What is real? If it is our senses—what we can see and hear, touch and taste and smell—then I think we have our answer." He winked. "But there's much we don't know."

"We can go back," Robby said.

"The roads are open," Haze added.

Corker placed his hand on Hiro's shoulder. The long fingers wrapped around it, squeezed gently. He didn't say it, but Hiro knew what he was thinking. The roads were still there. In order to take them, they had to choose a toy. He wasn't Viktor the Red anymore. He didn't know who he was. That was the work he had to do.

"Not for me."

He watched them plod down the driveway. Before they climbed inside the truck, Corker shouted.

"Don't forget, you have a paper due!"

They turned around. Corker smiled a grim but friendly smile. Then closed the door. They climbed into the truck and stared out the windshield, unsure of what just happened. A dragon and bobble-headed robot stared back. Hiro rubbed the snowflake between his finger and thumb.

Robby started the truck. "That's definitely Corker."

40

I stood in the dimness of the front room. Between parted curtains, I watched them climb into an old truck. The tires were bald; the passenger door a different color. The sort of vehicle I wouldn't allow in front of my house; the kind of vehicle that would force me to talk with neighbors until it was removed.

I watched them sit quietly. Stunned. An unseen weight tilted the world, and they felt it. Reality was out of focus. Nothing was what it seemed, and anything was possible.

Across the street, the Paxton children threw a ball in the front yard. The girls were on the front porch with their mother, scraping snow off the railings for miniature snowmen. The boys were playing a game without rules, one that involved tackling. They would wrestle until someone's feelings got hurt. I'd watched them play this game many times, lurking between the curtains, waiting for an errant throw to reach my yard.

There were boxes of baseballs and basketballs, wiffleballs and kickballs in my basement. The children knew better than to ask for them back. I once called the police when a Frisbee went into my garage. I showed the officers the mark it left on the trunk of my car.

Destruction of property, I told them. The father agreed to have the boys buff it out. I watched them do it.

What I hated most was the noise. The giggly laughter, the shrill screams and carefree frivolity were flames that boiled my blood.

The truck pulled away. Hiro, Hazel, and Robby would go home to celebrate Christmas. How did I know they were coming to my house? It was a tiny voice in my head. Not an actual voice, like the ones Viktor the Red had become so accustomed to. This was normal inner dialog. Thoughts. *My* thoughts. Although *this* tiny voice was different. It was unfamiliar.

I had been awakened in the early morning hours by EMS workers after the longest night of my life. Even in my confusion, I understood what had happened. The EMS workers were not easily convinced to leave. My vitals were sound, but I was confused. Dehydration, I told them. Low blood sugar, perhaps.

I lay in bed for the rest of the night, a cast-iron replica of myself. Sinking into the mattress like stone, trying to make sense of what had happened. It was a magic carpet ride into the past. All the doors inside me had been thrown open. I had been dragged through all the rooms to revisit memories I barely recalled. An awful, painful ride.

My punishment.

The longer I lay there, staring at the ceiling, pondering the possibilities, the more it felt less like a journey. I had seen things I had not been able to see about myself and no longer wanted to. I had been forced to relive them. Slowly, blood pumped through my veins, and something odd took over. Sensations in my chest and stomach. Cold steel in my legs.

Tremors of emotions.

We all have emotions, you might be thinking. Of course. It wasn't until that very moment I realized my emotions had been no more than thin ghosts haunting my body. They had been locked behind iron doors that were now open. The ghosts of the past soared freely with swirling tides in my stomach. They tightened my chest, quivered my cheeks, knotted my throat. Did I tremor with fear or weep in despair? No.

A storm was growing.

The house felt different. Foreign. The house I grew up in. I had gone from room to room, stood in the dark and felt the spirit of my father in each one. His presence oozed from the walls like corruption, bubbling beneath the paint, fouling the air. In each room, I recalled what I'd seen on my journey, each memory I was forced to relive. My chest was an iron cage. My fingernails bit into my palms. The ghosts spun inside me, a furnace stirring emotions until the pressure whistled in my ears.

I fell to my knees.

I screamed and cursed until my throat was raw and barking. Unable to get it all out, I continued until only whimpers escaped. There was so much emotion. A tidal wave gushed through the embankments.

I fell on the carpet, pajamas soaked with sweat, panting like a wild animal. It was then I turned to the cold fireplace. It was then a glimmer of realization that madness did not swallow me whole; perhaps the journey of memories I'd been forced to take wasn't a punishment after all.

I stared at a strange and foreign sight in my house. One that I had not seen since I was a child.

A gift.

I dared not move, afraid it would turn into a heap of ashes. I looked at the ceiling, imagined hoofprints on the roof. A jolly fat man coming down the chimney, even after all I had done. I moved slowly so as not to disturb the gift. If it was an illusion, I wanted to make it last.

I picked it up, felt the weight, the stiffness of the sides and sharpness of the corners. The smell of the paper and sound it made when I tore it open.

Even before I reached inside to find the bracelets, I realized this wasn't the true gift I'd received. My bones were shaking, my organs twisting. What I wanted most in all the world was what I'd tried to take from Toyworld.

I wanted to *change*.

I wanted to be someone else. Because there was something wrong with me.

The inner voice I heard, I knew why it felt unfamiliar then. All my life, it had been my father's voice. Now it was different.

It's my voice.

I knew where the bracelets came from, but I didn't have the courage to do what needed to be done. I was as fragile as thin ice. To be honest, I didn't know the children would come to my house. There was no magic there, no reading thoughts. I only hoped they would. I baked cookies and wrapped the gifts. I even doubted I could open the door if they rang the bell.

So I put a sign on it.

Timmy Paxton stood at the curb in front of my house. He wiped his nose on the back of a wool mitten. He could see me between the curtains. A football was on my front step. His brothers were shouting for him to hurry. Timmy could feel my expression, an expression my father taught me. One that turned children to stone. It was chiseled on my face.

I went to the kitchen and returned to open the front door. Timmy had not moved. His brothers watched from the other side of the street. I picked up the football in one hand. I walked through the snow wearing socks, feeling the cold bite my feet, and handed it to Timmy. A smile crackled in my cheeks and thawed my rigid brow. Timmy tucked the football under his arm. Before he could run back to safety, I handed him a plate of cookies.

I waved to his mother on the porch. She and her family watched like aliens had landed.

"Merry, merry!" I barked.

I went back inside and gathered wood from the fireplace. I took it into the backyard. Around a lonely fire, I sat on a log and stared into the steel blue sky, imagining colorful ribbons waving across the galaxy.

❄

The rumors started.

School is a volcanic vent for such things. Someone saw me smile; I think that was what started them. I remember how difficult it was at that age, when a haircut could send a child home in tears. Or funny clothes. I ignored the murmurs in the hall, kept the desks in line.

Hiro and Hazel didn't speak to me of the dream.

They approached my desk after class to turn in their papers. I put my finger to my lips before they could say anything. Perhaps I didn't want them caught in the rumor mill, as well. I also did not want to know if they'd gone back. I couldn't think or talk about that. Not yet.

Hazel's paper was exceptional. However, based on her previous work, I was certain she didn't do it. Her brother didn't have the aptitude for science, either. Hiro wrote it for her, of that I was certain.

He'd decided to write something different.

Hiro turned in a story about a world where a race of toys co-existed with humans, the socioeconomic impacts, political machinations, and the complexities of equality. It was accompanied by two illustrations: a colorful planet and a red skeleton.

It took three sittings for me to read. Emotion would well up from a deep aquifer. I wasn't ready to open that faucet yet. When I was done, my comments were written in red ink on the last page.

Beautifully written. But not the assignment.

Hiro was not hurt by the poor grade I gave him. I think he wrote it as much for his own self as he did for me. I found his project on my desk after class one day, a note written below my red comments in blue ink.

Thank you.

I quietly resigned at the end of the school year.

❄

I sold my house and moved away.

It was my father's house. I'd been living in his shadow all my life; the smell of the walls had steeped so completely into my being that I couldn't smell it until I left. I went north, found a small city where I blended into the population. I wanted to be alone without being lonely.

At some point, I got a job at a boutique toy store. One of those stores that specialized in custom-built dollhouses and unique playthings. It drew tourists and locals, especially during the holiday season. I had no such knack to build things, but I was quite good at wrapping gifts. I would watch small children light up when the bell rang over the door when they entered. Sometimes they would have conversations with a sock puppet or a plastic doll, and I would pretend they were actually hearing a voice adults could no longer hear.

Sometimes I joined them.

I became popular in the store. Partly due to my enthusiasm and willingness to close the store each night, which no one wanted to do. I would sit with the lights off for hours. The owner once asked what I was doing. I told her I was meditating. I had joined a group of meditators and found the practice helpful.

The toy store was my temple. Hope and joy permeated the walls. I would imagine whispering voices or movement on a shelf.

Tell them I'm sorry, I would whisper back.

I know what you're thinking, and I was, too. I was avoiding the pain. You would be right.

It took several attempts to find the right therapist. For the better part of a year, I avoided telling him about the dream. When I did, he smiled gently. Perhaps he saw it as a great metaphor. Or maybe he'd been there. I never asked. It had been almost five years since I'd closed my eyes and woke in that wonderful world. Five years.

I cried for the first time.

The dam finally breached. A lifetime of sorrow flooded out of the hole I had desperately tried to fill. I thought it would never stop. We continued talking about the dream so much that I was convinced my therapist had been there, too.

True freedom came when I forgave my mother, even if I couldn't understand why she would leave me. She had her own troubles, her own peace to find. My father, I knew what his childhood was like, how he became the person he was. I forgave him, too.

"You can start by forgiving yourself," the therapist said.

"What about Toyworld?"

He passed me a tissue. "They've already forgiven you."

❄

ONCE A MONTH, a different storyteller would visit the toy store.

The center of the store would be cleared on a Saturday morning. Children would sit on the floor or a parent's lap while a tale was spun. At times, adults were as enraptured as the children. That all depended on the storyteller.

It was a time of magical stories and wonderland liftoffs. Children transported to imaginary worlds and faraway places. And the store sold toys by the bucket. Sometimes, when the storyteller was famous —as famous as a storyteller can get—there would be toys custom-built from the story. Children carried them out the door with fairy dust in their eyes, squeezing a big-headed doll or talking to a pink pony with saucer eyes.

One Christmas, the storyteller was a woman with white hair clipped behind her ears.

She was dainty in size with sharp elbows and a petite nose. But when she took her sweater off, she was anything but delicate. A strong woman with a powerful smile that made flowers bloom.

Her story was about a man she called Nicolaus Santa, who got lost during the first expedition to the North Pole only to discover an ancient race of elven living in the ice.

I was captivated by the elements of science. The elven were technologically advanced, you see, cloaking their existence from humankind. I was already planning to buy her book and get an autograph before she left when someone asked her where she got her ideas. She looked puckish, her finger on her dimpled chin, blue eyes shifting around the room.

"Dreams."

I was smitten. And that, dear reader, is a monumental statement.

Never in my life had I experienced feelings for another person. Not like that. Swirling belly, light-headed and giggly. I would have embarrassed myself had I not gotten busy at the counter.

I stole glances as she signed books and took pictures; one by one she would smile and sometimes hug while muttering to each child. I strained to hear what she said to them. And then I froze. I listened again and nearly fainted.

"Merry, merry."

❆

We had coffee.

It took every gram of courage for me to ask. "I'm a fan," I lied. I was a fan, but not before that morning. We drank coffee and spoke about small things. I'd become competent at conversation, having engaged with customers for several years at that point.

"Can I ask you something?" I mused.

"Of course." Her smile churned butter in my stomach.

"Merry, merry." I said it like that. Just threw it out there like a worm on a hook.

She looked at me, waiting. Then she looked deeper. Put down her mug and wiped her mouth.

"Yes?" she said.

It wasn't a question, really. She knew what I was asking. Oh, the delicious, dainty scoundrel knew. She was going to make me say it.

Can you imagine the risk, to just ask someone about a world where toys are alive, and I went there and so did some of my students? She wouldn't wait for the check before diving through a window.

I bit into a dry scone. Nodding as I chewed, looking into her eyes. I wasn't going to do it. I wanted to have dinner with her that night, then breakfast in the morning. There would be a better time, once we got to know each other. I leaned forward and shrugged.

"The toys are alive."

The words just came out of me. I was as surprised as she was.

I didn't know where the courage came from and thought perhaps she didn't hear them. Maybe I didn't actually say them. She wiped the corners of her mouth and reached across the table. For a moment, I thought it was very forward of her to take my hand. I wasn't disappointed, but this was just coffee. She grasped my wrist and turned it over.

"Toyworld," she whispered.

She rubbed the red snowflake dangling from my bracelet. Later, much later, she would tell me that that was why she came to my store to tell stories, having seen it upon a previous visit. She was going to ask *me* to coffee. She hoped the bracelet was more than just an odd choice for a grown man.

"Please," I whispered, "tell me everything."

She did. Not right there and then, but over the course of months, she told me.

Viktor the Red, she said, had been before her time. She had awakened in the early days of what had been called the Great Recovery. She'd seen Belkin the Puppet on television with his top hat and stiff cane. He wore the red snowflake around his wrist. She had her own little family over there, living life as a fuzzy bunny with sparkly red shoes.

Later, I found Hiro's story, the one he'd turned in for his project. The bad grade on the back. We flipped the pages, her hand at her mouth. She nodded and laughed and hugged me some more.

If she ever had doubt, it was extinguished that day.

It was several months before I told her the truth. I wasn't hiding it from her, only listening to her tales.

At first, I told her I'd lost the ability to go back. When she asked for more, I said it was a long time ago and my memories were foggy. That was half-baked. I was afraid, terrified, she would leave.

And then, like the first time we had coffee, the words came out. It was on a Christmas Eve. We were ice skating at the outdoor rink in a quaint downtown area, holding mittened hands like teenagers. There were galaxies in her eyes. The words steamed from my frozen lips. I told her who I had been in ToyWorld.

And what I had done.

She squeezed my hand. "They forgive you."

We skated without another word. Children were looking and pointing. Parents smiled awkwardly at the man with tears running down his cheeks.

We skated until they closed the rink.

❄

I EVENTUALLY BOUGHT THE STORE.

At that point, I was making my own toys. It was a labor of love.

My lovely wife continued storytelling, traveling a lot less and doing it a lot more in the store. She wrote the books, and I built the toys: puppets and bears and dragons and monkeys. I was an old-fashioned toymaker in a fast-moving world. I was an enigma.

A scientist who believed in magic.

We were happy. Joyful. I think back to that countdown when Viktor the Red was moments away from taking all this away. The journey through the memories, the pain and sorrow, was the hardest moments of my life. It wasn't a punishment. Far from it.

I always suspected it was Santa Claus. Laugh if you want. Is it any more absurd than a dream world of toys? Even after all I'd done, who else would know what I really *wanted*?

One Christmas season, the store was full and the windows steamy. A storyteller from out of town had agreed to entertain our Saturday morning. She had emailed me, said she found my contact on the website. She only provided her first name. She wasn't famous or anyone to be recognized. I thought nothing of it. She was engaging and dramatic, singing and dancing and sweeping her arms. Children squealed and laughed. Their eyes as wide as their mouths.

"And then the train went *whoooosh* off the tracks. We soared through the clouds, into the valley that was near. Over the moon we could see, with merriment and glee, a sleigh pulled by a long train of flying reindeer."

The details of the story weren't what captured me. It was the way she told them.

Standing in the back, with his arms tightly folded, was her husband. He'd heard these stories a hundred times, maybe more. But he watched with a fascination that equaled that of the children. Then I realized it wasn't her he was watching. He was looking across the room, a smile hidden behind whiskers brushed with gray.

He was looking at me.

His face was round, and his cheeks were full. His hair was neat, as was the collar on his shirt. It had been decades since I'd seen him—three to be exact—but I didn't recognize him at that moment. It wasn't till after his wife was done and the store was buzzing with children, he approached without her, his smile growing the closer he got. And then I saw it, the look in his eye I hadn't seen since he invited me over for Christmas and I promised to accept the next year. A promise I never kept.

He held out his hand. "Merry, merry."

I took his hand with both of mine, shook with gentle vigor. The emotion that came so easily those days filled my throat. My words bubbled and stuttered. I swallowed them down. He leaned close to whisper in my ear, told me something I had been waiting to hear for thirty years. He whispered something I never thought I would ever hear again.

In the middle of my store, I hugged the boy who was now a grown man.

Our hero.

EPILOGUE

A silver train chugged through the middle of the valley where lights wrapped around trees and smoke puffed from chimneys, inflatable decorations danced in front yards and on rooftops. Music, heard across the village, played in the town square until midnight and would begin again at sunrise.

No one ever complained.

Below an expansive window set into the side of an enormous crystal wall, the lake had frozen over. The arena of the once infamous gala had been demolished, except for one wall, and the pit filled with water. In the summer, residents would fish off the arching foot bridge that led to the great pedestal that once held the fabled home of Viktor the Red.

Visitors would throw coins for luck.

In the winter, the small lake would turn to ice. The villagers would come to erect the Christmas tree on the pedestal. Visitors would arrive on the express train from all around the country to pay tribute to the Great Recovery. Stories of a time when Viktor the Red had stolen Christmas had been passed down for nearly two hundred years. Many toys, however, still remembered.

They had been there.

The tree would be decorated, the lights lit with a roar. People roasted marshmallows; toys dipped themselves in cauldrons of culinary delights. With music blaring, they would strap on ice skates and circle the tree.

Hiro watched from the glass wall, high above the frozen lake. He'd skated around the tree every Christmas since the celebration began the year the Great Recovery was announced. The year Viktor the Red fell and never returned.

Mads had made Hiro custom skates to fit his stubby legs. He still had them. They were falling apart, but he kept them to remember her.

The tail of the train pulled away from the lake.

"You're leaking."

A fire red dragon tugged on Hiro's arm. A bit of stuffing puffed out of a frayed seam. He was overdue for a re-cover. There were bald spots on his elbows; his glass eyes were cloudy. He'd had five complete re-covers in the last two hundred years TT (Toyworld Time). Haze had re-covered fifty-one times. She'd changed colors, tried different fabric, experimented with the latest fashion. Same dragon, different colors.

Always candy in her belly.

"Maggy can fix it," she said.

Hiro looked at the young woman across the warehouse. The machines that once lined the walls to distill Christmas spirit had been replaced with shelves. The floor was filled with workstations, each with an apprentice cutting fabric, setting a rivet or painting a smile. They followed Maggy's instructions, the master toy stitcher—a descendent of a long line of toy stitchers.

Maggy was Mads's great-granddaughter. There was more than one *great*, but how many Hiro couldn't remember. *Great-great-granddaughter?* Hiro grew up with all of Mads's children, and their children and their children—sitting in their cribs, seeing their first steps.

Even after all these years, the strangeness of time dilation never left him. He'd been a teddy bear for over two hundred years. Back in the skin (they no longer called it waking up), he'd just celebrated his forty-seventh birthday. Some days, his mind had trouble reconciling the difference.

Maggy was in the middle of the bustling room with a full-size puppet discussing the latest projects. Belkin had come to the workshop every night that month. His rounded face had been recently planed and varnished. It shined like lip gloss.

Flake stood on a workbench, arms crossed, while Snow interjected from the rim of the hat. Chase sat on the corner of a table, long tail swishing. Her purrs played like a satisfied instrument. Stretch was next to them but not listening. A red floppy hat covered the molded hair on his head. He waved.

Hiro waved back.

The only thing left from the time of Viktor the Red was the long, platinum table. A bobblehead robot was slumped on the edge of it.

"Where's your brother?" Hiro said.

"I told him to be here."

"Yeah, well, maybe it won't happen tonight."

Playfully she nibbled on Hiro's arm with spongy teeth (the latest fad). "It will. I can feel it."

Hiro hoped this night would be the night, but he didn't feel it like she did. He'd delivered the message, like he was told. Three nights they'd waited. Santa said it was time, just not when it would happen.

"One of the apprentices can take care of your seam."

They didn't make it one step from the window when a dollop of gooey light dropped from the ceiling. It fell onto the robot. No one was alarmed. They didn't even look up from their work. A horizontal line slashed across the television. The flat appendages jerked to life. Fireworks showered the screen.

"Sorry. Sleepover night. We got nine girls in one room and a vat of sugar. I didn't think I'd ever fall asleep," Robby said. "Did I miss it?"

He hopped off the table and rolled toward them. New spinners hummed on the ends of his appendages. Ever since his last upgrade, he skated everywhere like a middle schooler. He loosened his joints that were starting to rust (he needed to take better care) and executed a perfect camel spin. Hiro and Haze watched like bored teenagers.

"Merry, merry, Robby!" Stretch shouted. "How's the new claws?"

"What, these?" Robby snipped the air with pincers. "I could use three more!"

"Christmas present!" Stretch cheered.

Their conversation continued across the room. Annoyance from the apprentices filled the air. Hiro felt it ripple his fur like an electric breeze.

"So what's the plan?" Robby looked at the ice skaters below, jonesing to join a race. "We staying up here all night?"

"You asked that last time," Haze answered.

"What did top hat say?" He gestured to Belkin.

"Why would he say anything?"

Hiro knew why he was asking. He wondered the same thing. Belkin didn't have to say anything. His doubt about what they were waiting for shivered inside him like nervous bees.

"Never mind," Robby said. "I'm going down for an experience. You want anything?"

"You need to stay here," Haze said.

"Hiro?"

"I'm good."

Hiro didn't want him to leave. Robby's energy was soothing. He wasn't excited or nervous. He was happy to be here. Everyone else was edgy, especially Belkin. Who could blame him? He still carried a wedge of guilt from before the Great Recovery. His thoughts on tonight were like spotlights for everyone to feel. *What if this is a mistake?*

But Santa said it wasn't.

That was why they were waiting. Besides, they would know if it was a mistake by the toy that was chosen.

Hiro looked out the window. On the far side of the valley, just above the highest peak, a moon hung in the sky. Something streaked across the crescent. Haze pointed with her tail. Before she said anything, the air in the room rippled.

Belkin looked at the ceiling. Maggy called to her apprentices.

They felt it, too.

Everyone held their hopes back. Their thoughts didn't cloud the ether until a purple thread dropped into the room. It hovered over the platinum table. Hiro's fur stood on end. The atmosphere charged with static electricity.

Colors changed as the purple thread grew in intensity. Stretch's synthetic skin looked oddly green. The thread unzipped. A glowing orb of light burst from its pulsing depths and fired toward the shelves.

It lit a rocketman with integrated boosters first, then bounced to the other side of the warehouse to fill a bubble robot. Next was a spongy warrior, then a cow maiden, then a bug-eyed gremlin. Around and around it went like a three-dimensional pinball, settling in some toys for a few seconds while ricocheting off others. Sampling the inventory one by one.

There was every iteration of playthings on the walls, from custom jobs to mass produced. All the toys were all there. All but one.

No red skeleton in sight.

The apprentices held their breath. Emotions ripped through Hiro like electrified threads: excitement and surprise, anxiety and fear. The orb went faster and faster until the purple thread vanished.

"Where'd it go?" Robby's eye filled the screen.

They were searching for it. Waiting. Wondering if it was a failure, that a toy didn't fit (which worried Hiro quite a bit). Maggy was looking to her left.

A small panda tipped off the shelf.

It tumbled across the floor and bounced against the glass wall, facedown. There was a rush to surround it. Maggy held them back, to give the panda space. Hiro and Haze squeezed between the apprentices' legs. A new emotion emanated from the center of the gathering, beaming from the unmoving stuffed panda. It tasted murky and dizzy. No one moved.

Slowly, the panda's head turned. The glassy eyes looked out.

Maggy took a knee and held out her hand. The panda's snout twitched. She spoke softly, calmly.

"Welcome back," she whispered.

She picked the panda up and cradled it like a newborn. Relief flooded the room. It poured off Belkin in waves. His rigid mouth upturned slightly because he knew, they all knew, when the panda moved his arms that Santa was right.

A big red heart was stitched on the chest.

Stretch extended his elastic arm and tickled the Panda's tummy. He squirmed and snorted.

The panda struggled to sit upright. Maggy knew what he was looking for and held him to the glass wall to see. The ice skaters were below, the valley filled with merry lights.

Emotion dripped from the panda.

Hiro and Haze hugged. Christmas spirit flowed like a deep river. The Great Recovery was complete.

Belkin was the first to find the words they were all thinking. Looking out at the world filled with happy people and joyous toys, he said—

"Merry, merry, Viktor."

THE CLAUS UNIVERSE

Don't stop now. All of the Claus Universe is waiting.

https://bertauski.com/claus/

YOU DONATED TO A WORTHY CAUSE!

By purchasing this book, you have donated to the Imagination Foundation. 10% of the profits from ToyWorld is annually donated to find, foster and fund creativity and entrepreneurship in children around the world. Their efforts aim to raise a new generation of innovators and problem solvers who have the tools they need to build the world they imagine.